The Beast

The Beast, The Messenger and The King: Book One

Steven M Phillips

Cover design by: Luke Phillips @spooklgp

ISBN: 979 8 486 67442 6

https://stevenmphillipsauthor.com/

To my father: thank you for lending me so many fantastic books which have shaped this story and my life. You showed me the way to all the worlds which exist in our imaginations.

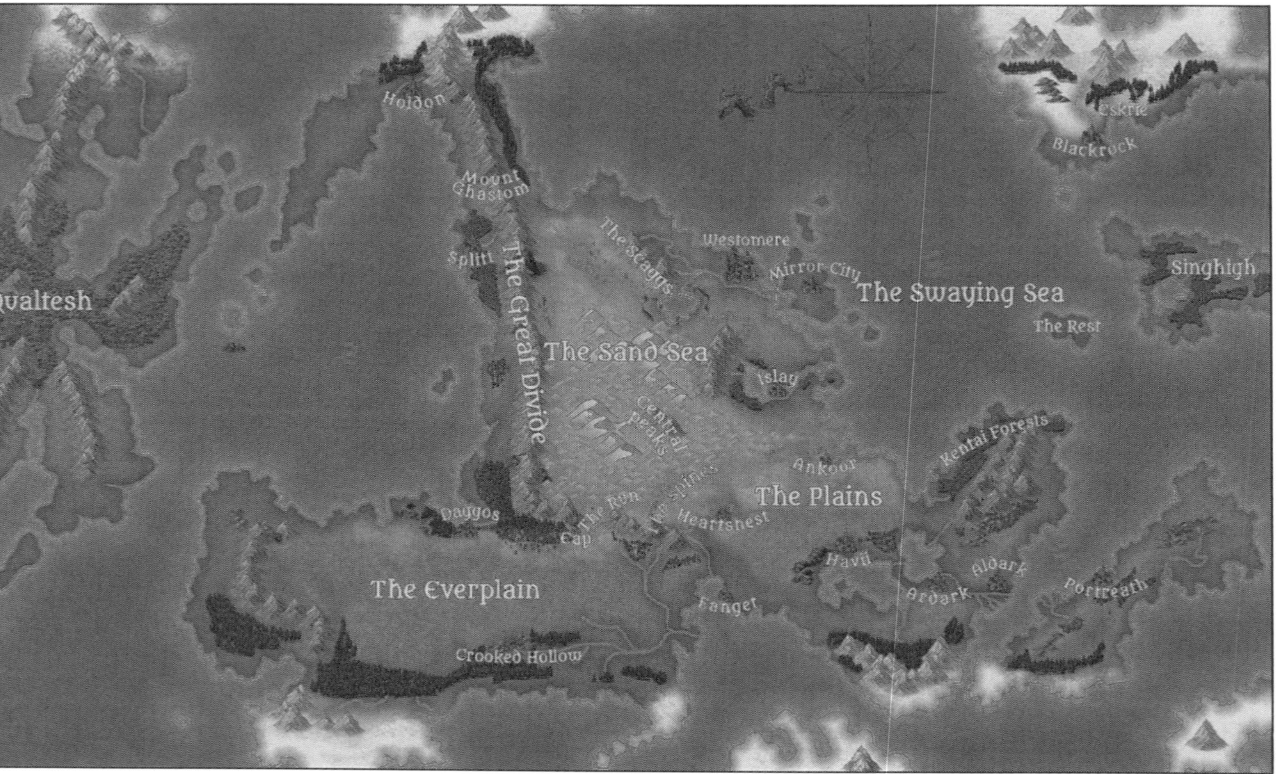
Qualtesh
Holdon
Mount Ghastom
Splitt
The Great Divide
The Scaggs
Westomere
Mirror City
The Swaying Sea
Eskrie
Blackrock
Singhigh
The Rest
The Sand Sea
Islay
Central peaks
Ankoor
The Plains
Kentai Forests
The Spines
Heartsnest
The Ron
Cap
Daggos
The Everplain
Havil
Aldark
Ardark
Portreath
Fanget
Crooked Hollow

PART 1

In the forest, the darkness pooled on the ground, shadows crawling into every crevice. The dark was a contrast to the bright light struggling into the woods from the fields outside. Only a gurgling stream broke the silence, its shattered surface reflecting its surroundings.

Swiftly, Bandolas rushed across the carpet of pine needles to hide behind another tree trunk. He froze in place, trying to make himself as small as possible. Concentrating intently, he slowed his breathing, trying to listen to the sounds of the forest. The small creatures were silent, no bird calls, no rustling of leaves.

A deep, rumbling thrumming started at the limit of his hearing, growing louder. It hummed in his ribcage and froze his soul. The sound of the beast. The intensity of the vibrations increased until it could be felt through all his bones, becoming punctuated by heavy thuds; the sounds of the creature's feet approaching.

For weeks Bandolas has hunted, hired by the Wizards of Eap to capture their abomination. Created to guard the sorcerers' tower, the beast had absorbed so much magic over the years that it was driven mad. Now it roams the land constantly eating, causing shame for the Wizards. Bandolas has in his pouch a contract to kill the creature, but fear has frozen him in his hiding place.

The only advice he had received was: "The beast senses movement. If you stay still, it will not see you!" How was he supposed to get close enough to kill it if he could not move?

An eerie, green glow lit the darkening forest as the beast approached, emanating from its strange stalk-like eyes, protruding through the antlers protecting its menacing head. Huge mandibles extended beyond its jaws, ready to capture prey and drag it into its vast maw, constantly gnashing, gnawing and grinding the bones of its victims.

The beast paused, close to Bandolas. Could it sense him? Bandolas held his breath trying to be a part of the tree, rough bark pushing into his back.

The smell of the beast became overwhelming and Bandolas almost lost his breakfast to the forest floor, swallowing back his rising bile as waves of stench flowed over him.

The beast moved on.

Without hesitation Bandolas moved, now was his chance. The beast was only metres away. He leapt, grabbing a handful of rough, brown fur and clambered onto the creature's tall back.

PART 2

Serena hated the chickens. They pecked at her as she tried to collect their eggs. They fouled the straw, so she had to rake it out and replace it every day. They smelled terrible and she spent so much time with them that she suspected she did as well. She lifted the hem of her skirts higher out of the mud of the foul enclosure, nudged one of the hens away with her heavy boot, and reached into her sack to spread another handful of grain.

As the birds dashed in to peck at the fresh bounty, Serena looked past the fences around her homestead to the slope of the nearby hill. She paused in her work and watched. A man had just crested the rise and was descending slowly towards the village through the grassland. He staggered every few paces and walked with a peculiar gait. He appeared to be pulling ropes behind him, hauling something heavy. A large mass covered in dark fur with something sharp enough to be digging furrows in the earth, leaving trails similar to that of a plough, zig zagging behind him.

Serena watched and waited. So far, the most interesting thing to happen in Crooked Hollow was when Big Sam Astor's best milking cow had birthed a calf with three legs. They had even renamed the tavern 'The Hopping Cow.' This was something new. This was something different. This was not normal, everyday, humdrum village life.

Crooked Hollow had been her home for twenty-one summers. The small homestead on the edge of the village: her prison, her school, her misery, and her life. When she was younger, her father had talked to her about life in the cities of Westomere and Fanget, where he had once adventured. He showed her how to hunt, how to care for livestock. Together they had fixed up the house and the surrounding sheds and fences. He had kept her mind busy and her hands busier still. The disappearance of her father five years ago had changed all that. Now it was just her and her mother, Tilda the seamstress. Old folk in town spoke of how she had once been a beauty and had stolen the heart of her father. She was the village surgeon as well as a dressmaker of some skill. Her steady hands had saved many of the local folks' lives. Now she was a miserable, drunken, unkempt old woman. Too tired to be of use to anyone.

Serena ran the home and the land, she kept them fed and housed, but only just. The local men had tried to buy their land, some had tried to buy her. But she had stood firm and true to her belief that somewhere there must be a better life. Some of the local lads showed interest in taking her hand but she knew that they were not what she wanted or needed. What she wanted was freedom and adventure.

This man dragging his load into their village, this was something new.

She rushed to the porch dropping her sack. Grabbing her staff and cloak, she ran off up the road heading for the village proper.

A crowd had gathered outside Peg and Joe's store. Watching warily as the man continued slowly down the hill.

"What should we do?" asked Holford, the elderly tavern keeper.

"Dunno. Not seen the likes afore." replied one of the elderly Fletcher twins.

"Should we see what 'e wants? P'raps 'e needs some 'elp." Slow Jacks suggests.

As the crowd start to fidget and mumble ideas at each other, no one steps towards the stranger. None go to help him. None would. The villagers were a cowardly lot, set in their ways and not used to change. They would wait to see what happened, never stepping forward.

Serena slowly eased through the crowd. Past the all too familiar faces and into the low grass. She began to make her way up the hill.

Behind her she heard their voices. She could feel their looks, like daggers in her back.

As she moved closer, she could see that the man looked exhausted, like he had been dragging the heavy weight behind him for days. He wore thick leather armour shaped to move easily with his body. Across the armour were many straps holding a plethora of pouches and a variety of weapons close to his hands. His hair hung over his eyes as he walked with his head bent down. A rope ran across his chest, held in his hands behind him, as he dragged his burden across the earth.

What he pulled was hideous beyond her imagination.

The man kept on walking. The effort of each step etched in the way his muscles strained, thc tightness of his shoulders and the ragged exhalations of his breath. Serena tore her eyes from the horror which the man was pulling.

"Sir, are you alright? Can I help you at all?" She asked feeling like an awkward country girl.

She moved to stand in front of him. He glanced up briefly, flicking the sweaty hair from his eyes with a quick movement of his head. Then he leant once more into the ropes and heaved forward straining hard with his legs to shift his load another step. He stumbled slightly to the side, righted himself and then heaved once more.

Taking a step backwards, to give the man room to keep moving, Serena tried again.

"Welcome to Crooked Hollow. My name is Serena. You really look like you could do with some help with that."

The man hunched his shoulders, leaned forward into the ropes and heaved again. His load does not move. Serena can see the sinews of his neck straining desperately. Then with a loud sigh, he dropped to his knees throwing down the ropes in disgust.

She could see the abrasions across his palms and the sticky blood drying on the ropes. He must have been pulling this thing for a long time. He looked beaten and broken. His head hung down, chin resting upon his chest as he slowly sank to sit upon his heels.

"A drink girl."

His deep voice croaked as he swayed slowly where he sat. He placed one fist on the floor to steady himself.

"I can get you one. Just wait here a minute."

Serena dropped her staff, lifted her skirts, and ran down the hill towards the centre of town. The villagers had not moved. They all began pointing at her as she hurried past them towards the well.

Holford called after her,

"So, what does he want Serena? He gonna cause us trouble?"

"What's he doing here?"

"Did you see what he's pulling?"

Serena ignored the questions. A half full bucket sits on the wall of the well. Someone must have left it there before the commotion started. She grabbed it by the handle, turned and headed back up the hill as quickly as she could.

The man had picked up her staff and was using it to try to get back to his feet. The wooden shaft slipped from his hands, and he collapsed back to his knees as Serena arrived.

"Stop that Sir. You are exhausted. Here, have a drink and take a moment. The whole village is watching."

Without looking at her he grabbed the bucket in both hands and tipped it up towards his mouth. The water splashed between his cracked lips and down his front as he greedily swallowed. He lowered the bucket to the ground and slowly put both his fists into the remaining water letting out a soft sigh as he did so.

"Thank you."

In that moment, Serena took time to look at him closely. He was tall and broad shouldered, his dark hair long and unkempt. The armour he wore was not like any she had seen, but it was obvious it would protect him well from all but the most vicious of attacks. He took his hands from the bucket and raised it above his head to pour what was left of the water over himself. As he did so, he let out a soft groan and held his left side.

"Are you injured?" she asked.

"It's nothing. Are there any oxen in town I can hire? I really need to get out of here."

He finally looked up and his eyes met hers.

"Not in that state. You won't make it far unless you rest."

He lifted her staff again, holding the shaft firmly in his hand as he tried once again to stand. Serena moved to place a hand under his arm and help him up. As she stepped close, he tried to move back, a dagger appeared in his free hand, held blade outwards towards her.

His arm waivered, his head tilted back, and he fell to the ground.

Serena rushed over, kicked the dagger away and held her hand close over his mouth and nose. She could feel his breath. He was alive.

PART 3

Bandolas slowly woke. He could not open his eyes and his mind struggled to keep hold of a single idea. He was lying on a hard surface in a warm space. Someone was close, they smelled of hard liquor. A sharp pain pierced his side and his awareness shattered.

Sometime later he opened his eyes. A girl was standing over him wiping his brow with a blissfully cool cloth. He tried to speak but she shooshed him and looked away and spoke to someone beyond his vision.

The next time his eyes opened, a woman was standing by his side staring straight at him. She wore a frown like others wear a shirt or scarf, deep creases splay out from the corners of her slightly yellowing eyes. As she moved closer, she raised a bottle to her lips and took a hard drag on the syrupy contents. Her hands ran over his chest down towards the wound on his side.

"Grit your teeth boy. This is gonna hurt." She said in a rough country voice before pouring the contents of the bottle onto him.

Fire erupted in his side and darkness claimed him once again.

As he came to, he was aware first of the sounds of farmyard animals, bleating, squawking, and braying. Bright sunshine from a small window was shining across him, gently warming his skin as a cool breeze prickled goosebumps up his arms. He could hear voices engaged in a heated argument getting closer. Both voices carried the lilting accent of the farm counties in the deep south of the Everplain. A harsh woman's voice spoke with finality,

"Nay Serena 'e will not die if he is moved. His fever broke in the night, the worst tis past. But he cannot stay 'ere. The village elders made it clear that 'e was not welcome, and we don't need another mouth to feed."

"But Ma, his wounds were infected and might still be, he would have died if you hadn't cut and stitched him. Perhaps he could help us out, god knows there ain't enough hours in the day for me to do all that needs doing. You could see him back to health and then…"

"No girl, and that's final. He looks like a man with business to get back to. Just because you 'ave taken a fancy to him with all that brow swabbing. He needs to go. Once 'e wakes, I'll see to it. Go bring the milk in and refill the hay or something. I got a date with a nice bottle of Whiskey that I've been saving."

"You ain't been saving it Ma, you drink it quicker than Slow Jacks can get it through his still."

There was the sound of a flat hand hitting flesh and then the older voice called out,

"No more than you deserve talking to me that way. When your tears dry, you'll thank me."

Then heavy feet banged across wood and a door opened.

Bandolas raised his head and saw a slim woman, reaching well into her middle years, with long hazel hair beginning to go to grey at the sides, striding towards him.

"Awake, are you?"

She moved over to a cupboard in one corner of the room, clinking about within for a few seconds before walking back towards him.

"Can you sit?"

Bandolas raised himself up onto his elbows.

He was in a small wooden cottage's main room. It was relatively spacious with two fireplaces, one at either end. The side of the room he was in was obviously a kitchen. Pans hung from the rafters along with various bundles of dried herbs. There was a large counter under a small window and several cupboards and shelves containing jars and storage baskets for foods. He was lying upon a sturdy wooden table with a chair either side. Everything looked well-made and well-kept if a little rustic. The other end of the room had two tall backed padded armchairs set by the fireplace. Two words sprang to mind: homely and cosy.

"It's a nice place you have here mistress."

"I ain't no mistress. You can call me Tilda. My daughter brought you in and I patched you up. Don't go prodding at your side for a day or two. Then change the bandages and wash the wound twice a day after that."

Bandolas looked down to see a thick linen bandage wrapped around his stomach and a blanket draped over his lower half. He moved to swing his legs over the side of the table and sit up.

"Take it slow lad. You've lost a lot of blood and it took a while for you to fight off the fever and infection."

He slid to the floor, careful of his side and the blanket fell off him. He reached down quickly to gather it up and hold it around his waist, realising that he was naked without it. The rapid movement caused his head to spin, and he felt weak and clutched at the table for support.

"It's alright. Ain't nothing I haven't seen before."

The woman poured water from a bucket into a cup and then added a brown liquid out of the bottle she had collected into another.

"Here plain water for you and the gods' water for me."

Bandolas took the cup he was offered and hastily swallowed it down.

"My, my. You do, do everything in a hurry don't ya."

She motioned towards one of the wooden chairs.

"Take a seat in that chair now and I'll fetch your clothes. You'll be leaving soon."

Tilda pulled aside a curtain in one wall to reveal a doorway leading into a room beyond. She disappeared for a moment and then returned dragging a large sack.

"Cleaned it the best we could. That's some fancy armour you were wearing. I hope you're not intending to use any of them weapons on me nor the girl."

"I..."

"Don't rush yourself lad. I'll leave you to it. You get dressed and sip some more water. I'll just be out on the porch with my drink."

She clomped past him and back out the door.

Bandolas sat for a minute, confusion burning through his mind. Where was he? What had happened? How long had he been lying there naked for these country ladies to see?

He sipped at his water, placed the cup on the table and reached for the sack.

PART 4

Serena thumped the wooden rail with the side of her fist in frustration. She knew her mother meant well but did she have to be so harsh about everything? The slap had shocked her. Her mother was a drunk; reclusive and bitter at life's events, but she had never struck out at Serena before.

For the first time, watching her mother cut the rotting flesh from the man's side and stitch the wound, she had been worried for both the surgeon and the patient. Her mother's hand, which had always been so steady and sure in the past, now had a visible tremor. The alcohol and the years were not being kind to her. The mood swings were getting worse, and she no longer cared what was happening in the world outside their doorstep.

Serena dreamed often of leaving, of life on the open road, of adventure in big cities and of meeting all kinds of people. Her father's stories of faraway lands where people rode great leathery winged bats through the skies and trees grew as large as mountains instilled in her a wanderlust, she felt she could no longer contain.

There was nothing left for her to learn here in Crooked Hollow. She was the best hunter, carpenter, farmer, dice player and archer in town. She did the accounts for half the businesses. But around here being the best at something seemed to be a bad thing. She knew that people whispered about her. Said she acted like she was better than them. It didn't matter how hard she tried to be nice and to fit in, somehow, they saw her as a threat and therefore they feared her.

Last time she had helped the Fletcher twins to fix a broken shutter on their lambing shed, she had her them whispering to each other that, 'she fixed it so quick she must be a witch.'

Words like that stuck in these parts. Words like that could get you killed.

So, she spent less time in town and more time on the farm. But it was not the life she wanted.

Perhaps this stranger with the dark eyes could be her ticket out of here. She just needed to convince her mother to let her go.

She looked out across the fields to where the man's cargo still lay. It had been two days since he had walked down that hillside. In that time no scavengers had come to feast on the flesh and no villagers had dared approach. It just lay there, antlers dug into the rich dirt, fur blowing in the wind, mouth staring straight ahead like a portal into a nightmare. How the man had ever come to be dragging this foul head must be a fantastic tale indeed.

She turned and walked back towards the cottage. She would have to face her mother again. Hopefully, she would not be too drunk yet. Or perhaps she would be so far gone in the bottle that she would sleep.

As she came around the side of the cattle shed, she paused and stepped back into the shadows. The man was coming out of the door of their cottage. He was wearing the simple loose shirt that he wore under his armour and the soft leather under trousers, which her mother had sworn many times over, as she had removed them to clean his wounds. He held the door frame with one bandaged hand as he awkwardly slung one side of his jointed armour over, obviously trying to get it on and failing. He threw it down to the floor and shuffled over to the bench on the veranda by the door.

He was a tall man, lean and well-muscled. His hair was long and dark, hanging loosely around his ears and over his eyes. Serena remembered those eyes well, dark brown, so dark they seemed to draw you in towards them to see them better. She had only looked briefly into them twice. But it was enough. She would do anything to have those eyes look into hers.

The man kicked at his discarded clothing and then slowly raised his head, looking around the farmyard. His face darted around looking first at the skies and then from one building to the next before his gaze settled upon her.

She had thought herself far enough away and deep into the

shadows that there was no way he could know she was there, but his gaze was unwavering. Like a hunting cat paused before it leapt for the kill. Serena's heart caught in her throat, and she could not breath.

A clattering came from inside the cottage and the sound of her mother swearing. The man turned his attention away and Serena turned behind the shed and walked slowly around to come into the yard from a different angle.

She ignored the glances from the man as she made her way over and into the only home she had ever known.

"Are you alright Ma?"

Her mother was kneeling on the floor by the table, a box spilled open in front of her. From the container a small pile of coins had spilled, as well as some papers and a few pieces of jewellery that Serena had never seen before.

"S'right girl. I just knocked this off the table. Was having a look for some memories."

Her mother seemed more drunk than normal for the time of day. It looked like she was crying.

Serena went to her and put a hand around her, helping her mother into one of the wooden chairs. She then knelt and collected the spilled contents of the box and put it on the table for her mother.

"What is it Ma? I've never seen these things before."

"It's just memories. Memories of better times. Bits I 'ave left of your father."

Her mother spoke on, tears slowly spilling down her face. Her voice sounded tired and half asleep. "A necklace he gave me when we had our first night together. The ring he used to bind our love. A letter he left for me when he went out to hunt, and I was alone. It's all I have now. The memories begin to fade."

"Ma, don't be sad."

"But I am child. I know that just like him you will leave. You'll walk out that door and you won't come back. If you stay this life will break you. There is too much of him in you."

Her mother reached out to gently pat her cheek, the same

cheek she had slapped earlier.

"Will you leave a letter when you leave so I 'ave a memory of you?"

Then she reached out and poured more whiskey into her cup and took a long slow swallow. Her head slowly sank onto the table, and she began to snore.

Serena went outside. She needed to think.

She stood looking out from the veranda over the farm.

"My name is Bandolas. Thank you for your help miss." The strangers strong, deep voice rolled over her.

Serena turned to look straight into his eyes and her world changed forever.

PART 5

"Heyah!" Serena shouted encouragement to Jess, the ox she is driving forward, "Come on boy heave!"

On the other side of the cart, Bandolas was shouting similar encouragement to Poppy, another of their oxen. The two steers were pulling ropes attached to the grizzled monster's head by its massive antlers. Slowly but steadily, they were hauling it towards the farm cart which stood with a ramp made of two wooden planks that Serena had been keeping, to make repairs to the shed doors later in the year, leading up onto its bed.

Serena had put her mother in her room, to sleep off the grog, and then asked Bandolas what had brought him to their doorstep. He explained his mission to kill the beast and the urgent need to carry on with his quest. She had realised that he would need transport and had offered to help if he would take her with him.

At first, he had seemed reluctant, but he needed her help and so the bargain had been struck. If she helped him to transport the decapitated head, he would let her travel with him to Eap. Then they could go their separate ways. Serena had offered the cart and two oxen to drive it and with a little ingenuity she had come up with a plan to get the head onto the cart.

Folk from the town came to watch for a while as the two of them worked. None offered to help. 'So be it.' Thought Serena, they would be a hinderance anyway.

The plan worked and the hideous head was loaded in the back of the cart.

It stank. The stench was the worst thing she had ever smelled. A mixture of damp, hairy animal, musk, rot, and death. Even through the thick cloth over her mouth and nose the putrid acridity of it caught in her throat making her want to gag.

As Bandolas pulled a heavy, oiled canvas over the cart's load, Serena watched the way he moved. Smooth and assured even though his wound obviously still pained him. Every movement he made spoke of confidence and danger. She went over to help him tie off the last of the ropes and to harness the oxen.

As they climbed into the driving bench at the front of the cart, he swept the hair from his face and looked appraisingly at her.

"Thank you for this Serena. Without your help and your mothers, I would surely have died. Now, I must see my mission through and collect on the reward. I must leave and soon. You are welcome to join me but know this: the path I take will be a hard one. The creature's magic still wards it from some predators, but others will be drawn to its scent like moths to a flame. With luck we will reach our destination without mishap, but I have learned from long years on the road that it is more likely to go another way. We leave in the morning. You had best settle your affairs before then if you still want to come." He gave her a long searching look edged with sadness before turning back to look ahead.

She wondered if this was the right decision, could she really trust this stranger with her life. Could he lead her to adventure and freedom?

They rode in silence, each caught up in their own thoughts and troubles, back across the fields to the farm as the last light of the day slowly faded into darkness.

★★★

Bandolas sat on the veranda in the cool evening air. A small, scented oil lamp sat on a table by his side. He worked oil into his leather armour as he thought about recent events. The old woman was still asleep. He was grateful to her for what she had done but also disliked her for the life she led. Living in this fertile valley, working the land, helping people. She was so blessed, yet she wasted it all in the bottom of a bottle. The life she could have had was what he dreamed of.

★★★

Then there was Serena. She made him uncomfortable, like an itch under his skin. She was beautiful and intelligent. She had proven to be resourceful and quick thinking but if he took her with him, would she just get in the way? He didn't want to be responsible for her. It was enough trouble looking after himself. Yet without her help, he knew he would never make it. His wound was serious. The pain in his side almost unbearable and he could feel the heat of infection starting to warm his skin. They needed to hurry.

★★★

Hand hovering over the bottle of ink, Serena once again paused in her writing. The words just would not come. How to say everything she needed to, how to phrase it so that her mother would understand. Shaking her head, she dipped the quill and began again.

★★★

Tilda sat up. Her head felt rotten. Queasily she got to her feet and wandered to the main room. A fresh pail of water sat on the table and the shutters have been drawn back. Serena must have started on her daily routine. From the angle of the sun through the windows, she would be out with the chickens. Tilda splashed water on her face and poured a glass of water. As she was drinking it down, she spotted a neatly folded paper tucked under the pail. With shaking hands, she opened the letter.

★★★

It read:
'I love you. I am sorry. I will return.
Serena.'

PART 6

Serena looked back from her position on the cart's bench next to Bandolas.

The road behind trailed down the slope, through the fields of low grass towards the town. It widened as it approached the first homesteads, allowing two carts to pass. The street led between the single-story buildings to the town square where it opened into a wider area containing the well and marketplace. The mayor's house and offices could be seen, with its small tower standing above the other houses. Opposite it stood the only true two-story building in Crooked Hollow, The Hopping Cow Inn.

Serena gazed with fondness at the shops surrounding the marketplace, remembering her father explaining to her where the different goods in the general store had come from.

"This is fine silk from lands far to the east across the swaying sea." He had said as he held the shimmering fabric for her to rub between her fingers feeling its smoothness and warmth.

She had been particularly obsessed by a small box with banded colours running through it,

"That is grown from stone-wood by druids living in the Kentai forests. They grow the wood over many years and each year the wood turns a different colour. It is hard as stone but not as brittle, resilient to fire and rot, prized by many and rarer than gold." Her father had told her as she brushed her fingers lovingly over its polished surface.

Everywhere her eyes passed she could see her father instructing her through her mind's eye. He had taught her how to ride and how to choose the best oxen for endurance outside the forge. Behind the Fletcher twin's house, he had shown her how to feather an arrow and which type of tip was best for taking down different game. In the woods on the Eastern slopes of the 'hollow' he had shown her the best ways to set traps for game and how to spot their trails.

Finally, her eyes passed over the farmstead in the distance on the far side of town. Her home for all her life. Without her father it was no home. Just a place that held memories, like one of the bottles fallen from her mother's hands, slowly emptying into the dirt.

"You alright?"

Bandolas's gruff voice asked from besides her. He did not take his eyes from the road ahead, but he obviously sensed her pain.

"I'll be fine. Talk to me, tell me a little of yourself."

She needed to hear his voice to distract her from herself.

He turned then from his task of guiding the cart to look her in the eyes. Such darkness seemed to dwell in their depths, they seemed to peel away layers of her soul leaving her naked in the storm of emotions within.

"There are many stories in my past. Most I will not tell. If we are to travel together, I tell you this, not as a threat but as the truth. Death stalks me and I it."

The oxen pulling the cart flicked their ears as if trying to hear better as the cart creaked over the lip of the hill to rumble through the Everplain.

"I do not know where I was born and, unlike you Serena, I have never known a home. I have travelled many lands. In my youth, I was a boy serving on a great sail ship travelling the plains and the sand seas."

Serena's father had told her of these 'ships,' great wheeled waggons powered by the wind which traversed the endless grass lands and the deserts. Once many years ago, Tired Jim the woodcutter's son had come into town all a fluster shouting that he had seen a sail on the horizon. Everyone in the village had dropped tools to sit on the lip of the hollow and stare out into the distance as a small triangle had slowly drifted along. It had been the source of endless gossip around the well for weeks afterwards.

"Later, when I came of age, I was sold to the flesh traders of Havii. I worked the land, then I worked the mines. Eventually, some soldiers bought my freedom. I scouted for one army or another for a time before my skills were noticed by those with power. I was paid well to hunt. People, animals, criminals, even kings. I fell on hard times when peace came to the lands, until my name was passed to the Wizards at Eap. I found myself hunting their 'beast' and it brought me close to your land. Now I need to return this foul head to them and collect my bounty. Perhaps it will be enough that I can retire to the northern coast and live out my days in peace. We shall see."

The cart drifted slowly down the dirt road, passing through areas Serena had rarely seen, and they sat in silence for a long while.

"You talk as if you are an old man, yet you are only a few summers older than I. Has your life been so bad? There must have been some joy. Something which makes you keep getting out of bed each day." She spoke with the gentle softness of one who cares for others.

Serena reached out to place a hand on his shoulder.

His flesh felt hard through his shirt and unnaturally warm. The waggon jolted in a rut on the road, and he moved away from her leaving her arm to swing back down to her lap.

"I think sometimes that I have seen too much darkness in my life. For some time now, the joy of the hunt has been the only brightness. But it is a cold light and I grow tired of its glare. Perhaps Serena, you and I met for a reason. I do not understand it, but I feel calmer in your presence, less in need to keep moving, less hunted myself."

He moved closer to her on the bench until their knees were touching.

"I cannot offer you any promises, but I will try to keep you safe until you figure out where you are going. What is the path of your life now that you have escaped your home?" He asked his question with solemn severity, he needed to know that what he did was right.

The land around them was flat grassland as far as the eye could see. The low hills surrounding the hollow were disappearing behind them as the sun began its slow descent towards the horizon. Occasional small stands of trees and bushes could be seen in low depressions in the otherwise featureless expanse of the grass of the Everplain.

"I wish to see the world. My father told me stories of his days adventuring, travelling the lands seeking treasure. Since his disappearance I have often wondered if he is out there somewhere. I hold no hope that I will ever see him again, but I believe there is more in life than the hollow had to offer. That place never changed, not the people, not their ideas, not their outlook on life. Just like you if I had stayed there, it was like death was hunting me. A slow death of the brain, of thought, of ideas. I wish to travel with you to Eap and see these 'Wizards.' To talk to them and find out about their ways. When I have learned all I wish to, then I want to travel, visit all the places my father taught me about. Does that sound stupid and childish to you?"

Bandolas listened to her lilting accent, fair in its own plain way. This girl was the match of any fine lady in his eyes.

"No. That sounds like a fair plan. Perhaps I might join you and see if I can find new light to fill the darkness of my life."

She could feel him turn to look at her. She felt him appraising her. She sat up slightly taller in her seat and let the movement of the cart sway their bodies together. He did not flinch away.

Clouds began to roll in towards them as the sun lowered in the sky. Rain would follow soon. It would be a damp night.

"When the road becomes wet the mud could clog the wheels, we would do well to find shelter before it gets dark."

Bandolas stood to get a better view out over the endless expanse of grass.

Serena pointed a short way to the east.

"We could use those bushes to hang a canvas from if we tied it to the sides of the waggon there should just be room underneath for us and the oxen. The waggon will keep the wind off us."

"You think clearly. Let's do it. Dinner is always better when it is dry."

Bandolas turned the oxen off the road and felt guilty as

Serena set to work on the shelter. She knew exactly what she was doing rattling off instructions for him to tie this and lengthen that.

Serena could not help noticing that there was a slight stiffness to his movements that was not there before, and he tended to keep his left elbow close to his injured side. She hoped it was just stiffness as the wound knitted together.

They ate a meal of dried fruits and bread. The rain drummed rhythmically on the canvas over their heads. The oxen smelled bad, but their warmth was welcome and soon Serena found herself drifting into sleep.

PART 7

At some point during the night, the rain had cleared, and the morning was crisp and clear. Serena looked out over the vastness of the plains. No longer could she make out the low hills of Crooked Hollow and they were in territory she had only passed into a few times with her father. She could not say where they were and the only defining feature to be seen was the thinning trail made by the road. She knew there were a few homesteads out this far, but not many. They mainly bred oxen and traded back at town for essentials which they could not get out here in the wilderness.

Bandolas was running through a series of slow controlled Movements. "What are you doing?" Serena enquired of him as she watched the play of his muscles under his thin shirt.

He lowered his hands and turned to her. "It is a form of stretching and training the body. The shadow fighters of Kentai practice it for hours every day. Here, join me. It would be good for you to learn some fighting techniques. This teaches you the basic stances and how to move between them."

She walked to join him trying to copy the way he stood.

"Relax and empty your mind of petty things, concentrate on your body and each muscle you use as you move."

He took a sideways stance, bent slightly at the knees with feet planted firmly, wide of his shoulders, hands held at stomach height with elbows out. She stood facing him. She followed the movements of his arms as he reached out and around to the left, turning his hips and then slowly returning to the first stance.

"Breath slowly and don't tense up."

Gradually he moved his arms and feet around himself and Serena could imagine how the Movements could be used in combat. This Movement a jab with the fist, this one a block with the forearm. The raising of a knee to block a kick and the sweep of a foot to knock an enemy from their feet.

"I can see how these Movements might be good in a fight

but how do you know which one to use?" Serena stumbled as she tried to copy a high movement with her foot and her skirts got in the way.

"You teach yourself to know all of the Movements by muscle memory. You do not think how you use them. Your body learns what to do. This frees your mind to think ahead. To see what your opponent's weaknesses are and plan when to strike at them."

Bandolas continued to move smoothly from one stance to another as Serena went back to tend to the oxen and prepare for the day's journey. She kept an eye on his Movements, mesmerising the angles of his body and the positioning of his limbs.

After a brief breakfast they packed up the last of the camp. They used a little of the water, stored in a small barrel on the cart, to clean themselves up. Then they set off across the plains once again.

The road they followed became more and more overgrown as the morning passed. A smaller trail diverted off to the west as they continued northwards. Eventually, the road faded until they were just rolling through open grassland. The grass themselves grew up to waist height and were just a uniform yellowish green on first glance. After hours of travel with nothing else to see, Serena began to notice differences in the grass about them, some had wider leaves others spiny almost spike like leaves. The colours of the leaves varied from variety to variety as well. There was every type of green imaginable but also some shades of blue and deep reds. Some of the grass grew in large clumps with broad leaves all sprouting from the centre. When Serena jumped down from the cart to inspect these, she found that the base of the clump worked like a water barrel, the leaves directing the water from the rain last night down to a central mass which retained the water that could be scooped out with a cup. Other grass grew as individual leaves spreading as a vast mat across the ground before them, almost spongy and springy beneath her steps.

They took it in turns to walk besides the cart encouraging

the oxen on and stretching their aching muscles. Sitting high on the driving bench of the cart and looking out across the plains they could see distant herds of deer. Large flocks of birds would occasionally rise from the grass in murmurations dancing through the air before settling down once again and disappearing amongst the stalks. Many smaller birds darted about in the grass hunting for insects and their songs filled the air. Occasionally, alone or in small groups, larger winged birds would swoop closer, riding the currents of air searching for small animals amongst the grass. For a while, a lone vulture seemed to follow the cart, perhaps following the smell of decay from the rotting beast's head which they carried.

The breeze made the grass sway in mesmerizing ways, waves of colour seemed to move across the land dancing across the vastness. It was beautiful yet stark.

Serena used her bow to bring down a hare which they startled from its cover and Bandolas skinned and cleaned it ready for the evening's pot. As the sun reached its zenith, Serena asked, "What is our direction and how long will the journey to Eap be?"

"We travel due North. If we keep this steady pace, we should pass through the plains in four moons time and be able to see the mountains of the Great Divide. Eap should be another moon's ride to the East from that point."

To pass the time during the afternoons travel, Serena busied herself altering her clothing. She had packed two dresses as well as the one she wore. One summer dress and one for winter. Her summer dress she cut into a shirt and skirt. The skirt she slit front and back, sewing the two halves together to make a workable pair of trousers. She did not want to be hindered again when practicing the Movements and stances with Bandolas and anyway trousers would be more practical for travelling.

She slit the winter dress skirt up one side and trimmed the hem shorter so it would hang halfway between knee and ankle, well clear of the ground. The fur around the collar she cut off but kept in her pack. She also loosened the bodice around the arms for easier movement.

The skies had been low and grey all day but as they travelled on the clouds began to break apart leaving woolly clumps roaming the blue skies their vast shadows moving slowly across the plains.

Over the next few days, the grasslands did not change. The waggon bounced and jolted its way along behind the stoic oxen. Serena and Bandolas walked more and rode less. In the mornings they practiced the Movements together, she picked up the motions and stances quickly and enjoyed giving herself over to the simple Movements, though she was always left feeling tired afterwards.

During the day Serena kept her bow close to hand to snag any birds or small mammals for their dinner. Bandolas spent more and more time tending to his various weapons especially his armour.

"You care for that as if it were your lover." She said to him one evening as he rubbed oil into the leather while she scrubbed the pans from dinner.

"If you care for the tools of your trade, they will care for you." He motioned for her to sit beside him. "Here take this." He handed her a long-bladed dagger. "This is a weapon designed to kill. Do you agree?"

Serena took the hilt as he offered it. The blade was heavier than it looked. A large round pommel sat at the end of a long leather-bound grip. The cross guard was simple and curved slightly forward. The blade itself was around the length of Serena's forearm. "Yes, it looks like it could kill."

"That one is also long and heavy enough to parry another's blade. The cross guard can catch or deflect a blow from even a heavy axe if used correctly. It is a weapon but can also be used to save a life. Yours. From now on carry it in your hand all day. You need to get used to its weight; it should become an extension of your own arm. You should feel naked without it. In the morning after we practice the stances, I will show you how to use it."

She looked into his eyes and saw a sparkle in them she had

not seen before, pride. This man took pride in the fight. Well, that was fine with her. She didn't leave home with him to learn nothing. She would learn what she could from him. She enjoyed being close to him.

Serena looked away as her cheeks warmed. "Your armour looks strange. Tell me about it."

He reached over and took her hand, for a moment she resisted, then he placed her hand onto one of the many thin plates of leather making up his armour.

"I spent a long time studying the weaknesses of other men on the battlefield. Metal armour made them slower than me, so I used my speed against them. Other men fight with no armour and rely upon their speed and instincts, so I made this to protect myself from their blows. The leather has been specially treated and is rare indeed. It cost me a lot of work, death and blood to be able to afford all the pieces. I went to the finest craftsmen I could find, and it took many moons to perfect. These smaller plates make it move with my body; the articulation made possible by these fine Stonewood rivets. The areas around the sides and stomach have smaller, thinner plates which overlap many times, so they are more supple and yet strong. See how the collar sweeps up and out," he says as he guides her hand over the curves," This deflects blows to the neck upwards and away from the face. The way the plates on the arms are arranged in different directions can cushion a heavy blow or entrap a blade between them."

Serena was no longer looking at the armour but gazing at his face, so alive with the telling of his tale. The armour felt smooth and warm beneath her touch cradled in his own rough hand.

"My armour is my life. Without it I am incomplete. In that way I guess it is like a lover."

Slowly, Serena moved her hand away from his and looked away into the night.

★★★

The next morning, they were practicing the stances. Bandolas corrected her posture a few times. Serena just could not seem to get the movement.

"Your timing is wrong. Your hip needs to lead the rotation. The power comes from twisting off your back foot as you rotate through your hips driving your elbow forward." He showed her the movement once again.

Serena watched him closely mimicking his Movements the best she could.

"No, not quite like that. You lose too much of your power if there is not enough rotation. Perhaps you are over thinking it. Try facing away from me. Picture the movement in your mind and let it flow through you."

Serena turned so her back was to him. It felt strange not to be watching him and instead for him to be studying her. She took the first stance allowing her muscles to guide her into the next.

"Good. Breathe and flow with the Movements." He said as he guided her.

She heard him step close behind her and then he tapped her left foot with his.

"You need to plant your feet wider."

She shifted her legs as he suggested and continued. As her arms stretched high, she felt his hands on her sides.

"Push through the back leg and stretch through your leading side more."

She felt his hand on the one side clench tighter directing her movement. She continued to move, the strain of her muscles bringing a shortness of breath. As she came back into the sure-footed stance, she felt his body move close behind hers.

"Now move with me." He whispered in her ear.

Together they moved through the motions, his hand clasped tight around her side. "Feel the timing and the rhythm as you flow through the forms."

She could feel the difference in how he moved, like a dancer light on his feet yet solid as a rock. He moved away and she continued the leg sweeps and high kicks. Moving faster as she felt the rhythm take hold.

"Yes, good you have it. Can you feel the energy pulse through you?"

Serena spun faster, she felt more agile, stronger and more powerful. She felt she could take on the world.

"Serena, never lose control. Slow it down!" Bandolas rushed in and grabbed her tightly to stop her Movements.

For a moment she strained to carry on; she realised how close he was. Then she clasped her arms around him her breath coming fast and deep. He stared into her eyes for a moment before releasing her and stepping back.

"You felt it didn't you? The Rush. Not many do. I can see it in your eyes like a tiny spark in the darkness." He knelt down motioning for her to do the same. Serena placed her knees on the dirt.

"I felt something. I don't know what it was. A sudden charging of my heart and quickening of my pulse. My mind somehow became faster; I could see where I wanted to be and then I was there. Flowing through the Movements. At first, I thought it was just being close with you. What did you call it? The Rush?"

"It was nothing to do with me Serena. The Rush comes from within us all. It is powerful, linked in some way to magic. Most people never experience it. But if you let it rule you, it can consume you. That is why the Movements are controlled. You have to be in control, never the Rush."

He reached out and took her hand, holding it gently in his. "Serena, I feel a connection with you. Perhaps more. I think you feel it to. But if you have this inside of you then first you must harness it. I have seen what happens if the Rush is not controlled."

"Do you have this Rush?" Serena asked, suspecting she already knew the answer.

"Yes. It is why I am the best at what I do. It helps me to be fast and to see clearly, there is more to it but that is for another time. Continue your Movements whilst I pack up the waggon. We should journey on soon."

Serena practiced for a while longer, but she struggled to

concentrate and free her mind to let the motions flow. She did not feel The Rush again that day.

PART 8

Bandolas was ranging ahead of the waggon, scouting for the smoothest route through the uneven ground. Serena guided the oxen through the grass keeping an eye out for any game she could shoot down. The blade in her hand felt heavy and got in the way of the reins when she had to turn the animals' heads.

A flock of large birds, perhaps crows, fluttered and cawed their way into the sky from the grass to the east and flew away towards the south. When Serena looked ahead again Bandolas was nowhere to be seen.

'Perhaps he is crouching down to relieve himself or has stumbled and fallen.' She thought, quickly scanning the grass all around. There was no sound but the wind. The small insect noises and chatter of the little birds had ceased. The world seemed to be holding its breath.

Then she spotted him. Moving quickly, running towards the waggon. He weaved his way through the landscape, dodging this way and that as he jumped unseen obstacles. As he ran, he waved, signaling for her to turn the waggon and ride westwards. She slapped the reins against the rumps of the oxen and called for them to speed up.

The creatures responded slowly but were soon trotting rapidly across the uneven ground. Serena bounced and jostled in her seat and stood up into a low crouch so her legs would absorb the worst impacts and not her rump. She glanced to the right to check on Bandolas's progress. He was getting close. She could see movement in the grass behind him, streaks of colour as the fronds parted around several different creatures swiftly moving through the grass. She could see different coloured streams moving from several directions all flowing towards the same point. Him.

Bandolas leapt up to the seat beside her, reaching quickly over into the waggon bed to pull the sack containing his weapons up. "Wild boars!" He shouted over the rattling of the wheels and rush of wind.

"A hunting pack, I came too close to them, and they gave chase. One of them managed to cut my leg with its tusk. Now they scent blood they will not stop."

Serena could see the boars weaving in and out of the grass around the waggon as it sped along. The people of Crooked Hollow were wary of these beasts, one of the biggest predators on the plains. They grew up to half the size of an oxen, were heavily muscled and their long legs carried them swiftly over uneven ground. These boars were not the type you found in the woods that could be hunted and turned into a tasty meal. These were apex predators. Their tusks were short yet sharp, used to wound and weaken prey from blood loss. They hunted in packs and had incredible stamina. Not as fast as the deer they hunted in the grass lands, they had a keen sense of smell and once they had weakened and wounded their prey, they would never give up the chase and miss out on a meal.

Serena called to the oxen for greater speed, sheathed her knife, dropped the reins -allowing the oxen to charge on their own- and drew her bow.

"We have to keep them away from the oxen, if they take one down, we'll be stuck out here." She shot an arrow into the rump of the closest boar, and it peeled away as another took its place, surging forward towards the thundering hooves of the steers.

She glanced up to see Bandolas had strapped his armour on and was attaching his various weapons to the belts, scabbards, loops and hooks that held them in place. She fired another arrow into the neck of a boar, only to spot that more were moving up along the other side of the cart. As she nocked the next shaft, Poppy kicked her hoof out at the boar closest to him and it stumbled, rolling under the wheels of the cart and squealing horribly.

"My weapons don't have enough range for this. There are too many for my knives. Can you keep them at bay if I steer?" Bandolas called.

Serena did not reply instead she fired at yet another boar closing in on Poppy. Her shot went just wide as her aim was thrown off by the cart bouncing over the rough terrain. As she reached for another arrow, she had to scramble to grab the rail as the cart turned sharply to the right. One of the boars was not fast enough and it went down under the thundering hooves of the oxen.

Her next shot found its mark thudding into the thick hide of another boar, which peeled off from the hunt.

"Can't they go any faster?" Bandolas called.

"Poppy and Jess are farm oxen, not the elite charging oxen of the kings' cavaliers. Just keep them running they won't let you down." She shouted as she took aim with another shaft.

As she sighted on another boar, there was a sharp cracking noise from the front left wheel and the waggon bed tipped violently. The front of the waggon seemed to dig into the ground, and she was thrown from her high perch into the mud and grass. Landing hard, she tried to roll to lessen the impact but, because her hands were tangled in the bow and string, she could do nothing to protect her head, which smacked viciously into an exposed rock.

She rolled onto her back and blinked hard, trying to clear the pain and her vision.

Bandolas appeared next to her, axe smashing into a boar's neck.

Serena sat and tried to push herself up with one hand whilst clearing blood from her eye with the other.

Bandolas was ten feet away whirling his sword at three charging boars.

She managed to get to her knees and tried to pull her dagger free, blinking to clear her vision.

Bandolas was next to her, rolling between two boars and slashing long red marks along their flanks.

Serena staggered as she tried to stand, attempting to take the first stance he had taught her, feet wide for balance, but she was struggling to raise her head up and again had to wipe sticky blood from her face in order to see.

Bandolas flowed through the air above the boars' backs, swift strikes from his blades slashing at their faces.

Serena fell once more to the floor, lying on her side with her cheek in the dirt, slowly her eyes blinked as her vision dimmed. Each time her eyes opened he had moved. Each time her eyes opened he was striking another blow, with axe, with sword, with dagger, foot and hand. He seemed to move with unnatural speed almost winking out of existence and appearing again next to another foe and dealing another blow.

The dirt felt cool against her brow, and she let the darkness take her away.

PART 9: THE MESSENGER

He released the buckles and swung his leg out of the saddle, reaching up to catch his spur into the circular ring set in the ceiling. Then he freed his other leg, catching his other spur into another ceiling ring. For a moment he swung upside down staring into the depths of the cavern below, then he reached out to pat Gisselle gently on her snout. She nuzzled back before moving off towards the dark shadows at the back of the cavern to roost with her kin.

He unhooked one foot and swung forward to catch his spur into the next ring along. It took a lot of skill to traverse the ceiling rings, but he had been doing this for most of his life and moved quickly and fluidly along toward the entrance to the tower ahead. One of the younger novices leaned out and waved a hand in welcome before stepping back to prepare his warmed cloak.

Having reached the wall by the doorway, he grasped The Rungs of the ladder unhooked the spurs and dropped down, twisting his body to land on his feet on the small platform at the entrance way. He paused for a few seconds to adjust his balance before stepping through into the welcoming warmth of the recovery hall.

A pair of novices moved forward to help him to remove his thick leather gloves and bulky fur jacket. Then another placed his warmed robe over his head. He shuddered at the delicious heat of it against his cool skin. Travelling as a Messenger was a cold business. The air tore the heat from your body, he was trained to excel in the cold air of the high atmosphere, but it was always a pleasure to return to the warmth of the land. A large fire was maintained at all times in the massive hearth, which took up a large portion of the wall opposite the entrance. In front of the fire hung several sets of sky armour and coats as well as matching robes for use on land.

He removed his hat and goggles and lifted the hood of his robe over his head, shuddering once again at the cosy feeling of the soft lined interior. He nodded his thanks to the novices, who had already started to clean and dry his discarded clothing, before stepping from the room to follow the stairs downwards to make his report to The Degan.

As he strode into the office, a large muscular man stood from behind his desk and came over to clasp arms with him,

"Welcome back Findo. Come in and warm yourself by the fire. There is a cup of wine warming for you over there." The Degan waved his massive arm towards the fireplace.

"Thank you, sir. How are things in Westomere? Has the wife given you any more children since I saw you last?" Findo's voice was smooth and charming as he gently chided his superior.

"No, not this time. You weren't gone long enough, but I have been working on it. Things have been quiet for a time now. The new king seems to have settled the arguments with Mirror City and trade has resumed. How went your mission?" The Degan settled back into his well-worn chair.

Findo moved closer to the hearth and held the cup of mulled wine in both hands the warmth seeping into his fingers as he blew gently on the contents before taking a sip.

"Splitt seeks to make war with the north, citing infringements of their mining rights along the mountains of The Great Divide. They petition the King to assist them to retake lands, which they claim rightfully belong to the Lords of Splitt. The North of course also claim the lands are theirs." Findo reached inside his robe and unstrapped a messenger tube from his thigh.

"Petitions from both sides are contained within. I made sure they were sealed appropriately. I hand them to you just as they were sealed before me. May the words contained within be known to be true and my duty is complete." He passed the tube to The Degan.

"No need to say the formal words to me Findo. I have known you too long. Are we not friends?" The older man smiled at Findo and carefully placed the message tube with some others in the basket by his desk.

"I'll see that these are sent on to the king. Now sit and

tell me what you saw from the skies. It has been too long since I have ridden myself. Have the dunes of the sand sea shifted?"

The two men chatted for a long time as the sun set outside. Other messengers came and went carrying the words of kings, courtiers, and lords. Some thought that the palace was the beating heart of the kingdom. Findo believed it was this room, in this tower. All the most important information in the world flowed through here, though not a word was ever read by them, as was their code.

The messenger service was run from this room. Though in reality, The Degan only oversaw the service. The sorting offices ran the messenger service, organising the message tubes and ensuring they were sent to their destinations. Most messages were sent by land or sea. The cost of sending a message by air were prohibitive to all but the richest and, of course, the King. So only the most important words were carried by the airmen. Findo had worked hard to be the best there was. Because of his job he was party to the gossip of the highest courts in all the lands, and he met the most important people, but to read the words which he carried would mean death. The code was clear. The tubes were sealed, and those seals were only to be broken by the recipient. If your seals were broken before delivery then you would be court-martialled and, if found guilty, executed.

It was late by the time Findo finally made his way down to his chamber near the base of the tower. Through his small window he could see the hustle and bustle of the city though he had no wish to join the throngs. He closed the shutters and heavy curtains of his room against the noise. The great city of Westomere might never sleep but he was in need of rest. He removed his spurred boots and robe and sank gratefully into the snug covers of his bed.

Early in the morning before the sun had broken into the sky, he was awakened by a timid knocking at his door. He slipped from the covers and threw his robe on.

"Come in." He called as he tried to tame his unruly hair. One of the novices opened the door and handed him a slip of paper. He looked nervously around the room before staring at Findo who felt uncomfortable on account of the boy's obvious adulation.

"Thank you. Please prepare Gisselle for flight later today. Make sure my gear is ready for my departure." He nodded his thanks to the novice who hesitated for a second as though he wished to say something, before he turned in silence and hurried to complete his duties. All novices were sworn to silence for their first year of service to learn the value of words and prove they could keep secrets. If they could not hold their silence for that year, they were turned away from the academy in shame. Most never made it.

Findo turned up the lamp on his table and broke the small wax seal on the note. The words were simple but clear. 'Meet me on the palace steps in one hour.' The seal was that of The Degan.

PART 10: MESSENGERS AND KINGS

The two men clasped arms on the steps of the palace. "Summons from the Chancellor. My guess is that the King himself wants a message delivered."

The Degan glanced at the young Messenger before turning to look out over the city. Findo followed his gaze. The steps to the palace formed a bridge out over the waters of the River Avoy, leading up to the tall island upon which sat the palace.

Before them sprawled the mightiest city in the world. Westomere.

Huddled close to the banks of the river lay the richer districts surrounded by a large defensive curtain wall, a remnant from times long ago when the city was smaller.

Outside this wall were the slums. A ramshackle area of small, cramped houses and businesses which ringed the city and was always clouded in a haze of smoke and dust. The majority of the citizens lived within the slums, striving to earn enough money to move to better housing, away from the crimes which were rife in such cramped quarters. Between the houses, straight and well-maintained streets ran like rays of sunlight outwards in all directions from the central palace. These roads were busy thoroughfares and were heavily patrolled by the King's men. Most of them were wide enough that a line of market stalls ran along their centres. The pitches were precious to the owners who would do anything to maintain their places.

Beyond the slums, the roads ran into the newer more affluent areas of the city. The King had decreed that housing should be provided for all and that it should be of a quality acceptable to all. The first of these new 'suburbs' had recently been completed and hailed as a massive success. Built with good roads linking into the main thoroughfares of the slums, sewer systems under the roadways and running water available on every street from a communal pump. There were shopping districts as well as factory areas. All housing was built of stone up to the second floor. It was a real marvel.

"Are you sure you're up to this Findo?" The Degan said.

"This is what I do. I carry messages, so that I can fly. I follow the code, so that I can fly. Come we should not keep them waiting." Findo put his arm on The Degan's shoulder and gently steered him towards the Palace.

The broad, white marble steps formed a ramp from the mainland up to the island. The river Avoy swirled underneath the ramp, filthy and heavily laden with sediment from further inland. The steps were crowded. People formed lines according to their business at the palace. Hawkers called out their wares and vendors sold food and drinks to the waiting people. The two Messengers made their way between the lines, no one would stop them, their uniforms marked them out, everyone knew better than to stop a Messenger.

The structure before them was not pretty. It did not try to be grand or entertaining. It was built for one purpose. To protect. Protect the land and the entrance to the river. Most importantly, to protect the King.

It squatted on the top of the craggy island. Thick stone walls with a series of towers surrounding an inner wall, which itself encircled the keep. The walls were imposing enough but the keep itself was a huge structure. It did not tower, like the fair castles of the north, it was not beautifully decorated as were the spires of Islay. No, it just sat dark and brooding, utilitarian in form and function.

The Degan saw them quickly through the formalities at the gate house and led them through the outer bailey. At the gates of the second wall, a junior from the chancellor's household met them and lead them on to the keep.

Once inside, he guided them through a labyrinth of corridors to a waiting chamber outside a large set of heavy oak doors. The man spoke with a high-pitched voice as though he had just eaten something disgusting,

"Make yourselves comfortable the Chancellor will be with you shortly." He said before bobbing a small bow to The Degan and scurrying off down the corridor.

The pair remained standing. They waited impatiently staring around at the blank stone walls before the doors suddenly opened and a tall slim man wearing a smart suit in the newest style stepped through. His intelligent eyes took in the two of them before he stepped over to firmly grasp arms with The Degan.

"So good to see you, old friend. How are things in the tower? I trust you have things running smoothly." The Chancellor spoke warmly.

The Degan pulled the man in and clapped his arm on his back. "You should come over sometime and we can share a cup or two and talk of old times."

He waved his Messenger companion over. "Findo here keeps me on my toes, the fastest and most reliable airman there ever was. Better even than me when they still let me fly."

The Chancellor offered his arm and Findo grasped it, surprised by how firm the thin man's grip was.

"For a time, the Chancellor and I ran together in the army, back before we got proper jobs." The Degan told Findo. "There was no one I would have trusted more to have my back in a scrape."

The two men clasped arms again before the Chancellor began to lead them down the corridor once again. They chatted amiably as Findo followed along behind them.

The Chancellor led them to the King's waiting chamber. Anyone who wished to see the King had to pass through this famed room. The walls glowed gently, they appeared to be made of some sort of glass, behind which burned a thousand candles. It was said that if you held murder in your heart that the light would see it and you would not be allowed to pass.

The Chancellor stepped over to some men to arrange their passage on leaving the Messengers alone for a short time.

"Always creeps me out this place does. Makes me feel like I'm hiding something." The Degan grumbled.

"Are the stories true?" Findo asked.

"I don't know. I've never seen anyone die here if that's what you mean. I never understand why there are no guards posted here though, so perhaps it is true. Anyway, if an assassin did make it through here, they still would have to get past The

Gauntlet." The Degan pointed at the doors ahead of them.

Just then the Chancellor returned with a guide. The guides were the only people who knew the way through The Gauntlet, a series of corridors and small rooms which led to the King's chambers. The Gauntlet was basically a maze, designed as a last line of defence for the King. The walls of the maze were said to move and change over time, great magics contained within them. Anyone who did not follow the correct path would be lost. Those that did not know the way and stepped from the path were never seen again. No one entered The Gauntlet without a guide.

The guides were the King's most loyal guards. Trained from birth by the shadow fighters of Kentai, proficient in all forms of combat and sworn to protect the King with their lives. It was said that they lived in the Gauntlet and that over the years it affected them in strange ways, giving them unnatural abilities. Because they spent so much time in there, they were also the only people who could navigate its dark corridors.

Their guide signalled for them to follow him and walked off through the doors. There seemed to be nothing special about him. Medium height and build, ordinary looking in every way. He would have been easy to lose in a crowd, except for the way that he moved. He had the grace of a cat, light on his toes. Relaxed, yet you had the feeling that he was coiled inside, ready to lash out and spring into action. Also, he was completely naked. The guides never carried weapons and never wore clothes.

He led them into a dark stone corridor, as unremarkable as the passageways through which they had travelled already. He made several turns and guided them through a low archway into a circular chamber. Without hesitation, he continued through one of four other archways. After only a few minutes Findo was lost. They continued to walk down corridors which looked identical, through rooms of various sizes and archways of a variety of shapes. Not once did the guide slow or hesitate. He just seemed to be wandering aimlessly on a whim, though he maintained an alertness at all times, yet soon he brought them to a doorway which he opened and led them through.

PART 11

Serena rubbed a fist full of grass along the back withers of Poppy. He turned to look at her, flicking his ears to ward away flies, then let out a deep rumble from his throat and went back to chewing the cud. She continued around to his other flank, brushing mud from his fur and checking for injuries. Both beasts of burden appeared hot and lathered from the chase and a little spooked, but they showed no sign of harm.

She came to, lying in Bandolas's lap as he washed the wound to her forehead.

"That will leave a small scar by your hair line. It bled a lot, but you should be fine. Lie still whilst I wrap a bandage around it."

He had tenderly washed and dressed the cut as she lay staring up at him trying to figure out what had happened. Once finished, he had helped her back to her feet and they had assessed the damage to the cart. The wheels were not designed for fast travel over rough terrain and the spokes on one side had cracked and broken. It was beyond repair.

Bandolas set to moving the corpses of the boars so that they could set up camp. He gutted, hung and skinned one, another he stripped the flesh from, covered it in salt from a pouch in his pack and hung the slivers of flesh out to dry in the sun.

"Without the waggon it could be a long walk. We will need all the food we can gather."

Once she had checked on the oxen, Serena let them loose to crop the grass. They would not venture far. She moved to go and help him set up a camp.

As they worked, she noticed that he favoured his right side, shielding his left with his arm. He also limped heavily.

"You should rest, I can finish this. Go sit and remove your armour and I will check your wounds. It would not help if either of us got an infection."

He looked at her with dull eyes and moved to sit by his pack on the ground nearby.

Once she had secured the canvases over the sides of the

waggon, she shifted their bedding rolls inside. It did not look like rain so Jess and Poppy could stay out in the open tonight. Then she walked over to Bandolas, earlier he had saved their lives, she owed him a great debt.

He sat with crossed legs, with his head bowed down low, hair hanging loosely. His armour was dangling from his shoulder, half removed.

"Can I help you?" she asked.

He did not respond.

She put a gentle hand on his shoulder, and he slowly sank onto his side, unconscious. Having worked alongside her mother for so many years, her training took over.

She pulled the armour from him and rolled him onto his back. Immediately, she saw that the wound on his side was bleeding, and his stitches were torn. The tear in his flesh did not look good. The edges of the wound were dried and rotten, the flesh surrounding it discoloured and dark. He had a terrible infection and had been hiding it from her.

She would need to cut away the dead flesh and seal the wound. In her pack were a small quantity of herbs she could use to make a poultice and draw out the infection. She started a small fire and put one of his knives in the coals to heat through.

Once she had stripped the rest of his armour from him, she found a couple of his smaller, sharper knives. In a pot over the fire, she boiled water and she tore their bedding to make bandages which she added to the pot. She ground the herbs as her mother had taught her to and mixed in a little of the hot liquid to make a paste. The knives she cleaned and laid out before her on some clean linen. Once she had everything prepared, she took a deep breath to steady her hands and began her work.

The rotten flesh went deeper than she had expected; she had to cut much of it away. When the knife on the fire was glowing, she pressed it into the wound, sealing the broken blood vessels within to stop the bleeding. He groaned as she held the hot metal to his flesh, his arms spasming by his sides and his back arching from the pain even in his unconscious stupor. When the grizzly work was done, she spread her unguent thickly over the ruined flesh and bandaged his side tightly. She then carefully ran her hands over the rest of his body checking for further wounds. He had many old scars but only a deep cut in his calf was fresh, she cleaned and dressed this and then rolled him into some blankets so he could rest.

As she put a thin stew over the fire to heat so that the meat would soften, she saw a small herd of gazelle bound through the grass nearby. One stopped for a time and watched her; head held high in curiosity as it flicked its ears. Then it swiftly turned and bound after its herd. The sounds of birdsong and small insects returned to the Everplain. For now, she felt safe. Safe but exhausted.

She cooled a portion of the stew as she ate her own and then carefully fed it between his lips, wiping away the excess carefully with a small cloth. She left the dishes dirty and tied Jess and Poppy on long tethers to the waggon so they would not wander off. Then she lay down by his good side, pulling a blanket over them both, and fell into a weary slumber.

Several times during the night she woke as he trembled or cried out. He was beginning to get feverish, and she cooled his brow with a damp cloth and tried to get him to take some water between his lips.

She rose with the sun, turning her mind to the cart.

The waggon itself seemed to be in good condition. The problem was the front left wheel. Several of the spokes had shattered, the felloes and the metal rim had bent, warped and snapped. With the right tools and materials, she thought she could fashion a new one, but out here… there was no way.

Still, she tried.

Using various of his knives she freed the tyre band. The felloes had broken loose, and a couple of the joining dowels were snapped but she could put them together. The main problem was that most of the spokes had snapped and without them there would be no support for the weight of the cart on the wheel. She could probably fashion a few from a couple of the cart's railings but not enough.

Still, she tried.

PART 12

Bandolas awoke around midday. He groaned as the sun stung his eyes. His left side felt as though it was on fire. It itched, stung and ached. He put his hand on it to discover that there was a heavy thick bandage tightly wrapping him from his ribs down to his waist. After trying to sit and discovering that the pain worsened, he lay still for a time. He could hear bird song; the rustling of the grass in the wind; snorting from the oxen, Poppy and Jess; what sounded like wood being shaved and swearing. Lots of swearing, huffing and frustrated banging.

"Come on you bloody hunk of wood, cut straight. Why won't the blade just follow the grain?" He could hear Serena's vexation in the tone of her voice.

"You know, I could help you with that." His voice was thick, his throat tight. The words seemed weak to his ears.

Suddenly she was there. Kneeling by his side holding his hand tightly. "Thank the gods you are awake. How do you feel? Can I get you anything? Do you want to sit up?"

He stopped her by placing a finger over her lips. "I feel terrible. What happened?"

"You lied to me." she said. Then she pulled her hand from his and walked away.

For a time, he just lay there.

"Serena. I'm sorry. I didn't want to burden you. I…" He could not find the words.

She came back carrying a small bowl. "Here, drink this. You lost a lot of blood and will need to regain your strength. One of the wheels on the waggon broke. I was thrown to the floor. You fought off the boars and then you helped to set up camp. You should have said how bad your wound was." She looked him in the eyes and reached out a hand, which she gently placed on his chest.

"I thought you might die. You still might. The infection was bad and had started spreading. I had to cut you very deep to clear it. I cauterised and cleaned the wound as best I could and have poulticed it against further infection. If we're lucky you'll live."

As he looked back at her, he saw tears begin to well up in her eyes. He reached a hand up, cupping the back of her head and pulled her close. His lips pressed gently against hers, the tears running between them. He let her go and she pulled away.

She held up his head and made him drink some of the thin watered-down stew. It had little taste, but it did make him feel a little better. She brought over their packs and helped him to sit propped up against them. Then she handed him the bowl and walked back over to the nearby cart.

He could see that she had been busy whilst he was out. Serena had taken the back panel and most of one side off the cart and constructed a sturdy enough workbench. On the bench and lying on the floor all around it were various pieces of wood. He could see that she had put some of the wheel back together but that it would not function properly and keep its shape there were too many missing parts.

Gods he needed something for the pain. Even the slight movements of his chest as he breathed caused his whole left side to hurt like a fresh stab to his side. He watched her shaping pieces of planking with his knives and slowly he sank back into darkness.

★★★

Serena looked up from her work. He was asleep again, head lolling forward. She reached up and touched her lips where his had touched hers. How soft they had been when every other part of him was lean and hard. Her heart beat a little faster as she thought of the feel of his skin under her hands. If only that thought was not marred by the sight of so much of his blood. The skies were beginning to darken as clouds rolled in from the west and the breeze began to pick up. She would need to move him into the shelter soon. The knives she had been using she returned to their sheaths, the belt which held them she strapped around her waist so as not to lose them. She began to tidy her work away. Checking on the oxen and tightening the ropes on the canvas of the shelter.

★★★

Sitting in their small shelter at the side of the waggon, he felt like he had aged 10 years that day. When Serena had woken him and helped him to move, he had nearly passed out from the pain. Every small step had been an agony. By the time they had walked the small distance to the cart he had been bathed in sweat, barely able to raise his head. She had settled him, wiped a cool wet cloth over his face and chest and wrapped him in heavy blankets. Now the oxen lay next to him sharing their warmth. The wind blew fiercely through their small camp causing the canvas to shudder and thrum. Rain would follow soon. He could taste lightning on the air. This would not be a pleasant night camping.

Serena sat on the other side of the small storm lantern she had unpacked from the chest on the waggon, using the weak light to try to fix two broken shafts of wood together. She aligned the broken ends and pushed them together. Then she wound thin cords of rope around the join. When she flexed the spoke it held for a moment and then came apart. She threw the parts down and pouted.

He motioned for her to come and sit next to him. "Bring those." He pointed to the broken shafts.

★★★

If only they had some glue. Something to bind the broken pieces strongly together. Serena knew they would need a miracle to make it out of the plains now. She sat beside him. The two broken ends of the spoke in her hand.

"Hold them together, like you did a minute ago." He said smiling weakly at her.

She did as he asked holding the spoke out towards him. He tried to sit up straighter but winced in pain. Then he closed his eyes, and she could see him breathing deeply, just like when he practiced the Movements.

He reached out and grasped the broken spoke between his finger and thumb just to the side of the break. Slowly he slid his grip along the wood. She glanced at him and saw his eyes were rivetted on the join, unwavering. He removed his thumb from the spoke but continued to slowly brush his finger across the cracks, breathing slowly and deliberately. A faint spark seemed to fire in his eyes. She watched the slow progression of his finger as it moved back and forth over the break.

She did not start when she began to see a small wave following his finger along the wood. She did stare in wonder as it became a fresh sprout following the path his finger traced. As his hand passed back the other way a new thin twist of wood followed it and wound onto the first. Each pass of his finger brought forth more twisting vines binding across the join in the two halves of the spoke. Soon the break could not be seen as it was covered in tiny ribbons of new wood connecting across it. He stopped and looked at her.

"The Rush can do many things if you can learn to control it." He said this, then his eyes rolled up and he collapsed into slumber.

Serena stared at the spoke. She tried to bend it, but it was strong once again. Bandolas was keeping too many secrets from her. There was so much to learn from him. She must help him survive.

PART 13

The night's rain had turned the area into a quagmire. Thunder and lightning had kept Serena awake for much of the night. Now she stomped about the camp and worked on the wheel. As the mud began to dry it clung to her boots making each step heavier. The weight matched her mood.

She had kept an eye on him all night watching as Bandolas had slept fitfully. His fever was low and now that the rain had passed, he slept on. The oxen grazed nearby on the lush green grass.

Giving up on her repairs, Serena retrieved her staff from the waggon bed.

After checking on Bandolas and wetting the cool cloth on his forehead with fresh rainwater she had collected during the night, she practiced the Movements. She ran through those he had showed her. At first, she felt awkward and jerky. Slowly, she stopped thinking about the world around her and the difficulties with the waggon, she concentrated on the motions and her breathing, relaxing her mind to concentrate on her body, the way her muscles moved, the correct posture of each stance. Time became meaningless as she moved around the camp.

Without realising it she had her dagger in her hand and was adding it into the Movements, swiftly thrusting forward with it, the blade flashing in the morning sunlight as it slashed through the air. Serena began to feel a quickening to her pulse, the world around her started to slow. She swirled past Poppy who flicked his ears towards her as she rolled under him. Bandolas's words came back to her, 'slow down, never lose control.'

Serena paused in her Movements. She was breathing heavily, her body ached in a good way, but her mind raced in a thousand directions which she was not ready to face yet. She walked over to her staff and picked it up. She tried a couple of sweeps of it. It felt good in her hand and provided more reach than her blade did. She worked through a few of the

Movements, incorporating the staff but she found that its length meant that she often needed to hold it two handed. She began to practice how she could create new stances, whirling the staff around her head and about her body. Soon she was caught up in The Rush, her mind raced ahead of her movements. The staff flowing around her sweeping low to the ground then swiping upwards, whirling around in her hands.

★★★

Bandolas awoke. For a while he watched. Serena was in the midst of the Rush; she moved as a blur seeming to flicker from one position to another. He did not know how long she had been caught up, but he knew if she did not stop, she ran a real risk of dying.

Using one of the poles holding the canvas up for support he slowly rose shakily to his feet. Then step by slow step he shuffled forward until he stood in the centre of their camp. The grass all around had been knocked flat by her passing. There was no way he could catch her or stop her in his current state. All he could do was wait and hope her path moved close. He began to breath rhythmically, watching her Movements. She drew close a few times, but he was not ready. He drew his knife, holding the blade along his forearm his grip reversed. His eyes closed and he listened to the sounds of her staff cutting through the air. He moved his feet further apart for stability and waited.

★★★

It was like hitting a stone wall. Her staff swung through the air in a beautiful arc and slammed into something immoveable. The wood cracked sending splinters through the air. She stopped, frozen in place staring into his eyes.

"How long?" He asked her.

"I, I, don't know." Serena's voice faltered. She looked at the position of the sun, realising that most of the morning had passed. When she had started the Movements, the sun had been low and now it shone near its zenith. A wave of nausea flowed through her and her knees nearly buckled.

Bandolas lowered his arm and reached out to catch her, but he ended up nearly collapsing himself as pain ripped through his injured side.

"You need to eat right now. Then drink as much water as you can stomach. The Rush charges a heavy price for its use, and you need to pay it. Go now." The tone of command he used left her no room to argue and she hurried off to grab their supplies.

Serena went straight to her pack and grabbed a fist full of nuts and dried berries from a pouch. She stuffed them into her mouth ravenously. As the flavours coursed over her tongue, she could not believe how hungry she felt and for a while she just stood there at the back of the waggon shovelling hand after hand of food into her mouth and hastily chewing and swallowing. When she had finished the mix, she grabbed a large piece of jerky and began to chew on that. It was harder to eat and so as she chewed, she moved over to where Bandolas had sat back down under the canvas.

He handed her a cup. "Drink."

She downed the water and he quickly refilled it. "Drink more."

She did. He filled her cup six times before she held out her hand to stop him.

"Why do I feel so bad now?" Serena asked.

"The Rush is like a fire. If it burns low and slow the fuel lasts a long time. If it burns hot and out of control it can consume everything around it. When you use this power, it uses you as fuel. If you are not in control, it will use all of you."

Bandolas looked into her eyes. "You must not lose control again. Find a thought to tether yourself to, a memory or a person and keep it in your mind as a reminder to come back. If you don't and you get caught up in it, the flames will rush through you burning up all your body until you die. Now, eat some more and rest. We will need our strength tomorrow to get this waggon moving." He slowly closed his eyes as Serena thought about what he said, she hungrily chewed on another piece of dried meat.

They both relaxed for a while before Serena became restless. She groomed the oxen and tethered them by the waggon before tidying her workbench. She thought about how the Rush had taken her. The thrill she had felt and the awful realisation that she had lost control. Completely. If Bandolas had not been there she would never have stopped. She would still be caught up in that magnificent feeling.

Once Bandolas was awake again she helped him to sit and changed his bandages whilst inspecting his wound.

"It seems to be 'ealing alright. The bleeding has stopped. We should stay for a few more days and give your wound a chance to 'eal properly before we move."

"If we get the waggon fixed tomorrow, I can rest in that as we move. We shouldn't stay for too long. Any predators out here will have sensed us and no doubt some are moving in. They might be wary at the moment but if we stay still, their number will grow, and they will become brave. Never stay in one place too long." His voice was weary. "I need to show you some things in the morning. To help you to control your powers. I worry that you are not ready. Most that I have heard of with these powers come into them slowly, from a young age and with people around them to help them. But you are like a charging bull, suddenly appearing and smashing through everything. What you did today, the way you were moving and the Movements you were using, you were creating new ways I have never seen before, things beyond my training. Do you know how? Or why?"

"I just did what you showed me, and then tried with the dagger and my staff. When I used the staff, it was like I couldn't 'old back. It just felt right. The more I moved, the more I realised I could do."

"It is very rare indeed that anyone can ever move beyond what they are shown. Few ever make new Movements or create new ways beyond their trainer's knowledge. Perhaps the Wizards at Eap will be able to tell us more or help you further. We should rest now. I will think on this overnight."

PART 14: MESSENGER AWAY

Findo hung upside down from the ceiling rings. He reached out to check the straps on Gisselle's saddle. She looked around to see what he was doing and nudged his hand with her nose. He gently pushed her head away humming softly for her to be still. The drop below him was far enough to kill a man on impact. Soon enough they would be in the air, and he needed to complete his flight check ritual to calm his mind.

Satisfied that everything was secure he swung down into the saddle, nimbly clipping the spurs on his boots into their mountings. Gisselle shifted her weight to grasp the rocks above more firmly. Findo adjusted his pack behind him and leant into the chest support, facing the chasm below. He buckled on the thigh straps securing himself onto the saddle and reached forward to brush the quills of Gisselle's mane.

She was a Kystraal, a large flying mammal. Evolutionarily, she was related to bats. Her kind had been bred for many generations for their strength, stamina, and intelligence. Around the same size as an ox, only much less bulky, her short rear legs were nearly useless on the ground but had a powerful grip and were ideally suited to grasping rocks in cave ceilings and on sheer mountain sides. Her front legs were exceptionally long, supporting her huge wings. The muscles of her chest and shoulders built for driving her through the air. Her body had two different layers of fur. An inner soft downy layer which helped to keep her warm and an outer layer of thick, coarse fur which ran smoothly over her, shielding her from rain and wind. She also had a mane of quills. Large hairs which had adapted to be hard, similar to the central quill of a bird's feather or to the protective quills of a porcupine. These quills were hollow and lightweight but hard and acted as a kind of armour around the Kystraal's neck and chest. Unlike most bats, Kystraal were not nocturnal, they did not have large ears or short noses. Giselle had a slightly elongated neck, small ears and large eyes. Her snout was long and aerodynamic with tusks which curved from the front of her muzzle backwards towards her chest.

Findo grasped the reins, which looped onto Gisselle's tusks and gave her a gentle nudge with his knees.

She dropped like a stone. The wind tore at Findo trying to tear him from his seat, but he was firmly anchored. He wrapped his arms around the chest support before him and let Gisselle have her fun. The floor of the cave was rapidly approaching as the Kystraal opened her wings at the last second, the force of her turn pushed Findo firmly into the saddle as she banked and flew out of the cave entrance into the bright afternoon sunlight.

She climbed rapidly, her wide leathery wings beating at the air as she rose. Findo reached out to brush her quills as he hummed satisfaction to her.

He glanced down at the city below and the palace fortification on its island in the river. He had said the words to the King himself, "I take these from you as they were sealed before me. May the words contained within be known to be true, until my duty is complete."

Now he carried three messages to be delivered to the three cities in the West: Heldon, Splitt and Daggos. The King wished to stop conflict between the cities from becoming war.

His first stop was to be at the northern city of Heldon. The city guild was to halt its mining operations along the Great Divide until the guild heads met for a conference with the King in Westomere.

After the north, Findo was to deliver a message to Lord Wilhelm, the ruler of Splitt. He was to cease all hostilities with the north and relinquish his claims to any mines north of Mount Ghastom, until he attended the conference with the King in Westomere.

Finally, his last message was to The Pirate, Oakhands, leader of the free peoples of Daggos a port city of ship builders. The message called for the shipwrights to cease trade with Splitt and Heldon until further notice, and for their fleet to patrol the oceans of the west and dissuade any hostilities between the two cities in conflict.

Findo pulled gently on the reins and Gisselle banked to the north, still climbing towards the clouds.

PART 15

Serena looked over at Bandolas who dozed in the seat beside her. His recovery was going well, though he still needed more rest. His mobility was improving, and the wound had stopped weeping. In the mornings he carried out some simple exercises whilst directing her in her training. She practiced the Movements both with and without weapons for an hour every day before breakfast. Once they broke camp, she would run ahead of the cart scouting the land to increase her stamina. As the sun grew high in the sky and the temperature increased, she would join Bandolas in the cart and he would talk of the places he had been and the things he had done. During the afternoons he would doze as she drove. Evenings were when they set up camp, tended to Jess and Poppy and worked on their equipment. Serena often set traps nearby to catch small game for the next day.

Everything had become routine. At first the adventure had been exciting and the sights new and interesting. Now the monotony of the plains was getting on Serena's nerves.

The most interesting thing to happen since the attack of the boars was three days ago, when a heard of buffalo had passed them. They had had to stop the to camp for most of the day as the herd was so large, Bandolas had estimated the size to be over seven thousand animals. The dust had hung in the air for hours and the ground was churned up making for slow going in the cart. They had kept a watchful eye out as a herd that size was likely to be followed by predators, but they did not spot any, except for a huge, winged shape riding high on the thermals above the mass of buffalo.

For three weeks now they had been heading due north and still there was no break on the horizon. The grass waved gently in the wind; clouds moved over the sky their shadows crawling across the land.

A covey of grouse startled from the grass off to the left of them, and Bandolas jolted awake. Serena reached for her bow.

"'ere, sleepy 'ead, take the reins. I'll go catch us some

dinner." She threw the reins into Bandolas's lap and dashed from the cart.

She slowed as she approached the spot where the birds had landed. Slowing her breathing, fingers ready with an arrow on the string. She began to step to the rhythm of the Rush; she could feel it building inside her. She concentrated her mind on the hunt whilst partitioning off a small part with an image of her father. As Bandolas had instructed her she had built a room in her mind with some special memories locked away in it. If she felt herself slipping away in the Rush all she had to do was break down the door of that room and the memories would bring her back to herself. So far, she had not needed the room, her control was improving.

Suddenly, in a flapping of wings and a cacophony of warning calls the grouse burst into the air in front of her. She drew and aimed. The world slowed around her. She could sense where the birds were going to be, it was as though she stood amongst them and just needed to reach out and place the arrows where they needed to go. Shot after shot flew forth. She stopped because there were no more arrows in her quiver. Twelve grouse lay in the grass before her, each with an arrow perfectly placed.

Bandolas had stopped the cart and was walking over.

"You never cease to amaze me. Never have I seen someone shoot like that. You are finding ways to use the Rush that not even the stone druids have tried."

She turned to him dampness in her eyes, "But we only needed a brace, I killed them all. I couldn't stop shooting."

"You did the impossible and should be happy. The Rush didn't take you." He stepped towards her.

"But it did take me. I couldn't control it. Everything 'appened so fast. There was no time to take or lose control." She shook her head, her long hair falling over her eyes. "Another thing to add into the morning routines. If I can practice it then I can learn to expect it."

"Yes. Then you can learn to control it. It is called the Rush because when you are caught in it, it pushes you forward like flowing water or a strong wind." Bandolas put his arms around her as he spoke, calming her. "You must learn to slow yourself by pushing against that flow. If you let it take you it will wash you away. Your memory acts as your anchor, but even an anchored ship moves with the tide. You need to learn to push back and stand your ground."

They gathered the fowl together and put them in a sack to clean and cook that evening. As Serena clicked her tongue and shook the reins for Jess and Poppy to get underway again, Bandolas nudged her in the ribs. "Can you see that, on the Eastern horizon?"

The cart started to trundle forward. Serena looked out towards the east. Endless expanses of grass. "Where? I can't see anything but grass."

Bandolas pointed.

She looked for a long time before she spotted what she thought at first was a distant hawk or vulture. Right on the horizon was a small speck. As she kept looking, she thought it appeared to be triangular in shape.

"That's a sail. We need to get moving. Hopefully, they haven't spotted us yet or they are travelling elsewhere. If they turn and the sail starts to get larger, we will know they are coming for us." Bandolas moved into the rear of the cart and started to strap his equipment on.

Serena urged Jess and Poppy to more speed, she kept her bow, staff and knife close beside her.

After a quarter of an hour the sail stopped moving along the horizon. "Ready yourself. They have spotted us and are turning. They will need to sail into the wind which means it will take them a while to get here. Let's hope they give up and move off." Bandolas leaned on the rails behind Serena. He Pulled a looking glass from one of his pouches. "They are having to tack northwards now. We have a while."

They spent the next hour watching the sail slowly moving northwards and then turning and heading westwards, all the while slowly getting bigger. Bandolas told her how a ship was controlled and the mechanics of sailing, he seemed reminded of his youth travelling on large ships. Serena was happy to let him talk, his voice calmed her.

As the sun began to set, they did not stop to make camp for the night. "With any luck they will lose us in the dark. Keep our course the same. They will presume we will try to turn in the dark and make a run for it. With luck they will second guess us and go the wrong way."

"Who could they be? Why risk riding on in the dark?" Serena asked worriedly.

"At best merchants hoping to make quick coin out of us. At worst, pirates, or slavers. I'd prefer not to find out." Bandolas continued to watch behind as Serena coaxed the oxen on.

As the light faded away their pursuers disappeared southwards. Serena and Bandolas began to relax, the tension of the pursuit weighing heavily upon them. Serena slowed the Poppy and Jess as it was becoming difficult to see in the darkness and she did not want to risk injuring the animals.

Bandolas continued to scan the horizon behind them, carefully watching for signs of pursuit.

"Damn! Do you feel that?" He asked.

Serena listened and watched. "What is it?"

"The wind is shifting direction."

The cart trundled slowly on.

A light appeared far away behind them. Slowly it moved back and forth zigzagging as the ship tacked into the wind searching for its prey.

Occasionally the light would stop. A couple of times it disappeared. It always returned. Serena gave the reins to Bandolas for a while and jogged besides the waggon trying to ease the tension in her neck and shoulders.

The night passed. As colour began to bleed back into the morning sky and the stars faded it was obvious that the oxen were exhausted. Jess was huffing and both animals were lathered. They could not go on like this.

"Bandolas, we need to stop. Let Jess and Poppy rest, they need to eat and drink. Let our pursuers come, you and I can take care of them." Serena's voice was tight with apprehension.

"You're right. There is no way we can outrun them. But before we fight, let me try to talk to them. Apparently, diplomacy is all the rage in Westomere."

They stopped the cart and unhitched the oxen to graze. Then they stood, fully armed, watching the ship roll in.

The vessel itself was not much wider than their cart, but it stood much taller and was about twice the length. The main body of it was shaped like a graceful boat, sweeping up to a long and sinuous prow. At the front of the ship was a large wheel. From the rear of the ship two long outriggers rolled along on a series of smaller wheels. The mast was tall and carried a single triangular sail. Towards the front of the vessel stood a lean and muscular man flying a kite. The kite was a large rectangle in the sky and was attached to a small mast at the front of the ship. The man used it to help steer the ship and for extra speed. Now the winds were favourable, and its target was in clear sight, it did not take the ship long to close the distance and soon it was rolling to a stop before them.

"Ho there friends. What brings you into the wilds of the Everplains?" A large man with a bulbous nose leant casually over the side of the ship to call down to them.

"Simple travelers making our way north for a new life." Bandolas replied.

"Well now, if that were true you wouldn't be dressed like that would you. Try again." The man said as sarcasm dripped from every word of his oily voice.

"We are travelling north, this man offered to escort me to Eap where I wish to beg the Wizards for their help." Serena said desperately.

"Hmm, some truth you speak but not all. There is more to this." The man turned back to call to someone unseen on the boat. "Boys, drop the ramp. These fine people have offered to share breakfast with us."

He turned back and winked at Serena, "You don't mind cooking up a little something does you darlin', we had a long night you see and me and the boys didn't get much chance to eat."

The man ducked out of sight.

PART 16

With various rumbling noises from inside the body of the boat, a section of the side began to lower slowly down.

As it hit the ground, two burly men stepped out, crossbows raised. Over the railings above, a young girl pointed a bow down at them. The man with the bulbous nose casually walked out from the shadows within the vessel.

"Keep your arms away from your weapons and we should all get along fine. Now darlin', about that breakfast you promised, will it be long?" The man's greasy voice slipped from his tongue like eels' breath.

Bandolas raised his hands away from his hips, fingers splayed. "Serena, could you start a fire and put some water on to boil. It appears these men would like to talk. Don't start anything. Let me handle this please."

He walked towards the man and reached out his arm. "My name is Bandolas, Serena is the one fixing your food."

The man with the bulbous nose stepped forward and clasped arms with Bandolas, "Captain Glime, you can call me Captain. This 'ere is me crew. Tall Jacks," The captain pointed to one of the men with a crossbow and then gestured on, "Devlin, and the girl on deck be my daughter, Sandy."

"Nice to meet you captain. What brings you out so far into the Everplain?" Bandolas walked slowly to the back of the cart and pulled two small chests out. He put them near the fire which Serena is building and gestured for the captain to sit on them with him.

"Good trade is scarce at the moment. The world seems to be holding its breath. Talk of war in the west and there's been no word from Havii or the twin cities for moons. We been trading small towns and villages around the outskirts of the grasslands for a while, but people are getting nervous, and coin is short."

The captain looked long and hard at the canvas in the back of the cart. "We saw you travelling way out here and wondered what would bring fine folks to these parts?"

As the captain had been talking Tall Jacks had lowered his crossbow and walked over to the back of the waggon. Devlin however kept his bow raised and aimed at Bandolas. The girl, Sandy had also lowered her bow but watched Serena's movements carefully.

"From her accent I'd say that she 'as travelled from the farmlands way down to the south. The question is why does she need a man so well armed as you to transport her to the Wizards at Eap? No need for a reply. And why is there such a large item hiding under that there canvas? I think to myself that perhaps it is not the girl but the cargo which you transport." The captain stares hard at Bandolas for a long time.

The silence became uncomfortable.

"Now, now my new friend, no need to start reaching for your knife. I can see that you could be a bit of a handful with a weapon in your hand. Let's none of us do anything hasty until we have all broken our fasts. How's the food coming along darlin'?" The captain turned his gaze from Bandolas for a second to look at Serena.

Bandolas moved like a viper, but the captain was faster still. Putting his hand quickly on top of Bandolas's stopping him from drawing his knife. "No need for that friend. This is your last chance. I don't want to have to take your weapons from you or harm you. From the way you're wincing I would bet you have already come to harm." The captain slowly sat back down releasing his hand from atop Bandolas's and raising his hands in a sign of peace.

Serena walked over with a steaming cup for each of them. "Tea for you both." She raised her voice to the others. "Warm drinks for you over 'ere. The morning broth will be ready soon if you 'ave any bowls that will help as we only have the two we use."

"Ok captain, we can talk." Bandolas sighed in resignation. Serena could see the fight go out of him as he sagged slightly, lowering his eyes to the ground.

"Good my boy. First we will eat." The captain turned to shout at the boat. "Sandy, fetch some salt and a few bowls, grab a small cask of grog whilst you're at it. Devlin, whatever you do, don't lower your bow. Not until our business is ended. Jacks, help with the breakfast would you."

They all sat warily drinking and then eating. Serena and Jacks had brought over a bucket and another chest for them to sit on. Sandy had brought out a small bag of salt which she offered to Serena to season the broth. "Father likes a meal with strong flavour." She placed a little cask down next to the captain before she took her bowl and went and leant against the side of the ship. Devlin stayed where he was, crossbow casually raised, pointing towards Bandolas.

"Thank you, darlin', that was very nice. Keep the salt, a rarity on the road, as payment for the meal." The captain pulled a handkerchief from his pocket and wiped his chin. "Now to business my new friends."

"Captain, we have nothing for you to trade...."

"Look son please don't lie to me." The captain stopped Bandolas in mid-sentence. "I like to do honest trade where I can." He pointed at the waggon. "Now will you tell me what is under that canvas that you are being so secretive about, or do I have to go and take a look."

Bandolas slowly stood up, keeping his hands held out wide away from his weapons. "You will have to take a look. If I tell you, you won't believe me anyway."

"Now that's the truth. I do believe I'll take a look." The captain walked over to the waggon and drew his sword. He pushed the corner of the canvas back with the tip of his weapon. "Hells, what a mess!"

Jacks walked up to peer over the captain's shoulder and visibly paled at the sight. Both men hurried over to sit back down again.

"Wizards?" The captain asked.

"Yes."

"Bounty?"

Bandolas did not reply.

"Bounty?" He asked again.

"Yes."

"Rather you than me son. I heard that they had lost control of one of their pets. You did well to kill that thing. Be that where your injury came from?" The captain asked, his voice had changed, and he now appeared more fatherly in his demeanour.

"I hunted it for several moons. When I killed it, its last act in life was to slice my side with its antlers. Serena helped me to heal. There have been setbacks."

Captain Glime stared hard into Bandolas's eyes. "Well, we can't leave empty handed. You must have something to trade?"

"What are you offering in exchange?" Serena jumped into the conversation.

"Darlin', your lives of course." The captain had not taken his eyes from Bandolas's.

"Sir, we have a sack full of grouse we caught yesterday. They should feed you and your crew well for a few days. Looking at your ship, I would say that if you re-rig your mainsail and lengthen your kite runner you could easily increase your speed by a good few knots. I used to sail these lands when I was younger. What's her name?" Bandolas gestured to the ship.

Captain Glime drew a knife from his hip and leant forward. Slowly, he reached out his hand.

Bandolas offered his own and the captain grasped it and turned it palm up. He ran his knife across Bandolas's palm and then his own. The two men grasped hands. Their blood mingling and dripping to the floor.

"The deal is made. I'd been thinking that the riggin' had been looking a little slack lately, you know your stuff lad. Her name be Swiftfire, would you like a tour on board?" The captain's attitude had completely changed. All tone of threat left his voice. He now seemed like a proud father wanting to show the world to his new child.

"Devlin, put your weapon away. Jacks help the girl with the sack of birds. Trade is done. Now we are all friends together." The captain offered his arm to help Bandolas up and ushered him aboard the Swiftfire.

INTERLUDE 1: A THING OF BEAUTY

Cxithh sank back luxuriantly into the pillows of his day bed. He slowly drew his knees up enjoying the feeling of his silk pantaloons against his thighs. He relaxed and lazily reached out a hand to collect his drawing pad from the floor next to him.

There was nothing he liked better after a long day in the office than to draw something beautiful and let his mind wander away from his troubles.

He casually flicked through the pages, reminding himself of the images contained within, until he stopped on his latest work. Completed less than an hour ago.

The image perfectly captured her sensuous curves as she lay on the bed before him. He lovingly stroked his long fingers along the lines of her neck, sweeping down the curve of her arm and under the voluptuosity of her perfect breasts.

Looking back at this fine drawing relaxed him enough that he could allow his mind to wander again over the events of the day.

He had spent moons gaining favour and influence, burying his strings deep into the heart of Splitt, a master puppeteer making lands idiotic ruler, Lord Wilhelm dance to his tune.

With Cxithh's assistance the Lord had increased productivity from Splitt's mines by 15% on the previous six moons. Trade tariffs had almost doubled the income to the court, and the Lord and his men had become richer than they had dreamed possible.

Cxithh had introduced the use of slaves, supplied from his allies in the distant city of Havii, to do much of the menial tasks around the palace. The Lord and his court had quickly taken to the idea and now slavery was once again a growing trade, every citizen of rank wanted to own one, following the latest fashions of court.

Now that the citizens had more time to think, he gently guided their thoughts to expansion. Moving new mining acquisitions further north along The Great Divide, bringing in new and varied materials for the great artisans of the city to shape and mould to their whims.

It had become a time of booming economy, as the world guzzled up the fine art which the city was churning out in vast quantities as well as the coal and other ores which were the life blood of trade.

The problem was that other realms did not take kindly to Splitt's expansion. The North threatened war and the King had sent a Messenger.

Cxithh had gently pulled a string and Lord Wilhelm had done his duty. Now the Messenger was gone, and it was time to shore up his position in the court.

Continuing to trace his fingers over the nakedness of the girl's image on his page, Cxithh's calm was broken as a fly landed lightly on the back of his hand, tickling his skin. That was the problem in hot, humid countries. Blood and death attracted flies and other vermin too quickly.

He reached out and softly rang the bell cord hanging on the wall. The slaves would come and take her body away before it started to rot. She had been one of the finest models in the city and had made a fine muse, for a while.

PART 17

A week had passed since they had met Captain Glime and his crew. Serena looked back at the terror of being pursued and intimidated with fondness now. Gods, they could do with something to break the monotony of the grasslands.

They had spent a day and a night in the crew's company. Bandolas had relished every moment. He had chatted with the captain and Tall Jacks as he had helped to tighten the rigging. They had even let him demonstrate to Devlin how to fly the kite to take better advantage of a longer kite runner. Serena had enjoyed riding in Swiftfire as she had sailed over the flat terrain. She was certainly more comfortable than the old farm cart.

Afterwards they had shared a keg of rum in the evening. Serena had gone to her bed early, unused to the hard liquor, but Bandolas had stayed up late into the night with his new friends, exchanging tales of the road and of the seas.

In the morning they had said their goodbyes. Before they left, the captain had asked for one last look under the canvas.

"It's an ugly thing, stinks as well. You mind that once you get in the forests to the north that you find some Kanva weed to burn. It'll help keep the bugs away. Good luck to you and fair trade to all."

Bandolas and Captain Glime had grasped arms one last time before they had all left on their separate journeys once again.

"Serena, it won't be long until we are back in lands where people live. We should try to avoid others where possible. We were lucky back on the plains, but things could be very different closer to the divide. If people spot us and get a look at our cargo, then word of our journey could spread. Less kindly types would see us as easy pickings and want to take the cargo for themselves to claim the bounty. You can fight but are you ready to kill?"

Serena put an arm around Bandolas's shoulders. "With you near me and guiding me I think I could do anything. But killing a man is not something I wish to do."

She spoke with less of an accent now, knowing that it made her easily identifiable as a 'southern farmer.' When they reached the city, she wanted to fit in, to fade into the crowd and not be noticed as different.

"Some people will not give you that choice. I know it is a dark way of looking at the world, but life has taught me that sometimes it is better to strike hard and fast than to let your opponent get close. If someone threatens your life you must fight with everything that you have and never give up. Fighting even if it looks like you will lose. The moment you stop trying, you give victory to them." His words were hard, but his voice was soft as he leant into Serena's embrace.

The cart began to jostle and bounce over the ground, for days now travel had been relatively smooth over the flat landscape. Bandolas slowed the oxen as Serena dropped from the cart to take a look around.

Sure enough, the previously smooth dirt of the Everplain was now rutted and uneven. Grass still persisted but hidden in amongst it were small bushes of heather, the roots of which bound the dirt into clumps and humps.

"We'll start to see trees soon and if you keep an eye to the north, the mountains of the Great Divide. It will still be a few days until we reach the forests of Eap. The going will be slower until we can find a trail." Bandolas called down, a big smile on his face.

That night they camped by a clump of low thorny bushes which provided some shelter from the wind. Jess and Poppy seemed happy as Serena brushed them down and checked them over for ticks and signs of injury. They nudged her and nuzzled at her wanting extra attention. It was as though they were as excited as she was to be leaving the plains and moving into new lands.

Bandolas watched Serena working as he set up their shelter and lay out the bedding. He knew that she felt something for him. Over the weeks together, relying upon each other they had grown closer. He hoped that that closeness could continue after they made it to Eap, but he was not sure if it was what she wanted. If he stayed with her then she might expect more of him than he could give. Would she want him to give up his homeless, travelling existence? Yes, she said she wanted to see the world, but they had to make money and the only way he knew how to do that was through death. Could he ask her to live her life like that, to become like him?

After dinner, when the plates had been cleared away, she came to him. "Take off your clothes." She instructed.

He raised his eyebrows playfully.

"Not like that, stupid. I need to check on your wound, make sure it's healing. I noticed you're still wincing when you reach across your body, and sometimes I hear you take a sharp intake of breath."

As Bandolas started to raise his shirt over his head she stepped in close to him. Trapping his arms over his head and wrapping her arm around his neck. He doesn't struggle as she steals a slow kiss from his mouth. Then she is all business. Running her hands down his side, prodding and pushing his flesh as if he were an animal at market.

"Lay down. On your side." She ordered him.

As he does so, she reaches over to pull the lantern closer, the fading light too faint for her to work by.

"The stitches were too loose, and the wound is sealing in an ugly scar. It looks as though the cauterised flesh has fallen away well and that the new skin is growing nicely but there is still the chance of infection. I'll need to cut away the old stitching as the skin is knitting without it now. It is going to hurt but if I don't do this the twine in your flesh itself could cause infection as it rots." He listened as she talked herself through what she needed to do. He knew her words were not meant for him.

He reached out and stroked her cheek, for a moment she looked him in the eyes. "Bandolas, I have never had to deal with a wound like this. So far, I've been lucky. We should really get you to a 'ealer…I mean healer as soon as we can."

"It's alright Serena. You have done well. I have not had a fever since the incident with the boar. Do your work and strap me up. I will keep getting stronger, you are a good healer."

She smiled at his words and set to work.

When she was done and had bandaged and strapped his wounds, she lay down beside him and he wrapped an arm around her. His arm was still around her when she woke.

Something was wrong. During the night, the wind had shifted. She could see the clouds scudding across the sky. A storm was coming.

"What's wrong Serena?" Bandolas asked.

"A storm is coming; the wind's cold and blowing from the north. We will be too exposed out here. Do you think we can find better shelter if we keep going?" Her voice was full of worry.

Quickly, they broke camp and stowed everything in the cart. It looked like they had a few hours until the weather would become too bad to travel and they decided to try to get to better shelter before the worst of the storm hit.

Serena ran ahead as Bandolas guided the oxen into the wind, trying to find the smoothest terrain. After a while, she began to wonder why the muscles of her thighs were burning so much, until she realised, she was running up hill. The land around them was no longer the flat expanse it had been for so many weeks. Now, it reminded her of the terrain around the hollow, slow undulating hills stretched off into the distance. She could see that dotted amongst the grass there were low lying bushes and shrubs. As she crested the hill, in the valley below and on the far slope, there were trees.

She moved ahead of the cart checking for the easiest path forward. The trees and bushes were scattered far apart but Bandolas called to her that they should keep going, that they were nearing the forests. On she ran up the next slope, angling slightly, following the easiest terrain for the cart.

The next crest revealed an even deeper valley, the far slope of which had a craggy outcropping of rock surrounded by a small stand of trees. She looked to the horizon as the first spots of rain fell on her face. It would have to do. The temperature was dropping, and she could see the mass of clouds building over them. This looked like a storm which could last for days. It was time to set up camp the best they could.

PART 18

They managed to get the cart close enough to the rock. The outcrop was only about three metres high, but it did have a slight overhang. A couple of straggly trees grew close enough that they managed to stretch the canvas over the stones, between the trees and the cart. It gave them a roof just higher than Serena's head, though Bandolas had to stoop slightly when standing.

The problem they had was that the wind blew the rain in through the sides.

"We need more canvas, or we'll have a very small shelter. The oxen will have to survive out in the rain." Serena yelled over the sound of the wind.

Bandolas moved to the back of the cart, He had already transferred all their belongings, so they sat tight against the outcrop away from the worst of the deluge. He pulled the coverings off the rotten monstrous head. Serena saw what he was doing and together they manhandled the heavy canvas into place closing up one side of their shelter, stopping the worst of the gale's wrath from blowing in.

Serena grabbed an extra coil of rope and went around the camp threading it through eyelets in the canvas to close the largest gaps whilst Bandolas hammered some stakes around the edges into the ground to close the bottom. Once they were satisfied with their handywork, they stepped inside.

Between the cart and the rock wall they had enough space to be able to set up their beds and to build a fire for food and warmth. It was a little cramped but surprisingly cosy.

As they had been working, the rain had turned into a downpour and both of them were soaked to the skin and shivering. Serena wrung her hair out and wiped water away from her eyes. Bandolas quickly lit the fire. When he turned from his work, Serena was standing looking out into the dark rain, she looked pale and was shivering uncontrollably. He did not feel much better himself.

"Serena, we need to get dry and warm before we freeze.

I'll go and check on Poppy and Jess you can get changed in privacy." He moved to step out of the shelter, but Serena grasped his arm.

"Stay." She said in a small voice.

He could feel her trembling.

"I'm too cold to undo the laces. Help me." She turned and looked into his eyes.

"I..."

"Quickly, it's so cold." She turned her back on him and started to fiddle with the string fastening her top around her neck.

He reached out and moved her hair to one side. Then with shaky fingers he unlaced her blouse. She pulled it from her waist, and he helped her to pull it over her head. She turned then and pressed her cold flesh against him, pulling his top free.

Quickly, they helped each other, fumbling and awkward, to remove their clothes. They embraced tightly beneath the covers of the bed sharing with each other their bodies' warmth.

Outside the rain poured down as the skies continued to darken. The oxen stamped nervously in the muddy ground. A small greenish glimmer went unnoticed as it left the empty eye socket of the rotten bestial head flying away into the sky heading northwards.

Serena awoke to the sound of the heavy rain pummelling their shelter, and the flapping of one corner of the canvas which had come lose in the wind. She leant backwards into the warmth of him, pushing her bottom into the space between them and cuddling into the arm around her. The repairs could wait.

★★★

She had just finished checking the ropes and hammering in a couple of extra pegs, when his shadow loomed out of the rain.

Bandolas had gone out to gather wood to dry next to the fire as their supplies were getting perilously low. He carried a large armful of deadfall and twigs. It would burn smoky and would not last long, but it would help to keep them warm.

There was no sign of the rain stopping any time soon.

As she checked on Jess and Poppy, moving them back closer to the waggon, he dug a trench outside the tent to divert the water which was starting to run in rivulets around the sides of the rock. When they were finished with their tasks, they were both cold and soaked again. This time they were both more confident helping each other to undress and they were getting better at keeping each other warm, although their discarded clothes never dried as they could have done, lying as they were in a pile on the floor.

★★★

It was two days before the rain eased.

Serena and Bandolas sat in their shelter watching the clouds slowly break apart revealing the bright blue of the sky. Water dripped from everything in sight. The grass was heavy and bent over as if in prayer to the new day. The air was crisp and clean. From the north the biting cold wind continued to blow.

Both were reluctant to give up this small sanctuary which had become their home for a few days, but eventually they moved to begin clearing away and packing up the waggon for their journey.

As they trundled over the rise of the hill they had sheltered behind, the world opened before them. Ahead they could see rolling hills stretching up to vast, snow-capped mountains in the distance. Below the mountains was an arboreal wonderland of trees, stretching far to the east and west.

"It will take a day or so to get to the forest proper where we will need to head east for a few more days to get to Eap. Can you see the large gap in the mountains over there?" Bandolas points to their right. "That's *The Run.* A gap in the Great Divide that leads to the lands to the north and the east. The Wizards' city lies at the entrance to The Run. I can't wait for you to see it."

Serena stared at the vista before her, pulling her cloak close over her shoulders against the cold wind. "It's beautiful."

That day they made good time as the trail quickly dried out. They followed what must have been an old drover's route up towards the mountains. By nightfall they were passing through rich and fertile land, the grass was interrupted by large stands of trees and woodlands. There was wildlife in abundance all around. Families of elk and deer grazed on the grass and low hanging branches. All sorts of small mammals scurried through the undergrowth and birds flew through the sky darting around in their pursuit of insects.

The next day they began to approach the edge of the forest. The huge trees loomed over the landscape gathering the darkness under their skirts. The wind began to ease and as they entered the gloom under the canopy of the trees, the still silence stretched over everything.

It became nearly impossible to navigate the cart through the dense underbrush and in between the trunks of the trees. Serena scouted ahead whilst Bandolas wrestled with the reins guiding the oxen through the complicated terrain.

PART 19: MESSENGER FLIES

The Pirate King of Daggos grasped Findo's arm firmly. "Make sure the King gets my words son. He has been good to us, but he is a long way from the West. If war is coming it will come to the land first. I will look after the seas, but only insofar as there is profit to be made. You tell him, his pockets had better be as deep as he promises. Gold will buy a lot of good faith. He had better be prepared to back up his purse with action. For it will be needed before the year is out. Carry my words swiftly back to your master."

Findo nodded to the man before him. He took the sealed message tube and strapped it to his thigh. "I take this from you as it was sealed before me. May the words contained within be known to be true until my duty is complete."

At this Oakhands the Pirate king poured out two measures of dark rum, offering one to Findo. The Messenger took the proffered drink and the two men nodded to each other and then knocked the smooth but fiery drink back in one. The deal was sealed. The Pirate then lead Findo back towards the Docks. He was a tall man, wide of shoulder and well-muscled. He would have stood out in any crowd without the theatrics, but he loved to be noticed. He wore a bright red coat which was braided with gold thread around the shoulders and collar, with a double row of golden buttons running down the front. His shirt was of fine black silk, open halfway down his chest. Around his throat, he wore long necklaces of pearls. Every finger sported at least one bright gold ring, some inset with precious stones. His long black hair was curled into perfect ringlets which fell around his shoulders.

His belt carried a variety of weapons, all shiny and encrusted in gems. At first sight many thought him gaudy, cheap and all for show. Those who knew him had learned otherwise. He was a master tactician, skilled with his rapier and a pioneer of using newly discovered explosive powders to create weaponry.

As they walked, Oakhands talked endlessly, gesticulating

wildly about. He paused frequently to sample wares from market stalls or share a few comments with passers-by. It was obvious that the people loved him and soon a small entourage of children trailed them down the street. As they entered the main wharf, he stopped and threw a handful of coins into the crowd of youths who cheered his generosity. He took a bow and they continued on.

"I envy your job son. What a thrill it must be to fly through the skies."

"It is an honour sir. An experience beyond words. Perhaps one day you could train to ride a Kystraal, and we could fly together." Findo smiled at the flamboyant ruler.

"If only I had time. Still, I have my ships which sail over land and sea. They will have to do. Good speed to you."

Findo bowed briefly and rushed up the gang plank of the ship before them. He deftly climbed up the rigging and made his way across the spar on the mainsail mast.

The city of Daggos did not have a purpose-built roost for Kystraal. Visiting Messengers had learnt to use the open rigging and clear sky around the docks to rest their mounts. Trips to Daggos were still rare enough that a Messenger and his mount drew a crowd. Many people were gathering on the docks, pausing in their work to watch. Oakhands was not the only one who could put on a show.

Findo cupped his hands to his mouth facing the clouded sky above and let out a loud humming followed by a piercing whistle. With one hand against the mast, he waved to the crowd, then turned and sprinted along the narrow spar he was balanced upon, high above the deck. He leapt from the end straight out over the sea and quickly began to plunge towards the dark waters.

Gisselle swooped down and he effortlessly caught onto the saddle, clipped in his spurs and she smoothly banked to brush her wingtips through the crests of the waves. Even with the wind rushing through his ears he could hear the gasp from the crowd on the shore.

He hummed softly in Gisselle's ear and with his knees urged

her upwards into the sky. They lazily circled the city as she gained height before they headed towards the east once again.

Oakhands watched them for a long time smiling to himself. That young boy sure did know how to upstage him. He surely would like to get his hands on a flock of Kystraal. As soon as he returned back to the workshops, he would have to get his engineers to figure out a way of getting his ships in the air.

★★★

Findo's trips to Holdon and Splitt had gone well. The Guild directors of the northern city had taken a night to consider the King's words before giving him their replies. In Splitt, Lord Wilhelm's advisor, Cxithh, had shown him around the galleries of the castle while Lord Wilhelm had handwritten his own reply. None of the rulers had even hinted at the troubles. This could only mean that they were hiding something, considered him a spy of the King, so were all smiles and fake joviality but all the while they worried what he would relay back.

The three message tubes were tightly strapped to his thigh. It was for the King and his advisors to unpick the words contained within. He would report what had been said in his presence and what he had seen.

From the skies he had witnessed that along the borders of the North, troops were slowly massing in the mountains and moving to and from the mines of the Great Divide. The shipyards of Daggos had seemed unusually quiet. The main fleet had supposedly put out to sea on exercises, whilst land ship production was down due to supply problems in the forests of Eap. Well, he could at least investigate that last one on his journey back.

Findo tightened the straps around his legs and pulled his furred coat collar higher. He adjusted his goggles and pulled his hat on tightly. Then he shifted his weight forward to lean into the chest guard, humming to Gisselle, instructing her to climb. He felt her shrug through the shifting of the saddle. She was feeling playful. His stomach lurched as she twisted and folded her wings, rolling to the side as she began to fall through the air. He leant into his back support pushing his head into the cushioned surrounds, knowing that the forces she would exert upon them now, could break his neck if he wasn't careful. His heart raced as she snapped her wings out and banked sharply in the opposite direction to her roll. He reached out carefully with his hands and grasped the reins. She was enjoying this, but she needed to be reminded of his control. He guided her through a series of aerial manoeuvres, she hummed deeply in her throat, letting him know that she enjoyed having him back.

Soon, they were gliding higher in the sky and riding the wind eastwards. Kystraal were powerful, designed for long gliding flight and they used much energy the more they used their wings. She had hunted when he had been in Daggos but would need to replenish herself again before they crossed the Sand Sea. He set her on a course towards Eap. He could rest in the area near The Run, and she could feed. The air above the forests was rich in birds and insects.

PART 20: TEARS

Serena ranged out into the forest. She and Bandolas had finished their morning routine, following the Movements, practicing with weapons and for her, learning control. He was healing well, and she was now showing him new Movements to incorporate into his routine.

The going had been slow at first as they wound their way through the trees but once they had picked up on an old loggers' trail, they had begun to make good time again. Jess and Poppy seemed happy enough. It had been pleasant to camp in the cover of trees with plenty of firewood to warm them through the night, and no rain.

Bandolas was breaking down the camp whilst Serena hunted for game. The ground was spongey underfoot and the cover was sparse as the dense canopy overhead allowed little light down. She pushed her way carefully through a stand of smaller saplings and made her way up the slope ahead, her bow in hand. She eased herself down low to peer over the ridge. Below was an idyllic scene.

A small stream ran through a shallow gorge, the sides of which were steep and rocky. Thick vines and hanging mosses draped themselves down towards the water's edge. There was a break in the canopy above and a shaft of bright sunlight fell onto the water, shattering into a thousand glimmering sparkles which danced across the lush vegetation. Insects buzzed and darted over the crystalline waters and birds fluttered to and fro. A young roe deer was bending down to drink at the stream.

Carefully, Serena reached for an arrow and nocked it to her bow. She calmed her breathing and waited. The deer raised its head. Slowly, she rose up, the deer was looking away from her, flicking flies with its ears. She drew and released.

Quickly, she clambered down to the stream and began the grizzly work of gutting and washing the body.

Bandolas must be wondering where she had got to. Serena swatted at a fly biting her neck and washed her knife in the stream. She had gutted the carcass and needed to get it trussed to carry back. She waved away flies which were being drawn by the blood, as she tied the animal's legs and hung it on a fallen branch. Hefting her load over her shoulders, she heard a loud buzzing and turned to swat away an exceptionally large fly, stumbling as the weight on her back shifted. She started to jog back towards camp, a droning, humming buzz following her from above.

As she moved swiftly through the trees, she became aware of harsh sounds ahead. Snapping twigs and branches, the bellowing of her oxen panicking and stamping about. More faintly she could hear the swish of metal cutting air and the sharp inhalation and exhalation of breath. It sounded like a fight.

She dropped her load and raised her bow as she came into camp. The droning noise was louder here. The air was thick with insects, most were small but larger ones dart in and out of the swarm. She could see that Poppy had bolted and was crashing through the undergrowth and Jess was lying at a strange angle half supported by his harness at the front of the waggon. The swarm was thickest around the fallen oxen. Bandolas was moving with incredible speed, his sword lashing out at the largest of the insects. He seemed to flow from one spot to the next, each pause in his movement brought another insect falling to the floor. Smaller throwing blades lashed out through the air like streaks of lightning as he threw them into fresh targets with his other hand.

Serena raised her bow and entered the Rush to join him. Arrows whistled. Her targets were easy to spot. Each one the size of her forearm with a dark black abdomen and a single flash of pearlescent colouring down the side. Four wings support the creatures in the air and their heads are elongated to a long point. She watched as one flew rapidly down to Jess, punching its pointed proboscis into his flesh then pulling back leaving a finger sized hole behind in Jess's flesh. When her quiver was empty, she snatched up her staff and whirled into combat. Every spin ended with another insect's body twitching on the ground.

Serena could feel herself caught up in the Rush, like a leaf in a stream that threatened to become a torrent. She knew she needed to regain control and as Bandolas flashed past her she heard him call out one word.

"Think."

She drew the door of her memories open, and a flash of images flooded her mind. Slowing, she steadied herself in the flow. They could kill a thousand of these creatures and there would still be more. Then one word screamed through her mind. 'Kanva'.

She remembered the words of Captain Glime. "You mind that once you get in the forests to the north that you find some Kanva weed to burn. It'll help keep the bugs away."

She spotted that Bandolas had not yet extinguished their campfire, no doubt he was keeping a mug of hot drink warm for her return. Her eyes scanned the forest floor looking for the plant she needed. Kanva weed was common throughout the lands. Its thorny stems and thick waxy leaves uninteresting to look at except in early spring when it blossomed with small purple flowers.

Bandolas cried out and stumbled to his knees, rolling to avoid the insects darting down upon him. He sprang back to his feet, sword slashing as bodies tumbled to the floor all around him.

There behind the waggon she spotted it. She threw her body into motion, swatting anything that moved before her as she ran across the pine needle strewn floor. She stepped onto a fallen log and sprang up to jump off a thick tree trunk. Clearing the cart in one, rolling motion, she landed gracefully amongst the Kanva weed. She grabbed wildly at the stems, snapping the brittle stalks, heedless of the cuts to her hands as the thorns tore her flesh. When she could hold no more, she sprinted for the fire, dumping her cargo and drawing the long knife that Bandolas had given her all those weeks ago.

She slashed two more bodies from the air and then knelt to blow into the flames as small whisps of smoke began to fill the air. The dry, thorny stalks caught quickly, and the leaves began to curl. A thick pungent smoke choked her as she inhaled to blow on the rising flames. She ran back to the clump of weeds to gather more.

These she twisted together to make two bundles as she ran back to the fire thrusting one end of each of the twisted bundles into the flames. The smoke rose all around her. She threw one of the smoking bundles toward Bandolas hoping that the smoke would protect him. Then she dashed over to Jess waving her smoking torch before her and the insects backed off. It was working!

She could see that Jess's side was covered in puncture wounds, in places the flesh had been stripped away, revealing the rib bones underneath. Jess was not breathing.

She moved, swept up in the Rush, carried away on a wave of pain. The door of her room of memories was open but it barely kept her from being washed away in the flood.

She gathered more weed to feed the fire. The insects were no longer attacking her. She moved through the camp, long coils of smoke drifting in her wake. As she passed the fire the heat drew her attention and she saw that it was getting out of control, she had stacked too much fuel upon it. She grabbed the barrel of water from the cart and doused the flames. Steam and smoke sprang into the air as the fire hissed its displeasure. Serena allowed the Rush to dissipate just like the flames and looked around.

There were chitinous bodies everywhere. The droning seemed to hang in the air for a moment before fading away. Her eyes stung from the smoke and her throat was raw. She looked down at her hands to see that her palms were bleeding, the skin lacerated and torn. Absent mindedly, she tore a strip of cloth from her skirt and bound her wounds. Then she began to gather their things which had fallen from the cart.

"Serena." His voice was quiet.

She turned to look for him, but he was not there.

She looked again at the ragged corpse of Jess, who had carried them so far and had been a part of her life for so long. Tears began to wash small streams through the soot and dirt on her cheeks.

"Serena."

She moved towards the sound.

He was sitting around the far side of a large tree, his back to the trunk.

"What? Jess is dead and Poppy has run off. How are we supposed to move the cart without them?" She crossed her arms and huffed at him, sitting relaxing when they needed to get moving.

"Serena. It's bad. I..."

She dropped to her knees, noticing how pale and wax like the flesh of his face was. She put a hand to his forehead and his skin felt cold. There was blood leaking out from beneath his armour, in between the overlapping leather plates, a lot of blood.

"One of them stabbed me."

She moved his hand off his stomach and lifted his armour. There was a hole and dark blood was pouring out. She put her hand over the wound to try to stop the bleeding, but his flesh was slick with it and her hand kept sliding about.

"Put your hand here." She instructed.

"Not the only one." He said weakly as he leant forward.

A quick inspection of his back revealed that he had another hole in the back of his left triceps and one more just above his right kidney, next to the scar which was barely healed. Both were large and deep. It looked like the insects had taken an apple corer to his flesh and taken a plug of his meat. Somehow the insects had found the weak points in his armour when no man could.

"Serena. Sit with me."

She stood and made to go to the waggon.

He grabbed her hand and pulled her down.

"No. It is too late for that." His voice was getting weaker.

"Hold me, Serena. Let me love you just a little longer."

She sat and held him, his head resting heavily against her chest. The last sound he heard in this world was the beating of her heart. She felt him stiffen and then relax.

Serena stayed for a long time holding him, stroking his hair and whispering small nothings.

PART 21

Darkness had fallen, covering everything. At some point it had seeped in between the leaves of the canopy high overhead and drifted downwards. Shadows had crawled out of the crevices and folds in the ground and between the trees, spreading outwards to meet the growing darkness from above. With the blackness had come the cold, slinking behind the dark and gathering slowly over the ground, pushing its way through to pierce into everything.

Poppy snorted. He was wary of every sound. He had not liked the stinging, biting buzzing things and had run away until they couldn't harm him. As it had started to get dark, he had stopped eating the leaves by the stream and had thought of Jess his friend and the other ones who stroked him and gave him tasty treats to eat. He had made his way back towards them. There was a bad smell in the air, and he had hesitated to get closer, fearing the creatures in the air which bit, but he felt lonely and had eventually pushed on.

Now he stood over the one he had known all his life. She seemed to be resting. He breathed her familiar scent in and huffed it out harshly at the stench of blood and death mixed with bad burned foods. She did not get up to brush his burs away, so he nudged her, trying to get her attention.

Serena came back to herself. She was unbearably cold, and her muscles were cramped. She pushed the weight from her chest and patted Poppy's big damp nose. Slowly she stood up, stretching, and looking around.

Then it all came back to her. She collapsed to one knee as the sobbing returned. Her mind did not seem to be able to hold her thoughts and her vision blurred.

Poppy pushed his nose into her lap. The warmth was comforting. She breathed deeply and his familiar scent, that of the farm and her youth brought her back. She felt as though parts of her were missing. Her thoughts scattered easily but there was a small thread amongst the confusion. She wanted to live. She wanted to make life worth something. The life of Jess, of her father and mother and that of Bandolas. She knew next to nothing about him but had entwined her life with his. Now she needed to find a life of her own.

It took a long time before she could think more clearly. She rested by the waggon, though she did not sleep.

When it was light, she brushed Poppy down. Carrying out the simple chore helped her to ease back from the abyss opening in her mind. She thought of Bandolas, and tears welled in her eyes again, but she forced herself to begin the Movements. The Rush did not come, but she calmed. Her thoughts began to turn to how to move on.

She felt angry, bitter and alone. The emotions reminded her of her mother, and she understood. Perhaps for the first time she really understood.

First, she went about the task of freeing the cart from Jess's body, using Poppy to help maneuver it. Then she covered Jess in stones and soil that she gathered from close by to try to stop predators from getting to him. For a long while she knelt with her hand on the last stone, unable to find any words to say her thoughts seeming to be stuck in thick mud, weighing her mood down. Tears fell and then tears dried as she moved and set to work on the waggon. Stripping it down, removing the sides and the seat. Making it smaller and less bulky so that Poppy would be able to pull it unaided and it would be lighter to heave over the uneven ground.

Finally, she went to Bandolas.

It took her a long time to prepare his body. She did not want scavengers to move his bones and gnaw on his fingers. She cleared the ground around the area and built a pyre out of deadfall and the unwanted pieces of the cart. She stripped him, dressed his wounds and put him in a clean set of clothes before she placed him on the pyre. She wanted to say some words over him before she lit the pyre, but she found there was nothing left to say. He was already gone. She stood and watched, as it slowly burned down to glowing embers. Carefully she stamped out any loose coals, fearful that the flames could ignite the forest around her.

That night she slept deeply, both her body and mind exhausted from the misery and sadness of her losses.

In the morning, the hole in her heart was still there, but a steel core of anger and determination was beginning to burn within her. She would complete Bandolas's quest and collect the bounty. She would build herself a new life in memory of their short time together.

She strapped on his armour and weapons. Then she ran through the Movements. Afterwards she carefully gathered more Kanva weed, putting a small amount in a pot to burn as they travelled. Once she was satisfied there was no more to be done, with a heavy heart, she harnessed Poppy and led him from the clearing heading east, towards her future.

INTERLUDE 2: PRETTY THINGS

The sculpture was truly spectacular, exquisite in the finest details. Cxithh could almost feel the breath of the hound upon his face as he leant closer to examine the textures of the fur around its mouth. He almost smelled the blood of the squirrel captured between the dog's jaws and heard the small bones cracking.

He stepped away, moving on down the gallery gazing at the paintings and ceramics all around him. Nothing else captured his attention and quickened his blood. His slippered feet whispered over the polished stone flooring as he passed through this week's offerings from the finest artists in the city.

Every week the displays were changed, and the doors opened for the public to visit. It had become a popular event in Splitt, the rich and noble queued outside whilst he checked the latest offerings, looking for that certain special something, which one of the artists had put up for his judgement. He had started this competition soon after he had come to the city. It had been a way to get to know the people and their talents. Yes, it had cost him dearly to put up the prize money, but the gains had been worth it. The art works displayed here now sold for many times their original value. He, of course, took only a small cut.

Now, the finest minds in the city called him friend and he had a small army of loyal artisans whom he could call upon to help him with his tasks.

His eye caught on a small lacework cloth. His finger darted to his ledger, and he turned a few pages.

'Exhibit 240. Hand woven lace based upon the designs of the Isle of Then, in the Swaying Sea. Woven from the silk of Havra worms interlaced with fine steel wire.'

"Paufry, come over here." He called to the head curator. "This fine silk shall be this week's winner. Arrange the sign and have it announced to the crowd."

Cxithh hesitated for a second. "Have the artist who created the tableau of the hound over there, come up to my offices. I would very much like a conversation with them."

He turned and wandered back towards his offices. His plans were progressing well. The armies were still massing on the northern borders, and output from the mines was increasing since the latest shipment of slaves had arrived. The King's Messenger had come and gone, through these very rooms, and been none the wiser of the greater scheme. For how long would he be able to keep his dealings hidden from the King?

The Princes of Havii had taken the Twin cities of Aldark and Ardark and were slowly expanding their territory, their forces keeping a tight hold on their borders, allowing no word to escape. The problem was that time was now against him. The longer it took the more likely it was that rumour would reach the King. If that happened, he was prepared, but it never hurt to have a little more control.

As he entered his private rooms a slave came forward to take his robe and ledger. "Is she here?" He asked.

The slave nodded and left.

Cxithh moved forward to the door of his sitting room, pausing before the entrance. He drew in a deep breath, calming his mind and reaching out from within himself to find the flow of magics. As he sensed it, he tethered himself and leapt into the Rush.

He could smell her heavy perfume lingering in the air. From the table by the door, he picked up his case of fine charcoals and pad of paper. Then he swept forward into the room.

Upon the walls his artworks were displayed in fine golden frames against deep red wall hangings. The floor was covered by thick rugs of deep pile and swirling dark colours. The air in here was warm and spiced by the scented oils burning in the shining brass braziers. A single chandelier lit the room. The cut glass baubles hanging from it splintering the light into beautiful patterns which shone upon the walls. In the centre, stood a large and sumptuous bed and next to it a simple cushioned chair and small table. He placed his art materials onto the table and turned to the girl. She was perfect. Her long curling, blond hair cascading over her shoulders and down her spine. The curves and arches of her body exposed to the light. She stood with her back to him and coquettishly looked over her shoulder at him.

"How do you want me sir?" Her voice carried the accent of the north.

"Surprise me my dear." Cxithh sat down in his chair and turned to a new page.

The truth was, he was a terrible artist. On his own he could do a reasonable drawing, but it was in his use of the Rush that his skills really lay.

He sat for a while his eyes drinking her in. She was quite a talent. Flexible and inventive in her choices of pose. He drew the charcoals across the paper half-heartedly as he watched her every movement and memorised every detail of her skin.

When he rose and approached her, she did not shy away. She allowed him to stroke a finger down her spine, then rolled over and beckoned him close. After a brief while, he reached under one of the silken pillows and withdrew what he had concealed there. She did not cry out as he slipped his blade between the vertebrate of her long neck. Her weight slumped in his arms as she lost all sensation in her body. It was a shame that, in that instant, she lost control of her bladder, but it was not enough to stop him.

As she lay there, he cast his thoughts to create a wall of silence around them and her screams went unheard. He shifted her limbs on the bed placing her into the ideal pose and then stepped back to check on his work. Apart from her panicked eyes she was perfect, but he could replace those from his memory. He took his small blade and gently pierced her thigh close to her femininity. He cut deep until he knew he had nicked the femoral artery. As the blood began to pour out, he dipped each of his charcoals into it, releasing a small amount of the powerful Rush coursing through him. Her life blood mixed with his magic.

He stood next to her, keeping eye contact with her as the slow realisation of her doom dawned on her and then the spark went out of her eyes, and she became a dull and lifeless corpse.

Sitting once again in his chair, he let the Rush flood him as he channeled it through his charcoal, rich blackness spread out from the point against the pure white page, sinuous lines crawling towards the edges. He held the charcoal still as the image slowly crept its way from the centre, details gradually clarifying until he held a masterpiece in his hands. Her perfection was forever captured in this image. Stored within it was her lifeforce, twisted to his will, to be used in the future should he need it.

It was time to talk to Lord Wilhelm. They needed to advance his plans. It was time for the North to fall.

PART 22

The forest stretched out before Findo, and it was magnificent. A mix of arboreal giants stood tall all around him. He sat high in the branches above the litter and chaos of the leaf strewn floor. He let his eyes dance through the canopy of leaves marveling at the different shades of green, back lit by the sun. It was peaceful here.

In the sky riding on Gisselle's back, there was always the rush of the wind, the flapping of loose clothes or giant wings, the whistle of the wind forcing its way through small spaces and the vicious slap of the cold driving hard into you.

In this space between the treetops and the ground, it was warm and quiet. He could relax for a while whilst the Kystraal hunted. Nowhere to go, nothing to disturb him. He sighed and leant his head back against the trunk, closing his eyes and soaking in the peace.

In just a couple more days he would be back in Westomere, his messages would be delivered, and he hoped he could grab some ground time. He really wanted to visit Lady Beholt's bath house and sit in the warm waters floating weightless, letting the heat creep back into his bones. This had been a long hard trip.

The things he had seen weighed on his mind. Splitt was definitely up to something. Surely, they were not prepared for war, they were a nation of artists lead by a man famous for his vanity and self-importance. Lord Wilhelm was known around the world as a shrewd businessman but also as a coward. Just one look around the Galleries showed that it was a land of soft hands not a place for taking up weapons to strike out at its neighbours.

The Northmen however were hard, and they were adamant that Splitt and Lord Wilhelm were moving upon their lands. However, he had only seen northern troops strengthening their own border garrisons.

Flying over the forests, he had seen a few abandoned logging camps, but from the air there was no sign of trouble.

Gisselle had been a little skittish as she scented prey below, but he had not seen anything out of the ordinary.

He had hoped that spending some time in the trees he might see or hear something, but no, all was peaceful.

He dozed for a while, allowing his cramped muscles to relax.

All too soon his peace was disturbed. There was a crashing coming through the undergrowth, below on the ground. Sounds of breaking branches, rustlings, the crunching of leaves, a faint mechanical squeak and a female voice gently calling encouragement.

He continued to sit and watch.

A very oddly dressed woman came into sight. She wore the strangest armour, and had weapons strapped all about her. She seemed to be harnessed, pulling heavily on her ropes, leading an ox who was strapped behind her to a flatbed waggon. The waggon carried something large under a heavy canvas.

As they came closer, the waggon stopped moving, its wheels obviously caught on one of the many roots protruding from the ground. The woman heaved at her straps, calling encouragement to the animal behind her and the waggon lurched as they pulled it over the obstacle. They made about another five metres before they were stuck again. This time they could not shift their load.

She unstrapped herself and went back to the wheel which was stuck. She called to her ox, and she pushed and pulled at the wheel. He could see the strain on her muscles as the ligaments in her neck stood out. Finally, the waggon moved over the knot of roots and rolled on. She moved back to the front and once again placed the ropes around her to help the ox to heave the waggon on, even though she looked exhausted and almost unable to stand.

"Hello there." Findo called out in greeting.

She dropped to one knee, a bow appearing in her hand its arrow pointing straight at him.

"Woah," He called raising his hands. "I'm not here to

cause you trouble Miss. Just felt it was a bit rude to sit up here and watch you struggle."

Ever so slowly the woman dropped the point of her arrow.

"Looks like you could do with a little help and as it happens, I'm just hanging around up here and have a bit of free time. What say you to a bit of help?" Findo asked as politely as he could.

She took a few deep breaths and returned the arrow to its quiver at her hip. She slung the bow over her shoulder and picked up a staff, which she had dropped at her feet, never once taking her eyes from him.

"I don't know you and I don't know your business. Why don't you just move on? Then, I can as well." There was a hardness to her voice, like there was a monster inside her waiting to be unleashed.

"Well, I would leave but I'm waiting for someone and might miss them if I go." He called back.

Her eyes quickly darted around the trees; she shifted her footing looking nothing less than deadly. He had seen this kind of alertness before amongst the King's guards and the guides.

"It's ok. She's no threat to you. She just went off hunting and should return in an hour or so. How did you come to be lost in the forest?"

"Who said I'm lost?" She moved forward with a hunter's grace making room around herself to fight.

"It's just that you are pulling a waggon through dense forest when just to the north is a perfectly good road. I presumed you were lost as you aren't on that roadway. I could give you a hand and get you moving again. Like I said I'm just waiting for a friend. A great man once said, 'A good deed will reflect back at you.' I like to help, and I hope that in doing so help will be there for me when I need it."

She just stood staring up at him as her ox began to graze at the meagre grass around it.

"Think of it like this, perhaps in the past you helped someone out when they were in need. Now I am offering to help you. Good deeds reflecting back."

"You have a long knife at your hip. Drop it." She commanded.

Without making any sudden moves he slowly drew his knife and carefully dropped it blade first. It sank into the soft loam of the forest floor as if sinking into its sheath with a soft 'shing.' He noted its position.

"Now stand and slowly turn around."

He did as she asked keeping his arms held high.

"Those things strapped to your leg. What are they?" She asked.

"My name is Findo Gask. I am a Messenger in the service of Westomere under the patronage of the King. These are message tubes."

"So, the weird clothes you wear are part of your uniform?"

Findo chuckled at this. She must be from somewhere far away not to know of the Messengers.

"Yes, in a way, these clothes are mostly for protection as I travel. It can get very cold." He slowly opened the front of his heavy coat to reveal the thick fur inside and to show that he carried nothing concealed underneath. "I gave you my name and an offer of help. What may I call you?"

"Serena." She seemed to relax a little, resting one end of the staff on the ground. "Your help would be appreciated. But how are you going to get down?"

"Like this."

Findo crouched and dropped backwards, as he did so his spurs caught on the branch and he swung underneath, releasing himself to arch through the air and grasp a smaller overhang below. Using his swing for the momentum he needed, he grasped onto a thinner branch from the tree opposite and allowed it to bear his weight as it bent down. From this he caught one spur onto the next branch down and fell in and around it, so that he was swinging upside down. He spotted a smaller tree and released himself to catch hold of it, the top bent until it was parallel to the ground, and he then let go to fall the last few feet to the forest floor. As he landed, he rolled to his side.

"Don't." Said her voice in his ear and he felt a cold blade at his throat. He slowly raised his hand away from the hilt of his dagger still sunk into the dirt.

How had she moved so fast?

"Alright." He croaked, raising his hands again. "I'm sorry. I just didn't want to lose my blade and you look pretty tough in that armour with all those weapons. Can we just start over?"

She put a knee firmly against his back shoving him onto his stomach amongst the leaf litter. He heard her take his blade and back away as he rolled onto his back.

Her long hair was plastered with sweat across her face, her eyes were rimmed red and she seemed to be trembling.

"Keep the knife. You look like you can hardly stand. I've got some cheese and a little bread in my bag." Findo opened his coat again to reveal the shoulder bag concealed at his side.

She sat down heavily, the spark seeming to go out of her eyes.

"Just don't make any sudden moves or I will."

He believed her.

PART 23

Serena took the offered bread and cheese; she had hardly eaten at all since the swarm had attacked. The bread was delicious, and the cheese was rich and creamy with a saltiness which made her mouth water. As she ate, she kept a close eye on the young man.

He was not a big man, similar in height to herself but he had a handsome face and carried himself with confidence. He had the cocky ease of youth that she had seen many of the young men in her village fail to pull off. Most notable was his peculiar uniform. On his head he wore a large hat, which was almost a helmet. It was domed and smooth on the outside but as he removed it, she saw that the inside was thickly lined with fur. It had large flaps which covered his ears and were held close to the head by the straps which ran down and over his chin. Attached to the hat were large round glass cylinders.

"What are those?" She asked pointing with his knife.

"Goggles. They go over my eyes and stop the wind from hurting them. Do you want to try them?" He held out the hat and 'goggles' to her.

She shook her head. Why did he need to protect his eyes from the wind?

His coat was bulky, the outside looked like oiled cloth, smooth and shiny, but the inside was thick fur. When he had opened his coat, she had seen that he wore several layers of clothing underneath. The only times she had seen people wear clothing like that was when the fur traders came to town in the depths of winter. But it was warm in the forests. Why would he be wearing winter clothes.

"Have you and your friend just come down from the mountains?" She asked.

"You could say that. We were certainly very high up. Is it alright if I take my coat off?"

He seemed no threat now that they were sitting. So, she nodded her agreement, quickly scanning the forest around them as he was disrobing himself.

His trousers were a thick but supple leather with peculiar straps and buckles hanging from them as well as the tubes strapped to his thigh, which he had said contained messages.

The strangest thing about his outfit though were his boots. They were knee high, strapped and buckled tightly all the way down his calves. The toes were rounded and looked a bit like the blacksmith's in the village, which she knew had wood stuffed around the toes to reinforce them in case he dropped anything heavy whilst working. The heels were the weirdest things. Large metal hooks swung back from them and curved around towards the sides of his feet. She had noticed that he had used them to hang upside down from the tree branches as he had swung down to meet her.

"You wear the strangest things." She said without realising she had spoken her thoughts aloud.

"I could say the same of you. I wear the tools of my trade. If you do, then I guess I have reason to be worried. Everything about you says *killer*."

Serena glanced down at the armour she now wore, and the weapons strapped about her. Somehow it all seemed to fit her better than the farm clothes from her old life. She knew that 'killer' was an apt description for Bandolas. But that was not how she thought of herself.

"Not 'killer.' Perhaps fighter would be a better description. I fight for myself, to survive. Perhaps you and I are not so different. I also carry a message."

She was worried that she was making a bad decision. When the Rush had been with her, she had known what to do but since she had dropped out of it, she just felt tired, and help seemed to be a very welcome thing. She took a gamble. She could always kill him if it didn't work.

"Perhaps you and your friend could help me. I have a message to deliver to the Wizards at Eap."

"Well, who would have known. You, a Messenger as well." He smiled at her, a big, broad, toothy smile. "I have to be honest; I can help you on your way back to the road but as soon as Gisselle gets back, I'll have to be on my way. I have promises to keep that involve the delivery of my messages. I can't be delayed."

"I could pay you." Serena didn't know how yet but she did not want to travel alone.

"I'm sorry but I can't spare the time to get to Eap. I have much further to travel than that and need to go quickly."

"They must have sail ships which travel from Eap. Perhaps you could get passage on one of those." Serena began to feel like she was pleading with him too much and decided to stop.

"I..." He hesitated, looking up above them. "Um... I need to travel faster than that. You see I am one of the King's Messengers. I travel through the sky. I fly. That's why I have all this gear. It protects me when I am high up where the air is thin and cold..." He trailed off seeing the look of disbelief in her eyes.

"Look, believe me or not, I need to get going as soon as my friend gets here. Until then I can help you. Fair enough." He held out his arm.

Serena looked deep into his hazel eyes. He seemed genuine and she was exhausted.

"Thank you." She reached out and grasped his arm as she had seen Bandolas do when he had struck a deal with the captain.

She handed his knife back to him and went over to the waggon.

Findo walked straight up to Poppy and let him sniff his hand. Then he rubbed his nose like they were old friends and stroked his neck.

"A fine animal. Not as large as those in the King's cavalry but he looks like he has plenty of muscle. Should be able to shift this cart easily with our help." Findo went towards the back of the waggon.

"What are you carrying?" He nodded towards the canvas coverings.

"You don't need to know." Serena replied.

"Judging by how deep the wheels are pressing into the soil, something heavy. It would be easier to shift this if we could drop some of the weight."

"I already stripped the cart as much as I could and dumped everything which is not essential. Can you help or not?" Serena's patience was getting thin as she grew wearier.

"I am trying to help. Let's get you to the road, shall we? It's that way." He pointed into the forest, how he knew the direction she didn't know. Everything looked the same.

She nodded and they set to work. Each of them guided a wheel as Poppy pulled. Working in this way they could guide the waggon around the worst of the bumps in the forest floor. When the waggon did stick, with two of them pushing and heaving it was quick work to get it moving again. Soon they stood on the roadway, a clear flat track running in a straight line through the trees. Sun light shone down through breaks in the canopy overhead. The surface of the road was gravelled and free of debris.

"I don't have anything to pay you with." Serena looked guiltily at her belongings trying to see if there was anything she could give him.

"That's OK. I didn't ask for anything, just trying to do my bit reflecting back a little help to someone who needs it. What happened to you anyway? You look like you have been through some bad times."

"My companion and I..." Was that all they had been? Companions? "We travelled from the south of the Everplain."

"Through the storm I saw. That must have been tough" He looked at her with new wonder.

"Yes, and when we got to the forest we were attacked by a swarm of insects, huge, strange insects. They killed Jess so I only have Poppy now and they killed, him." A wave of nausea and dread washed over her, and she sank down to the sit on the floor as tears welled in her eyes.

Findo rushed over to her and knelt next to her. "Can you describe the insects?" He seemed anxious and worried.

Serena sniffed, "They were about the size of your forearm with big, pointed noses which they used to stab at us."

He stood up quickly, "Shit. Dirth. I need to get Gisselle

back, now!"

Findo raised his head up to the sky and cupped his hands around his mouth letting out a loud deep humming noise followed by a piercing whistle.

"How did you get rid of them. No one survives an attack from a swarm of Dirth. They kill and then they strip the meat, all they leave behind are the bones of their victims."

"We cut down hundreds of them with our weapons but there were too many. It was only by burning Kanva weed that I drove them off." Serena stood up next to him drying her eyes.

"You fought them? What are you? Have you got any of that weed now?" He fired the questions at her quickly.

Serena ran to the back of the waggon and reached under the canvas to pull out an armful of the weeds as he hummed and whistled again.

"Light it then. She may be in trouble."

Serena presumed that 'she' was his friend and that his calls were a signal. She went to the side of the road and cleared an area to make a fire. Before long a cloud of thick smoke was curling up around them. He kept whistling as she searched the nearby area for more weed. There was not much. Serena started to worry that whatever he was doing would attract the swarm.

A shadow swept over them.

Serena glanced up to the sky but could see little against the light.

"Thank the King, she's here." Findo turned and walked towards Serena.

Then a buzzing came from the forest behind them.

Poppy began to snort and pull at his harness. Serena went to him and held his neck. Whispering in his ear. "It's alright. I won't let them harm you." She eyed the woods and hefted her staff in one hand.

Findo snatched a length of canvas from the cart and began to waft it at the fire, sending sparks into the air and the smoke drifting all around them, stinging their eyes.

The humming grew closer. Serena felt she could see a writhing blackness in amongst the trees.

He kept fanning at the flames and the smoke curled in the air, drifting towards the swirling mass of insects. They backed off, the buzzing slowly diminishing into silence.

Poppy stilled.

Findo stopped fanning the fire and left it smoldering as he went to put the canvas back on the waggon. He froze when he saw what he had uncovered in his haste.

"What….?"

"The message I take to the Wizards. One of their creations."

PART 24

The shadow darkened the forest again, accompanied by a loud flapping noise. Serena instinctively ducked as she ran over to Findo, grabbing the canvas and stuffing it over and around the grotesque monster's skull sitting in the back of the waggon.

He seemed to snap out of his trance and hummed loudly, looking up at the treetops. The smoke still swirled around them from the burning Kanva, but a loud buzzing drove in towards them from the trees.

Serena pushed Findo to the floor and rolled away drawing her bow and loosing an arrow at the Dirth, which was flying above them, heading towards the treetops.

Her aim was true, and the creature tumbled to the floor a feathered shaft protruding from its abdomen.

Findo jumped up from the dirt and drove his dagger through the things head, and its twitching ceased.

"Nice shot. Thanks for saving us there. Must be the good reflecting back?"

"It looked like it was chasing something, wasn't going for us, we just happened to be in its way."

Findo pointed towards the treetops. "Serena, meet my friend. Gisselle."

Serena looked up. There, hanging upside down from the branches was a huge creature. She instinctively shrank backwards towards the cover of the waggon, raising her bow. The animal gazed down at her and stretched it great leathery wings before wrapping them like a coat tightly around its body.

Stepping quickly in front of her, Findo put a finger on the point of her arrow and pushed it downwards. "No, it's ok, she's my friend just like Poppy is yours."

Serena looked at him and then back up at the giant bat like creature.

"What is it?"

"She is a Kystraal, and a more loyal companion I could not

wish for."

He walked over to the nearest tree and swiftly began to climb the trunk, using the weird hooks on his boots to dig into the bark for grip. Rapidly, he gained height and made his way across the branches to the Kystraal. He ran his fingers over her muzzle and along her neck before ruffling the mane around her throat. Then with practiced acrobatics he twisted upside down and mounted a saddle upon the creatures back. Leaning his chest into the high pommel. From this position he reached forward to hum into Gisselle's ear. She turned and looked back at him, and Serena could feel a deep humming through the air. Findo patted his friend a few more times before climbing back down.

"She says, she was happily hunting when the swarm came upon her. She managed to climb high into the air but when I called her back, the insects were waiting for her, and she had to fly wildly to evade them. She thanks you for creating the smoke and killing the Dirth." Findo smiled his broad smile at Serena.

"She said all that?"

"Well not in so many words, but that was the gist of it."

"What now?" Serena asked.

"I guess now we part ways. I need to fly on and we both have messages to deliver." He looked up at Gisselle and then back at Serena.

She turned her head away but not fast enough to hide the look of disappointment in her tired eyes.

Findo hesitated for a moment.

"I think I could accompany you a little further. The Wizards need to be warned that there is trouble here on the road. I reckon that this swarm is why the loggers are fleeing the forest and there are so few travelers about. I can send Gisselle on ahead to wait in the eyrie."

"I don't want to trouble you; you have helped me so much already." Serena seemed to be a little nervous of him now.

"Climb up with me and meet her properly. She is weak on the ground and finds it hard to take flight again." Findo gestured towards the tree.

Serena shook her head, "I cannot climb as well as you. I don't think I could make it."

"I'll help." He said simply, and giving her no chance to refuse, took her hand and walked her to the trunk.

It was not easy, especially seeing as she was so tired, but he helped her with her footing and soon they were up in the high branches and Serena was face to face with Gisselle. The Kystraal sniffed at her hair and pushed back against her hand as Serena stroked her muzzle. Findo showed her how to rub the quills of her mane and as Serena did so Gisselle pushed hard against her hip. Findo quickly put an arm around her to stop her falling as Gisselle kept nosing her waist.

"What have you got in your pouches? She seems very eager to find out." Findo asked.

"Just some dried jerky and trail meat. Can I give her some?"

"Oh, yes. She would love that. You'll be friends for life if you feed her."

Serena reached into the pouch and held out a handful of dried meat strips. She was surprised by how gentle Gisselle was as her soft lips nibbled the strips off her palm. Once all the strips were gone, she nuzzled and sniffed around Serena's waist again.

"Sorry girl but it's all gone. Perhaps I can find you more later." Serena hugged Gisselle tightly around the neck.

Findo helped her back to the ground after grabbing his pack from the back of the saddle and humming, clicking and whistling with his friend once again.

"She will rest here for a while and then head to the eyrie. I have told her I will meet her there tomorrow. If we push on through the night, we should make it by noon."

They spent the rest of the day chatting and walking besides the cart. Poppy seemed content with his new companion and steadily pulled the waggon eastwards. As night drew close, they rested by the side of the road. Serena collected branches from some Kanva weed growing in a clump nearby. Findo shared some more bread and cheese from his pack, and he opened a jar of pickled apples, which tasted divine spread over the simple fare.

As the shadows crept in behind the trees and the sky faded from blue, they rode on with Poppy plodding ahead. Findo talked of life in the cities and the majesty and beauty of the cloud tops high up in the sky. His words gentled her mind and soon she was asleep, her back leaning against their hideous cargo. Findo did not wake her as he watched the forest around them. He was content to let her rest so that she would be ready for the day ahead.

Later he woke her, and they guided the waggon to the side of the road. Serena unhitched Poppy and briefly groomed him. Then she gave Poppy the last of the grain and let him graze on the nearby grass. Findo curled up on the ground wrapped in his coat and hood and fell straight to sleep after asking her to wake him at the first sign of the new day. Serena moved a short distance from the camp and relieved herself behind a tree. She checked her gear and made a few adjustments to the straps of the armour. Then she ran through the Movements, letting them calm her mind as she considered the day ahead.

She had no idea what to expect. All she knew was that Bandolas had been heading to Eap to claim a reward for hunting and killing the beast. He had said that the Wizards wanted proof of the kill and so he was returning to them with the head. Now, she was determined to complete the quest for him, in memory of their short time together. Perhaps they would know something more of the Rush and be able to teach her. Or they may be able to guide her as to what to do next. They may even be able to give her employment. Bandolas had warned her not to get her hopes high where the Wizards were concerned as they were insular and distant with outsiders. Their only want in the world was to study and increase their knowledge.

Soon enough she would be moving into her new life, whatever that might be. Surprisingly, she had already made two new friends, Findo and Gisselle had come to her just as she was beginning to think all was lost. Talking with Findo and spending time with them both had reminded her that there was a whole world of new things waiting out there for her to discover, wonderous things like Gisselle.

She finished and walked back to camp to wake Findo.

When she arrived, he was already up and harnessing Poppy, talking in a gentle calming voice as he worked.

"Come on boy, back up just a little more, that's it. Good boy. Now hold still as I tighten these straps. Your momma will be back soon, and we want you ready for her. That's right she is kind of pretty and a bit scary. Good boy … "He glanced up at her. "Oh, I didn't see you there. Are you ready to get going?"

Serena smiled and combed her hair back from her eyes with her fingers. "Ready when you are."

She turned and lead Poppy on towards the east and a new day.

PART 25

The morning was warm as they walked besides Poppy. The road wound its way through the forest, slowly rising and falling with the undulations of the land. They were into the foothills of The Great Divide. Findo had removed most of his gear as the air became humid. The sun was much warmer here than in the south of the Everplains. The trees grew huge and the underbrush was thick.

As they walked, they shared stories of their pasts, she of her life in a small backwater farming town, he of his years of training in the service of the Messengers. When she pushed him for details of the things he had seen and places he had travelled he went quiet.

"Words won't do it justice. You need to see and experience these places for yourself, I don't want to spoil the fun of the adventure for you."

This did not satisfy her curiosity, but she did feel that he was being fair to her. It was her main intention in life after all. To explore all the places her father had told her of. Why spoil the surprise?

The road began to slope downwards, and the trees became less dense. They began to pass other roads leading off into the forest and soon they encountered other road users. People walking with packs, some pulling hand carts and others with oxen pulling waggons. Most were heading in the same direction as they were, towards Eap.

Findo chatted happily with the people they met, gleaning what news he could. Most of them were farmers or traders heading to the market town around the great Wizards' tower.

There were rumours of war, civil unrest in the cities of the south, trouble between the western cities. Most of it was gossip and rumour mongering. No one could say that they had first-hand accounts of anything, just what they had heard in the markets. People seemed to open up to him straight away, telling him of the hardships on their farm or the bumper crop of tuber weeds they had. One man with six oxen pulling a big waggon of uncut logs started telling Findo all about the difficulties he was having keeping his two mistresses a secret from his wife!

Findo listened carefully to everyone, asking subtle questions to keep them talking and then happily waving his goodbyes as they moved on down the road.

"Make sure the canvas is pulled tight on your cargo. You don't want people to see what you're carrying. It won't be long now." He advised her.

After checking all was well with the cart, they passed a sign at a crossroads. "What's that for?" Serena asked.

"Shows which way to the places nearby. Eap is this way. Back the way we came is Sandlewoods and Daggos. That way to Shroom Hill and if you go that way it goes to Pendledance and Fedgwick."

Trying not to show her ignorance, Serena stared at the painted sign. She had never been anywhere where there were so many places that you needed signs to show where each one was.

"If you look over there." Findo pointed. "You can see a mile marker. That moss covered stone. Look closely and it says how far it is to Eap."

Serena went over and sure enough the stone was carved with an E, an arrow, and the number 3.

Only three more miles. Her heart skipped a beat. She suddenly felt like this was a bad idea. She was out of her depth in a world she did not know.

"Come on Serena, you'll love the view in a minute. The waggon master on the last fur traders caravan, said that it was not far after marker three that you could see the tower."

Sure enough, as they rounded a bend and the land dropped away to the right, the trees had been cleared and they could see out to the plains below.

South of their position the grasslands rolled on to the horizon. To the east, The Great Divide swung south, great snow-capped peaks splitting the world in two. To the north, the mountains were broken. It looked as if someone had plucked a mountain out of the chain, like a tooth had been pulled, leaving a gap between them. This was The Run.

On the western side of The Run, climbing out of the cliffs was the Tower of Eap. The rock face grew upwards from The Run, carved and twisted, as it rose up it tapered up from rock into a man-made tower. The cliffs were at least one hundred metres high and the tower growing up from the top an equal height. The whole thing seemed somehow organic, as if the mountains themselves had grown a thorn, in which lived the Wizards.

It did not look welcoming.

At the base of the cliffs, a large wall protruded in a semi-circle, protectively surrounding the citadel. Tumbling down the hills around this was the town of Eap. Serena could see land ships moving into dock. Large frigates stood at rest being loaded and unloaded. Smaller ships, like the Swiftfire, came and went moving across the plains or up towards The Run. Buildings were painted in a myriad of bright colours competing with each other to be the most eye catching. Several roads, like the one they travelled, could be seen tracing paths into the plains or into the hills like a net spreading out from the town. The areas surrounding Eap were a patchwork of fields and farmsteads, growing crops and livestock to feed the populace. Serena had not known that so many people could live in one place.

"Serena, as we get into town, let me do the talking. Any guards we meet should let us pass as they will recognise me as a Messenger. You, however, they will distrust instantly, a woman wearing armour will draw attention, especially armour that is so distinctive. If they insult you, please don't react. Things are done differently here." He looked over at her and ran his eyes up her body. "And please keep your weapons sheathed. It's not against the law to carry a weapon, but a naked blade tends to mean that you are ready to fight, and to die."

Serena nodded her understanding. She thought for a second that perhaps it would be easier if she just changed back into her old clothes.

No. She would never do that again. This was her new life. Bandolas had died for her. She would wear this armour in memory of him.

They followed the road. The traffic increased until they were just a part of a slow-moving line of carts, waggons, and shuffling people. The fields around them faded away and the buildings reached out to swallow them.

Every street was busier than Crooked Hollow at harvest market. The ground floor of most buildings were shops with signs and stands displaying their wares. As they moved further into the town the buildings steadily grew taller until they were four or five storeys. The upper floors were built outwards over the street. Washing and wares were strung on ropes high overhead, fluttering in the constant wind filtering down the narrow passageways.

The noise increased. People shouting, children crying. Laughter and music. There were less carts and waggons on the streets as they drew closer to the tower. Most business was in the markets and docks lower in the town. The road opened up into a large clear space, on the far side were the huge walls surrounding the tower. Surrounding the square were smart taverns and cafes, the pavements bustling with a myriad of market stalls.

Findo guided Poppy on across the open ground towards a large set of gates in the high walls ahead of them.

A small line of people waited to be seen by some official looking men in uniforms.

"Shut your mouth Serena, you look like a country girl who has never seen a town before. Stop gawking wide eyed at everything."

"But I am a..."

Findo cut her reply short. "You're a skilled bounty hunter come to collect your payment. Act like it or you will be turned away at the gates."

Serena breathed deeply and calmed her mind. He was right. She had not thought this through enough.

"Serena. Be the person they expect you to be. Act like the person you want to be. People see what they expect. If your actions don't match those expectations, that is when you will get called out." He smiled his big smile at her.

They joined the queue.

PART 26

"Name and business?"

A large man in a spotless green uniform that had more shiny buttons than the other soldiers, spoke to each person in turn. He wrote notes in a ledger he carried and then barked commands to the two men by the gates.

Most people he turned away.

So far, Serena had only seen one man let through the gates. The two soldiers had opened a small door and let the scholarly looking man inside before closing the door again.

There was a family in front of Serena and Findo. They wore rough spun clothing and the mother kept fussing at her son's hair and clothes. He looked to be about twelve, tall for his age and scrawny. He stood proudly, ignoring his mother's fussing. Findo, of course, chatted with the father.

Apparently, their son had developed a habit of catching small animals and skinning them. One day they had returned to their farm after working the fields and found him sewing the skins onto one of the mousing cats. It was strange enough that the cat had let the boy do this, but the father swore that as they were telling their son off, the cat had gotten up and flown out of the door. Yes flown, like a bird.

They were here to apprentice their son to the Wizards.

Serena suspected the story was made up and that they were just too poor to feed the entire family. She could be wrong.

"Name and business?"

"Mrs. Drewer. We have brought our son to 'prentice with the Wizards. He made a cat fly you know."

"What else can he do?"

The woman seemed slightly taken aback by this. "Uh, um, he once kept the stew hot all day without a fire."

The large, uniformed man stepped closer to the boy. "That true son. Did you do all that."

" 's true. I am great at magics. Been practicing ain't I." The lad seemed very sure of himself.

"Ok. Where are you staying?"

"Why do want to know?" The woman replied.

"So that we know where to find you if the Wizards are interested. What is the address that you are staying at?" The man seemed uninterested, like he just wanted to get to the end of his shift.

"We ain't got no rooms yet. Came straight 'ere we did." The lady looked worried. "Just let the lad in and we will be on our ways."

"That's not how it works maam. Either you give us an address, or you move along. Stanley, show these nice people the way will you."

One of the soldiers by the door had been sitting writing at a small table. He did not so much stand up, rather, he slowly unfolded himself upwards. He was a behemoth of a man. At least half as tall again as Serena and twice as wide. His uniform was ill fitting and strained at the seams. As he walked towards them, he collected a large, polished wooden club from the end of his table.

"It's ok, we'll go and get some lodgings and come back with the address later." The woman led her family quickly away before Stanley even got close.

Poppy took a few steps forward at Findo's urging.

"Name and business."

"Findo Gask, King's Messenger. My Kystraal, Giselle flew on ahead of me and should be roosting in your eyrie. I claim my right to passage. This is Serena, famed bounty hunter. She travels with me as protector to the words I carry. She also lays claim to bounty set by the Wizards and wishes to collect."

The man looked them up and down as Stanley moved closer.

"Open the gates and let us through, or would you delay the words of the King and risk the wrath of the Wizards?" Findo stood tall, staring down the older uniformed man.

A few seconds passed, though to Serena it felt like an eternity.

"Stanley, open the gates and let these good folk in. Take them to the courtyard. I'm sure someone will meet them there." The uniformed officer nodded to Findo and moved on to the next people waiting in line.

"Follow me and stay close." Stanley had a surprisingly high voice for one so large.

"Thank you, Stanley. Lead on." Findo said as Serena slapped the reins to get Poppy moving again.

After passing through the first gates there was another set of heavy gates ahead and for a few moments they were trapped within the great walls. Stanley spoke to more guards at the second gateway, they briefly looked up at Findo before moving levers to open the way in.

Once through the wall, Stanley led them through the strangest area that Serena had ever seen. The road passed between two high fences, which formed an arch over the roadway. Vines and creeping plants wound up through the fence. The whole thing was reinforced every few metres with large metal supports. The fence was made like chain mail, loops of metal all interlocking. Through the fence they could see beautiful gardens, a landscape sculpted by man to imitate the best that nature had to offer. Moving through the gardens was an odd assortment of creatures.

Many looked like an amalgamation of different animals. Some were huge. Each was contained in its own fenced off pen. It reminded Serena of cattle brought to town for market and displayed for prospective buyers to look at before the auction.

This must be where the creature that Bandolas had hunted and killed had escaped from. To Serena's eyes it was a menagerie of torture. Some of the creatures mewled in pain, others limped heavily or dragged limbs, which did not work, behind them. Some however, stalked their cages, roaring their defiance at the sky.

They passed more guards standing to attention by a gate which led through a smaller wall, beyond it was a cobblestoned courtyard before the base of the tower itself.

Across the courtyard was a dark tunnel boring into the base of the cliff. Around it the rock looked like it had been melted like candle wax and formed into patterns, random shapes and grotesque gargoyles. Looking upwards the cliffs rose until the tower itself sprouted out from the mountain side, spearing towards the clouds. There were windows, balconies and openings throughout the cliffs, but the tower was smooth stone. Not a single aperture to mar its surface.

"Wait here. Someone will come." Stanley glanced nervously through the fencing and headed back towards the gates the way they had come.

"Impressive isn't it." Findo said looking up at the tower.

"Yes." Serena stated flatly. "Why do they have all those creatures behind the fences?"

"Experiments. The Wizards look to improve upon nature. They use their skills for many things. Gisselle and her kind were an early experiment, many years ago."

"But Gisselle is beautiful and intelligent. Most of these creatures are nothing but twisted abominations. Nature should not look like this." Serena was deeply disturbed by what she had seen.

"They are just a small part of the Wizards' work. The world would be a much more uncivilised place without the Wizards and their inventions. You know it was a wizard who first came up with the idea of land ships, and the messages I carry are sealed using a special wax and stamp created by the Wizards."

"It's just wax isn't it. What's so special about that?" Serena asked.

Findo pulled a tube free and showed the seal to her. "Hard as stone and if it is broken by anyone but the intended recipient, then the message gets destroyed and an alarm is sent to the person who sealed it letting them know. It is rare for this to happen but a Messenger who has a seal broken is hunted down and executed in the name of the Messenger service."

She looked closely at the seal. It had a symbol of an anchor and waves on it.

"Who sealed this one?" She asked.

"The Pirate, Oakhands." Findo put the message back in its

straps against his thigh.

"My, you do meet important people don't you. Isn't he the leader of Daggos?" Even in Crooked Hollow stories of The Pirate's adventures on the seas were told.

"I see many people, famed and not. It is my job."

Findo seemed reluctant to talk more so Serena went over to the waggon. She checked her weapons and stroked Poppy. This place felt strange, the gargoyles in the cliffs stared down on them unmoving. The dark tunnel was silent. The animals in their pens roared and called to each other. It all made her skin crawl.

After an hour of standing and waiting, they sat together on the cart and shared a small meal from their supplies.

"You've been here before then?" Serena asked.

"Once, when I was younger and still training. The Degan brought me. We toured all the eyries of the major cities and towns so that Gisselle and I would know our way. I've never had reason to come back, until now."

"It is good to see a Messenger," croaked a voice behind them, "we have not seen one for many moons. Does the King shun us now his war is done?"

They both turned to see a small old man standing at the rear of the cart leaning on his staff. He wore a stained and ill-fitting robe which once may have been a brilliant red colour but was now grubby and worn to a deep claret. His hair was long and hung limply around his shoulders. His clean-shaven face was wrinkled with age, but his eyes twinkled with inner fire and intelligence.

"It is good to see you again Master Humbold. The King has not sent messages? I thought he was in constant communication with Eap." Findo seemed confused.

"Ah yes, you once visited with The Degan. I recognise you now. You have grown." Master Humbold shuffled closer. "We have had no word from the King in three moons. News comes via the ships through The Run, but the world is slowly going silent. It seems that it is holding its breath before the storm to come. What word do you carry?"

"Come Master, you know I cannot say the words. I can tell you that trouble is brewing in the West. Armies are massing between Splitt and the North. The King hopes to hold a great council and quell the dispute before there is war." Findo jumped down from his perch and walked towards the old man.

"Hmm, bad days there are ahead. We here will stay our ground as always and watch and observe. It is not our want to work with men, just to share our discoveries." He stood taller and raised his eyes to Serena. "And you girl. Why do you bring your trouble to Eap?"

Serena jumped down to stand tall before this strange man. She took a calming breath before speaking.

"I have been companion to Bandolas. The Wizards charged him to hunt down and kill this escaped beast." She pointed to the bulk covered in canvas in the cart. "He was successful, but sadly died on the journey here."

Serena glanced down as her voice caught in her throat. "I have come to collect the bounty in his stead having helped him in his quest."

"No, no, no. That is not why you are here at all. You think it is, but you are wrong. You are lost."

The old man's words stung Serena.

"I have come to collect on his bounty." Serena felt a wave of anger wash over her at this man's words. She grabbed a corner of the canvas and pulled it back. "You see. This monstrosity escaped from here. He hunted and killed it. I helped him to get it here and now I mean to collect the bounty."

"But you did not kill it." The old man seemed to have grown in stature, standing taller than before, he leaned forward his penetrating eyes boring into Serena. "If you did not kill it then it is not your bounty to collect. You are just a girl playing dress up in a man's clothes. We owe you nothing."

Findo could see Serena resting her hands on the hilt of her dagger her fingers trembling with barely controlled rage as she breathed deeply. He moved closer to her.

"I may not have made the kill, but I have risked everything to bring you word and evidence of it. The least you could do is thank me."

"Thank you dear, but there was no need for you to come all this way. We have known for quite some time that the beast was dead. It was, after all, our magic which made it. We felt the bond break some weeks ago now. You really did not need to travel all this way. You may leave now." He made a shooing motion with his hand.

That sent her off the cliff and into the surging waters of the Rush. She let it flood her completely, holding nothing back.

Findo blinked and Serena was by Master Humbold, her knife at his throat.

"I have travelled far and risked all to be here, and you would dismiss all I have done as insignificant."

The Master seemed calm as he slowly stepped back from the blade at his throat. "Ah you have learned more than I thought on your journey. Still, you should leave now, girl, before you lose more of yourself."

The events of the next few moments would stay with Findo for the rest of his life.

The Master's staff moved with unbelievable speed to strike at Serena but somehow, she dodged backwards sweeping her foot low towards the legs of the old man. He, however, used his staff as a lever point on the ground to swing himself into the air, feet aimed straight for Serena's chest.

Somehow, she twisted her body allowing his feet to fly past her as she raked her knife along the man's back. He landed heavily and rolled back to his feet swinging his staff in an arc around himself knocking the blade from Serena's hands. She spun and rolled away, as the man steadied himself against the back of the cart.

He flicked his wrist, and a shower of insects flew into Serena's face. She closed her eyes and raised her arms to defend herself. Breathing slowly, she listened. There was a scuffing noise in front of her, as if of a shoe moving against cobblestones. She gathered herself, shaping the Rush around her and thrusting it outwards with all her might.

Master Humbold was thrown backwards through the air.

Serena opened her eyes at the sight before her. Her knees failed and as she fell to the ground, her last thought was that she had failed Bandolas as her mind emptied and darkness closed in.

Findo looked towards the tunnel in the cliff as men began to run across the courtyard shouting in astonishment. The old Master whom he had met all those years ago sat in the back of the cart impaled on the horns of the beastly head, which had been its cargo for so long.

It might be some time before his journey could continue.

PART 27

She slowly awoke. Her body ached everywhere. It made no difference if her eyes were open or shut. Darkness had consumed her world.

Her skin felt cold, and she could feel that she was naked. From the pressure under her, she could tell she sat on a hard wooden seat. As she tried to move, she discovered that her ankles and wrists were strapped to the arms and legs of a chair and that something was wrapped around her head holding it up against its back. She could wriggle her bottom and move her elbows and knees but not much else. She felt a deep ache inside her chest and inside her mind.

For a while she yelled into the darkness. Then she screamed. When nothing changed, she decided to listen.

Then she slept.

When next she awoke nothing had changed. She yelled into the darkness once more. There was no reply. Not a sound.

Eventually she had to relieve herself where she sat. At least the warm trickle was a change, though over time it was just a cold and clammy dampness.

She struggled at her bindings but gave up as her muscles began to ache and she feared that she was tearing her skin.

The darkness was unending.

She breathed and calmed her emotions.

Picking through her memories, she pieced together the last events she could remember. Findo had been with her. The old man had taunted her, and her anger had risen up.

She remembered that when she had reached for the Rush, she had let it take her completely. She had ignored Bandolas's teachings and lost control. The last time it had happened she had ended up exhausted. As he had told her, the Rush had consumed her energy to fuel the things she had done. She recognised the ache in her now as the same. She felt burnt out from the inside.

She breathed deeply and hesitantly reached for the power

within her. It was there, but it was not the Rush she remembered. It curled inside her mind like a slow, meandering stream. She felt hungry and thirsty, but in the darkness, there was no succour.

She slept.

Her eyes opened again on darkness. She was still bound to the chair. She yelled and screamed, straining at her bonds, aware of her nakedness and the filth she sat upon.

She needed to try something new. Slowly, she began to smooth her fingers over the wooden arm of the chair she was bound to. She concentrated on feeling the grain, learning the contours and shapes. As she caressed it, she allowed her mind to lazily drift in the stream of power flowing in her.

The darkness became her friend. Because she could not see, it was easier to picture what she wanted.

Her fingers smoothed the wood.

Looking into the darkness, she could have let it drive her mad. Even on the darkest of nights there was some glimmer of light from somewhere. Here there was nothing. The air was slightly cold but not uncomfortable. The floor was stone and was chilly against her bare feet. The wood held the warmth of her skin, if she did not move too much, but was cold if she shifted. Where her fingers worked the wood was warm, not unbearably so, but it had a warmth that radiated back into her, a warmth which brought her comfort.

She could feel that what she did was working. As she probed around with her fingers, she could feel where the wood had thinned in one place and thickened in another. She continued to smooth it and to shape it with a trickle of the Rush. It was Bandolas who had shown her this was possible and inside she was delighted that she could do this.

She moved the wood slowly, layer by layer, away from the centre of the arm of the chair. When she was satisfied with her work, she drew her arm forward, pushing her bindings into the gap she had created, she strained for a moment and her arm came free.

Sudden light blinded her eyes, and she used her free hand

to shield them. As they slowly adjusted, she could see that she sat in the middle of a cage. Metal bars surrounded her on all sides. Looking up, she could see that bars also ran across just above her head. She was in a barred box inside a larger room. Her cage was barely bigger than her and her chair. Straight in front of her on the other side of the bars sat a man holding up a glowing white sphere in one hand.

His voice was soft as he spoke. "You are special. How did one such as you come to be able to manipulate the Rush?"

Serena did not reply. She sat studying him.

He was perhaps in his middle years, dark hair kept cut just above his ears. His face was slightly angular with high cheekbones and his nose was a little too long and pointed. His robe was a deep midnight blue where the light shone upon it, appearing to disappear into the blackness of the shadows where it did not. Whilst not large, the man appeared muscular and well built, not at all the way Serena imagined a wizard to look. This man was, however, undoubtedly a wizard. The ball he held in his hand glowed with a blueish white glare with no attachments to it. It just sat in his hand, starkly revealing her nakedness to him.

He did not seem threatening as he sat watching her, watching him.

She began to caress the wood of the arm which bound her other hand.

He raised one finger on his free hand that was resting casually on the arm of his chair and slowly moved it side to side, a clear signal saying no.

Serena stopped what she was doing and sat still. Breathing slowly and holding onto the small stream of power in her mind.

"It has been a long time since an outsider has killed one of our own. Especially one who is not a wizard." He began to stand up, letting the ball of light drift upwards from his hand. "When you have managed to free yourself, you will find me downstairs. I will have the servants prepare some roast lamb and potatoes, bring you a bath and your cleaned clothes. I hope that once you have eaten you will be polite enough to answer a few questions."

He began to walk towards an opening in the wall behind him. The man paused for a second and looked back over his shoulder. "Your friend said you were clever, before he left. He also spoke in your defence before the conclave. If you should ever see him again, thank him that you still live."

The man turned and descended out of sight taking the light with him.

PART 28: THE MESSENGER FIGHTS

His arms wrapped firmly around the chest guard in front of him as Gisselle rolled and banked hard to the left, Findo found himself looking straight down at a caravan crossing the sand below. He had no time to see details as the Kystraal folded her wings and sent them spinning downwards.

He pushed his head back into the brace behind him knowing that the forces coming up would be beyond his muscles to control. He had hooked the reins away, giving Gisselle permission to take the lead, in this situation she would know best. His job was just to hang on and do what he could to protect them.

It had been a day since they had left Eap. Serena had still been unconscious. He had given his statement to the Wizards' conclave, written her a short note, and used his Messenger credentials to get out fast. He could do no more for her and, knowing what he did now, his mission seemed more urgent than ever.

They had flown high and fast through The Run, heading on a straight course back towards Westomere. They made good time and Gisselle was happy to be flying again having been well fed and rested at the eyrie. As they crossed the Sand Sea close to the Central Peaks, Findo had spotted dust rising from the desert floor in a long line. Nudging Gisselle lower with his knees, they had seen a vast caravan of sleds, waggons, and people in a long line, making its way northwest across the dunes.

Findo had never seen this number of people travelling across the Sand Sea and had decided to get a closer look. Giselle rode the thermals well and they had stayed high for an hour or so, keeping the sun behind them to avoid being spotted. Using his spyglass, Findo had observed that the waggons were similar to ones used in Havii, slavers' carts, full of flesh for the markets of the south. The problem was, they were not in the south or even heading south. He estimated that there were several hundred people walking, probably around the same number in the carts. Riding on the backs of Hindra, giant lizards native to the dunes, were dozens of guards, easy to spot because of their mounts and their black robes and armour, the uniform of the princes of Havii's elite soldiers.

Findo's best guess was that Havii was trading flesh with either The North or with Splitt, bolstering their armies with slaves. He needed to get back to the King and report his news.

As Giselle had turned to fly on to the northeast, a cry had gone up from the camp below and the guards had opened one of the waggons. They had been spotted. From within cages the guards released two large Ithras, flying insects with powerful jaws from the jungles of Qualtesh.

In classes long ago, when training as a Messenger, he had been told of these creatures. They were one of the few living things which could bring down a Kystraal.

He swallowed down his panic as he spotted movement to their side, Gisselle opened her wings turning suddenly to the right. As she did so, Findo looked up to see an Ithra, which had been following them, falling towards them, as it flashed past its legs raked against Gisselle's neck, shearing off several of her protective quills. She quickly turned to pursue.

He could see a flash of wings behind and to their side as Giselle rolled and banked closing in on the insect ahead of them. Findo knew they were outnumbered, and Gisselle would tire quickly doing aerial manoeuvres like this. He needed to even the odds.

Messengers did not carry bows or spears as part of their kit. His only real weapon was his long knife, but they did carry a net, usually used to stow extra equipment or to secure kit when roosting. They were climbing now, and Gisselle was losing distance to the lighter insect. Findo hummed and let out a shrill whistle as he stood up in the saddle. His Kystraal responded by levelling out her flight, continuing her pursuit at a lower altitude than her prey.

Findo could hear the rapid beat of insect wings coming from behind. He released the buckles binding one leg and turned quickly to cast his net out in a motion just like a fisher man.

Luck was on his side. The Ithra which had been closing on them from behind flew straight into the net as it splayed out into the sky. Its body caught up in the strands as the net closed all around it and the creature plummeted to the ground sending up a cloud of dust and sand on impact.

As Gisselle pulled her wings back looking to pick up speed in a controlled descent, Findo sat back down and braced himself. It was up to her now.

Again, the remaining Ithra flew down upon them from above, trying this time to catch its claws into Gisselle's body. She was aware of its ploy and banked at the last moment. The creature flew past and the Kystraal chased swiftly after it.

They skimmed over the tops of the dunes and for a moment Findo thought that she had lost their quarry. She flapped her wings hard to gain height and he could see that the Ithra had sought to hide in a shallow dip between two dunes. He felt a deep thrumming inside his mount's chest, she was not happy that she would have to land. He hummed back, unstrapping the rest of his harnesses so that he was free in his seat. Gisselle dove hard.

At the last moment, she banked sharply left circling tightly around their quarry and Findo, using all the strength his legs could muster, sprang from his seat, knife in hand. The impact with the insect was hard, his blade skidding along its chitinous exoskeleton before it caught between two plates. Their bodies slammed into the flowing sand of the desert floor and his knife and arm were driven deep into the Ithra's thorax.

He lay still for a moment catching his breath, before rolling away. Coarse sand stuck to the ichor coating his blade and hand as he pushed himself up to look around.

The sun blazed down, and he shielded his eyes from the glare of the bright sand. He could hear cries from men in the distance. No doubt the soldiers were coming. He pumped his legs trying to get up to the top of the dune, each step made difficult by the shifting sand. He saw her coming, flying low, hugging the contours of the land. As he reached the summit, he leapt high, trusting her to catch him. For once their timing was not perfect, he slammed hard into the side of his saddle and her shoulder caught him in the soft part of his side driving the wind from his lungs. She turned slowly, giving him time to scramble into his seat before she began to laboriously flap her wings, climbing back into the sky heading for home.

PART 29

Hands shaking uncontrollably, she struggled to do up the last buckle on the armour. She was drained beyond anything she had known before.

After the wizard had left her, it had taken hours to free herself. When she had found her way through the dark to the staircase, she had hardly had the strength to shuffle on her bottom down them, like a child.

A door had blocked her way, but when she feebly scrabbled at it, he had opened it. Neither of them had spoken. He had led the way through a large room which she could not remember the details of to this smaller chamber. She had tried to stand, but in the end had had to crawl at his feet as he showed her the way. He had offered no help and she would not have accepted it. It had not mattered to her that she was naked and covered in filth. He had promised her a bath and some food. That was all that she wanted.

The bath had been painfully warm when she finally managed to drag herself up and into it. She had half fallen, half slumped into the water causing great cascades of it to splash over the sides. He had left her then. She had just sat in the water staring upwards at the wooden beams of the ceiling until sleep had taken her into its warm embrace.

When she had awoken, the water was cold and filthy. She had done her best to scrub her hair and her skin, and had found a stool nearby with her clothing, her armour and weapons rested on a chest by the door.

With the final buckle done up, she put a hand against the door frame and gathered herself before pushing back the curtain and reluctantly walking through.

"Hello Serena, my name is Tempest Brooke, I serve as your guardian whilst you are with us. Anything you wish for, just ask and I will try to help. You have passed the first and second tests of the conclave and are welcome to stay here for as long as you like. Your entrance caused quite a stir." He pulled a chair back at the large table in the middle of the room and gestured for her to take a seat. She wanted to stand. To defy this man. However, she hurt too much and did not dare fall over and show weakness again. She shuffled over and he pushed her chair in as she sat.

On the table was a single plate of roasted lamb, potatoes, and salad, neatly laid out with cutlery. Two glasses also sat there. One by her plate the other opposite her, towards which he moved. The room was lit by a single candle, in a simple stand, at the centre of the table between them.

He collected a carafe from a dark wooden sideboard behind him and filled her glass, setting the jug near to her so she could refill as she wanted.

"Drink, eat. You have drained your body and need to start to build yourself back up." He sat down in the chair opposite her.

Her voice croaked as she spoke, her mouth dry and throat sore. "Why?"

"I will answer all of your questions in time Serena, but for now, please eat."

She sat with her head hanging low, arms propping her up on the table either side of the plate. It smelled delicious. With a trembling hand she reached out for the glass, it shook so much as she tried to raise it that she ended up using both hands.

The water was cool and fresh, it burned slightly as she swallowed but she felt her parched body respond almost immediately and she drank thirstily, water spilling from her lips down her front.

"Your body is in shock. The Rush took much from you." He nodded to her as she picked up a slice of juicy lamb with her fingers.

She had noticed how gaunt she appeared as she had dressed. Her clothing hung loosely on her frame. She could see the bones of her fingers clearly through her thinly stretched skin.

"In time you will recover. Until then, I would suggest you refrain from attempting to use your power. It could cause your whole-body system to crash again. Especially if you draw too much."

Serena sat and ate. She forced herself to clear her plate. When she finished, she drank another glass of water. All the while she watched him, watching her.

He did not move much, and when he did it was with an economy of movement. He seemed completely relaxed, sitting almost casually. But she could tell that if needed to, he would pounce rapidly with a cat's quick reactions. He reminded her of a hawk. Hovering, observing, waiting for its prey.

For the first time, he broke eye contact with her as he stood. "This will be your room. You have seen the other. In this corner is a bench, the chest at the end contains ample bedding to make it comfortable. The sideboard contains some spare clothing should you need it. You have seen the room upstairs."

He moved to a heavy wooden door opposite the staircase. "This we will leave locked for now. We wouldn't want you to get lost in the tower."

By the door hung a length of rope. "If you pull this a servant will come. You may ask for food, drink, water for a bath, any small things which you might need. Rest for now. I shall return in a few days."

He brought a box over from the sideboard and placed it beside her hands. She opened it.

"They are dried and candied fruits. I always find sweet things help me to restore my energies." He turned and pulled on the rope.

"Oh, your friend left you this." He placed a scroll of paper on the sideboard. The door opened and he left. As it closed again, it thudded shut and there was a click as the lock engaged.

Serena stared blankly at the wood of the door. As she tried to make sense of what was happening, she reached into the box and then placed one of the candies into her mouth. She sat savouring the sweetness for a long time before she rested her head on the table and drifted into a deep sleep.

PART 30

Over the next two days, Serena ate. She pulled the cord by her door numerous times. On each occasion it opened, she would ask the servant outside for something to eat or drink. To begin with she had just asked for simple things. As time went on, and she began to feel better, she asked for more and more extravagant dishes. Things she had heard of but never tried. Each time she was given exactly what she had asked for.

She had nothing else to do so it became a challenge to her. "Bring me pheasant served on a bed of wild rice with roasted root vegetables and a sauce made from plums." she asked. Half an hour later, it was delivered.

"I wish to eat some traditional spiced dishes from the twin cities, followed by a selection of desserts from Splitt." Within the hour she was full, surrounded by empty platters from which she had eaten the finest foods she had ever tasted.

Eventually the game grew boring. She had slept, she had taken another bath. Each time she rang the bell, her servants would speak to her to determine her wishes, but they did not engage in conversation, pointedly refusing to talk to her or answer questions.

"I am sorry miss, but for now we are not permitted to talk with you. We have been tasked with seeing to your wellbeing but are not to discuss matters with you until you are recovered enough to go before the conclave."

Through the door she could see nothing but a blank stone wall opposite. The servants made sure the door was never left open for long.

The scroll still sat on the sideboard. She had not wanted to read the words it contained. She felt that Findo was just another person she had let down in a growing list, her mother, Bandolas, even her father. She worried that his words would just open more wounds and she was not ready for that yet.

On the third day, she woke, bathed, and dressed in her full armour. She strapped on her weapon belts and climbed to the room at the top of the stairs. She placed a candle in one corner, dragged the remains of the cage to one side and began to work through the Movements. She moved slowly, making sure of her breathing, checking that each muscle stretched and flexed appropriately. She let her mind feel her body.

She was still physically weaker than she had been, but her strength was returning rapidly.

Gently she reached out and let her mind caress the Rush. No longer was it the thin stream as when she had last been in this room. Now it was a raging torrent once again. She let a small trickle into her actions as she sped up her Movements. Serena was cautious, however, and soon slowed to do some simple stretches, allowing her power to dissipate.

When she returned to her room, Tempest was waiting.

He sat casually draped in his seat. As she entered, he looked up at her. "I see you are feeling better."

Whilst he spoke, one of the servants came in carrying two large platters of food. Tempest rose from his chair and took them from the man placing one either side of the table. He closed the door behind the man and gestured for Serena to sit.

She did not need to be asked. The food looked fantastic, and she had worked up a hunger.

Eggs, fried ham, newly baked bread and cheese. There was even fresh peach juice in small glasses. Neither of them talked as they ate, each watched the other, assessing.

When they were finished, he pulled the cord by the door and a servant cleared the plates away. As the servant left, he did not close the door. Serena stared at the open portal.

"There is no need for that now. You are free to come and go as you wish. It is good to see you recovering so quickly." Tempest hesitated, as if unsure of what he was going to say next.

"The conclave would like to interview you now. Come with me." He stood and walked from the room giving her no time to react.

Serena grabbed the scroll from the sideboard as she dashed to follow him, tucking it into one of the pouches on her belt.

Outside her room was a ramp, its cobblestoned floor

circling upwards and downwards. It formed a corridor which was wide enough and high enough for an ox to pull a cart. On a bench against the wall by the door sat one of the servants who had attended her and brought her food. He stood and nodded to Tempest who stopped and leant close to him whispering briefly in his ear. The man gave her a quick look as if to say goodbye and walked down the ramp and around the bend out of sight.

Tempest led them uphill.

"You must have questions for me. What would you like to know?"

Serena walked slowly behind him, studying their surroundings. "Why am I here?"

Tempest looked back at her briefly, "Because you have power. Because you are a woman. Because you used your power to kill a wizard. Because you came to us."

He paused to let her catch up with him. "Perhaps you came to ask us questions or it is we who have questions for you."

As they continued to walk side by side, they passed doors on both sides of the ramp. "What is in these rooms?" She asked.

"Some rooms are where Wizards live, some are where they study. Up here in the tower most are empty. There are not nearly as many people here now as there were in the past." He seemed saddened by this.

"Am I a prisoner?"

"Yes, and no. Whilst it is true that I will not allow you to leave, once you have faced the conclave that may change. In truth, I am not sure we could stop you if you wished to leave." He seemed sincere in this.

Serena realised that if this was true, then perhaps they had other reasons for wanting her to stay.

The ramp continued to spiral upwards, the doors were not spaced evenly, and it was hard to tell how far they had travelled or when they had completed a full circle. Serena tried to build a mental map starting at her room and spiralling upwards but there was no regularity to anything except the constant angle of their ascent.

"The conclave will ask you questions. Answer honestly and in full and the questioning should be over soon. Then they will decide what to do with you." He glanced at her and smiled weakly.

"Is it not my decision what I do?"

"I wish it was." He looked away and hung his head.

They walked the rest of the way in an awkward silence.

PART 31

The ramp ended at a large set of double doors. Tempest stepped up and pushed them open. The incline continued a short way upwards, leading to the floor of a large circular room. Serena estimated that, by its shape and size and the time it had taken them to climb, this must be the top of the tower. The room was sparse. Just a large circular space with a high beamed ceiling. In the centre of the room stood a heavy wooden table. Around the table seated in elaborate cushioned chairs sat ten men. Two chairs were free, one at the head of the table and one on the side.

Tempest walked to the chair at the side leaving Serena to take the chair at the head of the table. As she approached, the men all stood up and turned to look at her. They watched as she pulled the chair out and faced them. They appeared to be waiting. Serena felt awkward, not knowing what was expected.

Tempest smiled at her and gestured for her to sit. As she did so, the other men sat as well, there was much scraping of wood against stone and shuffling as everyone got comfortable.

Opposite Serena sat a large chubby man, with large bushy eyebrows and a large balding head. His robe fitted him like a broken tent, all loose and heavily folded. The material was a bright yellow, edged around the collar and cuffs in deep blue fur. He seemed to have a perpetual frown and tucked his chin in to peer through his brows at her.

When he spoke, his voice was rich and deep, "You have been brought before us today as we have found you to be a user of the magics. Are you aware of your powers?"

Serena hesitated, her voice sounded very small as she replied, "Yes."

"How long have you had the power?"

Serena tried to think, "It has only been a few moons since I was first aware of it. Bandolas, the man who killed your beast, helped me to control it."

One of the men seated to her left choked as he was taking

a sip of wine and several of the others laughed at this.

"Control. You did not show control when you killed Master Humbold. You had no control." The fat man seemed to be angry with her.

Tempest held his hand up. Gradually the others turned to him.

"She has passed the first two tests. That shows she can control the power. We all remember our first time."

"But she's a girl, they have no control." A small thin man on her right said angrily.

Another stood up and banged his fist on the table as he shouted, "This is a waste of our time, magics are fading and we should be out there studying why, not sitting in here talking to a stupid girl who has no control and killed one of our number."

Tempest raised his hand again and waited until everyone was quiet before he spoke, "She has passed the first two tests. She may be unskilled, but she has the Rush. Two days ago, she was drained. Yet this morning she was washing in the waters of the Rush once again enhancing her natural physical abilities. When was the last time any of you did that?"

Serena had no idea what they were talking about, so she just listened, learning all she could.

Tempest continued, "I brought her here so that she could answer your questions. Ask them, deliberate on her answers and then make your decisions. Do not act like fools and dismiss this opportunity before you even give it thought."

"Girl. Do you know what the first test is?" An older, grey-haired man sitting beside Tempest asked.

Serena thought about this. Her first instinct was that it must be being able to feel the Rush, but she had spent some time in her room thinking on everything Tempest had said to her and if that were true, then the boy at the gates might qualify and Bandolas certainly would have done. "Giving all of yourself to the flow of the Rush and holding nothing back, with no reservation, committing to that action with no fear of the consequences."

The men all glanced around the table at each other nodding.

"Not the words that we teach, but that is the essence of it. Only by giving everything can the gifted survive. Control through sacrifice we call it."

The fat man glared hard at her from the opposite end of the table. "And the second test?"

Now she understood, "Drawing on the Rush even past the point when it should not be possible. Drawing it from all around you when you yourself have no more to give. That was how it felt to me in the dark room where you locked me."

She was getting angry with these men.

"Yes." The man closest to her on her right said. "She can use the Rush, so can many people. She is nothing but a witch. We cannot think to let her stay."

"Why not?" Tempest leant forward, "Do you worry that your pathetic use of the power will be eclipsed by one so young?"

The man shook his head, "Tempest are you blinded by a bit of skirt. That is what is wrong. She is a woman, come her moon times, her weeping between the legs will cause her to lose control. We all know women make bad judgements during their time. We cannot afford for one to be here amongst us with no control. Making bad decisions."

"You are a sexist fool, Marquand. No woman has ever passed the first two tests. So, what! I say we let Serena take the third." Tempest's face was red from the strain of holding his temper.

Everyone around the table started speaking at once, shouting each other down. It appeared that they all had reasons why a woman should not be allowed to take the third test. Serena just sat calming herself and watching Tempest, who also now sat calmly watching the others.

The fat man banged his pudgy fist on the table, "Enough. Sit down. Calm yourselves."

He waited for everyone to be seated and silent again before continuing. "Girl. Why did you come to us? What is it that you want?"

All the men turned to look at her.

Serena stared at her hands, resting gently upon the table.

"I came to you to claim the bounty owed to Bandolas for killing your beast. I want only that from you."

"Did you kill the beast?" Marquand sneered.

"No."

"Then we owe you nothing."

"Bandolas killed it for you. I travelled with him and when he died, I vowed to see his quest to the end." She looked up at Marquand.

"I travelled far and sacrificed much to be here, to deliver the beast's head back to you. I had thought…"

The fat man interrupted her. "You had thought that we would heap riches upon you, and you could return home and live happily ever after. A fairy story. Grow up girl. We pay on our contracts, but it is not your contract to collect. Are you family to this Bandolas?"

"No."

"Then why should we pay you anything?"

"I helped him," Serena looked away from them, "I loved him."

"And just because he spent time between your thighs, you think that we should pay you like a whore?"

"That's not 'ow it is. You twist my words." Serena stood up not noticing that in her anger she had slipped back into the accent of her youth and the Hollow. "I came to return your property to you and finish what my friend had started. Yes, selfishly I thought, there might be a reward. I want to travel the world and see the things my father told me of when I was young. I see now that it was a dream. I am a capable fighter and tracker and could take on new bounties, if you have any. Earn my own rewards."

"We don't hire foolish girls. We don't take in women as Wizards. There is no place for you here."

"You are correct gentlemen. This is not my place. Show me to the door and I will be on my way."

"I have a question." A small unassuming man, in a smart robe with shiny buttons all the way up its front, sat forward. He was the only other person in the room to have stayed seated and quiet through the rest of the interview. He nodded his head to Serena in a gesture of welcome. "Knowing what you do now, do you wish to learn more about your powers?"

"Yes."

"If we offered, would you stay and study with us?"

"I would think about it." As she began to calm she regained control of her voice and tried to speak with an accent of authority.

"If we said you had to leave, would you go and would you tell others of what you had seen?"

Serena thought for a moment as she wrestled her anger back under control. "I would leave. I would speak of what I have seen, but only if asked. I am not a gossiping washerwoman."

The others had all settled back in their chairs. Contemplating her words. The quiet man continued.

"If we offered the third test, would you accept it?"

"Honestly sir, I do not know. I did not come here to be a wizard. I would like to know more about this power, but it is not my reason for coming here."

"I ask you again for your answer to a previous question. Why did you come here?" The others all leaned forward; Marquand seemed about to say something but picked up his wine instead.

"A man walked into my village – Crooked Hollow – pulling a monstrous head behind him. He was wounded and needed help. My mother, with my help, healed him. I have been unhappy at home since my father disappeared five years ago. When Bandolas left to travel here with the head, I left with him."

Marquand interrupted her, "You ran away from home."

"Marquand," The quiet man continued to speak softly, "Please refrain from interrupting our guest. Let her answer the question in her own time and in her own words."

Serena inclined her head in thanks and continued, "We

travelled across the Everplain in one of the farm carts, with Jess and Poppy, two of our oxen. It was a hard crossing and it brought us closer together. We fell in love." She paused in her tale; the quiet man nodded for her to continue.

"When we reached the forests, we were attacked by a swarm of insects including some really big ones which Findo called Dirth."

"Yes, yes, he told us of the swarm. We will deal with it, we can't have the roads being threatened, not in these times. How did you survive? Nasty things Dirth are." The fat man spoke, his jowls wobbling beneath his jaw.

"Bandolas killed many, I shot some with my bow and took down more with my staff."

"You used the Rush?" This from Tempest.

"Well, yes."

"And you killed them all?"

"No. I remembered some advice we heard on the road, to burn Kanva weed. The smoke drove them off." She stopped talking. Words failed her.

"Go on Serena. Tell the rest." The quiet man coaxed her on.

Her voice was hollow and emotionless as she continued, "Jess and Bandolas died. I was lost in the woods with Poppy when Findo found us. With his help I got here. You know the rest."

"It seems some of us have underestimated you. None of us would have done the same in your shoes. Your journey is remarkable enough, especially the bits you left out, for example the storm you survived and the attack of the boar."

Serena looked up at him, how did he know?

"My dear girl, the beast was my creation, even in death it carried a spark of my magics. I have watched you for a while now." He looked around at the other men. "I say she can take the test. I know my words carry little weight in this room, but the girl has proven resourceful and powerful. I for one would prefer to have her as a friend rather than an enemy." He shrank back into his chair, steepling his fingers under his chin.

The men all looked at each other, each considering their thoughts, they seemed unwilling to say more or ask more.

Eventually Tempest stood, "My fellow Wizards, have you heard enough? Do you have any more questions?"

None spoke up.

He turned to the fat man, "Master Dunwith, have you heard enough to make your decision?"

The fat man nodded slowly.

Tempest looked at each man in turn. Each man nodded.

"Then decide now. Can Serena take the third test?" Tempest asked. "Raise your hands for aye."

Tempest raised his arm.

The old man next to Tempest raised his hand from the table as did the quiet man.

Master Dunwith looked around the table. He took a breath and held it for a moment. "I vote that she can take the test, but not yet. If she can learn better control. If she can learn to shape the world around her, then she may return in one year and we will vote again. For now, my dear. You must leave us."

He looked at the others, "Would that satisfy you all? Let her prove herself first."

There was a chorus of 'ayes.

"Master Brooke. Take her away now. We have much to discuss of the world. The Messenger brought unsettling news and I sense dark magics at work. Return when the girl is gone."

The quiet man rose from his seat and came over to Serena as she stood. He offered his arm which she clasped. "My dear, I do hope you return, for now go and see the world. Learn what you can in the time we have given you and return to us."

"Thank you Master…"

"Thatchem. Good luck." Master Thatchem shook her arm once again and then returned to his seat leaving Serena with Tempest.

PART 32

They walked for a while in silence. Tempest seemed to be waiting for her to speak.

"What now?" She asked when she could bear the silence no longer.

"That is your decision, I cannot speak for you." He stopped and leaned casually against the wall. She had to stop and look back up at him.

"I can speak of myself however." He gestured for Serena to lean against the wall opposite him. She complied and realised that in doing so he had let her stand at the same height as himself, so that he did not tower above her.

"Thank you, go on." she said.

"For some time now, the magic of this world has faded. There are less people born with the ability to touch the Rush and our numbers in the tower are the lowest they have been since this place was built. No man has come to us in the last decade with the potential which you have shown. No woman has come to the tower in over four hundred years, and she caused the War of Tears."

Serena had no idea of what he talked, she knew little of history, perhaps if her father had been around longer, she would have learned.

Tempest continued. "All of us here in the tower can sense a great need in the world, something has gone wrong, but we do not have the knowledge to fix it. Some of us argue that we should change our ways, go out into the lands and learn what we can, invite people of knowledge from all around the world to share ideas. But most see that as radical ideology. The Wizards have been a closed and secretive order for too long. We have stored arcane knowledge and used magic to our own ends, it has become tradition to try to protect the world from behind our high walls, looking down on mankind from our tall tower."

He scratched the stubble on his cheek before looking up at her, "Having watched you, seen what you are capable of,

Master Thatcham and I believe that it is time that we open our doors to the world. Perhaps new people, people like you, can bring us fresh ideas. Stimulate our learning and be a positive change. I am sorry for the way we have treated you, but it has been our way for so long and change is hard."

Tempest looked deeply saddened and vulnerable in that moment.

"My advice to you, Serena, would be to go out into the world and learn what you can. Learn first what you want. Learn what knowledge you can and use that knowledge wisely. Learn to use the Rush, every person born with it is different, therefore the things they can do are different. Most who can touch the magic will only be able to do small things with it, like running a little faster or being able to shape small things made of wood or stone. A very few rare people learn to shape the world around them in different ways, for example to turn the air cold around them or, as you have done, to shape the air to push objects with great force. Learn your talents, try new things and see the world. When you feel you have ideas to share, return to us and we can learn together."

Serena fidgeted with the hilt of her dagger as she considered his words, "I understand what you are saying but I have no idea where to start. I am alone now in a huge world. I feel small and stupid and should never have left home."

"Don't say that. Every journey begins with the first step, and that is the hardest one to take. Don't let doubt or inexperience stop you. Remember this, you have friends, and you will meet new ones down the road. I will always be here for you, the Messenger …"

"Findo?"

"Yes, Findo. He cared for you; he was a friend was he not?"

"Yes, I suppose he was."

"Do not fear the unknown, be brave and strong and take that first step, wherever it will lead. Down that road is new knowledge and new friendships. There is not much you cannot achieve if you set your mind to it, you have proven that much." He gave her a wry smile. "Come, let's get you fully equipped to face the world."

As they descended the tower, Serena quizzed him on places she could go to and what knowledge she should seek out. It seemed to her that Kentai, with the stone druids and the shadow fighters could be a good place to start.

They collected her staff and pack from her room, and he led her to the kitchens where they sat and ate for a while. He ordered some food to be packed for her journey and left her to eat saying he had business to attend to but he would shortly return.

Serena sat in a small booth to the side of the busy kitchens, watching the men at work, whilst picking at a crust of bread and thinking. She remembered the scroll which Findo had left for her and carefully cracked the wax seal on it.

Serena,

I am sorry that I had to leave. Master Tempest has assured me that you will be cared for and treated fairly. I sincerely hope you get what you came for.

I have to leave and deliver my messages to the King. I have already delayed too long.

I am worried about the rumours I have heard and things I have seen. The Wizards confirmed that Havii has closed its borders and that there has been no word from The Twin Cities for many moons.

If you are at a loss for work, then I offer it to you. Investigate what is happening in Havii and the South. I would go myself but must complete my mission. I will implore the King to release me to travel and join you. On the second full moon from now, look to the skies and you should see Gisselle flying over the Pillars of Kheem. You will find a way to let me know you are safe, and I will come to you.

If you are not there, then I will understand and free you from this service.

You are a very troubling person. I hope that you have not stirred up too much mischief in the tower.

Findo.

Serena felt relief. Talking to the Wizards had drained her of purpose. Findo had sent her a lifeline. She clung to it. With renewed hope for a future, she now had a mission. She would see it done and learn what she could of the world and its magic along the way.

When Tempest returned, he seemed distracted and less inclined to conversation. "Your words and actions have stirred up the conclave. Some may seek to detain you further. I would see you on your way. Are you prepared to take your first step?"

Serena stood and hefted her pack, "I believe I am."

"That is good, follow me." He led her from the kitchens and through a warren of corridors and rooms descending further into the mountain. Some of the places they passed through were busy with people working, cleaning, carrying piles of scrolls. Some looked to be scholars. When she asked, Tempest told her they helped in the Wizards' studies with research. Most people were well into their middle or aged years. Serena only saw one person close to her own age, sitting alone on a cushion in a room off a corridor which they were hurrying down.

"How do you wish to travel from here?" Tempest asked over his shoulder.

"Um, I could take Poppy. He has served me well so far."

"Which direction do you take?"

"Through The Run towards Kentai." Serena answered.

Tempest stopped suddenly and Serena almost ran into him. "It may be better for you to travel by ship. I do not wish to frighten you, but some look for recompense for the death of Master Humbold and would detain you further. You may do better heading to the docks and trying for the next ship."

"May I say goodbye to Poppy first?"

"Yes, but we must hurry."

Before long Serena stood stroking the flanks of her last remaining link to the farm she had grown up on, tears flowing down her cheeks. She hugged the friendly ox around the neck, breathing in his strong musky odour. On the floor at the side of the stables sat the skull of the beast she had risked so much to deliver here. Discarded and abandoned.

She patted Poppy one last time and then went over to the head. Tempest stood at the door watching outside. She took her knife and eased the antlers away from the bone. She undid her bedding from her pack and rolled them in her bedroll. Tempest glanced her way as she worked and nodded his approval. She would take something from all of this, these mementos.

Then Tempest led her out of the Temple grounds through a series of tunnels and corridors which led through the curtain walls and back to the gates. She was glad she had not had to see the mutated animals in their cages again.

"Head to the docks, if you can find Captain Bartham he is a good man and can be trusted. Otherwise book the first passage you can. Do not delay. Marquand and his cronies will not be happy that Dunwith ruled in your favour." Tempest reached in his robe and pulled out a small purse which he placed in her hands. "There is not much but it should buy you passage."

"Thank you, Master Tempest, I hope that all you have done for me is worth it. When I can, I shall return and share what I have learned with you."

Tempest nodded once, then turned and stalked away.

Stanley still sat hunched at his table, large club resting close to his hand. He gave Serena a polite wave as she walked off, heading down into the town.

PART 33

It was exhilarating sitting near the prow of the ship as it raced forward, the wind full in the sails and the kite runners tight and humming. Serena pulled her hair, which was whipping around her, back from her face and stared ahead.

She had found Captain Bartham easily enough. When she had reached the docks, she had headed to the busiest wharf with the best-looking ship. Dodging through the deck hands moving cargo she had approached the gang plank and been stopped by an unassuming, plainly dressed man.

"Where do you think you're going miss." He had asked in a friendly tone.

"I'm looking to cross through The Run. This looks like a fine ship, so I thought I'd come and ask." Serena tried to appear sure of herself. Projecting the image people would want to see.

"I don't need any more sell swords. My crew keep things safe." He eyed her up and down, taking note of her armour and weapons.

"You mistake me sir. I look to buy passage. You wouldn't happen to know where I might find Captain Bartham?"

"Maybe I do? Who's looking for him?" The man lowered the ledger he had been holding to take notes of the cargoes being loaded aboard.

"Master Tempest from the tower sent me." Serena noticed that a few of the men close by had stopped their work and were casually watching and listening to their conversation.

A fellow appeared, looking over the rail of the ship, "Hey, why are you slowing down. I want to catch the evening wind." He called.

"It looks like you have just found him." The man with the ledger said to Serena before turning and shouting up to the man on deck.

"Sorry boss, this rather charming girl seems to have distracted the boys. She says that Tempest sent her."

"Send her up, I want the Kite in the air before the hour is

done."

Serena was then directed to climb aboard the ship. As she did, she looked around. The vessel was much larger than the Swiftfire had been. There seemed to be a crew of at least twenty men all busy in the task of moving or stowing crates and bails of cargo. The vessel stood as tall as most two-storey buildings and was long and sleek. It had a high prow which swept down over the leading wheel to the main body of the ship. To the rear, two arms swept out holding the ship off the ground on rails with rows of small wheels. The ship had one main mast with two more which could be lowered out to the sides on a system of ropes and pulleys.

Unlike the Swiftfire, this ship had a raised deck and most of the cargo was being stowed below.

Captain Bartham waved for her to join him as he swiftly made his way to the back of the ship and up some stairs, pausing frequently to speak to the men he passed, offering them words of encouragement or advice.

"Stow that below and make sure that Ned is evenly distributing the weight."

"Tighten that line."

"Coil those ropes, don't want no-one tripping over lad."

Once up on the raised deck at the back of the boat, the captain turned to her. "Tempest sent you, did he? What does that man want now?" He stood sizing her up.

"Nothing, he didn't send me to ask anything of you. He said you could help me out with passage through The Run." She tried to stand tall, hands resting gently on her weapon belt.

"He did, did he? It'll cost you fifteen gold and we sail to Heartsnest. Any closer to Havii is too dangerous. Will that suit you?"

Serena looked in her purse and started to count the coins. Captain Bartham moved quickly to cover her hand with his own.

"Girl, you're as fresh as a daisy ain't you. Never get your money out in sight of a sailor. If they see your coin, they will find a way to try to take it." He relaxed as she put the purse away.

"I can give you a small room close to mine. I suggest you keep the door locked when you sleep if you don't want company. Otherwise, you have free run of the ship, as long as you stay out of the way. Payment at destination. Would that suit you?" He reached out his arm.

Serena grasped it and gave it a firm shake.

"Do you carry those blades for show, or do you know how to use them?" He asked.

Serena moved fast, her knife pulled back and then released through the air before her heart had taken a beat.

The captain turned to look at it, quivering in the corner of the deck below, a rat skewered through its neck.

"You might be wet behind the ears, but you have some skill. Perhaps you could come in handy after all. I presume Master Tempest sent you to escape some trouble." He glanced around the lower deck, men were securing the cargo with rope and pulling in the gangplank. "Let's sail together shall we."

He was an ordinary looking man, but he had an air of command about him. As he called out orders to his crew, they quickly set about their tasks. The man from the dock came and joined them.

"You're sailing with us then?"

She nodded.

The man introduced himself as Geoff, quartermaster and first mate of the Bladewing. He spoke briefly with the captain and showed him the ledger, the captain gave it a cursory look before turning back to check on his men.

"Captain given you quarters?" Geoff asked.

"Yes, thank you, he said my room was near his."

"I'll show you where to store your pack. We should be underway quickly now the wind's turning. Looks like the desert is taking a deep breath this evening, you'll want to be on deck for this run."

They walked and he showed her to a small cabin not much larger than the bed within. She asked what he meant by the desert breathing. He chatted away explaining that each day the wind blew like a tide. Through the late morning and afternoon when the sun was high, the wind blew through The Run towards the Everplain. In the evening and through the night the wind turned and blew in the direction of the Sand Seas. Most folk called it 'The Breath of the World.'

"You can tell by the way the clouds are starting to swirl and deform northwards that it's going to be a strong one tonight." He clapped his hands and almost skipped as he showed her back up on deck.

Serena spent a while trying to work out what each sailor's job was as they moved around the ship constantly, some climbing the rigging, others pulling ropes to let the main sail slowly unfurl.

A short, stocky sailor took up station near the front of the ship. He wore a system of harnesses and Serena recognised him as the ship's Kite flier, just like Tall Jacks on the Swiftfire. He tethered himself directly onto the deck and then grabbed hold of a wooden pole with more ropes passing through it. These ran ahead of the ship where some young boys ran out unfurling the silken material. The Kiteman raised the pole up high, a signal to the boys below he reached forward as far as he could, and the boys threw the Kite into the air. The man heaved backwards hard, and the silk caught the wind, flying up into the air. Two other sailors stepped in and tightened the ropes securing the Kiteman to the deck and hooked another rope running from the pole he held into a large metal clasp in the deck. The Kite was much bigger than the one on the Swiftfire, a huge rectangle of shimmering cloth, taut in the wind.

Gradually the ship began to roll. As it did the men released more sail, the Kiteman steered, and they picked up speed as the wind pushed the Bladewing forward.

That had been about an hour ago.

Serena sat above the forerunner, a big wheel reaching out under the prow of the ship, watching the ground rush past. The Kiteman had been joined by two others, each with one hand on the steering pole assisting him as the wind heaved at the ropes attached to the Kite. The main mast was at full sail and the two side masts had been lowered and their sheets bulged with the force of the wind.

She had always thought that sailing would be smooth and that the sound of the wind would be calming. This was anything but. The deck vibrated, bucked, and lurched as The Runners ran over the ground, ropes sang, canvas slapped, men shouted to be heard as they worked the ship. Through it all, Captain Bartham's voice rang out ensuring everyone strived to make the most of the wind.

The steep sides of the mountains grew closer as Eap, and its tower shrank on the horizon. The sun slowly setting and turning the sky red.

Serena thought of Bandolas in his youth working a ship like this one, feeling his joy at the speed the craft flew over the land, as the wind wiped the tears from her eyes.

PART 34: THE MESSENGER LISTENS

"Sire, we have travelled here from Holdon with the greatest of haste at your behest, please do not dismiss what we say without hearing us out." Guild director Cobin pleaded.

The King stood and stared the man down. "You tell me nothing I do not already know. I asked you here to prevent a war, yet you tell me that you have mobilised troops and fortified your borders. These are not the acts of peaceful people, but of those that seek conflict."

The Northman who spoke for his people raised his hands trying to calm the situation. "We only seek to defend ourselves from the aggressions of Splitt. Our mines were taken by armed groups, and they will not stop there. They seek to take our lands."

The ambassador from Splitt wagged his finger at the Guild Director. "We took back mines which were stolen from us over the years, nothing more. We do not amass armies to strike into our allies' lands. We seek to trade and profit. It would appear, that you men of the North, are the ones looking to steal lands. Why else would you gather your fighting men like this?" He pointed at the map laid out on the table.

"All of your words are more slippery than eels. I feel no truths being spoken in this room. I called you all here to answer for your actions. I will not stand for war." The King spoke with barely contained fury.

Findo stood against the wall behind The Degan, who in turn sat next to the King. Along this side of the table sat various lords and dignitaries of the court as well as the Chancellor. Behind the seated men stood their aides. On the other side of the table towards one end, sat Ambassador Keen from Splitt, with a team of aides behind him. There were several empty seats and then six of the Guild directors representing Holdon, no one stood behind them.

"Sire, if the Ambassador can promise that Splitt will take no more from us and that trade will continue to be fair then we shall stand down our armies. The problem is that, since taking our mines, they have driven prices up, selling to us at rates never before seen and we know that they trade with others at half the price. They only take, we require some give."

"Ambassador," The King sat and leaned both his arms on the table, "Do you deny that Splitt has taken the mines by force?"

"No Sire, that much is true, but we only took back mines which historically belonged to us. The North stole them from us by nefarious means over the course of years, seeking to undermine our legitimate rights." The Ambassador sat back in his chair voice low and smooth, his demeanour relaxed and confident.

The Chancellor sat forward. "Director Cobin, is it true that the Guilds had acquired the mines from Splitt?"

"Yes, over the past century we have traded rights to the mines north of Mount Ghastom with Splitt. Paid for in coin and concessions."

The Chancellor leaned in and spoke quietly to the King.

"It appears that Splitt has taken these mines outside of agreements made within law. It should renounce all claims to them and allow the people of the North to reclaim them as is their right. In recompense for their loss, a fee of two in every ten of profit made from these mines should be paid to the Crown who will hold it for a total of five years. After that it will be paid over to Splitt to be used as welfare to support the poorest of their peoples." The King continued as the Guild Directors and Ambassador shifted uneasily in their chairs.

"One quarter of the troops stationed at the borders will immediately stand down and return to their trades. The people of Splitt will make no retaliation against the North and all embargoes will be lifted, trade shall be resumed at fair and standard rates. I hope I have made my position on this clear, gentlemen?" The King paused as if waiting for a response.

There was an uncomfortable silence.

"Now, it has been reported to me that Havii has closed its borders and there has been no news from the South for some time. Does anyone know of this?"

The Ambassador waved one of his aides forward, they spoke softly together for a few seconds before he spoke, "We have heard rumours of trouble in the South but nothing substantial."

"What about slaves? I am reliably informed that caravans have been travelling northwards across the Sand Sea. There are only two lands they could be travelling to." The King left his implication hanging in the air. Slavery was banned in the Kingdom. Anyone participating in slavery would be dealt with harshly.

"Havii is a long way from the North. What use have we of slaves when we struggle to find enough work for our own people without the mines." One of the other Guild Directors spoke up, a dour man with an unfortunate deformity around one eye which made him look permanently startled.

Again, one of the Ambassador's aides stepped forward to whisper in his ear. "I know nothing of slaves and we, just like you, have had no contact from Havii for several moons. Perhaps they are the ones we should all be worried about. For years they have been using their fighting pits to train men. Perhaps it is to the South that our attentions should be turned. Our country is one of trade and artistry, what use have we for slaves?"

The Ambassador appeared to be getting bored, he yawned behind a gloved hand and slouched in his chair.

"I shall have an agreement drawn up. Tomorrow we shall reconvene for your countries to sign it. Consult with your aides and each other, if you have any news of value concerning the South reveal it to the Chancellor's office. The new day will bring peace between your two nations." The King stood and swept from the room.

The Ambassador and his retinue left shortly afterwards, soon followed by the Guilds.

The Degan turned to the Chancellor as the King's aides began to gather their papers and leave. "Will they sign?" He asked.

"The Guild do not like it, but they will comply with the King's wishes. Splitt has never been strong enough to stand on their own, in the end they will take the offered money and be content. It is a shame that Lord Wilhelm did not make the trip, but his Ambassador will see the sense of the situation in the end. What troubles me more is that neither country claims to have heard from The Princes of Havii. Where are the slaves going and who is trading in their flesh? We must find out more from the South. Have the Messengers truly heard nothing?"

"All I know is from the few reports I have had. Rumours and gossip. It is as though a wall has gone up to the south. Messengers have travelled that way, but they have been turned away at the borders. None of the flying corps have been called in that direction for a while and they have been kept busy with this business between Splitt and Holdon. Findo here has been the closest, you have read his report, and that was weeks ago now."

"My sources went silent when the borders closed. There is more going on here than we know. First Mirror City rebelled, the troubles in the West and now something is brewing in the South. I do not like it one bit. Let us hope that the agreement is signed tomorrow, and we can lay at least one problem to bed."

The two men talked late into the night, Findo sitting silently listening, wishing he could be back in the air on Gisselle. Tomorrow he would ask to carry a message to Havii or the Twin Cities of Aldark and Ardark. This could be his chance to find Serena and discover what she had learned.

INTERLUDE 3: MARRED BEAUTY

It was night. The sky was dark and thick with cloud. No moon or stars shone in this small mountain pass.

Ahead, further down the slope, there were fires. Soldiers, wearing the star emblem of the Guilds of Holdon, sat around eating and drinking, joking with each other and sharing tales. They rested behind their tall wooden barricades thinking themselves safe.

All around them, a thousand men moved into position. They swarmed over the landscape climbing the slopes and flowing down the valley, an unstoppable tide of humanity washing down to surround the defences before them.

Not a sound was made by a single person, except for those in the camp.

Cxithh channelled his power pouring silence over them all.

He gave a short nod to Captain Fairview. The man raised his fist to his chest in salute and then turned to walk down and lead his troops to take the Northmen's frontier fort.

At the allotted time, when all were in position, Cxithh released his latest creation. Oily darkness trickled from his hands, it flowed outwards like a cloud of thick smoke, boiling larger and larger, drifting down the vale towards the unsuspecting soldiers in their border camp.

As the smoke hit the walls it rose upwards like a great wave crashing against a cliff, before tumbling down amongst the tents and the men.

Still there was no sound. The blackness oozed and bubbled through the camp and then continued in its path downhill through the valley. The fort was left in darkness.

Drawing the last energies from the dried husk of a borrowed body, Cxithh cut his mind loose, leaving Captain Fairview and his men to their work, his job was done.

★★★

"Sir? What was that?"

The question startled the captain who had been standing staring blankly at the scene before him. He quickly regained his composure. “Best not to question lad.” He replied. “Now, run and tell Lieutenant Guthrie to signal the men to hold their positions.”

As the young lad ran off to relay the message, Captain Fairview looked back up the slope to where the slave had stood moments before, commanding him with that voice he detested. The shrivelled husk of a corpse now lay there, motionless on the ground. He would not go near those magics, better to leave the bones for the vultures.

He motioned for his elites to move and led them in a fast march to the gates of the fortifications.

Their dark armour clanked and rattled as they moved. Chain mail making its distinctive slithering ringing, in rhythm with their steps. A shocking contrast to the unnatural silence of moments before.

They had won many battles, in the early days with their swords, more recently by reputation. When people heard that the Cull were coming, they would throw down their weapons in fear and stand with arms raised standing in puddles of their own piss. At least that was how the men joked around the campfires at night.

The reality was that it had taken years of training in the fighting pits of Havii, and then more years battling in whichever army paid the most. Eventually, he and the men he had gathered around him had earned their reputation and the Princes of Havii had granted them their freedom. He had chosen to stay and fight for them. It was all he and his men had ever known.

Moons ago, he had stood before the Princes, and they had introduced him to the worm they called Cxithh. Since then, he had met him many times, although never in person. He always appeared in the body of a slave, but you would never mistake him for one. Whatever vessel he possessed was recognisable by its dead, staring eyes and of course, the voice. The charming, gentle, well-spoken voice of an oiled serpent, slippery and full of venom.

The captain’s army had been sent northwards in secrecy.

They were to carry out the commands of the Princes through the words of their servant. Cxithh.

Now his men stopped at his signal. Standing before the strong wooden gates of this border fort, high in the mountain pass north of Mount Ghastom. No sound came from the other side, no calls from sentries in their lookout towers. All he could hear was the faint sound of loose canvas flapping in the wind.

He walked forward alone and pressed his palms against the great wooden doors. With a hard shove, the gates swung smoothly open.

His men moved as one into a tighter defensive formation, weapons raised and ready. Spearmen at the front bracing for a charge that never came.

Raising his fist in a signal for his men to hold he walked forward.

The soldiers, who only a short time before had walked patrol, talked, and laughed around fires, eaten and carried out their night duties, were no more. In their place were broken things, horrific twisted lumps of muscle and bone only just recognisable as ever having been human. Bits of armour and clothing stuck out of the warped piles of meat. It looked as though a mad butcher had put each soldier through a malformed mangle and then left its product discarded behind him on the floor.

Captain Fairview turned and relayed orders for his men to burn everything. They would set up their own defensive positions whilst they awaited their next orders. He could not help but think that, perhaps not before long, soldiers would not be needed to wage war if destruction on this scale could be wielded by those with magic.

★★★

Cxithh's eyelids gradually fluttered open. He was uncomfortable with this feeling. He had never channelled so much before. He breathed deeply and felt for the Rush inside. He was disappointed to have drawn so much from himself. It would take days to recover.

From the walls all around his room dry, brittle paper fragments began to fall. His once beautiful pictures were now blank. The magnificent displays spent and turning to dust. He marvelled at the power that he had absorbed from his creations, what he had just achieved and the possibilities for the future.

Gently, he reached out and daintily rang the small bell on the table next to his chair before reaching and gathering his art supplies into his lap.

A slave came in, followed by a young and incredibly pretty woman. The slave lay the tray of food he carried on the table, before backing out through the door, closing it softly.

The woman began to undo the buttons on the side of her dress. "Where would you like me sir?" She asked coquettishly.

Cxithh smiled as he picked up his charcoal and turned to a fresh sheet of paper.

PART 35

Serena leaned back against the railing on the quarterdeck, watching the sailors going about their work. She had found it difficult to sleep as the vibrations of the ship and the violent jarring as it passed over rough ground had kept her awake. Eventually, the strain of the last few days had pulled her into slumber.

She had awoken early and had made her way back up on deck. Captain Bartham had talked with her briefly checking that no-one had disturbed her in the night and making sure she had everything she needed, before hurrying off to direct his men.

There had been a brief flurry of activity as the ship turned to a new course heading eastwards, but the wind was favourable, and the ship was rolling along easily with the breeze behind her now.

Most of the crew had either gone below decks to their bunks or sat around playing dice in small groups. Serena noticed a few men sitting together near the mainsail. They were chatting as they worked on small white objects with a variety of little tools. She moved down the steps and approached them. They seemed to be carving intricate designs into pieces of bone. A pile of crates gave her a perch from which to watch as they worked.

The men sang a wordless song, the rhythm matching the movements of their hands as they chiselled, scratched and bore intricate patterns and pictures into the smooth surfaces of the bone pieces. Serena found it both mesmerising and fascinating as she watched the patterns slowly emerge. One of the men, older with a balding head and dark weathered skin, noticed her and waved her over.

"Hello there, miss, you interested in a bit of scrimshaw? Happy to sell you a piece from my collection."

Serena shook her head but asked, "What is it that you are carving? It does not look like wood."

She crouched next to the man watching him carefully

chisel the shape of a mountain into his work.

"No miss, proper scrimshaw is done in bone, whale bone. I was lucky enough to get my hands on a barrel last time we was in Daggos. This piece here is a tooth, you get a finer and better finish on it than with the plain bone, though it's harder to carve."

"What are you making?" She asked one of his companions who was working on a piece just larger than her thumb.

He looked up from what he was doing and brushed his long blonde hair from his face, "Shaping a whistle miss. They sell well to the children in the cities."

The last man in the group was carving designs into a knife hilt, the whole knife was fashioned from the bone and was one of the most beautifully carved items she had ever seen. "May I?" She asked pointing at it.

The man passed it over to her. She felt its weight and examined the blade. It would make a terrible weapon, but the design was spectacular. A miniature picture of the Bladewing, running at full sail through a mountainous landscape ran along the blade. The handle was entwined in spiralling patterns which confused the eye and drew you to the pommel, which was a perfect rendering of a boar's head down to the finest hairs.

She handed the blade back, "That is fine work."

The first man spoke up, "Good scrimshaw is worth a pretty penny in the South. We don't really do it for the coin though, the Captain likes us to keep our hands busy and we enjoy it. Helps to pay for our grog when we're in port. Hanlan here could get work in Splitt, if he wanted, but he enjoys the wind too much. Make yourself comfortable and join us if you like, got plenty o' bone."

Serena sat and the man, who introduced himself as Bry, showed her the basic tools and how to use them. Over the next hour or so, Serena managed to carve a passable tree, but it was obvious that these men had spent many hours practicing their craft, though it did give her an idea.

She spent the rest of the day chatting with the men, finding out about their lives. Bry had once worked at sea, which is where he had learnt to carve bone, he had married and settled in Daggos working in the shipyards, but his wife and son had died of pox a few years ago and he had returned to sailing, though now he travelled the land.

"I guess you never really lose your passion for the wind." He said a whimsical smile playing across his weather worn face.

Hanlan had been a woodworker in Eap, labouring for his father making simple furniture for peoples' homes, until he had racked up a large debt gambling in the drinking dens around the docks. He had taken to sailing to escape his debtors, hoping to one day return home and make amends with his family.

The third sailor, Den, came from a family of sailors and it was all he had ever known or wanted to know. "I gets to see the world and the ship gives me all the family or friends I could need."

Around them the landscape gradually changed. The grass yellowed and grew shorter. The ground drier and dustier. The air became warm, and fewer clouds marred the perfect blue sky. They were getting close to the deserts of the interior. Large herds of bison and antelope could be seen moving across the plain.

At one point, near to the middle of the day, they saw several insects which were about the size of a six-month-old ox, moving together following a herd, hunting. The sailors told her they were Eltrath, fearsome hunters.

"They group together to kill their prey but are usually solitary, except in spring when they meet in greater numbers to mate and lay their eggs. They are not usually a threat to us; they keep to these lands between the grass and the desert proper. They are not fast, but they never tire, they kill by separating off a member of the herd and then wear it down to the point of exhaustion."

Serena shuddered as she watched the insects until they disappeared into the distance.

During the afternoon, Captain Bartham ordered all men off

their bunks to attend to their duties. Serena retreated to her place by the rails on the quarterdeck as the sailors hustled to their tasks, responding to commands from the captain and from Geoff, who had come back on deck. The sails were reduced, and the Kite drawn in as the ship slowed down to a walking pace.

A group of sailors, including Den, lowered four long pointed boards, around the length of a man, over the side. Each board had a double row of wheels on the base. Four muscular sailors wearing harnesses like that of the Kiteman – in fact Serena thought she recognised two of the men as the ones who had helped control the Kite through The Run – climbed quickly down to the ground and strapped their feet to the boards.

Another group of men ran out in front of them trailing lines and carrying silken pouches. Serena rushed to the aft rail so she could watch what they were doing as the ship trundled on. The men threw their silks into the air, perfectly timed to catch a gust of wind and four rectangular Kites sprang into the air.

Geoff came over to stand with Serena watching the action below. "The Kiterunners do our hunting. Hopefully, they can catch a boar, or an antelope and we will all eat well tonight."

Serena watched as the Kiterunners quickly raced passed the ship, zigging and zagging between each other and whooping as they went. Each man had a short throwing spear strapped to his back.

"Looks dangerous." Serena said, never taking her eyes off the men who were quickly disappearing towards the northern horizon.

"Often only three men return. It is physically exhausting and highly skilled. The men get paid well enough as reward though. They'll be back before dark as the wind will drop then. It could be a still night tonight. Rest now if I were you. The men like to drink and sing if the wheels are not turning." Geoff moved off to harry the sailors back to work and Serena wandered back to her cabin as the ship began to pick up speed.

PART 36

Her fingers caressed the ridges and tines surrounding the plate of the antler sitting in her lap. Serena breathed deeply, remembering her time travelling with the beast's head to Eap with Bandolas, as she closed her eyes and drew a trickle of the Rush forth.

She had tested the bone of the antlers and found it to be harder than expected and slightly flexible. The plates were large and thin yet deflected her heavy knife when she had struck them. The beams and tines had fitted her palms well and her idea had grown.

She worked by touch, her fingers slowly rubbing against the smooth material, eyes closed as she concentrated to hold an image in her mind. She sat on her bed with her back leaning against the hull, feeling the vibrations through her body and channelling them through her arm and down her fingers to the antlers.

She could feel sweat beading on her brow in the heat of her confined quarters, but she did not stop to wipe it away. Her hands continued to glide over the surfaces, slowly reshaping them. The weight on her lap suddenly lessened as one piece fell away. She finished shaping the piece she held and then picked up another.

Eventually, through the vibrations, she felt the ship begin to slow. Her work finished for now, Serena checked and tightened the straps of her armour and went back up on deck. Her legs were slightly unsteady beneath her, a sign that she had been drawing too much on the Rush. The sky was beginning to darken; pinks and violets were highlighting the horizon.

A man high up in the rigging shouted something she could not make out and the sailors all rushed to the rails looking northwards where his arm pointed.

Through the shimmering heat haze, three rectangular shapes could be seen moving closer. The Kite runners returning. There was a hum of disappointed voices all around and a bowing of heads. Then the man in the rigging shouted again. The heads all snapped up, eyes straining to see. Slowly, a fourth Kite appeared through the dusty miasma. The men all cheered. Serena could see Geoff patting Den on the back and smiling around at the men.

That night the wind stopped blowing. The sky was clear and black. On deck the men roasted the boar which the Kite runners brought back, and the captain had Geoff open a cask of rum. Serena drank only a little this time remembering her previous experience drinking with the crew of the Swiftfire. She sat chatting with Den, Bry and Hanlan, under a blanket of sparkling stars, late into the night.

As the rum took hold, the men celebrated and sang. They began with typical sea shanties, then they moved to ale house songs, the words to some were less than complimentary to women. One of the Kite runners stumbled over and swayed as he looked down at Serena sitting on the deck between Den and Bry.

"Come girl, a real man needs some relief after a successful hunt." He reached out to take her arm.

Serena scooted back and he missed her arm but lost his balance and fell on top of her, knocking her to the floor.

He breathed heavily in her ear as she squirmed to push him off, "Just where I wanted to be. Now, if you'll just stay still."

Suddenly his weight was yanked from her. Serena rose rapidly, her blade whistling through the air as she struck for his throat.

"Stop!" The captain's voice rang out.

She froze in place.

"Why captain? We are only having some fun after all our hard work." Another of the Kitemen was stalking towards Serena. She glanced about. Many of the sailors were backing away. As the four Kiterunners moved to surround her.

"You will find her not as pleasurable as you hope boys. I ask you to stop, not for her sake, but for yours." Captain Bartham's voice boomed out from his high position on the quarterdeck.

"You shouldn't ha' brought a woman aboard if you didn't

want to share captain. You knows the rules. What happens at under sail stays at under sail." The men were closing around her.

Bry let go of the back of the first man's shirt as he turned to glare at him.

"You might regret laying hands on me old man. Now back up and leave us be." He seemed to have sobered somewhat and shoved Bry back so hard he tripped over a bucket. The Kiterunners laughed at him and turned their attention back to her.

"Serena, put down your blade." Captain Bartham called out. "Make it a fair fight and let them live to tell this tale to future idiots, so they don't make the same mistake."

She understood and reached down to unstrap her weapon belt, dropping it to the floor at her feet.

"Don't stop there love. Show us a little more, a teaser if you like. Save us some time, why don't ya?" The tallest of The Runners moved behind her so that she was surrounded.

Her feet eased across the deck as she assumed the stance. Her breathing slow and shallow.

As Bry sat up, he thought he saw a glimmer of something pass through her eyes, but he blinked, and it was gone.

The man to her left moved to grab at her. As she pushed his hands away, the man behind her wrapped his arms around her and viciously pulled her arms behind her back.

The first man moved in close and grabbed her as she kicked at him, stepping in closer so that he was between her legs. The man pinning her arms moved back towards a pile of crates and pulled her onto his lap as he sat, holding her in place as the first man's hands began to scrabble at her waist band. The man on her left reached in and grabbed her breast in a meaty hand.

Some of the sailors turned their backs, some shouted in protest, others jeered and called profanities encouraging the Kiterunners on. As if this was entertainment to please the crowd.

A small voice in her mind reminded her to keep control as she unleashed hell upon these men.

Her head whipped backwards splintering the nose of the man holding her arms. As he let go of her to hold his face, she grasped the hand on her breast and twisted the fingers back. They made a sickening cracking sound as bone splintered. The man pulled his arm away and Serena gripped on using the sideways momentum to twist her body, tightening her thigh muscles around the man between her legs and throwing him to the ground.

As she rolled free and stood, the last man drew a short dagger and made a raking lunge towards her which harmlessly scraped over her armour as her fist connected under his jaw sending him flying backwards.

Each of her Movements flowed one into the next as she spun across the deck. As each man tried to rise, a hand, elbow, knee or foot would connect with his face. She aimed each blow carefully, just enough power to knock them back, allowing each to try his luck again.

The man with the broken nose hesitated, breaking her rhythm, as he signalled to his companions to back off and regroup.

They came at her as one. Looking to overwhelm her with numbers, she fed her speed and moved easily between their grasping hands, her elbows and fists smashing into the backs of their skulls. Serena danced away but did not give them time to recover before she swept the feet from under the first before smashing her fist into one of the other's throats. That man fell to the floor holding his neck as his face turned purple.

Brokenose threw a crate at her, charging in behind it looking to wrap his powerful arms around her.

Serena dropped to one knee as the crate flew over her head and smashed her elbow upwards into his groin. As he fell forward squealing in pain, she rolled and slammed her arm into the first man's mouth before he could stand, knocking a few teeth loose. She sprang to her feet and the last man looked at her and dropped to his knees holding both hands above his head in surrender.

Brokenose rolled on the ground holding his privates. A

couple of sailors had stepped in and were helping the third man who was having trouble breathing.

The first man rolled onto his back and spat out blood. He looked at her with unremorseful hatred as she stood between his legs. "Bitch!" He shouted before she kicked him hard in his balls. He folded up hugging his knees to his chest unable to make a sound through the agony which shot through him.

"Let that be a lesson to you all. Women should be treated with respect. If you think to do one harm, she will find a way to hurt you back. To your bunks men, we have a busy day tomorrow." The captain glared at his crew as they slowly shuffled away.

Bry walked over and clapped a hand on her shoulder. She breathed out and let go of the Rush. "I ain't never seen no one move like that."

Serena shrugged. "It's nothing." she said as she retrieved her weapons from the floor. "Thank you for helping."

"Wasn't nothing. I haven't seen the likes in years. You got a gift and should be proud of it."

She helped him clear the deck and tidy away fallen cargo before she returned to her cabin and locked the door. Just in case.

PART 37

As the sun rose, so too did the wind, whipping clouds of dust up from the dry plains. All hands were on deck as the Bladewing rolled across the barren land. As Serena moved along the deck, many of the sailors paused to nod at her or give her a word of congratulations. It seemed the incident the previous evening had given her a sort of celebrity status.

When he spotted her, Den came bounding over, "Can you show us a few of your moves? I wish I could fight like you."

"I'd love to Den but you're a little busy right now. Perhaps later if you'll show me how you carve the stripy symbols so precisely."

Den told her he would be more than happy to and returned to his station. Serena headed forward.

As she neared the Kiteman's station, she could see the short muscular frame of the head man – whose name she had learnt to be Dazram – was strapped in, Brokenose and another of her assailants with a heavily strapped hand were assisting him against the strong wind. They eyed her warily as she passed. Dazram called after her and she looked back over her shoulder, loose hairs flying wildly about her head.

"Nice job keeping these boys in check last night, I wish I had been there to see it. If you ever want a job up here, just give me a holler." He turned his attention back to the kite as it swung wildly in a gust.

Serena found Geoff standing at the prow with another man. They both had spyglasses to their eyes.

"Ah, good day to ya miss. How sharps yer eyes? The names Cobryn." The man held out his arm shouting over the rush of the wind and the noise of the wheel below.

Serena shook it, "Pretty good."

"Aye, their pretty I'll grant ya. Join us." He handed her a spare spyglass and waved her close.

He leant in to shout in her ear. "Just keep an eye out for bumps and lumps in the ground, most stuff we can handle but we need to avoid the bigger things like rocks and trees."

Geoff suddenly turned and waved an arm twice to the south, the Kite crew responded instantly, and she felt the ship turn a little away from the north.

"Tell me what you see. I'll relay the commands." Cobryn moved over a little allowing Serena room at the rail. She stared ahead, finding it difficult to make out anything ahead.

"Ya got to use the glass miss, if ya see it with ya naked eye it will already be too late. You're a spotter now. Get spotting."

It took her a while to get the hang of using the spyglass. At first everything was fuzzy and with the movement of the ship she found it hard to focus as the image kept jumping about. Every time she caught a glimpse of something, the ship would rock, or bounce and she would have to start all over again.

"Find a spot in the distance. Closer to the horizon, relax your arms and your knees. Get a feel for what the ground looks like and let it move towards you, don't try to find anything specific let the image come to you."

Serena relaxed, she found herself taking up one of the stances and she calmed her breathing. The images steadied and she found that she could see best if she looked half a mile or more away.

"Looks like a deep dip in the ground just north of our course." She called spotting an area of deeper shadows amongst the grass and dirt.

"How far out?" Geoff replied.

"A quarter way to the horizon."

"She's right." Cobryn called after a few seconds. He turned and waved his arm once to the Kitemen.

Over the next half hour, she spotted a few larger rocks and a small pack of boar. Cobryn told her to take a break and asked her to return in an hour. "Ya got potential. Things 'll get a bit tricky later. Make sure you're ready, we'll need all the eyes we can get."

As Serena made her way back to midship, Bry called her over. He was manning the water barrel. Handing out tin cups he filled with a ladle to the men as they needed it. He handed her a cup which she drank thirstily.

"Seems you're fitting in to being a sailor. You won your first brawl and now you're working as spotter." He smiled at her,

"Just be careful you don't let success go to your head." He winked at her letting her know he was being playful.

"Thank you Bry. Will you be carving later? I've got something I'd like you to take a look at."

"When we're through the Spines and the wind dies down, me and the boys will be at the chisels before bunks. You've tickled my interest now. We'll see you later." Bry turned to fill another sailor's cup as Serena handed hers back and headed to her cabin.

She quickly used the chamber pot and grabbed a corner of cheese to nibble on whilst she inspected her work on the antlers. Then she headed back on deck wondering what the Spines were.

After collecting a jug of water and a tin from Bry, she made her way back to the prow and offered a cup to Geoff, who handed his spyglass to another sailor taking up his post on watch.

"What are the Spines?" She asked.

"Columns of rock which rise up out of the dirt like the bones of long dead beasts. The safest course is to head north around them, but the captain doesn't want to waste time changing the wheels for sand sledges. It will be tricky to navigate in this wind and at this speed, but we have done it before. Just keep an eye out for Scalthryn, those big lizards have a tendency to run out and get caught in the wheels, almost like they're trying to stop us. The rocks can be hard to spot, same colour as the dirt. Look for the shadows and, if in any doubt, play safe. The rocks will shatter the outrunners and splinter the wheels. Then we will be stuck in a land that has no mercy for the likes of men."

Geoff really knew how to make her feel confident.

"You'll be fine. Think of yourself as just helping out Cobryn and I. Take your glass and let's get to it."

The ground was banded in dusty red and yellow hues, the grass remaining grew in small sorry clumps and the ground was flat rock and hard packed dirt. Far to the south, Serena could just make out the mountains of the Great Divide as they swept eastwards before resuming their southerly march. Here and there were scatterings of small rocks and other detritus. This really was a barren land.

She took up her post at the prow, Cobryn in the centre, Geoff on his left and her on the right. She was to keep an eye on the centre and south. Cobryn dead ahead and Geoff the centre and north.

They swept their gazes ahead searching for obstacles. "Centre south, big pillar." Cobryn called.

It took Serena several moments before she found it, and once she did, she couldn't believe that she had not seen it. A tall spire of rock, like a huge tree trunk jutted out of the plain just south of their course. Its top was rounded and the base thick and covered in small rocks and dirt. It was the same colour as the landscape, banded in red and yellow. A shadow pooled at its base, hiding from the sun's harsh glare.

She raised her glass and spotted several lower humps in the earth, the eroded remains of once great towers. She called out their positions, but they were not on the Bladewing's direct course.

Geoff and Cobryn called out frequently relaying the obstacles as they spotted them, as did Serena. The towers became more frequent and became larger in size as they grew closer together.

The tallest were over twice the height of the Bladewing's main mast and just as thick. The sides eroded smooth by the wind revealing the layers of rock from which they were formed.

Serena was aware that the sailors were working hard to reduce the sails and the wings were being raised. The ship slowed a little, but the mainsails were bloated with the force of the wind. In places the ground was thick with small columns, the broken and eroded remains of once mighty towers. A sailor took up position behind Cobryn to relay his orders as the three of them were now too busy calling out the positions of their spots to relay the orders themselves. Cobryn listened to their reports and called his course alterations which were relayed, and the Kitemen responded. The Bladewing flew on as the towering monoliths gathered closer all around.

As the Bladewing turned to avoid a rock fall, rounding the base of an immense tower, Geoff called out, "Scalthryn, three, running south across our path."

"Sharp south, full flight." Cobryn's command rang out as he swung his glass to spot the lizards.

The deck shifted underfoot, wood creaking under the stress.

As the ship moved, a small column of rock, barely discernible against the background landscape came into Serena's view. Around it swarmed several Eltrath. The insects seemed to be watching the Lizards which were running across the course of the ship. Serena could see that as things stood, they were heading either towards the spike of rock or going to run down the Lizards.

"No!" She screamed. "Hard north! Eltrath and rock on new course!"

"She's right. Hard north with all you've got!" Cobryn called once he had spied the obstacles.

The deck lurched again, and several sailors lost their footing. The ship groaned as the Kitemen struggled to change direction so suddenly.

The captain's voice could be heard distantly at the aft of the Bladewing as he directed men to trim sails, re-stow loose cargo and help fallen men.

The ship was not turning fast enough.

A great cry went up from behind Serena and she quickly glanced back. The Kiteman with the injured hand had fallen to the deck, the pole which they used to control the kite swung wildly, without his support, and struck Dazram across the jaw. He dropped his weight down and spread his hands wider but with the uneven weight of Brokenose on the other end the kite was now flying in the wrong direction, pulling the ship to certain doom.

A channel opened in Serena's mind, and she let the tempest loose.

She moved.

So quick was her reaction that men later would say that she had not moved at all but just stopped being in one place and started being in another.

With one hand she grasped the hook through the deck, her other around the pole and she pulled. Brokenose was in her way, countering her movements, so she kicked him hard in the ribs, knocking him from his station, using the momentum to swing her legs up around the pole, releasing her other arm to grab at the rope around Dazram.

Using her entire body, she pulled. And the Kite moved to the north.

The ship responded, groaning as its course was changed once again.

Dazram slapped at her hard, "That's enough. Get in front of me and help me control this thing!"

She dropped to the deck, planting her feet wide and leant back into Dazram's solid frame as she grasped the pole, her hands besides his.

"Hold the course." The spotters yelled and she followed Dazram's lead to straighten the Kite.

Together they steered the ship free of the Spines and it slowed as the captain called for his men to haul in the sails.

"Daneil, Gaz, haul in the Kite. The girl and I need a drink." Dazram said to Brokenose and the man who had lost his grip with the bandaged hand.

They moved to unstrap the head Kiteman and began to haul in the ropes as Dazram slapped her across the shoulders. "I knew you'd make a good Kiteman." He smiled broadly at her. "Come I predict that I can find us a shot of rum to reward your hard work."

PART 38

The ship was rolling at a walking pace. Captain Bartham, Geoff and a couple of other men had gone over the sides to inspect the hull and the outrunners for damage after the hard riding through the Spines. The rest of the crew had been given a break and had either returned to their bunks or were lounging around on deck. Dazram had sat for a while with Serena, but she had shown little interest in conversation with him, and he had taken his leave to check on his men.

Bry, Den and Hanlan had joined her. Their aimless chat had slowly brought her back to herself and she went to her cabin to collect her things.

"Bry, do you think you could find a way to attach these to my armour?" She showed him two curved plates that she had formed from the antlers.

"Aye girl. I'll need to cut some pieces loose and restitch them. Den here can work on some fastenings to hold them in place." He scratched his thumb nail over the surface. "Stronger than your leather and well formed. Not carved but shaped by hands. Your own work?"

Serena nodded.

"We'll have it back to you by morning."

Serena unbuckled her armour and handed it to him. It felt strange to move about without its now familiar weight.

"Hanlan, could you carve the handles of these for me?"

"Sure, what do you want?" He looked at the two knives she offered him. One with a blade the length of her palm, the other longer and thicker, the length of her forearm.

"They need a sure grip. I don't know what to put on them, but you have shown me things designed for such ugly work can still be beautiful."

Hanlan reached out and took the blades. He caressed them almost lovingly. "I have a few ideas."

She left them then, the day's events had used much of her energy, and she wanted nothing more than to lie in her bunk and close her eyes.

★★★

A repetitive rattling sound woke her. Someone was trying to open her door. She rolled over and the light flooding through her small porthole shone in her face, momentarily blinding her.

She could feel the familiar vibrations of the ship moving at speed and the humming of its hull.

The handle of her door rattled once more.

"Who is it?" Serena asked, tucking her loose shirt into her britches and strapping on her weapon belt.

"Bry. I got something for you. Open up and I'll show you." His voice sounded odd somehow.

Serena moved to turn the key and open her door. A sound made her hesitate. A shuffling, scraping sound of a boot. She had never seen Bry wear footwear, most of the sailors went barefoot.

The Rush trickled into her movements and her senses heightened as she took a deep breath. She swung the door open and took a quick step backwards.

The man whose fingers she had broken and whose place she had taken at the Kite stood behind Bry with a knife held firmly against the older man's throat. Bry held her armour in his hands. She could see that he had completed the work she had asked him to do. He and Den must have worked on it all night.

A small trickle of bright blood ran down Bry's neck, bouncing as he swallowed and it moved over his Adams apple to the hollow at the base of his throat, pooling there, glinting in the light of the new day.

Serena moved. The knife moved faster, leaving a long ugly gash just beneath the grey stubble of Bry's throat.

She watched as his eyes widened in terror, he gasped breath frothing with his own blood. His attacker pushed him forward into her cabin, her way blocked by his falling body, and she was forced against the wall as he grasped at her for support, his frantic hands tearing at her blouse.

She let him fall, the sound of his head striking the side of her bed resounding through her small room as she gathered herself and leapt forward.

The Kiteman was rushing in, reaching back with his bloodied knife to strike at her. She moved with all the speed the Rush allowed punching forward with her fist. The poor man could never have seen it coming, Serena held nothing back as she pushed everything she had into the blow. She delivered her anger through her clenched hand.

His chest imploded, ribs caved inwards, shards piercing heart and lungs. The pressure of the blow forced air from his mouth and nose in a bloody spray across Serena's face. The force lifted him from his feet and carried him out of her door, across the narrow corridor and into the wall beyond, and still her momentum carried her forward, arm smashing through the wall leaving his body impaled upon her arm.

Serena stood there, up to her shoulder in gore, screaming wordlessly into his face as she watched the light go out of his eyes.

A firm hand on her shoulder brought her back to herself, she turned to see the captain standing looking at her wide eyed.

"Stop now. See to your friend." The captain gestured with a turn of his head to her cabin.

She pulled her arm back from the hole she had created, and the body slumped heavily to the floor. As the sounds of many feet slapped down the wooden floorboards outside her room, she dashed to Bry's side and lifted him easily onto her bunk.

There was a flood of blood flowing down his chest from the deep slash in his throat. The cut was brutal enough to have severed his windpipe and he was choking for breath, suffocating in his own life's fluids.

Closing her eyes, Serena channelled the raging torrent within herself, feeling her way across the tissues of his wound with her fingers. It would not be enough. She needed more.

She breathed. With each inhalation more power flowed in, and she poured it forth, shaping tissue and reforming flesh. When she was done, she stood. Uncaring that her torn shirt revealed her breasts to curious eyes. She pushed past the men standing all around her doorway. Men leaning against the walls as if exhausted. She paused to pick up her armour. Captain Bartham stepped out of her way, his face drawn and pale, as she made her way up onto deck.

Blood dripped from her fingers onto the boards as she walked to the barrel which Bry usually manned. She stripped off all her clothes and dunked them inside. When enough of the blood was washed from her trousers and shirt, she used a discarded rag to wipe the viscera from her skin and gathered great handfuls of water in her cupped palms to pour over her flesh.

Men watched, mouths agape. She made sure they would see her.

Then she dressed and strapped on her armour. Her breasts now cupped behind a shield of bone, shaped from the antlers of the Beast. It was no longer misfitting. No one could miss that Serena was a fierce female warrior.

She tightened her weapon belt, turned and followed the path of blood across the deck back to her room.

The captain was yelling orders and the men had already carried the cadaver away.

"You went too far." He said as she moved past him.

"No. I did not. I went just far enough." She snapped at him, "One of your crew tried to kill one of my friends, his intention was to kill me or at the very least hurt me. For that he paid with his life."

"That is not what I meant. Whatever you did, drained me, it drained my men and weakened us. If you are part of this crew, you cannot take from us, it is witchcraft and sorcery. I had thought you better. I would never have expected this from a pupil of Tempest. Stay here in your cabin until we reach port. I want no more trouble from you." He closed her door and she heard him calling orders as his boots stomped away.

PART 39

Confined to her cabin, she spent her time caring for Bry. The wound in his throat seemed completely healed but the bump on his head looked bad. Just above his right temple, a large swollen area of skin.

She hoped that rest would help him. She had not been able to rouse him for hours, she just sat at his side whispering stories to him and hoping he would recover.

Den popped by, calling through her door that he had brought food and drink. He came in and sat with her for a while. It was obvious that he felt uncomfortable in her presence. He was worried about Bry and asked a stream of questions. How had she cured his slit throat? When did she think he would wake up?

When Hanlan came, Den was quick to make his apologies and return to his duties.

"How is he?" The delicate artist asked.

"I don't know. I healed his cuts, but he has a lump on his head, and I don't know what to do. He hasn't moved the whole time I have sat with him."

"He's a tough old nut. You'll see. By morning he will be up on deck handing out water and gathering gossip like he always does."

Hanlan reached into a bag he had brought with him and handed her knives over. "Beautiful blades they are. I never handled nothing like them before. As I carved, it was like I could have done it blindfold, like the blades already knew what they wanted to be, and I just let it appear."

Serena held the large blade up to the light. The hilt felt right in her palm, a twisting mass of intertwining vines perfectly fitted her palms. As the vines flowed down into the blade, they blended into the image of a savage beast roaring its anger silently towards the point. It was perfect.

The smaller blade was carved in the image of a man, his head made up the pommel whilst his body fit well in her hand and his legs ran down either side of the blade. The images were not perfect recreations, the artist never having seen either of them, but they could only be Bandolas and his Beast. Serena hefted the blades in her hands, they were light but balanced well, she tried a series of Movements, whirling them through her fingers and around her small room. Then she carefully placed them in their sheaths on her armour.

"Thank you Hanlan. I will find a way to repay you for your work. They are perfect in every way."

"It's alright miss. It was not hard. As I said, they already knew what they wanted to be. You just help Bry, make sure he gets better."

For two days she stayed in her cabin. Den or Hanlan brought her food and drink and helped her to move and clean Bry. But mostly she sat alone with her thoughts.

On the morning of the third day, Bry opened his eyes. The swelling on his head had gone down but he had a bad bit of bruising. Serena woke stiff and tired lying on the floor next to her bed. Bry was trying to sit up.

It was immediately apparent that he was a changed man. She helped him up on deck, Den and Hanlan ran over and crowded around them.

"What's wrong with him?" Den asked bluntly.

Bry's left arm hung loosely at his side and the left side of his face held no expression. He seemed to have difficulty holding his head up, every time he lifted it to look around it lolled randomly to one side or another.

As they walked, with his right arm grasping tightly over Serenas shoulders, his left leg dragged across the floor.

"Sssno, nees, ta, stare. Be alsright." Bry said slurring his words.

Captain Bartham and Geoff came over calling for the other men to get back to work.

"I told you to stay below." Captain Bartham snarled at Serena.

"I just thought it would do him good to get some air and move about. You can't heal properly in bed."

"The sight of him might scare the others. They're jumpy

enough already after what you did. Seeing him, who knows how they'll react."

Bry pushed himself off of Serena and grasped hold of the captain's arm, "Shtill work, I cans. I'sh get beshter. Pleash." He pleaded, staring hard into the captain's eyes.

"I seen soldiers returned from battle with head wounds, just like this. Some recover with time, others...." Geoff seemed to want to say more but trailed off.

"Den. You're relieved of your duties and are assigned to Bry. Help him in his duties, after the years he has served on the Bladewing she owes him and will care for him. As for you miss, stay out of the way. No more incidents. We should reach Heartsnest before nightfall if the wind keeps up. I expect you gone as soon as we make port." Captain Bartham marched off to his usual position overseeing the ship from above on the quarterdeck.

"Don't mind him. He's just fearful of you and scared how the men will react to you." Geoff moved away to see to the men and left the four of them alone.

Just then, a cry came from high in the rigging and all eyes turned upwards. A sailor called and pointed to the East where they were heading. Men scrambled to the railings.

"Sails. Three. Closing." The man called down.

Geoff ran forward pulling his spyglass from his belt.

Serena, Den, Hanlan and Bry made their way to the railing to see what they could.

Over the next hour, Serena paced the decks as the three ships flying the colours of Havii approached. She had entreated the captain to let her help, but he had flatly refused.

"I have enough trouble with these slavers without you getting involved. The best I can hope for is that they take our cargo and let us go, the worst is that they take us all." He had said the last time she had tried.

When she had approached Dazram, hauling in the Kite he had just grunted at her to stay out of the way. "You'd do well to get below and hide, fine flesh like yours will sell well in the city. Clear off and leave us to our work."

He had shoved her aside and joined Brokenose folding the Kite away.

At the prow, Geoff had been a little more informative, "We could never outrun three ships against the wind. The captain will seek a deal so the men are fine, and we will take the loss of the cargo. You...I don't know what he'll do. I had thought he had a soft spot for you, but since the incident...Who knows. I'll do what I can."

As the Bladewing rolled to a stop, Brokenose and Dazram made a run for it. A few of the crew helped them to lower the skimmer boards to the ground and in no time their Kites were up, and they were tacking across the plain away towards the Spines.

It was not long before the slavers' ships were upon them, and their own skimmers lowered down to set off in pursuit of the Kitemen.

"Cowards." Serena muttered to herself as she leant on the water butt next to Den and Bry.

"No miss, they are not cowards. Their skills are highly prized. The slavers might let us sailors go but they would have been taken. We should think to getting you out of sight." Said Den. Bry made noises in agreement and made to push Serena.

She stood her ground. "I will not shy away. Let any man try his luck with me. You have seen what I can do."

She stood taller and rested her hands on the handles of her knives.

"Anyway. I am on a mission from the King."

Bry and Den looked at each other doubt in their eyes.

Captain Bartham started barking orders and the men began to loosen ropes holding cargo and haul up crates onto the deck.

PART 40

The slavers' ships rolled up and surrounded them.

Two of the ships were a little smaller than the Bladewing but the other was a huge, bloated thing. Black with large red eyes painted on the prow and a design above the frontrunner wheel making it look like an animal, with mouth agape, snapping at its prey. It was different to all other land ships that the Bladewing's crew had ever seen. It did not look built for speed, with a wide low hull and high castles to the front and rear. It did not have outrunners but instead the keel of the ship was made up of a line of metal wheels. Two more lines of larger wheels ran out at an angle from the sides of the hull. It did not have a central mast. In its place it had two masts one slightly forward and the other slightly behind midship. From the rails all along the sides were wing sails. It had no Kite, but a complicated series of metallic ropes attached to the forerunner wheel to steer it. As the dark ship swung into place, it was obvious that it was not slow and was very manoeuvrable.

A voice called from the high deck of the rear castle. "Present yourselves on the ground, with your cargo, and your fates will be decided. Run and you will be captured, beaten and taken for the Princes' pleasure. There is no escape."

No sailors could be seen on the large ship and, on the two smaller ones, the men aboard all held weapons in hand but lounged around on deck, idly watching the Bladewing and her crew.

Captain Bartham and Geoff oversaw that their men unloaded the cargo with haste and then they lined them up like soldiers ready for inspection.

"Men stay your hands. Be calm. I will negotiate for your freedom. Stand tall and remember who you are. The crew of the Bladewing. Sailors of the Plains as free as the wind!" The captain spoke softly but with conviction and the men stood taller, proud of who they were.

The side of the black ship cracked open and was lowered to the ground on chains. As the planking hit the dirt, a platoon of soldiers wearing surcoats of metal plates linked with chains marched forward, their spiked helmets glinting in the sunlight. Behind them stalked a nightmare.

Over seven feet tall, chest bare to show his solid mass of muscle and moving with the grace of a true predator. From five points all around his skull, long twisted horns protruded, curving around his head to meet just below his chin. His legs were thick and brawny. Over his skin were scrawled patterns which moved as his sinews tightened and loosened with his stride.

The soldiers surrounded the Bravewing crew and then banged their shields to the ground and raised their spears in the air.

The monster walked forward.

"For the pleasure of the Princes, I greet you." He was well spoken, the voice of a nobleman emanating from the body of a monstrosity.

"Due to reasons which I will not go into, the state of Havii claims you all as its citizens. You are cordially invited aboard my fine ship, The Dread. You may choose to stay where you stand now if you wish but if you choose to do so, please be aware that there will be consequences." As he spoke two men with barrels and hoses strapped to their backs ran from The Dread and quickly climbed aboard the Bladewing.

Serena could see the captain sweating and rubbing at his arms.

The slaver's Kiterunners returned at that moment, hauling behind them Dazram and Brokenose who were dragged into the circle of soldiers and forced to their knees.

"It is good of you to join us. Your captain here was just trying to decide whether to join me and enjoy working for the pleasure of the Princes, or to die. Before he speaks, I would like to hear your opinion on this matter." The goliath moved smoothly over the ground to tower before the kneeling Kitemen.

"What say you? Join the state of Havii and serve or take your beating and die?"

As he spoke these words, flames began to lick up the central mast of The Bladewing as with a great whoosh the fire which had been set aboard it caught. The two men who had climbed aboard leapt down from the rails and scurried back aboard The Dread.

Dazram tried to run.

One mighty fist beat him to the ground.

The Kiteman reached out and began to haul his now useless legs across the ground, arms frantically scrabbling. Fist after fist rained down on his back, beating his body bloody. Then the monster lifted the gruesome corpse of the Kiterunner high above his head and threw it into the conflagration of the Bladewing.

He turned and spoke once more.

"So, captain, you and your men are already clearly beaten. Why risk your lives, when you can join us, for the pleasure of the Princes?"

"I surrender my cargo and my crew to you, for the pleasure of The Princes." Captain Bartham looked like he had just chewed on a rock, but he had no choice.

"Now captain, if you could introduce me to that fine lady who stands with your men that would greatly please me."

Serena stepped forward head held high.

"I need no man to speak for me. I am Serena. Bounty hunter." She began to pick up pace, "You sir have not given us your name."

She sprinted towards him, unleashing the Rush within.

Two of the soldiers moved to intercept her. They were fast. Almost as fast as her. The first swung his spear, trying to sweep her legs but she easily stepped over it. The second planted his shield and thrust his spear at her ribs.

She dodged around the point and used his shield to plant her foot upon as she sprang into the air.

The monstrous face just stared at her as a massive fist swiped her and sent her spinning to the ground. When she regained her senses and crouched to spring into action again, the Rush was gone, and a wall of shields surrounded her bristling with spears pointing at her core.

"My dear. I am Malthrain, and soon you will understand that you, are mine." He chuckled as he walked away.

A man stepped from the line of shields and slammed the butt of his spear into her head.

PART 41: MESSENGERS

His argument with The Degan had left Findo in a sour mood. He stood as the novices brought over his travel clothes. Justice and Bartholomew were in the recovery hall with him, novices helping them into their coats as they talked.

"The King got quick decisions out of them then. Treaties all signed, and peace declared between the lands. I have to admit I am looking forward to seeing Splitt again. You know my mother was born there." Bartholomew chatted away as he was helped into his fur lined gloves.

"Aye you tell us often enough how your mum could paint the spots on ladybugs. I haven't had the pleasure of delivering to Holdon before. What's it like? You were there recently, weren't you Findo?" Justice asked.

Findo nodded, trying his best to be cordial with these young Messengers. He had helped train them both up and they had done well in their service so far.

"Just keep your wits about you, both of you. Those tubes you carry might well be the most important messages you will ever carry, but don't be thinking that they mean peace. Not from what I have seen. There is more to this. You just stay quiet and let others talk around you. Listen for all that information a loose tongue could let slip. There is a lot more going on and we still don't know how Havii, and the slavers are involved." He walked around the others as he talked, helping to check their equipment.

"As you fly, keep your eyes to the ground. Look for signs of people on the move. Spend a little time following the mountain passes and let your courses meander, a few extra hours on your flights and you could find the secrets to this crisis."

"Look Findo, we heard you arguing with The Degan, but the King declared the matter over. The Ambassador has sent word to Splitt. The Guild Directors have set sail to return home and the treaties are signed. We're carrying copies of them on us for pities sake. It's over." Bartholomew said.

Findo grasped the front of Bartolomew's heavy coat and pulled him close, "Do you doubt what I have seen with my own eyes. Massed armies are not easy to just send home. Men like to fight. Then there is the question of the slavers. All I am saying is that you should gather what information you can but be careful." he hissed.

The two Messengers nodded that they understood.

"Where are they sending you that's got you all riled up anyway?" Justice asked.

"It seems the King feels the need to get himself a wife and looks to extend the hand of friendship to Eskrie. He sends me to Blackrock asking for a portrait of the daughter of Lord Shiven, and a request for her to visit Westomere. The King also sends messages to Singhigh and Portreath concerning daughters of Lords there." Findo tapped the tubes strapped to his thighs.

"I hear that Singhigh is a beautiful land, I always wanted to go there." Bartholomew looked wistful. "Why do you sound like you don't want this mission? We serve at the King's command; you've never questioned it before."

"I just want to know what is going on in the South and find out why there are the troubles in the West. I feel I have questions which no one can answer, and I met a girl…"

"Ah, did you now. So, all of this is about a girl. She must be quite special to turn the head of the infamous Findo Gask." Justice winked at Bartholemew.

"No, nothing like that. I asked her to do something for me. Find some answers. I promised to meet her but, with my mission, I am not sure I can make it."

"You're sworn to the Messenger Service. You taught us that. We heard you when you were 'talking' to The Degan. You want to go scouting, it's not our job. We report what we see, but it is not our place to go looking for trouble." Justice checked his stirrups as he spoke. "I take these from you as they were sealed before me. May the words contained within be known to be true until my duty is complete."

He spoke those words solemnly, "We carry the words of

others. We help to make the world a smaller place and a safer one. Nothing more. Let others do the groundwork and worry about war. We fly!"

With that Justice headed out of the door to the eyrie.

Bartholomew stood for a moment before offering his arm. As Findo took it and shook it he said, "I know you just want to do right, but let it go. Do your job and enjoy your time in the air. Not many people get to do what we do."

"You're right. Look at you, student become the teacher. Thanks." Findo grasped his arm a moment longer before watching the younger man head out of the door.

One of the novices brought over Findo's gloves which had been warming by the fire.

Findo just wished that The Degan had not turned him down so bluntly. He would have to have words with him again when he returned, hopefully without the raised voices, fists banging on tables and general bad feelings. Yes, he would have to repair those bridges, but for now he would enjoy the wind in his face and the feel of Gisselle beneath him carrying him to far flung lands.

On the wall was a map of the world. His mission would take him far across The Swaying Sea. north and west. Gisselle would need to fly high and slow if they were to make the trip. There were not many islands they would pass over on the first leg, and she would need time to recover. With luck though, he would still be able to make it, the first new moon was days away. That meant he had just over a moon to deliver his messages, return and convince The Degan to send him south.

There was no time to waste.

PART 42

The town of Heartsnest lay around them in ruins. In the distance fires still burned. Lines of people, roped together, moved through the streets being led to work, mostly clearing rubble and searching for any items of value in the wreckage. From several of the buildings nearby, those which were relatively intact, Serena could hear the cries and sobs of women. She could only guess at what horrors they were facing as lines of soldiers waited their turn outside.

The central square of the town had been cleared and was now serving as the invader's headquarters. To one side, The Dread was at rest, now loaded with the cargo she had taken. The men of the Bladewing had sat in her hold on the journey here locked in darkness. There had been no soldiers guarding them, but the doors of their prison had been solid. Not one of them talked of escape.

They were led out to stand in a long line in the centre of the town square. Soldiers stood to attention along each edge, weapons drawn, blocking all hope of escape.

From one of the streets, a ragged line of townsmen, roped together by their hands, was led to stand next to the sailors. Down the line from Serena stood the captain and Geoff. As she glanced over her shoulder, she could see Bry, leaning his good arm against Den's back for support.

Several men in simple white tunics, each cut from a single piece of cloth and cinched in at the waist by a rope, began to set up a wooden fence, penning off an area of about five metres along each side. Others carried sacks of sand which they emptied onto the floor inside the pen. A large ornate chair was brought out from inside The Dread and placed carefully to one side of the pen near the centre. Malthrain lumbered over to it and casually draped himself into the seat so that he could see inside the fenced area.

A soldier walked along the line of townsfolk, untying their bonds. There was nowhere they could go. Another made sure that each sailor stood next to one of the defeated people of Heartsnest. Serena nodded to the man next to her. He refused to meet her eye, staring numbly at the back of the captive in front of him.

A tall soldier with tight fitting leather armour stood at the front of the lines with the 'pen' behind him. "You are all men of Havii now. Prove your worth on the sand today and you may rise through the ranks to become a fighter and free man serving at the pleasure of The Princes." He called loudly.

"If you do not have the fight in you, or you are a coward, you shall be taken as a slave. Your body will become the property of the state and you shall spend the rest of your lives in service to it as a slave dressed in white. Choose your fate today, it may be the last choice you are given."

The man then gestured to the first two men in the lines to step forward. They were led before Malthrain who spoke softly to them. Serena could see the sailor shake his head and stand taller, then both men climbed over into the fenced area. The townsman was given a wooden club and the men began to circle each other.

The fight did not last long. The sailor quickly disarmed the townsman and used the club to knock the fellow to the floor. Malthrain waved and said something which she could not hear, and the men were taken aboard The Dread.

The process was repeated again and again, and the lines slowly dwindled. Some combatants were given weapons, most fought bare handed. Each fight was stopped before any real harm was done. Those who chose to fight were taken aboard the ship. A few dropped to their knees pleading mercy and were hauled to one side where they were stripped, beaten and then hauled away down one of the streets, out of sight.

Geoff had a hard time of his fight, neither man managing to land a blow on the other. Malthrain stood and moved to rest his meaty arms on the top of the fence, calling words of encouragement to the men as they swung wilder and wilder punches. Geoff retreated, kneeling and struggling to breathe. The man he fought lunged forward and Geoff rolled towards him knocking him down and they began to wrestle in the sand.

Malthrain clapped his hands, and both were led to The Dread.

Captain Bartham's fight finished after one blow and he was taken to the ship while his opponent, who had made no effort to fight, was stripped, beaten, and hauled away.

It was not long until Serena stood before Malthrain. He appraised her, briefly wandering his eyes over her. "You carry yourself well and are equipped admirably. Do you prefer the blade? You have many strapped to that fancy armour." he asked her.

"I am well versed in using the bow but have no qualms fighting up close." She replied trying her best to stare him down. Her side was bruised from the blow he had dealt her earlier, and a headache still rampaged around the base of her skull from the soldier's spear.

"And you dear fellow, do you prefer the blade?" Malthrain reached out to raise the man's chin and look in his eyes.

The man spat in his face.

Malthrain sighed and slowly relaxed back into his seat, wiping the globule of spittle from his cheek with a small cloth he pulled from his pocket.

"You have both dared to strike at me today. Not many do. From now on your fates are one. You will fight for me, but I will make sure that any blow which is dealt to either of you is then repeated upon the other. If you lose an eye, so will she. If she is cut, you will be. The only exception to this that I will make, is that if one of you dies, I will see that the other will suffer much, much longer before their own demise. Now join me to watch the rest." He waved his hand, and two simple stools were brought over.

"Sit." Malthrain commanded and they did.

The interrogations and fights continued. The questions he asked of the men seemed random at times. He would ask one how his family were and another whether he had killed before. The next he might ask if they had travelled beyond The Sand Sea and then the next how many women he had bedded. From the answers and reactions, he seemed to glean some knowledge of each man and he judged them. It seemed to

Serena that the fights were just for show.

Hanlan and Den were amongst the sailors directed aboard the ship and then Bry was helped over to stand before them, the soldiers hauling him roughly.

The townsman next to him was young and a good head taller. Still, Bry stood as still as he could and met Malthrain's eyes.

"Lad, you look well built. What trade have you?" The monster enquired.

"I'm a 'prentice smith sir. Been beating iron these past five years." The youth replied, wiping his hands nervously against the front of his trousers.

"Have you any experience working with the softer metals?"

"I once made a copper kettle for Mrs. Stubbins down Winch Lane, mighty pleased she was."

"My meaning is unclear. Have you worked in precious metals, gold or silver?" Malthrain leant forward.

"No sir. Though I hope to one day make my own wedding band."

"Hmm. If I were to offer you a weapon to fight this man with, what would you choose?"

"He don't look much up for a fight sir. It would be mighty unfair." He hesitated and then blurted, "But if I had to, I would choose a hammer. Only thing I know."

Malthrain lost interest and turned his gaze upon Bry.

He stared at him for a long time.

"Do you have no words for me old man?"

Serena couldn't bear to watch as Bry struggled to stand, head twitching, the left side of his body hanging limply.

Bry turned and shuffled, limping to the fence. Awkwardly he climbed over it, losing his balance and tipping to the sandy floor inside.

Serena stood to go to him and help.

Malthrain grabbed her arm forcing her to sit once more. He hissed at her. "You cannot help him in this. If you move, I will cut your new partner's nipples from him and feed them to you. Remember what happens to him also happens to you. Stay still." He took his hand from her and went to stand at the fence.

"Bring the lad a hammer. A big one." He commanded.

The youth climbed into the fighting area and was handed a huge two-handed Warhammer. Even though he was well muscled it was obvious he struggled to lift the weight of the head.

Bry still knelt in the sand.

"Alright young apprentice. Show me what you can do."

"But 'es half dead already. Old as my Grampy." The lad was obviously uneasy.

Malthrain roared. "Then kill him quick boy. Pick that hammer up and smash his skull. Beat him like you beat the iron on your anvil. Do it. Do it now!"

The lad lifted the hammer and ran forward, raising the weapon above him. He drove it down with all his force the head making contact and sending up a spray of sand.

The lad had no experience, fear and recklessness along with the ridiculous weight of the weapon's head meant it landed wide of the mark.

Bry reached out and grabbed the lad's shirt front, pulling him forward to topple on the sand. Slow to react, the youth rolled onto his back as Bry scrabbled to climb on his chest. The older man grabbed a handful of the coarse sand and shoved it into the boy's eyes, grinding it in with his palm.

"Enough." Malthrain said and Bry rolled away.

"Take them both aboard, make sure his eyes are washed and dressed. We need a new smith. Put the cripple to work preparing the forge. He can be the smithy's new boy and work the bellows."

Serena couldn't meet Bry's eyes as he was hauled past her. She didn't know if it would have been better to have let him die than to leave him broken like this. She would find a way to help him. She would find a way to help them all.

PART 43

That night they rested fitfully in the hold of The Dread. Soldiers came and passed out bowls of stew and hunks of bread to everyone. Then they cleared away the dishes and brought in bedding, much of which looked to have been looted from the town. Throughout the night there were sounds of construction outside, hammering and sawing. Harsh voices calling to each other.

"They'll be building gallows to hang us all on." Brokenose speculated. He had come and sat with Serena, Bry, Den and Hanlan. None of them had the energy to tell him to leave.

"Could be building cages to carry us away." suggested Den.

"Whatever they are building; we all need to stick together. They outnumber us and are better equipped, but a chance will come, and we should be ready." Hanlan spoke up, sounding braver than he looked.

"Whatever it is, this girl is our best chance to survive. She kicked my sorry ass. I intend to keep close to you. If you decide to make a move, I'll have your back." Brokenose held out his arm.

Serena couldn't quite believe him, he and his Kiteman friends had assaulted her, but allies were hard to come by and he seemed to genuinely want to make amends. She took his arm and shook it. "This does not mean I forgive you. You need to earn my trust." She spat the words at him quickly, as though the taste of them revolted her. "For now, we should get some rest. What do you think they want from us?"

"Fightsh. Needs mo fight shlaves. Fo sha pitsh." Bry slurred.

"What are the pits?" Serena asked.

Brokenose cut in. "The Princes of Havii train their armies to fight in arenas. Each man has to prove himself one on one against the others. Only when you have proven yourself to the slave masters do you get chosen to stand in the army. If you are a soldier, you are treated as a free man," He hesitated "Well, as free as a slave can be."

"They say that every person in Havii is a slave to someone above them, and all of them serve under the Princes." Whispered Den in wonder.

"But you said that the soldiers were free men." Serena said stifling a yawn.

"Free to keep slaves. The lowest slaves, who wear white, serve the freemen. The soldiers serve under their officers, and they under the generals. Everyone serves the Princes and they for their part provide for all. No man is to go without food or shelter." said Brokenose

"What about women?" Serena leant forward.

Brokenose hesitated, he seemed worried that what he had to say might upset her, "Women wear white. They are the property of every man. A freeman can claim a woman as his own and have a family. But all women are all men's property."

"How is this allowed to be. Why do the other nations allow them to act this way?"

"Well, many years ago the rulers of Havii slowly expanded their lands and captured all of the South, forcing their laws on all the cities. Those of the North led a great army and defeated Havii. The lands were broken up and the rulers of Havii were forced to agree that only in their own lands were they allowed to continue to have slaves. All other nations imposed heavy sanctions on goods from Havii and it became a very isolated city state, shunned by all. Slavery of all kinds was banned by the King in all other lands."

Den spoke up, "It seems that they no longer hold to those rules."

★★★

Serena did not sleep well that night.

In the morning they were led outside to the square. Each person was given a bowl of porridge and a piece of fruit. They ate huddled in small groups sat on the ground.

Serena sought out the man she had been paired with.

She found him sitting on his own, close to the pen, wiping the last of his porridge up with his fingers.

She sat next to him. Brokenose hovered nearby.

"That your man?" The townsman asked.

"No. Just someone I had a fight with. What's your name?"

"Devlin, but most call me Tracks."

"Why Tracks?" Serena asked.

"Since I was young, I always loved the wilds, spent most of my time there. I'm a trapper see. Spend my life out on the plains or down by the rivers trapping big game. The furs fetch a handsome price and I like the time alone. Less distractions out there with the plants and animals than in the town. Folk took to calling me Tracks, saying I never leave any. Of course, they're wrong but it adds a couple of silver to the pot when negotiating prices if people think you're special." He eyed her armour and weapons.

"What should I call you?"

"Serena."

She considered spinning him a fancy tale but decided to leave it at that.

"Well Serena, I'm no stranger to a fight but most of my experience is with animals and although some of these folks look a little wild, I must admit I am a little worried. I heard gossip in the hold last night that you are quite the killer."

Serena hung her head, ashamed to hear that others thought of her that way. But what did she expect after the events of the last few days?

"It's true that I have killed. Just a few moons ago I was a simple farm girl, living a simple life in a quiet village, miles from anywhere. So much has changed." She stood and offered him her arm. "Come and join me."

He looked at her questioningly but accepted her arm and she pulled him to his feet.

She led him to an open area where less prisoners were sitting around, close to the new wooden constructions which slaves in white were still working on relentlessly.

The whole square was now surrounded by one storey tall wooden frames. Their purpose was still unclear, but it reminded Serena of the frames of new houses she had seen around her village only all joined together completely surrounding the town square.

"Devlin, each morning, if we can, I'd like you to join me and follow the Movements that I do. You should find that it loosens you up and prepares you for the day. Over time the Movements will sit in your memory, and you will find that they help in a fight. They have helped me."

"Please Serena, call me Tracks." He watched as she took up the first stance. "I guess that as anything that happens to you will happen to me. I might as well join you for this too."

Brokenose watched from a distance as Serena showed Tracks some of the basic Movements. At times she would stop and help him to adjust his footing or change the angle of one of his arms. After five minutes or so Den and Hanlan came over and joined in. Some of the slaves started to jeer. They clapped and laughed when Den fell over trying to balance in one of the moves. Brokenose moved over and talked to the men who laughed. They went quiet and turned away watching as soldiers filed into the area from one of the streets.

A horn blared and the soldiers moved to stand, spaced apart and to attention, all around the sides of the square. The sailors and townsmen gradually began to stand up, nervously whispering between them at this new threat.

Malthrain walked out of The Dread. His body oiled and glistening in the morning sunshine. Slaves brought out his chair and set up a canopy over it, shading his seat.

He held his arms up and slowly the whispering ceased.

His orator's voice carried through the silence. "Welcome to your first day as fighters. Today you will be given weapons. My most skilled men will show you how to use them to the best effect. You will train all morning without rest. If you disobey an order, you will be stripped, beaten and given the white. If you are too slow, you will be stripped, beaten and given the white. I train freemen, not slaves. Each of you, if you so choose, can rise up through strength of arms and become a freeman." He walked forward, passing amongst the captives. Eyeing them up as if he were at market choosing the best cattle.

"Listen to your instructors. When the sun reaches the highest point in the sky, you will be given water and bread and allowed an hour of free time."

"In the afternoon, you will run, you will march, you will sweat, and you will wish you had never lived. If you fall behind, you will be stripped, beaten and given the white. When I am satisfied that you have worked hard enough, you will be given your evening meal." He paused as he looked down at a heavily muscled man. He reached out a meaty hand and felt the man's biceps and chest. Then he back handed him sending him sprawling to the floor. The man made to move; his hatred clear in his expression. Soldiers nearby lowered their weapons and took one step forward. The man eyed Malthrain's back as he walked away. Then he relented and sat down rubbing his jaw and spitting out blood.

"Before you go to your beds, you will fight. One on one against an opponent. If I think for one moment that you are not wholly committed to their death at your hands then you will be stripped, beaten and given the white." He surveyed the nervous faces all around him. "Tomorrow we will start again. In two weeks, we will travel to Havii, and I will present you to the Princes. Their best men will want to fight you and kill you. They claim to have the best fighters in the land. I mean to prove them wrong. I believe in you. I believe in your training."

His voice rose louder and louder, spittle flying from his lips. Men all around seemed roused by his speech, Serena realised that he was winning some over to his side. "Soon, the best of you will be freemen and will be famed throughout the land for having beaten the Princes' men, all the riches of the world will be yours. Train hard and together we can rule the world!"

A cheer went up from the soldiers at this and many of the captives joined in, caught up in the moment.

"If you can, stay close. Hopefully, we can use the mornings to continue to train together." Serena said to the men around her as the soldiers began to split them all into groups, each with their own area of the square.

Malthrain sat in his seat, he missed nothing as he watched everything.

Serena's group was joined by a few more men. They all eyed her warily. Some of the sailors still had kept knives at their belts and a few of the townsmen had swords or staffs. Whilst she stood out in the crowd as the sole woman and the only captive wearing armour, bristling with weapons.

The weapons they had made no difference. There was no escape, not yet…

A tall, deeply tanned balding man of middle years marched over to them. He wore a red sash over his armour and had a long-curved blade strapped to his waist. Six soldiers followed in his wake and spread out to mark an area for the group to work within.

"Call me *Sir.*" The balding man commanded. "I am to be your instructor. Obey my commands, listen to my advice and work hard." He looked each of them over, assessing them.

"Line up!" He yelled.

Tracks, Den and Hanlan moved quickly to stand at Serena's side. Brokenose quickly joined them as did a few of the other men. Two of the townsmen, who had sniggered at their group doing the Movements, lined up separately.

One of the soldiers moved from his place around them, he drew a short wooden club from his belt and smacked the first man in the back of his legs, causing the man to fall to his knees. Then the soldier twisted, and the club connected with the second man's skull, just above his eyebrow. He fell like a sack, unconscious before he hit the ground.

The last couple of men who had been slow to join the line quickly stood with Serena and the others.

Sir, moved to stand by the man on his knees. "Do you have any skill with weapons?" He asked.

"I use a bow to hunt." The man said looking terrified.

"Ever been in a fight?"

"When I was young, got in scraps all the time."

"Stand up and get in the line." Sir said to him.

The man heaved himself up and hurried over. Sir following his every step. Once he was in place, Sir stood face to face with him.

"What do you say?"

"Thank you..."

"Thank you what?" Sir shouted in his face.

"Thank you, Sir!" The man shouted back.

Sir began to walk along the line. Two of the soldiers dragged the unconscious man away as others dropped some weapons on the floor inside the area.

Sir stopped in front of Serena. He stood uncomfortably close to her. He was almost a head taller, and she had to look up to meet his eyes. His breath smelled faintly of garlic and stale wine as he spoke down at her.

"Never trained a girl before. You have seen what happens if you're too slow or not up to the task."

Serena nodded that she understood.

"Malthrain says you're special that you can touch the Rush. Well, around here that doesn't really count. If you use it, then all you do is make yourself weaker. If you don't... I doubt you'll last a day."

"We shall see, Sir."

"Yes, we shall." With that he turned and one of the soldiers handed him a weapon from the floor. He began to pace before them.

"This is a halberd. You grasp the shaft with both arms spaced apart like this." He took up a stance hands wide on the shaft. "The wide axe head is for cutting your opponents at range like this."

He spun and swung the weapon in a wide arc.

"You can also use it like a spear or pike thrusting with the point." He moved forward demonstrating the motion.

"It is also good against mounted opponents as well as foot soldiers. The hook here." He showed them the hook on the reverse of the axe blade. "Can be used to catch onto clothing and pull a man closer or from his mount."

He continued to demonstrate different moves that could be

made and then had them all armed and following his moves. Later, when he was satisfied, they could all use the weapon offensively and defensively, he had some straw filled sacks brought over and they practiced the moves against those.

Serena had no time to see what any of the other groups were doing but she could hear shouts, commands, and the ringing of metal.

Finally, they faced off against each other. The aim was simple. To land a blow.

The blades were not sharp but the weight of them, especially if swung, was enough to break a rib if you were unlucky. By the time the lunch horn blared, she and the nine men which made up the group were sweating, tired and bruised. All were glad to sit on the ground and share the food and water brought to them by slaves in white, who refused to meet their eyes, looking only at the ground.

Fresh soldiers filed into the square and replaced those who had been on guard. Sir left with them.

PART 44

In Serena's group, as well as Tracks, Den, Hanlan, and Brokenose (whose real name turned out to be Tobias) were: Gaz, a joiner by trade, young and blonde haired, he was strong and fast; Keith, an older man who had once served in the town guard before retiring to help his wife run a general store; Woodsy who had once trained in Ardark as a healer before returning to Heartsnest to help on his family's farm; Howth, who had taken easily to the Halberd and claimed he was a lumberjack; and Dill, the man who had told Sir he could hunt with a bow, who was actually a chandler.

They ate their meal in relative silence. The guards watched them constantly.

All around the square men sat in huddles eating. Surrounding them the wooden structures continued to take shape. A terrace of small rooms, all open to the square.

More quickly than they would have liked, the break was finished.

Each group of men, carrying the weapons they had trained with in the morning, was shepherded to form a line. They were made to stand in pairs, each group together. For every ten men there were six soldiers. Three on either side armed and armoured.

Malthrain had retreated back inside The Dread.

From one of the roads, a giant lizard paced into the square to stand at the side of the lines. Upon its back sat a man with dark skin, almost the colour of night. He wore a strangely peaked leather cap with a mane of red hair flowing from its top. He stood tall in his saddle and called out to all assembled before him.

"My name is Colthar. I am your running master. As the sun begins its decent through the sky and beats its fiery breath down upon you, I will try to break you. Some of you will break. Some of you will cry. You will feel pain. But I do this to make you strong." The lizard he rode upon licked its eyeball and moved its sinuous tail, rasping against the ground. "Listen to the beat of the drum."

A soldier at the head of the line began to beat out a low, slow rhythm on a large drum strapped to his chest.

"Feel it in your bones." Colthar paused and moved his fist up and down in time with the rhythm.

"Now stamp your feet!" he shouted.

Slowly, men began to join in and stamp in time with the drum.

"Good. Now we march!"

He pulled on the reins and guided the lizard to the head of the line, leading them out of the square, through the ruins of the town and into the plains. For a long time, they marched slowly. The soldiers correcting men who fell out of rhythm or moved out of place.

The drum never faltered. Occasionally, Colthar and his lizard would drop back along the line of marching men. Always watching taking mental notes of who was doing well and who was looking weak.

As the sky began to change colour with the sun low to the horizon, the beat began to quicken. By now Gaz and Dill were both limping, their shoes not up to the task. The line snaked its way around a low hill upon the top of which Colthar and his lizard sat like it was a large nest, and the pace began to quicken.

The soldiers moved closer to the men, hands never far from their wooden clubs.

Serena pushed sweat slickened hair from her forehead and panted for breath. In front of her, Tracks kept pace, never breaking stride. To her side, Den struggled, occasionally stumbling on the uneven ground. Serena was quick to grab his elbow and steady him. He was having difficulty jogging and holding the Halberd, it kept banging into his thigh.

"Cross your hand across your chest to hold the weight of the head against your shoulder, use your other hand to take the pole's weight and keep it clear of your legs." she advised him. He shifted the weapon and seemed to find a better grip.

The group ahead of them were carrying long swords

sheathed at their belts. The weapons slapped against their thighs and tended to suddenly slip between their legs, tripping them. The soldiers did not allow them to stop, and the men had to scramble back to their feet and run to catch up. Those that fell were often hit with a club, making matters worse.

By the time Heartsnest came back into sight, the whole line was running hard. One man, from a group several ahead of Serena's, had fallen. When he did not get back up, two soldiers had peeled off and beaten him badly. His screams had fallen silent as a particularly vicious blow had caved in his skull sending a spray of blood over Tracks and Brokenose as they passed.

When they made it back into camp, it was all most of the men could do to collapse onto their backs in exhaustion, weapons discarded on the ground like fallen leaves.

Fresh soldiers lined the square. The structures surrounding it were complete, the slaves in white gone to some other task.

Malthrain sat imperious in his chair, watching everything.

A detachment of soldiers moved through the exhausted crowd getting everyone back to their feet and lined up before a large tent which had been erected in the centre of the square. Gradually the line moved through the tent. Inside water and food were handed out to each man in wooden bowls. Soldiers checked each person for signs of injury, those who were limping badly were moved to one side, where slaves in white washed and dressed their wounds.

Once they had eaten, Serena's group moved to the wash station and cleaned their bowls before returning outside to wait for Gaz and Dill.

When they stepped back out into the cooling evening air, both men looked happier than they had all day.

"Feels good to have some clean cloth wrapped around my feet. They had to cut and peel off my old sandals. I am not looking forward to the march tomorrow." said Gaz as he and Dill joined the others.

"Just keep your feet dry tonight, try to let the air get to your skin. If we can't find you some boots tonight, in the morning we'll get your feet wrapped well before the march." Woodsy told him.

It seemed strange to Serena that in just one day, her group had become exactly that. Looking around the square, all the different groups were still together, bonded now by the training and the march. People, who the day before had been strangers, now chatted quietly like old friends sharing their joint misery.

Slaves lit torches around the square as darkness descended to cover them. Then soldiers directed everyone to move to 'the pit'. This was what they called the small fenced off area where the fights had happened the previous night.

As they all stood shuffling their feet in the cooling air, standing close around three sides of the pit, a double rank of soldiers armed with shields and spears moved up to surround them. To either side of Malthrain stood the captains from the morning, each wearing polished armour which appeared to glow as it reflected the orange light from the torches.

Malthrain stood and held up his arms for quiet. He waited until all were still.

"You have survived your first day. I am sure that some of you wish nothing more than to go to your beds." He looked around at their weary faces. "But it is not yet time for rest. Each of you will be tested on the sand. Your captains have reported back to me on your performance in training. Your names have been gathered and put into this chest."

Two slaves in white hurried forward to hold a small chest up besides Malthrain.

"I will draw two names from it. These two fighters will face each other on the sand of this pit showing no mercy. They will fight to win. Be warned. Hold nothing back. For if you do, you will be stripped, beaten, and given the white. If you fight hard, you shall be given quarters in the Gojon, the buildings which I have had built for you. Each of you will be given your own cell, with bed and bucket to be your place of rest for as long as you serve me. Train hard in the morning, run fast in the afternoon and fight well in the evening, then you may rest well at night!"

As he had spoken his voice had risen with his arms until at the last word his arms pointed to the sky and his words rang with ferocity.

Ever so slowly he lowered his hands into the chest and pulled out two small flat stones. He spent a moment looking at them and then raised them up between his thick thumb and forefinger. "Chester from the spears and Madraid from knives. Step forward men. You have the honour of being the first to bloody the sand."

Two townsmen stepped out of the crowd and walked to stand before him. Their captains stepped up and spoke briefly with each. They were given their weapons and climbed over the rails into the pit.

"Fight." Malthrain called stepping eagerly to lean his arms on the rails as he watched.

People in the crowd began to shout encouragement as the two men circled each other. The man with the spear seemed to have the advantage in reach and Madraid could do nothing but dodge and retreat. He was backed into a corner and Chester made some quick jabs towards his ribs. Madraid dodged and rolled under the spear's tip, Chester was too slow to retreat and one of the knives grazed his ribs opening a long shallow slash in his flesh.

"Enough." Malthrain called. "Take him to have that stitched and then show them to their cells".

"I guess he doesn't want to kill us after all." Den whispered.

"He won't let us kill each other. He needs us to fight for him. He is putting a lot of effort and money into all of this." Brokenose said quietly. "You don't let your prize cattle die, do you? You might whip them to teach them a lesson but, in the end, you feed them well and train them to pull a plough or walk to the milking shed."

The fights were kept short, most lasting only a minute or two. Malthrain stopped most after the first blow was landed. Not one person refused to fight. They had all seen what would happen if they did. At least in a fight they stood a chance.

Den fought well against another man from knives, using the long reach of the halberd to keep his opponent away.

Brokenose faced one of his crew mates from the Bladewing who fought with a staff. It was obvious he was not experienced with it and Brokenose disarmed him and pinned him to the ground quickly.

Some men stayed behind after their fights to watch. Most limped off to their cells to rest.

Gaz, Dill and Hanlan all lost their bouts but fought well enough, each took a few more bruises but no bad injuries.

Keith's halberd swung low as his opponent charged him and it cut deep into the flesh of the man's calf, cracking bone. The man writhed in the sand screaming and it took four soldiers to carry him off to the healers' tent. Keith stayed with the others to watch the fights.

As time dragged on and the fights continued, Serena became more nervous. She knew that if she used the Rush, she could beat any of these men but would the cost in energy be worth it? She hoped that her instincts would be enough.

Tracks was called up. His opponent had a flail, a wooden club with a chain on one end attached to a heavy metal ball. They circled each other wearily before Tracks thrust for his opponent's stomach. The man stumbled backwards falling to the floor but managed to get the chain of his weapon wrapped around the head of Tracks's halberd. The two men wrestled for control of the halberd before Tracks dropped it, charging at the prone man. Somehow the man managed to regain his feet and dodge, his weapon coming free of its tangle. As Tracks made to lunge at him again, the fellow swung a blow into Tracks's ribs before he was tackled to the ground. Tracks wasted no time and rained blow after blow at the man's face. Malthrain called an end to the contest, but two soldiers had to go into the ring and drag Tracks from the unconscious man as he continued to smash his fists down.

Tracks was pulled from the pit and forced to his knees in front of Malthrain, spears held to his throat.

"You disobeyed an order. I asked you to stop yet you

continued to beat at my property. For failing to stop when commanded, you will go without rest for one hour for each blow that you landed on that man. However, you showed true blood lust and that is something which cannot be trained into a man." Malthrain pointed at the unconscious man being carried away. He consulted with one of the captains.

"Tonight, you will not sleep. My men counted twelve blows that you landed after I called a halt. There are eight hours until dawn. You will walk the length of the yard all night. Tomorrow after you fight, you will walk the length of the yard for four more hours."

A note of recognition ran over Malthrain's face then. "You're the one I partnered with her."

He turned to survey the waiting fighters. "Come to me my dear. Don't be shy."

Serena pushed her way through the waiting crowd.

"You saw how this man disobeyed a direct order did you not?" Malthrain asked.

She nodded weakly.

"You will walk with him and suffer his punishment by his side. Now I believe I saw him take a blow during the contest. Would you agree that he was struck?"

Serena felt sick. Again, she nodded.

"Take off your clothing." Malthrain ordered gesturing to them both.

Voices all around ceased their whispers as Serena immediately began to unbuckle her armour. Tracks watched her for a second before he started to pull his shirt over his head.

They both stood naked before Malthrain, skin covered in goosebumps in the cool air. Tracks tried to cover himself with his hands in embarrassment, but Serena stood tall, chin held high, staring unwaveringly into Malthrain's bloodshot eyes.

Malthrain moved over to Tracks. He examined him closely, leaning in, lifting his arms and pulling and poking at his flesh.

"You have the fresh bruise on your ribs from the flail, just here." Malthrain pushed a finger hard into the reddening bruise and Tracks winced in pain.

"Also, you have a bruise to your thigh just here." Again, he poked. "How did you get that?"

"Practicing the halberd this morning." Tracks tried to stand up taller as he said this, trying to mask his fear, but it leaked into the strain of his voice.

"Ooh, this one across your back looks painful. Your captain needs to show you how to protect your back whilst wielding the halberd." Malthrain stood and turned to Sir.

"Fetch a halberd and a flail."

Sir walked quickly away.

"Now my dear. What about you?" He leant in close. Serena could feel his warm breath against her skin as he looked at every inch of her flesh. He poked at her thigh and lifted her right breast with a finger.

"Remarkable. Not a scratch on you."

Tracks fell to his knees as Sir returned with halberd in one hand and flail in the other.

"Now dear, this might hurt." Malthrain stated.

"Halberd to the back, make sure it hits just below the left shoulder blade. If you're not sure check his bruising for position first." Malthrain directed Sir.

Serena heard Den shout 'no!' just before the weapon hit her. She stumbled forward and couldn't stop the cry as the pain of the blow lanced through her back and side. Den's shouts were quickly silenced by a look from Malthrain as he tried to see who had shouted.

Serena shakily stood back up to stand tall, chin raised staring at Malthrain.

He walked around her examining the bruising from the blow. "It is lucky for you that we use blunted blades, still you will need to visit the healers before you begin your night walk. Now the leg. Aim the blow to hit here." Malthrain poked painfully at her flesh.

Sir hit her thigh hard with the butt of the halberd. Her leg went dead, and she fell to one knee. This time she did not cry out. She rubbed the bruise and shakily stood once more.

Malthrain waved Sir away and handed the flail to another captain.

"Would you be kind enough to raise your arm above your head dear?" Malthrain asked.

She considered in that moment whether she should call the Rush and end this. But she didn't know enough about his power. He had beaten her from the air like a rag doll the last time she had tried to use it and she doubted she could use the Rush in the same way she had with Master Humbold at the tower.

She raised her hand resting her palm on her head.

"Don't break anything." Malthrain said to the captain just before he swung.

The blow knocked the air from her lungs, and she doubled over trying to hold on to the pain in her side as she struggled for breath.

"Get up dear and let me check you."

She stood and once again his breath was on her flesh.

He nodded, seemed satisfied and walked back to his chair.

Serena met Tracks's eyes briefly, she saw his pain for her and looked quickly away.

Malthrain dipped his hand once more into the chest and pulled out a stone. The name on it was called out and a man came forward. Serena recognised him as one of the men who had trained with longswords, who had run before them that day.

"No need to dress dear. You can fight like that. It will make it easier to see the wounds that I will inflict on your friend here." Malthrain pointed at another of the captains who stepped forward bearing a gleaming longsword.

Sir stepped over and handed Serena his halberd. Another man handed Serena's opponent the longsword and they both climbed into the arena. She noted how much harder it was to do things gracefully when you were naked with hundreds of eyes watching your every move.

The man tested the weight of his weapon and tried a few swings and thrusts. Serena stood stock still facing him, halberd resting on the ground held in one hand by her side. The man began to circle her. She did not move. The crowd all around edged closer to the pit watching intently.

They collectively held their breath as the man made a thrust forward. Serena did not move as he rapidly danced backwards expecting a swing from her that never came. He was right to be wary. Perhaps he had heard the same stories as Tracks.

His next move was a wide arching swing aimed to hit Serena's chest. She ducked it easily as she swept one foot low, spinning away from him. His blade knocked the halberd to the floor. She spun counter to his arc and, as he tried to reverse his momentum and bring his blade back around, she punched him in his side and twirled away. His sword passed through the space she had just occupied, and he stepped back into a defensive pose holding the point out before him.

Serena planted her feet apart, side on to him and waved him towards her with a movement of her fingers. He lunged and she stepped back.

She waited and the next time he lunged, she back handed his blade and pushed his back as he stumbled past her, losing his balance to sprawl in the sand.

Serena backed away and crouched.

The man was angry now. He stood up; the crowd were starting to cheer them on. He dashed forward wildly swinging his sword two handed over his head.

Then he stopped. Blade falling from his limp fingers onto the sand behind him. His gaze lowered to his chest where the spike on the top of the halberd had pierced his heart.

At the last moment Serena had lifted the head of the discarded weapon from the sand and braced it. He had run himself onto the blade.

His was the first death on the sand.

Malthrain sat more heavily on his chair as she was led away to the healers' tent, her armour and clothing bundled in her arms.

PART 45: MESSENGER OF LOVE

The girl was astoundingly beautiful.

He watched as she chipped away at the ice with her spear, forming a small hole in the frozen river. He helped her to bait a line of hooks which she lowered down into the slow flowing water beneath.

She tied the end off on the end of her spear and rested it on a Y shaped pole which she jammed into the ice. Then they sat and she unpacked a meal from her gear which she laid out on a blanket. He couldn't help staring at her as she worked.

Her full, red lips and high cheeks blushed pink with the cold. The way her nose turned up just a little at the end. Her long wavy blonde hair and blue eyes.

She looked up and smiled at him. His heart skipped a beat and he looked down, feeling like he had been caught stealing by staring so long at her.

"Would you like some pickled fish?" She asked with her melodic sing song accent.

Why did the King have to torture him so?

The journey to Eskrie had been long but they had made good time. Upon arrival in Blackrock, he had handed his message directly to Lord Shiven. Once he had read the message, the Lord had immediately sent for his daughter. Then she and Findo had taken a trip in the wilds so that he could get to know her better, to be able to make an accurate account for the King, Lord Shiven had said.

So, Findo found himself out on the ice fishing with the most beautiful girl he had ever seen.

"I'm starving. I'd eat pretty much anything you offered at this point." He said reaching to take the offered fish.

She hesitated, pulling her hand back. "Anything?" She said smiling coyly at him.

Flustered and unsure of how to respond Findo froze. She punched him in the arm and laughed. "Perhaps I'll let you try a piece of me later, if we have no luck catching fish."

He laughed awkwardly and took the pickled fish. It was

only because he was so hungry that he managed to stomach the tangy, oily slime that slid around his mouth and down his throat. Luckily, there was bread to go with it, and wine.

Their protectors stood a short distance away on the banks chatting and smoking from long pipes. They paid little attention to Findo and Lady Grey. They were on the lookout for bears and game.

The line began to bounce, rattling against the spear and Lady Grey quickly grabbed it and began to haul it in. Findo rushed to help her. His thick gloves made it difficult to grasp the thin line, so he took them off. He was surprised at how powerfully the fish fought and it took them several difficult minutes to land it. She quickly pulled the hook from its mouth and then gave the fish to him.

It was the strangest creature he had ever held. Streamlined, its silvery scales glistened in the light. Its fins spread out flat to either side from its lower body like fanned arms and the tail hooked downwards and split into two finned 'legs'.

"It's a Bothan, bottom feeder. It is perfectly adapted to moving on the underside of the ice or on the riverbed, it uses its tail to grip on in stronger currents where it waits for prey to wash towards it."

Findo thought that in this case she was the Bothan, and he was being washed towards her beautiful mouth. He handed the fish back to her and she skilfully gutted it and put it in a sack with chips of ice.

By this time his hands were becoming numb, and he blew on them and rubbed them together to try to warm them.

"I can help with that if you like," she suggested opening the front of her heavy fur coat. "Put your hands on me and I'll warm them."

Findo stared at her, wanting to touch her but knowing that he should not.

The men on the bank called to them waving that they should come over. He helped her to pack away their things and followed as she dashed across the ice. He was not so graceful and slipped frequently on the glassy surface.

"Lady, we should get you back to Blackrock. It's not safe out here. One of the scouts has reported signs of bear nearby. If they are ranging this close to the city, it is a bad sign." The captain of the guards reported.

"No captain. I wish to see for myself. Perhaps something has driven a lone bear south or it might be injured and wandering alone having been driven out from the pack."

She handed the sack of fish to Findo and grabbed a bow from one of the guardsmen. "Lead on then." She started to walk forward, and the men had to rush to gather around her.

Findo followed along in their wake.

The scout led the way, following his own tracks back through the snow. As they approached a hollow ahead, he signalled for the men to crouch down. The guards spread out around Lady Grey, facing outwards. All had bows with arrows nocked and ready. Findo rested his hand on the hilt of his heavy dagger.

"Down in the hollow Lady, in the deeper snow. There are prints and signs of scatt. Looks like the creature is marking its territory." the scout whispered.

"Not likely to be injured then. Any idea which way it went?" Lady Grey asked pulling her hood closer against the chill wind which was getting stronger.

"No Maam. First signs, I came running back to you."

"Good. You and Jorry circle around the hollow and see if you can pick up a trail. Captain, join me to investigate the hollow. Men keep your eyes and ears alert to anything. We all know how sneaky these bears can be." With that she moved off down the slope.

Findo followed her and the captain.

The snow in the hollow was up to Findo's thighs and he had difficulty moving through it. "Lift your knees high as you walk. Place each foot flat and slow as you step, you should find it easier then." Lady Grey advised as she examined a large print in the snow of the opposite slope.

Then she turned and picked up a rounded pile of faeces. She pulled off a glove and pushed a finger inside.

"Still warm in the middle. Fragments of bone and shredded bark. It has eaten recently and passed through this spot less than a quarter turn ago. From the amount of scatt I would say that it is marking its territory. So, it has moved into this area believing it to be better than wherever it came from."

"What should we do Lady?" The captain looked worried. "I fear we need more men."

"Yes, you're right. We should head back, leave some scouts to see if they can pick up a trail. We should be able to drivc it off with greater numbers, but if it refuses to budge then we will need to kill it."

The scout returned and called down the slope to them. "Lady, it headed over that way and then looped around towards the river. I think it might be trying to track us. You should get out of here now. From all the signs it is the biggest I have ever seen south of the Giants."

They began to clamber back up the slope to the others, the captain calling orders for the men to spread out and be wary.

The party made their way back to towards the river then followed along the bank headed south towards the walled city.

PART 46

The first few days had been hard.

Tracks and Serena had suffered the worst. By the end of the third day, neither had cared when Malthrain had had them beaten and cut, matching each other's wounds, all they wanted was for the day to be over, the training, The Running and the fighting to cease, so that they could seek the sweet oblivion of a full night of sleep.

Now, a week later they fared no worse than any other. In fact, they were doing better than most. Their unit had become strong. Most groups had lost a few men to injury or the white. All ten of their group still fought. People around camp were starting to talk of them as the untouchables.

Every morning, before breakfast, they went through the Movements.

It was their thing.

They owned it.

Whilst all the rest lounged sleepily in their cells or sat together in the dawn light talking, Serena showed her group the Movements. Not one of them complained. They were all seeing the benefits.

Den commented that when he woke his muscles were tired and stiff but after their sessions, he felt lighter and ready for the day. Keith wished he had followed the Movements when he had been a town guard as he felt more supple and faster in his reactions. None of them had lost a fight in the pit since the first night, though they all had bruises and scars.

Dill, Hanlan and Gaz had become fast friends. During the bouts in the pit, they had started a system of bartering for bets. Now, everyone in the unit wore sturdy footwear, they smuggled extra rations and had even found a supply of herbs, salves and bandages, which Woodsy used to tend their wounds.

Sir treated them with grudging respect, he never slackened on discipline, but he spent extra time making sure they knew their weapons well, and he was harsh on any soldier who wrongfully beat them. He could see the value of his livestock. As their reputation rose, so did his.

After the morning meal, they gathered together to train. Only today was different.

A horn blew from high on the deck of The Dread and Malthrain stood tall by the railing. "Fighters. You have won my respect. You came to be mine, in many different ways, but you are all my fighters. Soon, we will be leaving to face the Princes and their men. We have only a few days left to hone our skills and become the best. I have brought some of my finest fighters to join you. They will kill you if they can. I have also purchased fighters from other pits to try their skills against yours. For the next five days you will not march in the afternoon. You will train for the pits. Each night the fights will be to the death or until a man yields. Fight hard and win your freedom."

From the road came the sounds of men marching in step.

The new men were formidable. They looked like well-honed weapons.

They marched imperiously past the scattered huddles of men in the square and formed up in neat formation before the pit. Each wore a breast plate of hardened, polished leather and a skirt of chainmail and long sturdy sandals. They carried a spear and across each back was strapped a crescent shaped shield upon which was painted, in black and red, a curled ram's horn.

Behind them, walked a large group of men and women wearing white. They gathered behind the fighters in a rough formation.

Malthrain walked out before them. His captains gathered around him.

"You men have proven your worth on the sand. You are my finest. For your victories in the pits each of you has earned the honour of being a free man. Yet your service to me and to the Princes is not done."

He began to pace before the men, speaking loud enough that his voice would carry to everyone in the square but addressing these new fighters. "You will join the ranks of these new recruits and train with them. You will see that they are skilled, but you will share with them your knowledge and your experience. It is your task to see that when they stand at the pleasure of the Princes, that all of us succeed. It is my dream for us all that each of us will earn the title - free man. That all of us will enter the great army of Havii. That all of us will win. Fame and fortune shall rain down upon our heads and before us no army in this world will be able to stand, and we shall be truly free!"

The men raised their spears as one unit and slammed the butts to the ground, again and again. Beating out a deep rhythm. Then they began to chant one word over and over again. "Malthrain. Malthrain. Malthrain."

The captains stepped forward and divided the men up, moving them to their allotted training areas. The servants in white filed off to the Gojon cells on the eastern side of the square, where they began to empty and clean the cells, many were women.

As they walked back to their training area, Serena spoke quietly with Tracks. "How many do you think? About fifty?"

"Yeah, about that. Means there are around a hundred and forty fighters now. With the new whites, there must be over two hundred in camp. Add to that the various crew of The Dread and the captains and guards that would put it at over three hundred souls here for the pleasure of Malthrain."

"Any rumours of dissent? There must be others who want to escape." Serena looked carefully around making sure no-one was in earshot.

"Not a word. Hanlan and Keith have been trying to chat to the other groups, especially during the fights, but everyone else seems as tired as we are. If we could get out of camp, where would we go? We would be hunted down easily."

"We must not give up hope. Our chance will come. Perhaps some of those in white might help."

Tracks slowed as they neared their area, "We need a plan. We won't be able to escape on our own and that means we will need allies. We need to start thinking smart and making friends. I'll talk to the others and see if anyone has any ideas."

Sir marched up with five of the new fighters in tow. Weapons practice began.

The new men were good. Fast, strong and well trained. But they were rigid in their thinking.

Sir had them demonstrate fighting as a unit with the halberd. Three of them covered the other two holding their shields locked together whilst the pair demonstrated thrusts and parries through the shields. Serena's group had to try to attack, but they could not find a way to strike at them.

Then Sir and the new fighters showed the group how to assemble the formation. Shields were provided and, by the time lunch came around, all fifteen under Sir's command were marching, forming up, locking shields and moving with reasonable precision.

As they were waiting for the midday meal to be brought around, one of the new fighters started talking with Brokenose.

"Hey, you guys are not what we expected." he said with a heavy southern accent. "We were told you were just townsfolk and sailors with only a week's fighting training. Yet you learn quick. You made the formation in one morning. It took me weeks to learn."

"That, my new friend, is because you were lucky enough to find yourself working with the best." Brokenose bragged.

"We will see how good you are on the sand after food." The new fighter held out his arm. "I'm Girau. It's good to meet you."

Brokenose took his arm and they shook. Over the next hour, Brokenose introduced himself and the rest of the group to the new men.

Girau came from Ardark By The Lake, one of the Twin Cities. He had been taken as he had fled the city a year ago when Havii had invaded. Since then, he had served for a while in white, until he had picked a fight with a soldier. His master had sold him on to the owner of a small fighting pit. He had trained hard and been taken to Havii to fight in the pits.

During his first match, he had been spotted by one of Malthrain's agents. Soon he found himself with a new master.

"They trained us hard but kept us away from the pits. All of us wanted to fight, to win our freedom, but all we were allowed to do was train. A week ago, we were told we had to march to this piece of nowhere, but that if we did, we would be free men. They let us choose a slave at the market and gave us armour and shields, then we came here. Now we train you so that we can all return to Havii and prove our worth in the pits. There is to be some sort of festival with the fights as the main event. The Princes will be there. I hope to kill one of their men, then they will have to make me one of their own men and I can fight in the army."

"A good goal. I hope that we can all kill many of the Princes' men and win our freedom." Keith spoke up.

"First we must fight on the sand here and earn our places." Girau replied.

During the afternoon they all practiced one on one. Sir did not push them hard, and they had plenty of time to watch each other, especially Girau and the new fighters. Sir encouraged them to find fault with each other's techniques and to advise better ways. Serena thought this clever of him. They all learned a little from watching and talking about the fights, they also had plenty of rest so they would be fresh in the evening.

As the sun began to set and they broke for dinner, there was a palpable tension in the camp. This time the fights would be different. The stakes had been raised. If you lost, it could mean your life. Conversations dried up and most men ate in silence, lost in thought.

Most of the free men went to their cells to spend time with their women. Some seemed happy with this, others not so. Serena found it quite uncomfortable trying to eat her food to the accompaniment of cries of pleasure and pain coming from the eastern side of the Gojon. She hoped it would not give others ideas about her.

PART 47

Three pits had been set up in the sand before The Dread. Malthrain sat in his 'throne' watching everything eagerly. The captains moved between the different arenas according to who was fighting, supporting their own.

The fighters stood around the pits, eagerly calling support to men from their squads. Serena's group kept close to each other. Dill, Hanlan and Gaz set up next to the main pit taking bets as usual. Trade was good, the new fighters had plenty to bet with and even the guards came by on occasion. It seemed Malthrain was happy to allow them to trade bets as it encouraged competitiveness.

There was almost a carnival atmosphere. The shock of seeing fellow fighters being carted off on stretchers after each bout had quickly given way to a kind of blood lust.

"If it keeps up like this, there will be half the camp left in the morning." Tracks leant in speaking quietly with Serena.

"Malthrain taught us that to give up was to be given the white. Now everyone has a point to prove. We don't even know how many fighters he wants to take with him to Havii. This is a total blood bath." Serena glanced over to Brokenose who was deep in conversation with Girau, leaning against the rails of the pit waiting for the next bout to begin. "At least we seem to be making some friends."

Hanlan was the first of their group called into the pits. He had a lucky draw against a man armed with a hammer. He easily kept the man at range with the halberd and took quick advantage of a slip in the sand by his opponent to spear him through the thigh. The other man however did not yield. He continued to fight even though he could hardly walk and had a stream of blood pouring down his leg. He glanced often to his captain and Malthrain as if expecting someone to step in and stop the fight, his eyes wide with fear. Hanlan circled him, making weak jabs with his weapon causing fresh wounds. The crowd began shouting "Kill him!"

"Finish him!"

"Smash his head open!"

Hanlan let the man come at him, using defensive strokes to deflect his weakening blows. "Just yield. It doesn't have to end like this." he called to his opponent.

"If Malthrain sees this he'll have Hanlan beaten." Serena said to the others. "What can we do?"

Brokenose stepped up to the rails with Keith and they began chanting, "Kill, kill, kill, kill."

The others joined in. It was the only way to save their companion.

Hanlan looked at them and Serena saw the look in his eyes change. He understood.

Hanlan stepped back from his struggling opponent to get the space he needed. Then he changed his grip and swung the blade of his weapon forward with a mighty two-handed blow. Blood sprayed the crowd as separate parts of the body fell to the floor. Hanlan hung his head as the faces all around him roared for his victory.

Brokenose was called up next. He won his fight with ease, taking the legs out from under his man and slitting his throat. It was not pretty but he got the job done.

The lumberjack from Heartsnest, Howth, and Woodsy were next. They were to face each other.

As they entered the pit, Sir handed each their weapon "I'm sorry boys but you need to fight. I wish it didn't have to go this way. Perhaps you are not untouchable after all."

After their initial reluctance circling each other, their training took over.

"Give them a good fight boys. Show them what the Untouchables are made of." Keith called from the side.

Woodsy landed a clattering blow against Howth's side and Howth immediately struck back. The crowd began cheering and they traded blow for blow all around the sand.

Howth hit a lucky strike against Woodsy's hand, and he dropped his weapon, diving across the ground to grapple for control of Howth's. It was obvious Woodsy's hand was injured, and Howth easily wrestled control away from him, spinning back across the pit, swinging his blade wide. He landed another lucky blow to Woodsy's upper arm and stepped back into a defensive stance.

Woodsy backed away, trying to reclaim his fallen weapon but his arm hung loosely at his side, and he struggled to lift it from the sand. Howth stepped forward and placed the spearpoint at his companion's chest.

"Yield?" he asked.

Woodsy raised his good hand and yelled. "Yield."

Guards pulled Woodsy from the pit, and he was dragged off towards the healers' tent.

"A brave man knows when to yield before an opponent. He will live to see another day. Perhaps even to fight with you once again on the sand." Malthrain addressed the crowd, his loud booming voice easily quieting the clamour all around. "He fought well and did not concede until all was lost. Sometimes, after we have given our all, it is better to live, better to stay alive so that the next day, we can rise up again, learn our opponent's weaknesses and strike them down."

A cheer went up from the crowd.

After that, more men yielded, but not many.

Dill, Gaz, Keith and Den all won their fights.

Serena finished her opponent with little effort, driving her knife up into his armpit as he took a wild swing at her.

After her contest, as had become the habit with her or Tracks, Malthrain made her stand next to him until the other had their fight.

They did not have long to wait before Tracks's name was called. His opponent was one of the new fighters, not from their group.

The man removed his upper armour and shield. He was all wiry muscle. He paced the sand opposite Tracks like a caged animal. In each hand he held a short, slightly curved sword. As he paced, he rapidly spun the swords around him and called to the crowd. He knew what he was doing.

Tracks took up a defensive stance. Malthrain stepped closer pulling Serena with him.

"This could be interesting, dear." he drawled.

The swordsman stopped his pacing and began to slowly circle around Tracks who took a wide stance and lowered the point of his weapon between them, looking to keep his enemy at a distance.

As the man stepped in, Tracks thrust with his halberd, the sword batted the point and both men spun away from each other to start circling again.

Serena took another step forward, there was something about the way the man had moved. She watched him closely.

Again, the swordsman stepped forward, as Tracks thrust with his halberd, the man allowed the spearpoint to pass behind his back as he spun and cracked Tracks on the head with his elbow before continuing his move, spinning so that both his swords passed just over Tracks's head as he ducked. Both men resumed circling the other, Tracks shaking his head to clear it.

Serena had seen enough. This man had used the Rush. She could see it dancing in his eyes and in the - slightly too fast to be natural- way he moved. She began to worry.

Malthrain leaned his horned head towards her. "You see my dear, you're not the only one who's special."

Slowly, Tracks was worn down. His opponent never made a move which did not land a blow. He used elbows, knees and the pommels of his swords. Serena winced at each hit, knowing that Malthrain would not forget a single one and that each would be dealt to her later.

Tracks began to take risks. He went on the offensive, swinging the halberd around himself, low and high, knowing that if he could land a blow, it would slow his opponent. But this man was experienced, his blades began to slash in. He jumped over the halberd as it passed low and rolled past Tracks, slashing his legs. He spun clear of an overhead swing and red lines appeared across Tracks's back.

The crowd were cheering.

Malthrain watched every blow with a grin behind his horns. Serena inched closer to him. He turned to look at her.

"Whatever you are thinking now, in this moment. Put it from your mind. You know that you are mine. Why don't you have dinner with me tonight? If your friend there survives." he licked his lips and turned back to watch the action.

Serena relaxed her tensed muscles. He was right, now was not the time. But soon, soon she would strike.

Tracks went down. He had overextended on a strike and, losing balance, he was easily pushed to the ground. As he rolled to his back, the swordsman put the points of his blades onto Tracks's chest, close to his shoulder joints. The crowd stilled.

Then one voice shouted "Kill." And the chant started.

The swordsman placed a foot on Tracks's stomach and pushed the blades into his flesh. Serena could see Tracks clench his fists against the pain. "Yield!" he called out.

The swordsman stepped away, leaving his blades quivering slightly, standing straight up, pinning Tracks to the ground.

Guards stepped in with a stretcher to carry Tracks away to the healers.

"Bring him here." Malthrain called.

Once they had laid the stretcher before him, Malthrain pulled the swords free.

"Take off your clothes dear." he said as he turned to face Serena.

Serena was used to this routine by now. She stripped and stood head held high before him.

In the past, he had always commanded others to inflict the wounds. Today was different, there was a fierce look in his eyes as he set to work.

No one watching could have mistaken the malice behind his blows. Not once did he check Tracks to make sure he cut her in the right place. Each blow was given exactly as it had landed during the bout. Twice, the captains had had to step in and help her to stand again.

All too soon she knew what must come next.

"Now dear." he said in his all too well cultured voice. "Take a seat."

He gestured to his chair.

Serena trembled only slightly as she sat down.

He placed the points of the blades against her, pushing her back. The swords began to cut her, she felt a warm trickle of blood run under her left arm and another running over her right breast. He pushed harder. The blades sank into her flesh.

Serena gritted her teeth and stared into his eyes.

Then he pushed the swords forward hard enough that they pierced the back of the chair.

Serena didn't even blink as she slowly breathed in and out. In her mind she was just dipping her toes into the mighty flow of the Rush, without that power she would not survive.

Malthrain turned to the guards. "Take him to the healers, make sure he recovers. I don't want to spoil my favourite game. Bring her and the chair inside. I'll take my dinner now."

PART 48

Malthrain sat at the other end of the table to her, resting his elbows on the smooth boards as he devoured roasted meats, the grease spilling down his chin as he sucked on another bone.

Serena watched his every move, her glare boring into him.

"You know dear, it is rude to stare." He drank heavily from a large glass of dark red wine. "Would you like something?" He waved his hands at the half-eaten platters of food before him on the table.

"Just tell me why I am here?" she hissed.

The pain in her body was a distant thing. She continued to hold the flow of the Rush in her mind, without it she would have passed out before they had even finished moving the chair up to his quarters on The Dread. The bruising ached. The slashes were no longer bleeding as freely but she could feel her back sticking to the surface of the chair as the blood there congealed. The blades still pinned her in place. Her arms were almost useless.

He stood and went over to a basin on a dark wooden cabinet. He washed his hands, towelled them dry and wiped his face. Then he fetched something from behind her.

He placed it across the blades sticking out in front of her.

"You can take this if you wish. Walk out of this room now wearing it and you can walk out of my life." He pulled a chair close and sat leaning towards her.

Serena looked down at the white robe. She could feel the draped material brushing against her skin.

"No."

"Why would you choose to continue with such suffering as you endure? Why fight?" he asked.

"It is who I am."

Malthrain sat back in his chair and idly played with one of his horns.

"You and I are not so different. *It is who I am.*" He leant forward and placed a callused hand upon her knee. "*It is who I am…*" he repeated thoughtfully.

He lifted the robe from the swords and casually threw it to one side.

"And who are you really, my dear?"

She stared hard at him, suddenly all too aware of her vulnerability. Naked, pinned to a chair by swords driven through her body. Blood and bruises covering her flesh.

"Just a simple farm girl who met a stranger and became the greatest fighter you will ever know."

"The greatest..." he repeated. "The greatest. I like that."

He slid his hand up her thigh and gripped her leg hard in his huge hand. "I like that very much."

"And who are you?" she asked not taking her eyes from his.

"Once, I was a man like any other. Skilled perhaps with a sword and with my wits, but I got into difficult circumstances and by chance fell in with the Wizards. That was when things changed for me. That was when they changed me. It was in Eap that I became the man you see before you now. They tried to cage me, so I ran."

He reached out and pushed some stray hair back from her face, "I ended up in Havii. There I fought and found fame. The greatest fighter they had ever seen, the Princes said. They gave me my freedom. 'Make more like you,' they said. 'Bring us the best fighters we have ever seen, and we will make you truly free.' It seems to me that we spend our whole lives serving other men. What would it be like, to be truly free?" He ran his finger softly down her cheek and followed the line of her jaw to her neck.

"You were the greatest fighter?" she whispered.

"It is who I am." He said as his finger traced its way down her neck and over her chest, circling her nipples.

"It is who we are." Serena tried to lean her head forward.

"You have yet to prove that." His hand grasped her breast painfully as he slid his other further up her thigh.

"No woman has ever won in the Princes' arena. That is not to say that some have not tried. What makes you think that you are any different?"

"It is who I am!"

Humour and anger warred across his monstrous face as he spoke, "Perhaps it is."

Serena relaxed. It didn't matter what he did to her. She knew she had him. She had found his weakness and she would exploit it, she believed that she would be able to use him to do what needed to be done. Just not today.

He stood and kicked back his chair, knocking it to the floor. "Guards. Take her to the healers."

PART 49

Tracks lay in the bed next to hers. His wounds had been stitched and dressed and they had given him something to make him sleep.

"You may want to bite this." A woman in white said offering a small length of wood wrapped in leather. From the look of it many had used it before, indentations from teeth were etched all along its length. Serena opened her mouth and bit down.

They lowered her chair so she was lying back. Guards hovered in the background nervously.

The woman who had spoken before leant down and whispered to her in a friendly voice, "Try to hold still. You will probably pass out for a while. I will work quickly to free you and get you on the bed so that I can cover you and the men will stop their stares."

Serena nodded.

The woman spoke quickly to the other slaves to be ready to move her. Then she grasped the handle of one of the swords and put her other hand on Serena's shoulder. She pulled hard and Serena bit into the stick as the blade pulled free. One of the other slaves put her hand over the wound trying to stop the flow of blood that welled out.

The kind woman moved to Serena's other side. This time the blade did not come free easily. The pain slammed through Serena as she bit down hard. The Rush poured from her as she lost consciousness.

When she awoke, the woman was standing by her, washing her with a wet rag. Serena lay on her side, a rough blanket covered her to the waist.

"Good, you're awake. I have almost finished cleaning you. The wounds on your back were bad. When we moved you from the chair, they tore open. I have stitched all your cuts as well as I can. In the morning I will need to inspect the damage to your arms, you may lose full use of one or both, it is too early to say."

Serena was surprised by how coarse her voice was as she asked, "Have the guards gone?"

"Yes, they leave us alone in here. They don't like to see the wounded." The woman had a nice smile. She looked to be a little younger than Serena's mother. She wore her hair short, cropped just above her ears which accentuated her long, elegant neck.

"My clothes?" Serena asked.

"I do not know. They did not bring them." The woman finished wiping away the blood and grime from Serena's arms and she moved away with the bowl and cloth. She soon returned and helped Serena to turn onto her back and sit up against some cushions.

"What is your role here?"

"I do whatever any freeman tells me to do." The woman looked away.

"Are you happy about that?"

The woman looked around and leant close to Serena's ear. "Be careful what you ask. There are always those who would pass on your words to others who are less kind."

Serena tried to grasp the woman's arm, but her hands felt numb, and pain jolted through her arms.

As she winced, the woman said, "Try to lie still. You should be able to move in a few days, but it is more than likely that by then you will be wearing the white and you will see for yourself whether it makes you happy."

"Who were you before?" Serena asked.

"I was and am a Stone Druid. I travelled to trade in Stonewood wares from my homelands in Kentai. We did not know that Havii were on the move again and the Princes had broken the agreements. That was a few moons ago. Since then, I have known a few masters. I have been lucky that I have skills which make me valuable. For several weeks now I have worked for Malthrain. Being in the tents keeps me sheltered from the nastiest of the men. But these times have not been kind. The rape is the worst of it, but it is better here than it was before, in the city, passed from man to man." The

Stone Druid spoke with a deep sense of bitterness and regret.

Serena could see the anger, sadness, and frustration in the woman's eyes. "It is for people like you that I fight. I would see that Havii burns, and all women are free."

The woman looked at her doubtfully. "How would you do that."

"I will be the greatest fighter they have ever seen. I will raise an army of free men and women behind me and burn their city to the ground."

"I like your fighting spirit, but I have my doubts that you will even be able to hold a weapon again, let alone fight."

"I am Serena. What is your name?"

"Coshelle."

"Well, Coshelle. If you bring a few more healers over, then I will show you that I mean every word I say." Serena held the woman's gaze for a long moment.

"You have my curiosity now Serena. I will give you this chance." Coshelle moved off and Serena relaxed back into her pillows. She had no idea if this would work or if she would end up being a broken plaything for the men. But she knew she had to try. The fight had to start somewhere.

Good to her word Coshelle returned with five other healers, all wearing the white.

"Coshelle, what do you know of the Rush?"

"It is rare in the world, more so than it used to be. Most who use it do so to change small things about themselves, some, like the Shadow Fighters of Kentai use it to enhance their bodies, making them faster, stronger or able to fight past exhaustion. The Wizards use it in many ways, they study the Rush and manipulate it to change the world around them. We Stone Druids use the Rush to shape the stone wood and to help the plants to grow. I have seen the spark of the power in your eyes. Why do you ask?"

The healer leant close as Serena whispered weakly, "I intend to use the Rush now. I would like to use you and your companions to help me. Would that be alright with you?"

"No one in Havii asks, they just take. Thank you for asking

Serena." Coshelle looked to the other slaves who nodded their agreement. "Do what you must, and we will help."

Serena took a deep breath and reached for the Rush. She let it flow over her. She fed it her need. She fell into the torrent and let it sweep her away.

Then she reached out and pulled more in. She reached outside of her stream and found others which she drew into her own. She flailed around feeling like a leaf cast over a waterfall being smashed by the force of it. Then she turned and she found the right direction. The surging flow sped around her, but it no longer controlled her. She began to shape it, a little at a time.

When she opened her eyes again, Coshelle was leaning heavily against the side of her bed. The slaves were on their knees. Serena felt energised. Her pain was gone. She knew that her wounds had healed.

Around the tent others in their cots began to stir.

"Serena. I am yours." Coshelle placed a hand over Serena's heart. "The druid law handed down over the last thousand years speaks of power like this. I believed it to be fairy tales. Now, I swear myself to you. Teach me to use the Rush in this way."

"I do not know how I do it. But I would gladly try to help you and would be thankful for your help. First, we need to stop these men in here from running out into the camp and talking."

PART 50

Serena left the tent at first light.

It had taken all night, but in the end she, Tracks and Coshelle had convinced the other fighters to stay in the tent and feign injury. She was not completely sure how, but in the process of healing herself she had reached further out and healed all the others as well. Although she was fine, the men were affected to a lesser extent. Many of their wounds had healed, but not all and some only partially. All, however, were better than they should have been.

It had taken much explaining for them to understand that it was by her hand and even more to ensure they would stay silent. For now, most had agreed to help her if she called upon them. Coshelle and Tracks were to stay in the healers' tent and make sure that they all complied.

For her own part, Serena was not going to hide. Her rapid recovery from injury would just add to the myth beginning to grow around her. Already she led the 'Untouchables', she intended to make sure everyone saw her today. Let Malthrain hear how she was not beaten by his actions. Tonight, let him see that she was indeed the greatest fighter he would ever see.

She met up with her group in their usual area. She was surprised to see that Girau and the other freemen had joined them.

"You look well. How…" Den began to ask.

"I'll explain another time. Today we train hard. I hope you are all up for this." She looked around at their quizzical expressions. "You all know that in the camp they are calling us the Untouchables. We should use that reputation. Show them we earned it."

"You talk like you are our captain. You are not." One of Girau's companions stood up to her.

"And you talk like a slave serving another master. You have seen us fight. You have seen me fight. You have heard the stories about me. I intend to see that those who fight with me win." she paused and scanned all their faces. Then she walked up to the man who had questioned her. "Do you want to win?"

"Yes." he said staring down at her.

"Then I am your captain. I have stayed quiet for too long. I do not wish to be a slave to other men. I choose to be free, and I believe that all of you want to be free. Follow me and we will make it happen. Let any man who stands before us in the sand quiver with fear to be facing an Untouchable." The men all around her nodded their agreement.

Serena slowly turned around, she walked to each man in turn and offered her arm. Some hesitated at first, but all of them looked at the fierce determination in her eyes, each weighed the rumours and tales in camp and the undisputable fact she stood before them unharmed and strong when she should be lying in bed wounded. All of them shook, the agreement had been made. They were hers.

She began the Movements. They all followed.

Over the morning meal they talked tactics.

What was the best way to defend against a sword? How to press the advantage against a taller opponent?

To begin with it was mostly Serena asking the questions of the more experienced fighters. Then the others started to ask questions, based upon the fights they had been part of or that they had watched.

Serena sat back and listened. They were learning.

When Sir and the guards arrived to begin training, he handed her armour to her. She thanked him and asked him if he could keep it safe for her.

"You will need it today." He told her. "I don't know how you are healed after last night, but others will notice. From what I heard coming over here, they already have. They will come for you. You will need it."

"Sir could you please look after it for me? If I survive the day, then I will gladly take it back and wear it once again. You are my real armour, you and your guards. It is your job to protect us, is it not?" She paused and for a moment it looked like he would object but she carried on.

"You train us. You stop us from running away. You keep peace in camp." She looked away from Sir to the guards.

"You win bets on us at the pits. You want to protect that investment. If you look after us, we will fight and win. You will get richer. Men will buy you drinks to hear you tell tales about the Untouchables and their brave guards who trained them to be the best. We do not want to run away, we do not want to wear the white, we will wear red. If you protect us, then we will paint the sand red with the blood of our opponents. You will be known as the ones who trained the Untouchables. You will be famous."

"You may be right girl. But you are still mine and it is time to train." Sir walked over to a heavy sack which the guards had carried over. "You will need to be versatile in the pits. All of you are competent with the halberd. Now you should learn to fight with other weapons. By getting to know them you will get to know their strengths and weaknesses. By using them you will learn the best ways to face them. Line up. Let's begin."

When they broke for lunch, Sir spoke with the guards before leaving to make his reports. They stayed close to Serena keeping a wary eye on her, but also on any men who approached too close to the group.

Brokenose came and sat with her. "You know you have a very special way of making friends."

"Someone needed to shake the camp up a bit. I don't know about you, but I don't want to spend all my time looking over my shoulder for trouble. We might not like having the guards close but at least now we can relax a little."

"If you didn't paint targets on our backs with everything you do then we wouldn't have to watch for trouble." Brokenose moved closer to talk more privately. "What are you planning?"

"All I'm doing is trying to make enough noise that everyone will be watching me. If they are watching me, they won't be watching you and the others. They will make mistakes. I just hope that we can begin to carve out our own little piece of the world. You and the others keep listening, gather information on the guards, the other fighters, find out what you can about The Dread. When will we be going to Havii? What will be our route? What will the pits in Havii be like? The more information we have the better prepared we will be."

"Alright Serena. You just stay safe and try to spring a few less surprises on us. When Malthrain carted you off last night I thought that was that, yet here you are. You're a tough little bitch."

"You're pretty tough yourself Brokenose."

"I wish you'd stop calling me that."

"If the shoe fits..."

★★★

They came for her during the afternoon.

Serena had just finished a practice bout against Keith. He had used a sword and shield. She had just her fists. She had shown how the Movements they all practiced each morning could be used to avoid his weapons and to find gaps in his defences. Brokenose and Girau had laughed hard every time she had smacked him on the arse before dodging away once again.

As she went to fetch a cup of water from one of the barrels spaced out around the yard, the guards who had been watching were quickly attacked and silenced as a group of men moved in to surround her.

'So much for the guards,' she thought as she turned to face the newcomers. The others were about twenty metres away. So far, they had not noticed what had happened as they were watching the next practice bout between Den and Hanlan.

The would-be assassins wasted no time, they came straight for her, knives held ready, some already slick with the blood of the guards.

So be it.

Serena pulled over the water barrel and pushed it towards the nearest men. The water sloshed across the floor turning the ground to mud.

She batted the blade away from the first man but allowed him to pull her to the ground. They rolled fighting for dominance and Serena came out on top. She ignored his hands grasping and tearing at her clothing. With all the force of the Rush flowing through her she slammed her palm into his head between his eyes and his skull exploded with the force. She grabbed handfuls of mud and gore and began wiping it across her face, arms and through her hair.

The other men had hesitated upon seeing her taken down. They came at her again now, with renewed vigour as she spun low taking the legs out from under a burly older fighter. As he hit the ground, she rammed an elbow into his throat crushing his windpipe.

She pumped speed and strength into herself, allowing the Rush to wash her in its tempestuous waters.

Men began to scream as she broke bones. She did not waste time taking the fight to them but let them come at her. Each was allowed one chance to strike. None were fast enough. Once their chance was over, Serena was relentless. She had killed the first man for show. She now aimed to harm. Badly. Over and over.

Six men lay screaming in the mud, another lay choking for breath and one lay dead. The last three men stopped short and dropped their weapons holding their arms up, "We yield." The youngest shouted desperately.

By now the others had heard the commotion and run up behind the men.

Serena paced back and forth, before them all, fighting for control of the Rush. She bared her teeth and roared her fury and the men dropped to their knees as her friends began to surround them and hold them.

Guards from further off were running to quell the fighting.

"Stop!" Serena yelled. She stood the barrel back up so that she could climb upon it and speak to the growing crowd.

"No one touch these men. They thought to attack me. They thought to weaken Malthrain's fighters by breaking the rules and fighting outside of the pits. Let him come and judge what should be done. If any man makes a move to help these men, I will see it as disloyalty to Malthrain. Disloyalty will result in being stripped, beaten and given the white." She stood tall upon her perch, her face, hair and clothing covered in mud and blood looking like a wild animal just the whites of her eyes and her teeth showing through the grime.

"If any dare approach, I will attack, and they will lose. Fetch Malthrain."

The Untouchables began to form a perimeter around her. The men on the floor continued to scream, many had bone sticking out of their flesh from the force of the blows she had inflicted upon them.

Soon a commotion approached through the crowd. First soldiers and then the captains, including Sir, appeared. They fanned out to surround Serena and her group. Then came Malthrain.

He walked tall, surveying all around him. He scanned the carnage scattered around the floor and then raised his eyes to meet hers.

"My dear, you should get washed. You look like a beast."

Brokenose repeated his word. "Beast."

Then the Untouchables took it up as a low chant as they faced the guards, unmoving. "Beast. Beast. Beast!"

Then they fell silent.

"Well, Malthrain. If you are inviting me for another exquisite dinner, then I shall make sure I am bathed and perfumed ready for your pleasure. But first, I ask a favour. You set the rules. Fighting is for the pits." she paused and looked at him waiting.

He nodded his horned head.

"These men sought to kill me. They were perhaps angry that I had found favour with you, as your greatest fighter. They tried to kill me outside of the pits, outside of your rules. *Your, rules.* Your punishment. How should these men pay for their crimes?" Serena jumped down from the barrel and strode towards Malthrain, ignoring the cries of pain around her.

"Those who break my rules are stripped, beaten and given the white." He waved to the guards who quickly moved in to take the three men on their knees away.

"Those men who have already taken the beating." He gestured at the ones on the floor, "They have a choice. They can crawl their way to the healers and take the white or die where they lie. They are not worthy of earning their freedom in the pits." he spoke loudly to the crowd which had gathered all around. "Save your energy for the pits, train hard, and you will earn your freedom. If any man feels wronged, he may speak to his captain and petition to settle his arguments on the sand of the pit. If you feel hatred for this woman, you can fight her one on one. If you feel that someone has done you wrong, you can face them one on one in the pit."

He strode forward and punched Serena hard in the face. She fell backwards into the mud. "If anyone feels they can take me in the pits they are welcome to try!"

Malthrain looked down at her as she struggled to get up again. Then he turned and strode away, guards and captains forming up around him.

Sir marched over and faced the crowd. "You heard. Train hard. Afternoon session starts now. Everyone back to your sections."

Guards were shouting at the men and the crowd began to break up.

"I don't know what you are playing at, but you had better win all your fights. You have made it hard for all of us." Sir spoke down at Serena as she rubbed her jaw.

"This only happened because your guards were not up to the job. Be thankful I did not tell Malthrain how lax you had been in your duty. I suppose I can tell him later if you'd like." She watched his face grow pale. "If you want us fit and strong then you would do well to see we get extra rations and that we all get some rest time during training so that we can prove once and for all that you are the best trainer of fighters there is in this camp. That is what I really want to report to Malthrain."

Sir looked relieved and nodded at this. "I'll see to it and double the guard."

"No need. I don't think anyone will have the appetite for a fight outside the pits now." Serena held out her arm. "We just want to be the best Sir. Will you help us to be the greatest fighters?"

Sir reached out and shook her arm.

"You should get washed up. You look terrible."

"I will Sir. I think I'll have my armour back now as well."

PART 51: MESSENGER WITH A GUN

Findo wondered how much longer this would go on for, as Lord Portreath continued his lecture.

"As you can see my friend, we have plenty of shit on this island. Guano from the sea birds all over the cliffs, guano in the caves from the bats. You could say that we have more shit on this island than we can use. We have known for years that it makes a fantastic fertiliser and that, by using it in the fields, we have increased our yields and can even force crops to fruit twice in a season."

Findo tried to stifle a yawn.

"It was after some floods a few years back that we discovered that, if washed in water and allowed to crystalise, you could harvest a more concentrated version of shit. My advisers like to call it Saltpetre, but I call it what it is, concentrated shit. Anyway…" the Lord continued to drone on as they walked through the cave complex.

Findo's eyes wandered to the Lady Portreath. She was not as stunningly beautiful as Lady Grey or Lady Shin from Singhigh, but she had a way about her. She did not fuss. Just got on with things in an efficient manner.

"So, when we discovered that you could mix these crystals with a little ground Charcoal and Sulphur to create an explosive charge, well that was when the inventors got really excited." Lord Portreath led them out of the cave and onto a windswept, open plain overlooking the sea at the top of the cliffs to the north of the city.

"It has taken a few years for us to perfect the mixture, and there have been many accidents along the way, but I think that I have a dowery that the King will not be able to turn down. If he takes my daughter's hand in marriage, I promise to change his armies forever. Behold the Ry-fell." Lord Portreath gestured to a group of men standing behind a large, ornate wooden table.

The men were soldiers dressed in their best uniforms. One of them came over and handed a strange contraption to Findo.

It was a wooden branch with a long metal tube attached to one side. The wood widened out at one end and went beyond the tube which itself ended and was sealed off with a bizarre mechanism. Findo turned the device around and peered down the tube trying to see if there was anything inside. The soldier reached over and took the object back.

"I wouldn't do that if I were you sir." he said before walking back to the table.

The other soldiers were pushing things into the tubes on other Ry-fells.

Lord Portreath started to talk again, "By mixing the powders in the correct way and adding in a projectile, adviser Ry made quite the discovery. Watch now. Oh, you might want to cover your ears."

The lord put his fingers in his ears and nodded to the soldiers. One of them released a bird to fly off into the air. The others put the Ry-fells to their shoulders and pointed them in the direction of the bird. Findo nearly jumped out of his skin at the loud explosive reports as the Ry-fells all fired and a cloud of smoke rose into the air. Lady Portreath pointed up and Findo watched as the bird fell lifeless to the ground several hundred metres away.

'Oakhands The Pirate would love these.' he thought to himself.

Over the next few hours, Findo asked many questions. He watched several more demonstrations and he fired a Ry-fell himself.

Eventually Lord Portreath led him back through the caves towards the eyrie and Gisselle.

"I hope I have done enough here son to convince you that my daughter would be the King's best choice. He will see the worth of this new weapon. I give this as a gift to you," The Lord handed Findo a long package wrapped in oiled cloth.

"And these." He also gave Findo three small pouches which Findo knew contained the black powder and shot needed to fire the weapon.

Lastly, he handed Findo a message tube.

"I thank you for the gift my Lord and I take this from you as it was sealed before me. May the words contained within be known to be true, until my duty is complete." Findo nodded to Lady Portreath and then shook arms with the Lord before he climbed upwards to the ceiling rings and loaded his new Ry-fell behind the saddle on Gisselle's back.

He mounted up and gave a quick wave to the Lord and Lady below before he nudged Gisselle gently in the ribs and she took flight. At last, he was headed home. He wondered what had been happening in the East, how Serena was doing on her quest and whether he could convince The Degan to let him travel towards Havii.

PART 52: MESSENGERS' REPORTS.

"One of them is lying. They must be. Their accounts are completely opposed to each other." The Degan was unsettled and angry. He did not like it when the men who served under him made mistakes. He took it personally, as though it was his fault. But then he always had. For as long as the Chancellor had known him, it had been his way.

"One of them says that they saw an army marching south. The other that there is an army marching north. We need to trip them up on the details. Perhaps it is time to take them before the King. Maybe he can intimidate the answers out of them where we have failed." The Chancellor stood up and spoke quickly to one of his staff. The man ran off to prepare their way.

"We need to be sure. One minute we have a peace deal between Splitt and Holdon and the next thing we know is that armies are marching and there will be war. They are two of my best Messengers and normally I would never doubt either of their reports. The problem is they cannot both be right." The Degan frowned deeply. "I thought that by coming here, you would be able to tickle out the truth."

"Old friend, things are never simple for leaders of men. You should have learned that over the years. You did the right thing coming to me with this. Perhaps if we put them both in the same room, with the pressure of having yourself, as their direct superior, myself, as the advisor of the King and the King himself, cracks may begin to show in their stories." The Chancellor gathered his papers and led The Degan out into the corridor.

Justice and Bartholemew stood outside, flanked by guards.

The Chancellor led them to the waiting chamber.

The Degan watched the two young Messengers closely. The bright light of a thousand candles reflected off their faces. Neither seemed more nervous than he should. Neither of their faces revealed a lie. They were not struck down by some unknown force because they had murder in their hearts. They were just two men of the Messenger service, trained to fly, trained to be loyal to the service and to the King. Yet The Degan knew they could not both be telling the truth. He was glad that the Chancellor had decided to take this to the top man. That he had spared the time to deal with this.

Two guides came. One, led them through The Gauntlet. The other followed behind, watching Justice and Bartholemew as if he expected them to turn into vipers. If either man made a false move, that guide would end his life without hesitation. The Degan hoped it would not come to that.

The King's meeting room was not large. It was not gilded or ornate. It was fit for purpose, like the man himself.

The rectangular room was dominated by a large wooden table. Beside the table were comfortable chairs. Along the walls, more chairs were lined up. The walls themselves were not covered in beautiful works of art, there were no shelves of books. There were two doors, both on the same wall. The short walls at either end held fireplaces, though it was a rare cold year when they were needed. The wall opposite the doors was painted floor to ceiling with a map of the world. The Degan loved that map. It made him dream of travel and exploration, he often wished he could spend longer in here just studying that map.

They sat Justice and Bartholomew at the table below the map. Between them stood one of the guides. The Chancellor and The Degan sat opposite them with an empty chair between them.

The King walked in from his apartments with the other guide.

"No need to get up. After all I am only going to come and sit with you all." the King said happily as he marched over to take his seat. The others all stopped trying to stand and relaxed back into their chairs.

"How can I help?" The King seemed in good cheer.

The Degan began, "Sire, these Messengers were the ones sent to carry your messages to Holdon and to Splitt along with the new peace accords. They have returned with troubling news. You should listen to their accounts."

"Interesting. What are your names men?" The King leant forward and clasped his hands on the table.

"Justice, Sire."

"Bartholemew."

"Alright then why don't you tell me your tale Bartholemew." The King waved for the messenger to begin.

"Well Sire, for a while we flew West together over the Scraggs and then over the barren lands and north along the Great Divide. Just south of Mount Ghastom, we parted ways. I flew over the high passes. As I descended and turned to head south towards Splitt, I saw smoke rising from a small town. I flew over and could see that the town had been burned down. I saw no signs of people, no armies and no townsfolk fleeing."

"Did you not think that strange?" the King asked.

"Of course, Sire. I thought it best to head to Splitt with all haste and report what I had seen. Perhaps they could have helped save the town." Bartholomew hesitated.

"Carry on now. Tell it all." The Degan encouraged.

"Perhaps I should have spent more time investigating. Findo told us before we left that we should find out all we could. I doubted him and wanted to get my message delivered and tell the city what had happened in this town. As I circled south and began to fly for Splitt, I did think I noticed movement in the hills to the north, but I did not take time to investigate." He stopped and licked his lips. "Could I get a drink of water please. All this talking is making my mouth dry, and I am a little nervous if I'm honest."

The King stood and walked to the far end of the table. "Carry on with your story." He waved through the doorway to his apartments and then walked back and sat down as Bartholemew continued.

"In the forests near the city of Splitt, there was much activity. Trees were being felled and areas had been cleared. It looked as though defences were being prepared and trenches dug."

A guide carried a tray with a jug and several cups into the room and set it down in front of the King, before hurrying away.

"So, you're saying that Splitt were preparing for an attack?" The King poured a cup of water and offered it to Bartholemew.

"Thank you Sire," The Messenger took the cup from the King and had a few sips before continuing. "Exactly that. When I approached the city, it was in turmoil. People moving around the streets, soldiers marching everywhere. I headed straight to the roost under the arched bridge and was met there by Cxithh, Lord Wilhelm's senior advisor. He took me straight to the palace. What a wonderous building that is."

"Yes, yes. We all know of the beauty of Splitt and the glory of the artisans. What can you tell me of the war? Did Holdon not hold to the treaties?" The King sat back in his chair as The Degan and Chancellor shared a look. They had heard this story before.

"Sire. I met with Lord Wilhelm and gave him the message and his copies of the peace accords. He read your words right there and he and Cxithh discussed them briefly. I was then given a tour of the Hall of Art whilst a reply was written, which I gave to The Degan on my return."

The Chancellor handed a sheet of paper from his file for the King to read.

I sincerely regret that it is too late for peace. We are besieged.

Holdon has not followed the agreements made. They have attacked deep into our territory. Your Messenger has seen the destruction of our towns with his own eyes. We will retreat and hold fast for as long as we can, but I beseech you, as my King and as the ruler of these lands to send armies to defend us.

I only hope that it is not too late.

With hope.

Lord Wilhelm

"What else did you see or hear lad?" The King looked troubled.

"Well, Lord Wilhelm left, because he was busy preparing for his war council, setting defences set up and all. Cxithh took me to his apartments and made sure I had a good meal so that I could fly here with all haste. I took the fastest route back. On the way, I saw a couple of burned and deserted villages as I passed over the Great Divide but no signs of armies."

"Did you see signs of their passing. An army on the march leaves scars across the landscape." the King pressed.

"I cannot be certain, but I believe I saw long trails of broken ground running south from the North Sire. It could well have been signs of an army passing."

"Thank you. May your words be always true." The King looked again at the letter and pondered Bartholemew's words.

When next he spoke, it was to The Degan and Chancellor. "If this is true then we need to contact the generals and mobilise our forces."

"I think you had best hear what the other Messenger has to report first, Sire." the Chancellor pointed out.

The King turned to Justice. "Make your report. Is it true that the Guilds have broken the peace?"

Justice leant forward. As he did, the guide standing next to him shifted his weight reminding the Messenger of his presence.

"Sire. My report begins the same as Bartholomew's. From Mount Ghastom I flew North. I followed a circuitous route over and along the mountains. Findo had seemed really worried about us making sure we looked for signs of trouble. Well, let me tell you, he was right. The very first mountain pass I flew through contained an army. They weren't wearing any colours, so I didn't know if they were from Splitt or from the North. Gave me a right scare they did. I had to get Misty, my Kystraal, to fly higher as I was worried we would be spotted. Every valley we flew over seemed to contain more soldiers. All holding the passes." He looked to The Degan who smiled back encouragingly, and he carried on.

"I decided to cut across the farmlands and over the bay to approach Holdon City. The whole land was occupied by an immense army. Just sitting there, tents set up all across the land."

"Could you tell which way they were going? North or South." The King leaned forward.

"I could not. The land all around was darkened and the soldiers were not moving. The army was like a giant beast resting in place." He took a breath to steady himself before he continued.

"I flew down into the city and Misty settled into their roost. All the Guild masters met me in the meeting rooms there. They told me that the army had arrived a few days before and set up camp. They had not been able to send out word as all the land around the city was held by the enemy, cutting them off completely. Sire, they were under siege. The army does not even need to attack them, they will eventually just be starved out. The Guild masters told me that the city was bursting with refugees from the surrounding lands and that if you did not send help soon, they will begin to starve. They gave me a message for you."

The Chancellor shuffled through his papers and handed one to the King who read it solemnly.

"You are telling me that Splitt is attacking Holdon." The king pointed at Justice who nodded.

"And you are telling me that Holdon are attacking Splitt, right?" Bartholomew nodded.

"Well one of you is lying. One of you is feeding me false information. One of you has broken his oath." The King stared angrily at the two young Messengers.

Both Justice and Bartholomew began to speak at the same time, each claiming the other was wrong.

The guide placed a hand on each of their shoulders and they quieted.

"Justice, why should I trust what Bartholomew says?" The

King asked.

Justice considered the question briefly. "Sire, he has been my friend for a long time. I would trust him with my life. But I know what I have seen. I tell you the truth. If he says that he saw what he says he saw, then I believe him as well."

"But how can that be? How could both lands be attacking each other in this way? It makes no sense." The King beat his fist in his palm.

"I can only tell you what I have seen to the best of my abilities. If that is wrong, then I apologise Sire."

The King turned his attention to Bartholomew. "Is your friend a liar?"

"He must be. I have known him for years and he had always seemed good before. But after seeing the destruction of that town and those villages and the panic in the people of Splitt. I know he must be lying because I tell the truth."

The King seemed to be done asking questions, he turned to The Degan. "What say you?"

"This is a mess. I have heard their tales three times now and neither of them has changed their story. The details are fixed. I have no idea who to believe and am ashamed that men in my service have brought false reports before you." The Degan looked away, embarrassment flushing his cheeks.

"Sire, how should we proceed?" the Chancellor asked.

"I know just the thing." The King stood and went to the doorway again. He spoke quietly with the guide there and then came back over and sat down.

The guide he had spoken to went around the table to stand beside Justice.

"I am sorry." The King said to the young Messenger.

The guide grasped Justice and hauled him from his chair, dragging him around the room and out of the door. The other guide, who stood next to Bartholomew, stepped behind him and placed a hand on each of his shoulders keeping him from standing.

Then the screams began.

The King sat calmly watching Bartholomew.

The Degan gripped the table edge like he was hanging from a cliff, turning his face away at each new and horrific cry.

The Chancellor poured them all a cup of water and sat back slowly sipping from his.

The cries stopped.

"Hopefully, we will have no reason to question you in this way, Bartholomew." The King turned his head as the guide returned to the room and whispered in his ear.

"Continue." He said to the guide who walked calmly back out of the room.

This time the cries were more muted but just as horrifying to hear.

The Chancellor placed his cup back down.

"Is this going to take long?" He said stifling a yawn.

The cries cut off in a horrible gurgle.

The guide came back and whispered to the King once again and then stood behind the King.

"It seems your friend will not change his story. I'm afraid it is your turn."

"No. No. You can't. It's not right. You can't torture me. I serve you. I'm loyal. I tell you the truth. Please!" Bartholomew struggled in his chair but the guide behind him held him still.

The Degan looked down at his white knuckles. He couldn't believe this was happening. The King was a good ruler not a torturer. He looked at Bartholemew.

"Please Bartholomew. If you have anything to say do so now. Tell us the truth." The Degan pleaded as he watched his young Messenger go limp. The flesh on his face seemed to pale and his head hung loose.

"Don't tell me he's passed out." The Chancellor stood and made to move around the table.

He stopped as a voice like honey on fine silk spoke out.

"You should send your armies now. If you wait, it will be too late." Bartholomew raised his head. His skin was grey. The guide let go of him as if his hands were burning.

The King met Batholomew's eyes which were now a

sickly, bloodshot yellow. "I hope that one day I can sit in this room and rule in your place." The smooth voice spoke from the throat of Bartholomew.

The King demanded, "Who are you?"

"My name is Cxithh. The man who will kill you, goodbye." Bartholomew raised his arm towards the King fist clenched pointing at his face.

Then the skin of his knuckles began to tear as bone protruded, a shaft extended outwards, growing quickly, straight at the King.

The guide moved fast, but the Chancellor was faster. He pushed the King back and put himself in the way as the bone continued to grow rapidly and pierced his chest, throwing him backwards and pinning him to the wall. The guide chopped his arm down and shattered through the monstrous bone cutting its connection to Bartholomew, who collapsed forward onto the table, dead, his body shrivelled to a mummified husk.

The Degan helped the King up from the floor and then went to his old friend the Chancellor.

"I thought you couldn't use the Rush anymore."

The Chancellor looked pale but was alive enough to joke, "I lied. Pull this out of me and call a healer. I feel a little faint."

From the doorway to the King's apartments, Justice ran in. "Did the plan work? Did he confess?"

The Degan turned to him. "No lad, he was merely a puppet. Turned from good by evil men. Now follow the guide and fetch a healer. Then go to the tower and gather the Messengers. We are going to be busy. We are going to war."

PART 53

Serena expected the evening to go badly.

Tracks and Woodsy were still in the healers' tent, hopefully carrying on the ruse that they were still injured and keeping the other fighters there under control.

Now the Untouchables needed to be exactly that.

There was a buzz around the pits. A sense of excitement. Every man there had proven his worth. Every man had some belief that they could win.

Some held grudges and Malthrain had given them a way to extract their petty vengeance by allowing them to petition for whom they were to face. Serena was prepared to have a busy night.

She and her men had finished training early. Sir allowed them some rest time and they had spent it lounging around their cells in the Gojon. Dill had handed out some extra rations which he, Gaz and Hanlan had acquired through their betting system. Serena was thankful for it; she had consumed most of her reserves using the Rush and felt certain she was going to have to dip further into that tank tonight.

She waited until the last possible minute before gathering the Untouchables around her. "Tonight, is the night boys. Let's put on a show. Make any man you face on the sand regret the day he did so. Watch each other's backs. Expect trouble. The guards should keep us safe, but they can't have eyes everywhere. Malthrain may seek to separate us or to cause us trouble, so be on the lookout but don't stand in his way. I'll deal with him if it comes to it." She checked her armour straps and her weapons then led them across the square to the crowds by the pits.

The others formed up behind her. When they reached the crowd, men noticed them and cleared the way. She marched up to their usual position by the main pit. Gaz quickly set up a table and improvised chalk board as Dill began calling that the shop was open for bets.

It was not long before Malthrain and the captains came out

of the belly of The Dread and took up their places on the other side of the pit.

Malthrain spoke to the crowd and then the fights began.

Each time one of the Untouchables were called to the sand the first thing they did was ask their opponent to yield. None did, but they made the offer.

Serena was surprised that there were no petitioned matches. No one had laid down a challenge. Each pair of names was drawn from the chest in the usual way, Malthrain announcing them to the crowd.

Serena had an easy match but, afterwards, was not called to stand and strip before the crowd. She returned to the others in confusion.

"I don't like this. It's not what I expected. Why has no one challenged us?" she said to Keith.

"I expect that after your show this morning they are just scared. Perhaps some will try to petition for one of us, seeing us as easier targets." he replied uneasily.

None of the fighters returned to their cells to rest after their bouts. Only the injured were carried away. The fights were hard and bloody. The support to the fighters given wholeheartedly. This was their lives now. To fight in these pits. Everyone seemed committed to this new life.

Then it was done. The last fight finished. There were no more names in the chest.

Malthrain sat casually in his chair the whole crowd watching him, waiting.

Slowly he raised his hand. The crowd quieted.

"You have all fought well. You have trained hard and proven your worth on the sand. Some of you have become exceptional. You shall be rewarded. Some of you have yet to shine, your time will come. Tomorrow we will leave this place to head for the city of the Princes. The journey will be hard, but so are you. I will leave at first light to prepare our way. My captains will see to you, under the command of Colthar. Take this opportunity to gather your strength for the fights to come." He stood and began to pace before them.

"I ask of you only one thing. That you are loyal to me. I have treated you fairly, given you shelter, food and healing. Some of you are freemen and possess your own slaves. If you follow my rules, then I will look after you. Soon we will stand at the pleasure of the Princes, and they shall witness our strength,"

There was the noise of a commotion from The Dread as slaves in white carried large casks and placed them down on the sand beside Malthrain before scurrying back inside.

He smacked one of his great fists down on the top of one of the casks, cracking the top open and lowered a cup down into it. He then drank the cupful down in one. "I drink to you all and look forward to seeing you once again in Havii. Tonight, you may drink and have a good time. Tomorrow you march to meet your destiny!"

PART 54

The caravan wound its way through the low undulating hills of The Plains. The countryside reminded Serena of home, only here the weather was warmer, the grass grew shorter and there were more yellows and browns in the colours of the land.

Guards roamed around them riding the strange lizard creatures she had learned were a kind of Scalthryn, bred for their size and ease of training. Colthar led the line, the red of his cap and darkness of his skin easily identifying him.

That morning The Dread had sailed out of camp at first light. The fighters, slaves and guards who had lived for the last few weeks in the square had packed their meagre possessions and formed up to march. They had walked through the empty and broken town of Heartsnest until they met Colthar, his mounted guards and the waggons of the caravan.

It had seemed strange passing through the town. In the square, they had been shut off from the outside world, unaware of what was happening around them. The slavers had picked the town bare. Now it stood empty. No people, no animals and no future. Everything of any value at all had been stripped away and carted off. They were the last people who would ever remember the small trading town by the river. It would not take long for the grass of the Plains to reclaim the town.

Now the waggons of the caravan were spread out in a long line. Those near the front were for the guards. Immediately behind these, the waggons were packed with slaves wearing white, while the ones behind those carried the supplies and the healers. The rest of the train was made up of flatbed waggons in which the fighters took it in turns to rest. Anyone not resting was marching alongside.

Serena was reminded of her journey with Bandolas when Poppy and Jess had hauled them across the Everplain. She was comforted by the presence of the oxen drawing the waggons and made time to help corral and bush them down each evening.

Before dawn each day, the Untouchables went through the Movements. Tracks and Woodsy had joined them on the first day returning from the healers, with them came seven new allies, fighters who had been healed by Serena that night in the tent. By the third morning, others had joined them. Geoff and Captain Bartham brought several more of the surviving sailors and some of the men Girau and Brokenose had befriended. The Untouchables now numbered around thirty men.

The guards kept a close eye on them. The other fighters steered clear.

During the day, as they walked, Serena would run forward and speak with Coshelle and the other healers ensuring they were safe. Each evening, Sir would come to them during dinner to 'check on his great fighters.' Each time he came, Serena would ask him for a little something. It began with a pair of shoes for one of the fighters so he could walk more and not have to travel in a waggon. Then she asked for an extra barrel of water so they could wash the dust of the road from their faces in the evening. Each time he was persuaded that it was worth it to protect his investment. Serena knew that each time she made a request, it hooked him to her more, each time he sold her a small portion of his loyalty by giving in to her demands.

They marched from first light until sunset.

Those in white would set up and break camp each day. There were as many soldier-guards as there were fighters and they worked in three different shifts.

Captain Bartham was keen to try and escape before they were too far into the Princes' territory, but they all knew it would be nearly impossible. The Scalthryn moved slowly most of the time but were faster than a man on the run and had greater endurance. Anyone running away would soon be brought down. On top of that, the guards could easily fight off a rebellion. All of them had, after all, earned their own freedom by fighting in the pits once.

Serena wanted to go to Havii. She wanted to find out as

much as she could for as long as she could. She needed to meet Findo again and report everything to him so that the King would send his armies and stop the Princes from enslaving any more towns like Heartsnest. She wanted to find a way of stopping the Princes herself and she wanted to burn Havii and the slavers to the ground.

To do all this she would need to find more support.

★★★

The city of Havii clustered around a hulking basalt hill that was all that remained of an ancient volcano. A lake to the south disappeared into the distance, sparkling and clean, the largest body of water that Serena had ever seen.

The buildings were ancient, made from the rock of the hill, dark stone carved by men in another time. Spires and turrets eroded by the centuries and festooned by vines and small trees taking root in the cracks. From this distance, it was hard to make out details but in its prime, this would have been a city of wonderous beauty.

The plains surrounding the conurbation were vast. A hard pan dustbowl organised into different sections, cut through by wide roads. Clusters of different coloured tents lined the roads, surrounding large, cleared fields where men marched, trained and fought. Here and there sat land ships at rest, the biggest could be seen in the distance, its unmistakable profile clear even through the haze and dust of the camps, their destination, The Dread.

From their elevated position on a low grassy hill, they could see other caravans approaching across the expanse of the plains from all directions. Each heading for a different encampment of tents. Though barren and dusty, the plains were full of colour as each area was marked by tents and flags in a multitude of rainbow hues.

Colthar rode his lizard along the line calling orders for everyone to march. He wanted to put on a show of force. Everyone had to dismount from the waggons and step in time to the drums as they approached the encampments. The oxen pulled the carts down the hill and the pace of the drums increased. They began to pass outlying fortifications and passed patrols of guards wearing the traditional plated armour and pointed helms of Havii.

Slaves in white scurried away from their passing whilst fighters stopped to watch the newcomers and size them up. The Untouchables stood tall and jogged in time with the drums. They did not look around them or wave, as others did. Serena wanted them to be noticed. From now on, she would toe the line for Malthrain, she would make sure their reputation spread. She wanted their opponents to feel fear before they even stepped upon the sand. It started here, with this small show.

The waggons pulled up beside The Dread and all the men, guards, fighters, and those in white formed up in neat rows in the cleared area before her.

Surrounding this area were tents decorated with thick red and black stripes. Guards wearing sashes of the same colours stood to attention all around. A flag flew from both masts of The Dread sporting a matching design. Malthrain stood at the high rail. Alone. Watching.

As was his way, he raised his hand for silence.

"My men. Welcome to Havii. The tents are yours to use for your rest. The ground you stand on is mine. Whilst you walk upon it, you too are mine. Here you will train. In five days, the festival will begin. Train hard and you will go to the pits and win. Win in any way you can. Win for yourselves, win for me, win for your freedom!" The men all cheered.

"Colthar, how was the journey?" he asked of his captain.

"The men were loyal and marched hard. We have made excellent time and arrived earlier than we had planned." he replied.

"Then you have all earned the rest of the day off to get acquainted with your new accommodation. You may leave the camp, if you wish, and explore the other training camps and the city. My only demand is that if you do so then you must wear my colours, you must not bring disgrace upon me and you must be in line at dawn to be counted, ready for training. Remember that I reward loyalty." He stood for a long moment scanning the men before him before giving his final command. "Dismissed."

The slaves in white began to file away to the largest tent, where others in white already waited. The guards who had travelled with them headed to the tents closest to The Dread and the rest of the fighters began to slowly drift off to explore the field and areas further away. Serena stood still, taking it all in. Her men stayed with her.

Then she began to give orders.

"Tracks, Brokenose take a few men and secure us accommodation close to the healers. Keith, Gaz and Den, start talking with the new guards, find out how we get the camp colours and what rules they have that we need to know. Everyone else, see to getting an hour's rest and securing us a good spot to train. Why waste a perfectly good afternoon." The Untouchables were the last to leave the lines.

PART 55

The moon lit the field in silvery light. The sky was clear, and it was obvious that the moon was swelling. During their time in Heartsnest, Serena had thought little of her mission. She had just been trying to survive. Now she looked up at the waxing moon and she knew that their time was running short.

The Untouchables were becoming a tight knit group of fighters, but more than that, many she now considered friends. They were essential to her plans.

Coshelle and the rest of the healers were invaluable, making sure they were patched up each day ready for the next and making links with others in the city who wore the white.

Serena made sure that all of them walked the streets of the camp and of the city. She wanted them all to be familiar with the layout. The easiest ways in and out. She knew there would come a time when they may need to move, fast.

The camps were organised and safe. During the day, most people were training in their assigned areas within their coloured zones. In the evenings, people were free to go where they wished. Everything was neat and tidy. Everything had a place. The soldiers were swift with punishments if you stepped out of line. These were military camps, precise and regimented.

The city was different. It was chaotic.

People bustled everywhere. Men wearing their riches paraded around like pompous peacocks. Soldiers in uniform marched in small groups watching everything. Men of every colour and creed walked around visiting the many delights the city had to offer. There were shops selling everything you could desire, from drinks and street food to weapons and slaves. Anything was available for a price.

The buildings were of carved black basalt. They were hulking things, perhaps beautiful in their day. Most were ruins now, time and misuse destroying their structures. Canvas roofs stretched between walls marked most of the buildings now. The streets were cramped and crowded. Unsuitable for waggons, those that could afford one were carried in palanquins.

Slaves in white scurried everywhere, carrying out chores for their masters. If they were too slow to move out of a man's way or seen in any way to have made a mistake they were hit, whipped, kicked and abused by those who counted themselves above them. Anyone who did not wear white could treat those that did however they wanted. The worst was saved for the women. It was not uncommon for a woman to be raped on thc spot.

Some of the buildings were better maintained and reflected how the city must have looked in the past. These were usually the homes of the very wealthy or were government buildings. Most of the buildings still standing were square, about four storeys tall with decorative domed roofs, spires and columns.

The city had its own climate. It was hot all year and moisture drawn from the lake made the air thick with humidity. Lush vegetation grew in any spot unclaimed by man.

The largest building was close into the towering cliffs of the extinct volcanic hill. The palace of the Princes. Into the cliffs themselves were carved many staircases and entryways. Tunnels bored through the rock.

The hill itself was hollow. The excavations of the rock to build the city had created a large bowl like depression in its centre. This was the pit, a huge arena. The sides were carved into steps down to the centre, creating a giant amphitheater, at the base of which was the Princes' Pit.

In the tunnels of the hillside, there were other smaller pits - for the less prestigious fights - in huge, cavernous rooms. None of them compared to the wonder and scale of the Princes' Pit.

"Come on Serena. We need to get back. Coshelle said she would have information for us on the slave housing in the city and we need to talk through tomorrow's plans before we get some rest."

Tracks was right, they needed to get back. Serena turned

around on the sand one last time looking up at the hundreds of tiers before her and wondering what it would be like with thousands of people all looking down upon you and cheering.

She quickly scaled the iron fence around the Princes' Pit and joined Tracks as he headed out of one of the many tunnels moving back down to the city.

★★★

"As far as we can tell, the patrols run all day and night every day. Usually there is around a quarter turn between them, give or take a little. They run about a mile out from the camps and, using the spyglasses Geoff got us, we could make out another patrol about a half mile further out from that." Hanlan reported.

"So, all land routes out are secured with a double perimeter of guards patrolling at very regular intervals. It would be difficult to even get a small party past. Would it be a better option to go by water?" Serena asked.

"Not at all. Every ship of note carries a full crew and guards. The docks are patrolled frequently and are behind a perimeter of guard stations. You can't even get close to them without the correct paperwork. There must be a better option." Captain Bartham reported.

The Untouchables sat around the tables in their mess tent talking altogether. With Serena sat Tracks, Brokenose, Hanlan, Captain Bartham and Coshelle, her closest advisors.

"Any news from the other camps?" Serena asked Brokenose.

"Everyone is just waiting for the festival to begin. There are plenty who are discontent with this life, but none that we have found or heard word of who are planning anything. I don't think we will find any allies. But if we start something, then others might join. It's hard to tell, and I make no promises. We will keep trying but I'm worried that our words might reach the wrong ears and then…"

"Ok. I get your point. What about those in white? Surely they would rise up and help us if they could earn their freedom?"

Coshelle leant forward, "Perhaps. There are many in the city and the camps who hate their lives but are too scared to do anything. You must remember that they are not fighters like you. Fear keeps them under control. There is a lot of fear here."

"There has to be someone. Somewhere in all this mess who wants a way out and who is willing to risk it all? They will be secretive, but they will be there. We must keep looking. We need allies if we ever want to live in freedom." Serena stood. "Get what rest you can. Tomorrow is the last day before the festival begins. We all need to do well so that we are confident going into our fights. We have been hidden in this camp for long enough. All of us will need to be untouchable in the days to come."

PART 56: MESSENGER'S CODE

The Spire was the home of the Messenger service. A two hundred metre tower of rock jutting out from the city which surrounded it. At the top was the cave where the Kystraal were housed and from which the pilots of the Messenger service came and went. Further down, brickwork interrupted the sheer rock cliffs as the buildings began. Offices, supply stores, bunk rooms and, at the base, the stables.

Findo dodged around the bustling men and women running everywhere. This was the busiest he had ever seen the tower since war with the Mirror city had threatened the Kingdom in his youth. Riders on swift young oxen were flowing out of the courtyards below, carrying the King's orders to raise the armies and mobilise for war. He fought against the flow of humanity dashing around him and made his way up the central staircase towards The Degan's offices.

As he walked down the corridor, he glanced out of a window at the city below. A city which appeared as it always did from this distance, calm and serene. It was only when you were at street level that you saw how busy the largest city in the world really was. Westomere sprawled into the distance like a sleeping giant. He knew that soon the streets would be much quieter as many of the men left for battles in lands they had only really heard of in stories.

Several men, dressed in the traditional dress of the Messengers, hurried out of the open door ahead. All had a series of message tubes strapped to their thighs.

Findo nodded to them as they passed headed towards the stairs downwards. "Until your duty is complete." he said to them in the traditional Messengers' goodbye.

Waiting in the corridor outside The Degan's office were most of the airmen of the service. As Findo approached, he heard The Degan call from within, "Enter!" in his deep gravelly voice.

They all filed through the door and stood before the large desk facing the imposing man behind it.

"No time to waste, you all have assignments. Take your messages and travel swiftly and safely. Do not take any risks. We need you airmen now more than ever. You carry the most important words from the King to his Lords. I trust you all to return in haste with replies. It is our tradition that, because of the nature of your work, you are granted extra leave and higher pay. Until the present crisis is over, all leave is suspended. I hope you said your goodbyes well and left your women satisfied, they will not be seeing you for some time and I hope their memories of you will last."

The men smiled at this.

"Collect your tubes from the ready room, the novices have been briefed. Any questions?"

The airmen stood solemnly, still and quiet.

"Do me proud boys. Until your duty is complete."

They repeated the words and hurried out of the door.

"Findo. Stay a while." The Degan gestured to a chair and the young Messenger relaxed into it with a questioning look.

The Degan stood and walked to close the door, then he went to a cabinet and fetched a bottle and two glasses. He poured for each of them and then settled back down looking weary.

"You did well with your report for the King. It took his mind off the crisis for a while. I'm not sure he will get to choose a bride soon, but the smile on his face as he looked at the portraits was a picture itself."

"That it was sir. It sounds like the business with Bartholomew was a nightmare. A magic user in Splitt who can control another's mind over that sort of distance. It beggars belief sir." Findo shifted uncomfortably in his chair.

The Degan took a small drink and studied his glass for a moment, "It is good to have you back. I hate that you are around so rarely. I need good men I can trust to talk to."

"Sir, I know what you mean. I value your advice, and I need it now." Findo set his untouched drink down on the desk. "I need to go south. I know that we don't scout. I know that we don't get involved in politics. But I made a deal with that girl I met in the forests of Eap. I asked her to find information on the troubles in the south with Havii and I need to collect her message."

"But we need you here, I need you here. You're my best and most reliable man."

"Sir. I told you that there was something wrong in the West. I tell you now that there is something wrong in the South. This could be our best chance to find out what. No Messengers have returned. No scouts have returned. I bet that even the Chancellor's spies have not sent word." Findo sat forward in his chair.

"You're right my boy. But it is not our duty."

There was a polite knocking at the door.

"Wait!" The Degan called.

"Sir. I will be back with the utmost haste. Is there not a way to send me south with a message. Perhaps to Kentai or back to Portreath. I could even carry a message to the Twin Cities seeking their aid." Findo pleaded with his superior.

"It would be best if you gave this up Findo. I just can't see a way, at the moment."

This time the knocking on the door was louder.

The Degan looked up at the noise.

"Please sir. I made a promise. It's a message I need to collect."

The banging at the door became more persistent.

"Let me think…" The Degan got up and went to the door, he spoke briefly with the aide outside and then turned to Findo.

"Finish your drink then meet me in the ready room in a quarter turn. I'll have a job for you then."

The Degan gave him a look of regret before hurrying off after the aide.

Findo sat for a moment. "Shit." he thought. "Serena had better be worth it."

PART 57

Before she left the tent, Serena spent some time at each of the tables speaking briefly with all the men. They seemed in good spirits. All were a little nervous of the fights to come but she told them to trust in their training and be ruthless in battle.

As she made to exit, Coshelle grabbed her arm.

"In my homeland, sometimes our work meant that we had to spend many hours in the Rush to complete our carvings of the stone wood. Little items, like the rivets holding your armour together, would take a man a few hours to achieve. Kings and Lords, however, rarely want little things. As you know, there are limits to using the Rush. It drains you. We Stone Druids use special food and drink to help us to recover quickly and to go on for longer. I have been trying to make some which will work here. Today I came across some supplies of sugars and of special herbs and nuts. Here." The Stone Druid handed Serena a small sack. "If you have need, then eat as many as you can. It will help you to last longer without drawing from others."

Serena looked in the sack. It contained hard biscuits which smelled of honey and herbs. "Thank you. Don't stay too long, you might be missed by your master."

"He will be too drunk tonight. He was going to the city to drink and to look for women. I feel sorry for them, but at least I should get a good rest!" Coshelle smiled and slipped off into the night.

Geoff caught up to Serena just outside her tent. "Serena. I found out that information you asked me about."

"Which information was that Geoff? It's late and I'm tired."

"The Pillars of Kheem."

Serena stepped closer, "What of them?" she whispered, full of anticipation.

"They are stone columns, like those of The Spines. One of the desert fighters from the next camp was talking about them. They used to be holy sites to his tribe, before Havii captured and enslaved his people. He was telling stories of how, when a member of his tribe had come of age, they had to climb these Pillars and pray to their god, Kheem, for a whole night, sitting at the top of one. I listened to his stories and to the conversation around his table for a while. The caravan which brought them in passed the Pillars on the way here, about a day out to the north."

"Thank you, Geoff. Now go and rest." Serena watched as he walked away. She looked to the sky. Full moon tomorrow and she had just found this out. Luck was on her side.

★★★

They went through the Movements.

Serena trickled a little of the Rush into her muscles and was surprised to see that the others still kept pace with her. That's not to say that they didn't struggle, but they moved fluidly and at a rapid pace. She smiled to herself and pushed harder.

One by one they began to drop out. Moving to the side, she watched those still moving. Soon there were only six of them left.

She slowed a little and turned her head so that she could see who was with her. Brokenose and Tracks were blowing hard, sweat pouring from their brows. They were by far the fittest of the group, but their Movements were getting out of time, and she knew that soon they would have to stop. What surprised her was that Woodsy, Den, Girau and Gaz were still going. She increased the pace again, using the added speed to help spin and kick high over her head. She noticed Brokenose and Tracks fall to the floor, spent, chests heaving to get their breath. Gaz stopped suddenly and walked off shaking his head. Serena went through a series of low sweeps with her legs and then rolled forward punching before using her momentum to leap high. She watched as Den and Woodsy landed awkwardly and rolled to a stop. She swept over to them to check they were alright.

Den looked at her in awe. "I could feel it. Like a storm blowing through me. I could feel it, Serena. The Rush. But I couldn't grasp it and use it."

She reached out a hand to help him up from the dirt, "Well

done Den. Perhaps with time it will come to you."

She turned to Woodsy. "How about you? You did very well today."

"There was something there, I knew it was there but...I don't know." he stood and clapped Den on the shoulder. "Maybe we will figure out the magic stuff after all. Now I feel tired and need some water. Come on Den, let's see if breakfast is ready yet."

Serena looked over their shoulders to the others. They were all just staring at something behind her. She turned around. Girau was moving in a blur. Each time she blinked, he was in a new position, constantly in motion. She recognised it straight away. Once that had been her, all those moons ago out on the Everplain with Bandolas. He was caught in the Rush.

She began to move with him. Her pace increased to match his. She edged closer.

His eyes held an unnatural spark, as though lightning resided inside them. He seemed completely relaxed, his motions fluid and smooth as he spiralled through the Movements, but she could tell from the slack look on his face that his mind was in the Rush. She hit him hard in the side of his head.

His body crumpled to the floor, dark dirt sticking to his flesh. He rolled onto his back and stared at her. "What did you do that for?"

"Just making sure you were not getting too big headed. How do you feel?" She sat down next to him as the others began to gather around.

"Like you just punched me in the side of the head." He rubbed at a spot just behind his ear. "That was a little scary. This torrent of force just opened in my mind and, however hard I tried, it just swept me away. I couldn't stop. I felt all powerful, like I was king of the world. Now I feel like I have been wrung out. Like all my energy has been sucked out of me."

"We will talk. I know exactly how you feel. Control is

everything. You will need to learn how to use just a little of the Rush so that you do not get swept away in it. You need to eat and drink more than usual to replace the energy the Rush has drained from you. Take it easy today. Tell me if anything happens and don't try to reach the Rush again unless I am around." Serena helped him up and others carried him towards their tents laughing and slapping him on the back as if he were a hero who had just slain the dragon and rescued the fair maiden.

This could be good for the group, or it could be a distraction from their task. Why had some of them suddenly been able to sense the Rush and even use it. Serena knew next to nothing about her powers and now she would be responsible for theirs as well. Perhaps it would have been better to stay with the Wizards and to have learned more. She walked back to the tents hoping that Coshelle might be able to help her.

Sir was waiting for her by their tents.

"Serena. Malthrain wants you aboard The Dread. Follow me." he turned and began to march away.

Tracks quickly handed her a cup of water, which she drank in one, and threw her a questioning look.

"Get everyone ready for training and in the lines early to be counted. You know the drill." Serena called to him as she hurried off after Sir.

PART 58

Malthrain sat in his chair at the head of the table. The captains were along the sides, with Colthar perched uncomfortably on a stool opposite him. Colthar never looked at ease when he was not mounted on his beloved lizard.

"Ah. I am glad that you could join us dear. I hope that training is going well and that everything in camp has been to your liking." Malthrain watched her every move as Sir guided her to a chair at the table before taking a seat himself.

"I have gathered you all here because, as you know, the Festival starts tomorrow. We should sort out our teams and organise who will be best suited to the different pits. You all know the strengths and weaknesses of your men. The Princes have sent word that only the very best will get to fight in the main arena. Only one man from each camp will face off there on the first night. After that, only those who have proven themselves will get to fight there. All bouts in the main pit will be against one of their champions. The Princes stack the odds in their favour. Most of our men will have to fight their way through the lower pits before they will even earn a chance of fighting in the big pit." Malthrain seemed irritated and stood up to pace around the table.

"We must organise our groupings so that we stand a fair chance of winning in every pit. That means that I want our fighters mixed up. Good and bad in every pit. Most will send their best to the tier two pits and their worst lower down. That way they will get noticed more quickly. Now, I think that that is a short-term plan. I intend to get the most men possible to the main pit for the final bouts of the Festival. That means that they might have to go from the bottom upwards. It will also mean that we should have some easy wins on the way up." He stopped and looked around the room for opinions.

"Would it not be better to put our best men at the top from the start? That way they will appear before the Princes quicker." Colthar leaned his elbows on the table.

"But it will also mean that they will fight the best from the start. I know that we have trained them well but so have all the others. We will lose our best fighters more quickly and may not have as many reach the final rounds." Malthrain's argument did make some sense to Serena. She had spent the last few weeks dreaming of glory before the Princes. But that would mean fighting their best. There was always a chance someone was better than her. At least if she had to work her way up from the bottom, she would get a little fame along the way perhaps earning a formidable reputation.

"How should we choose our groupings then?" Sir asked.

Malthrain began to pace again. "Each group should be an even selection of good and bad from across the camp."

"But won't that mean splitting up units. Some of the men have become close groups with a great team camaraderie." one of the captains suggested.

"On the sand, when you are alone against your opponent, what does that camaraderie really count for? What will matter is the cheers of the crowds and the strength of their resolve." Malthrain sank back into his chair, casually lounging in it. He seemed more relaxed now that he had talked through his decision.

"Seven pits. Seven teams. What say you my dear?" he locked eyes with Serena. "How should we choose."

She did not hesitate with her answer, "Your champion for the Princes' Pit, will lose and die on the first night." She did not look away from Malthrain as other captains began to scoff at her words. "Five of the remaining pits should be as you say, mixed teams, that way you will get the most fighters through to the following rounds. The lowest pit is different. That is where you set an example. On the first night, you want to shake the very foundations upon which the fights are based. That is where you put your best and most ruthless fighters. On the first night, you want that team to win every fight, and not just win but overwhelm, pound and smash. The seventh arena should be painted in black and red. Black stone and red blood."

The captains stared at her mouths agape, but she only had

eyes for Malthrain. He sat still, one hand gently caressing one of his horns. "That is why I invited her here."

He broke eye contact with her to look around at the captains. "She has a winning spirit. Black and red. I like that, it is poetic. Colthar and Sir you will work with this fine lady and pick the most ruthless bastards in this camp, men who will win without honour and without hesitation. The rest of you, organise your teams however you wish. Get them all outfitted by lunch time. This afternoon they fight in my pit with blunted blades to make sure they are used to their kit and to ensure the groupings work. No one leaves camp tonight, double the guard. Rest in the morning and then we warm up before the parades. By the end of tomorrow night, I intend for us to have found our fame and spilled blood, for the pleasure of the Princes."

"For the pleasure of the Princes!" The captains echoed.

They filled out of the room, Serena flanked by Colthar and Sir.

"You really are trouble. How you got the ear of Malthrain I don't know. Perhaps there is something sweet between your legs that we have not seen yet, and you have given him a taste of it?" Colthar spoke mockingly trying to get a reaction from Serena.

It worked.

She turned and swung a fist at him. He was fast and stepped back from her. She didn't slow and used her momentum to carry her forward bringing the elbow of her other arm around seeking to hit his chest. He continued to back away, stepping over a low sweep of her leg.

He used the Rush.

Colthar pushed Sir into her path, and she had to step around him as he stumbled forward in the tight confines of the ship's corridor.

Malthrain appeared in the doorway behind Colthar.

"Stop. I will not have a discontent in my ship. Take it outside on the sand." He loomed over them, stooping so that his head did not brush the planks of the ceiling. "This should be interesting to watch. Sir, prepare the pit."

"Bad move girl. You should have stayed home on the farm and not tried to play dress up in your pretty armour." Colthar seemed enraged, sparks dancing behind his eyes.

Serena took a breath and turned her back on him. Then she walked calmly through the darkness of The Dread with the sounds of Colthar and Malthrain's footsteps following her.

Outside, the fighters of the camp were lined up and being counted for the day. Sir was calling orders and the pit was being cleared ready for the fight. Serena walked casually up to the fence and swiftly climbed over to the sand.

Colthar paced like a caged animal before Malthrain who held up his hand.

"To honour this day where you shall all be sorted into teams for the coming festival, Captain Colthar has decided to give you all an exhibition bout. Gather close and learn what it means to be a veteran of the pits and a champion of the Princes." Malthrain's words rattled Serena.

This man had been a champion for the Princes, in the pits? What had she gotten herself into now?

Colthar stripped off his shirt. Beneath, his dark skin was scarred in many places, testament to the fights he had survived. He rolled his heavily muscled shoulders and drew his long-curved blade. He jumped the fence in one swift movement and turned, raising his arms to the crowd his roaring voice joining their cheers.

Then he turned to face Serena and drew his short dagger with his other hand. He stood calmly facing her across the sand, lightning in his eyes, poised and ready to strike on Malthrain's word.

"Fight!"

Colthar moved in a blur. Serena calmly stepped around him. She had not even reached for the Rush yet. She had known from the moment that he had dodged her attack in the corridor a few moments ago that she could best him. Now she had to put on a show.

She let him attack a few more times, dodging out of harm's

way at the last second. He was channelling more and more of the Rush into his actions, and she began to let a trickle into her own Movements.

Serena drew her daggers. The next time Colthar swung at her, she caught his blade between hers. He tested her strength, gradually pushing her back and then thrust his dagger for her heart. She let his blade strike her breast plate.

It did not yield.

Closing her eyes and breathing deeply she unleashed the raging torrent in her mind.

Serena fell backwards, Colthar's weight followed her down towards the sand.

She twisted as his dagger pushed past her. His sword, held between her blades, flexed and then she pulled it free of his hand.

Serena moved away to the side and Colthar rolled forward as their bodies hit the ground. They were both on their feet again instantly. Only now she had two weapons and he held only one.

She saw his eyes widen in shock and disbelief as he circled away from her.

She gave him no respite and followed as he retreated. She flicked quick cutting blows at his arms and legs which he deflected away with his blade until his back was up against the corner of the fence. Then she asked him one simple question.

"Do you yield?"

His reply was to leap at her.

She was prepared for this and ducked underneath him rolling into the corner herself. She used the strong upright to reverse her momentum and pounced straight back towards him as he rolled to his feet. She twisted an arm around his neck and placed one of her blades at his throat.

"Do you yield?"

He elbowed her in the ribs and kicked her shins. Serena pushed him away from her and retreated.

Colthar stumbled and picked his sword back up from the sand where it had fallen. Panic was starting to creep into his eyes. Serena could see that it was costing him to use the Rush for this long. His face looked drawn, and he breathed in great gulps of air.

He came at her swinging his sword. Each time the blade came, she batted it away and sliced the flesh of his arms. He increased his pace and ferocity.

They stood toe to toe. Him, swinging his sword. She, deflecting it away and leaving ribbons of red across his dark skin. Black and red. Malthrain's colours.

He slowed, swinging his sword wildly. Serena just stepped out of his way until he stood there, panting heavily, head hanging. Both his dagger and his sword dripped bloody trails onto the sand. His blood.

She stepped forward and placed a dagger point into his neck. "Do you yield?"

"Never."

With this last word she pushed her blade home.

As she walked away, she heard his lifeless body slump to the sand.

No-one cheered.

There was only one sound. A slow loud clap as Malthrain showed his appreciation in a solo round of applause.

PART 59

They were a ragged bunch. Some of them tall and heavily muscled. Most were lean and wiry. All of them had one thing in common. Serena had seen them kill without hesitation in the pits. They were tough. She hoped that they were the men that she needed.

In all, eleven men stood with Serena and Sir. Malthrain himself had helped to pick them. Now they stood before tables and racks which displayed their wares. Slaves in white carried equipment over. Swords, shields, armour, weapons of every description. Bry and the young blacksmith from Heartsnest were there as well, helping to check the fit of the kit and taking notes if adjustments needed to be made.

Bry seemed more able than before. He moved with only a slight limp and the tremors in his muscles were less frequent than Serena remembered.

The only distinguishing feature to all the equipment was that in some way it was adorned with red and black, the paintwork on a shield, a patch on armour, the leather twisted around a handle for grip.

From the Untouchables, Sir had chosen Serena, Tracks, Brokenose and Girau. The other men came from across the camp, but they all knew each other from the pits, the journey or the camp.

Their group was the first to choose their kit. Serena took only a halberd and a small leather and iron cap which Bry helped her to adjust for size.

"I'm so sorry Bry. I…"

"No needsh to be ssorry girl, you did your besht in a bad ssituation. I'm fine. Better than that, I am safe. I get to work with my hands, have enough food and a comfortable place to bunk. In some ways I am better off than before." As Bry talked he dropped his slurred speech. "I am not as broken as I make out. No one here notices the weak." He winked at her and she smiled.

"Clever. I'll remember to watch my back when you're

around."

"You're building quite the reputation girl. Stay safe. Just remember old Bry if you ever find a way out of here."

"I will." Serena squeezed his hand gently and then walked away to form up ready for the afternoon fights.

★★★

That evening the Untouchables sat in their mess tent once more. They seemed in good spirits as they chatted about their new groupings and plans for the pits. Serena tried to put on a jovial face, but she couldn't help thinking about Findo.

"You seem distracted. A problem shared can ease the burden." Tracks caught her arm as she tried to sneak out.

"Can you cover for me? I need to go somewhere." Serena tried to keep the fear out of her voice.

"Of course. Can I help? Should I get the others?"

"No. I must go alone. Just tell the others I needed rest or something. I'll be back to do the Movements in the morning." Serena turned to go.

"Just stay safe. We all need you." Tracks's words stayed with her as she tightened her armour and checked her weapons before collecting a small sack from her tent.

She hoped that she was fast enough and that the Rush would not fail her. She would need to be quick enough that the guards and sentries would not see her.

She breathed slowly and deeply and felt for the Rush. She separated a channel off from the main flow and fed it into her muscles. Then she ran. Fast. Northwards beneath the glow of the full moon.

If any guards saw her, it was only as a faint smoky blur. The only sign of her passing was a light breeze and a faint haze of dust drawn up in her wake.

She could not maintain the pace for long. Once outside the camp, she slowed to a jog, knowing that there were the two rings of sentry patrols moving somewhere out in the plains. Once she estimated she had gotten far enough, she stopped and lay down behind a small clump of long grass. She quickly ate one of the biscuits Coshelle had given her and enjoyed the herby sweetness. Then she raised a spyglass to her eyes and scanned the landscape for movement, planning out her route and gathering her energy.

She looked up to the sky. A few small clouds obscured patches of stars. This would have been easier if there had been more cloud. As it was, the moon bathed the landscape in its silvery light. She grabbed a handful of dirt from the floor and rubbed it into her face and the exposed skin of her forearms and hands.

Was Gisselle out there somewhere, looking down? What sign would she be looking for? Would Findo even remember the message he had left her so long ago?

She slowed her breathing and drew a trickle of power once again. She would go and find out.

PART 60: A MESSENGER AND A GIRL

The air whistled through Gisselle's stiff mane as she plummeted through the sky, her wings folded back and close to her sides. Findo clung to the reins, pressed against the chest guard.

The fires of the border guards rapidly grew as they descended. The moon was full. Findo had coaxed Gisselle to fly as high as she could so that they avoided being seen against the stars and the moon's silvery light.

They had been circling the Pillars since just after nightfall, searching for a sign that Serena was there.

★★★

Gaudan leant back against the rock he was using as a rest, his feet stretching close to the fire. Around him, the other guards talked and laughed. The still air of the night was cold, the opposite to the day's searing heat. This close to the desert everything was dusty. What he would give to have a bath and wash the grit from his skin.

Still, it was good to come to rest in camp. Their patrol had covered many leagues today, marching the line of the border under the glare of the sizzling sun. It had been weeks since any of the patrols had encountered anyone and that had been a short bloody affair. In the shadow of the pillars with the light of the moon illuminating the land for miles around, they could rest easy.

Born to a high-ranking freeman, Gaudan had grown up in his father's household under the watchful eyes of his mothers. His father was a generous man and he had had many brothers and sisters to play with. When he was of age, he had worn the white, working his father's small holdings outside the city. He had enjoyed tending the herd of boar in the orchards, his father produced some of the best ciders for the Princes' pleasure. The boar kept the pests away and cleared the spoiled fruits - as well as providing fabulous, dried hams and sausages. When he had reached his fifteenth summer, the age you left home and became a slave of Havii, his father had sold him to a master in the fighting pits and he had trained there for two joyous years, before earning the right to fight for the Princes' pleasure.

In the pits, he had gained the title of his beloved animals, the Boar. The only fight he had ever lost had been his first, he still carried the scars on his arms and chest. He had been known for his tenacity and belligerence on the sand. Never giving up, until his opponents were worn down and open for the kill. The Princes themselves had made him a freeman.

Since then, he had served in the army. He had been present at the sacking of Aldark and seen the brutality of war. He had also fallen in love with the camaraderie of soldiers. The deep friendships you developed sharing life on the march and risking your life for a greater cause. As he looked at the faces of the men around him now, he knew that he would sacrifice his life for any of them, and they would do the same for him.

"Hey, Gaudan the Boar, has the heat of the sun baked your brain? You look like you have drunk too much already my friend. What's with the stupid smile?" the big man sitting next to him kicked him playfully in the leg.

"Just happy to be alive and fighting by your side Kamta. Fill my ale up, could you?" Gaudan passed his empty mug over.

Kamta reached behind and filled Gaudan's mug from the barrel resting there.

"There you go. Any idea when we will be marching to join the main bulk of the army? Rumour is it will be heading north soon."

"You hear as much as me. You know Panni? The short guy from sixth patrol?" Gaudan asked.

Kamta looked at him puzzled.

"Only got half an ear… Boasts it got bit off in the pits…always chewing on black leaf." Gaudan tried to remind his friend.

"Yes. The one who always tries to sell you his ugly daughter."

"That's the one. Well, when we passed him yesterday and were sharing cups, he said that he had heard from a fellow in the twelfth patrol that once the festival is over then the Princes will want the border pushed further out as the army begins to march. Could be that we get to see action soon. I miss a good fight. With all the patrols ringing the land, we've cleared any trouble."

"Aye. Soldiering is mostly marching with the occasional clashing of swords and fear of death… Did you hear that?" Kamta stood and slowly turned around scanning the land surrounding them.

"What was it? Snake? Lizard?" Gaudan and the others quickly got to their feet, turning their backs to the fire to peer into the darkness.

To the south they could see a vague line of dust rising into the air, a faint sound similar to paper being slowly torn hummed at the edge of their hearing.

Weapons were drawn and the men efficiently closed formation as Kamta began to walk forward to get a clearer look.

He turned as a gust a wind swirled sand up around the base of the nearest rock column.

Then his head sailed through the air to land sizzling in the flames of the campfire. Within seconds, the fire went out as the bodies of Gaudan the Boar and all his companions fell, smothering the light.

★★★

Findo saw the fire closest to the Pillars wink out.

With no better target to aim for, he guided Gisselle downwards. She flared her wings as they approached the ground and they passed low and fast over the camp.

Through the blur of the speed of her passing, Findo could just make out the familiar outline of a certain girl in distinctive armour.

Serena was here.

As Gisselle flew low and slow over the ground, Findo released his stirrups and leapt from the saddle. He tucked and rolled as he hit the hard packed earth, coming to his feet to find a knife pressed under his chin.

"What was the name of my ox?" Serena asked with a deadly cold voice.

"Poppy. I always thought it a bit of a girly name for such a fine strong animal." Findo relaxed and stepped backwards a pace as Serena sheathed her knife and began inspecting the bodies in the camp. "You seem different. What's happened?"

Serena pulled a short sword from the pile of cadavers and handed it to him. "I've grown up. You look well. How's Gisselle?" Serena pulled a biscuit from a bag at her waist and started munching on it.

"She was happy to hear we were coming; she seems to like you. Serena, there is trouble in the Kingdom. The North is under attack and an attempt was made on the King's life. What news have you? I really need to report something useful when I return."

"I don't really know what I can tell you. The other patrols will have seen the fire go out and will come to investigate. We don't have much time." She sounded tired and worried. "I can tell you that Havii attacked and took Heartsnest a few weeks ago. They are expanding their borders and taking everyone as slaves. If I am not back before dawn, then people I care about will come to harm. We must be quick. Ask your questions." She glanced to the moon and then to the horizon as if expecting the sun to leap into the sky at any second.

"Is Havii a threat to the Kingdom?" Findo was straight to the point.

Serena sighed and turned to face him. She seemed slightly unsteady on her feet as she bit into another biscuit, speaking around the food. "Yes. The Princes have taken all the lands between Kentai and the Great Divide. They attacked and enslaved the Twin Cities and have expanded their borders outwards. All of the people of the South now live as slaves under new masters. Me and the crew of the ship I travelled on were taken near Heartsnest. Those that could were trained to become fighters for the Princes, those who win in the pits of Havii will enter the ranks of the army. I have only heard rumours, but it seems the Princes have amassed a large army and intend to expand their lands further. That's all I know."

Findo looked to the sky, tracking Gisselle's Movements. "The King is sending his army north. If the Princes strike for Westomere now, the way is open for them. How can we stop them?" He kicked at the dirt in frustration.

"I haven't been sitting around doing nothing you know." Serena stated flatly. "I intend to fight in the pits until I stand before the Princes. I only need one chance to kill them. If someone can show that that is possible perhaps others will fight against them as well."

"That's just dreams. You can't stop an army by killing its leaders. There are always others who will step into the role. Anyway, what you propose sounds impossible!"

Serena moved like lightning, grabbing the front of Findo's coat and holding him tight as he struggled to pull away. A dangerous light danced in her eyes. "I have been learning what is possible. I will kill those that enslave this land."

Findo looked at the bodies around them and remembered the things he had seen her do in Eap. "I believe you could."

Serena let go of him and pushed him away.

"You won't be able to do this alone. You'll need help."

In a cold icy voice Serena replied, "I have help. There are others who fight with me whom I can rely on. I just wish there was a way to speak to the slaves and get them to fight for their freedom. I can only work in the fighters' camps."

They both stood there in silence for a moment, Findo glancing to the skies. Serena scanning the land all around.

"I wish we had met again in better times. I'm just a Messenger. I deliver messages. I may not even be that anymore, I betrayed my orders to come and meet you. I am not a fighter. I want to help but I don't know how."

"I have come all this way because you helped me when I was lost. You gave me a purpose. Along the way I have found a new reason to fight. Perhaps Findo, what you need is a new message to deliver."

PART 61

Serena sat at one of the tables in the mess tent consuming mug after mug of lukewarm soup. It had been a hard trip back from the Pillars of Kheem and she desperately needed to replenish her energy with food and sleep. Sadly, sleep would have to wait for now.

"I'm here to help. I may not be a fighter like you, but I can look after myself. You and your buddies can do the fighting, I'm just here to try to help Serena find the right people in the right places to start an uprising." Findo defended himself.

"Skinny little man like you? How can you start an uprising? King's Messenger indeed. All you fly boys do is strut around with lords and ladies. You couldn't start a fight in a tavern full of pit fiends!" Brokenose seemed a little reluctant to accept Findo into the team.

Serena paused to wipe her mug with a hunk of bread. "I vouch for him. He saved my life the last time we met. If what he says is true and the Kingdom is at war, then we are the only people who can stop the Princes. Findo sent Gisselle, his Kystraal, with a message for the King. He will know of the situation here soon enough, but we cannot expect his help."

She looked around at the faces seated before her. "We are all too easily recognised in the camps as fighters. Our job is to be seen, to be recognised, to keep everyone looking at us. The Untouchables, mighty warriors of the pits." She paused to chew for a moment. "Findo can get amongst the slaves, spread the word. Coshelle can show him around. They can go places we cannot."

Brokenose did not look convinced, "And he is expendable. I will not shed a tear if he is caught, but will he squeal under a torturer's knife?"

"Look friend. I don't give a shit if you like me or not. I'm here to save a kingdom. Nothing will stop me from achieving that, so why don't you just stop flapping your lips and complaining and see about helping?" Findo sat forward, seeming to grow in his chair as he stared down the big man.

"You got balls saying that to my face. If Serena says you're in, then so be it. Just do your part and stay out of mine." Brokenose got up from the table and walked off to talk with some of the others.

"You have some terrible friends Serena." Findo said staring angrily after Brokenose.

"Yes, I do. The first time I met him he tried to rape me, and I nearly killed him for it. Now he fights for me, and I need men like him. Ruthless. But from you I need something different. Do you think you can find help in this shit hole?"

"I can try. I have spent most of my life delivering messages, giving speeches, talking with important people and listening. I'm exceptionally good at listening. I'm sure I can find the right ears to pass messages to. As long as someone can show me where to start looking." Findo was trying to sound confident, but Serena knew he was just putting on a show.

Coshelle said "I think I can get you to places where you can listen. You will have to wear white and blend in as a slave, but you should be alright as long as you don't get into any trouble. Tomorrow I will take you to the markets in the city. We will see what we will see and then report back. I suggest that tonight we all get some sleep. There are not many hours until dawn and the Festival begins."

Coshelle spoke the truth, Serena badly needed sleep.

"Findo go with Coshelle. You need to bunk with the slaves." Serena turned to the others sitting with them. "Tracks, are the men ready?"

"Ready as they ever will be."

"Then I suggest we all get some sleep."

With that Serena stood and wandered out seeking her own cot and the release from worry that exhausted slumber would bring.

★★★

Coshelle led Findo out of the camp and into the streets of the city as the sun was beginning to rise. The air was cool and raised goosebumps on his flesh.

"Do they make these any bigger. I feel very exposed in this?" he complained, remembering the luxurious warmth of his flying jacket.

"That's the point. Remember, you are now a thing. Property. Any freeman can see that, as you wear the white. If you are told to do something, you best to obey. Without question. Do not draw attention to us. Keep your head down, look meek and stay close to me." Coshelle wound her way through the narrow lanes following other slaves wearing white who were heading to the markets to collect supplies for their masters.

"But you are free to go anywhere?" he asked.

"Yes."

"Then why do the slaves not just walk away?"

"They would be spotted by patrols and returned to their owners after receiving a beating. If the owner no longer wanted them, they would be sold to another." Coshelle suddenly dropped to a knee and looked at the floor.

Findo copied her as a man wearing a fine robe and surrounded by large muscular men walked past.

"Who was that?" Findo asked as they started to walk once more.

"That was a slave merchant. It's best to stay out of their way." Coshelle pointed ahead. "We are nearly there. It's good that we came early. Less freemen go out in the mornings and it's easier to move about."

The alleyways opened into a large open square full of stalls selling everything imaginable.

"Let me do the talking. You are too new at this. You are just here to carry the goods we buy."

'And to listen.' Findo thought to himself.

Coshelle pushed through the crowded aisles, through a sea of men and women who all looked alike. The same downtrodden expressions, loose fitting white tunics cinched at the waist with simple cords.

The merchants called out their wares, groups of freemen lounged around in canopied areas set aside as cafes and drinking stalls. Occasional patrols of soldiers walked past, dressed in pointed helmets and polished mail armour.

The Stone Druid visited several stalls, herbalists and medicine suppliers. She passed notes of exchange with the merchants, stating that Malthrain was liable for the cost of the goods. Soon Findo was weighed down with sacks full of bandages, cotton thread and all manner of fragrant herbs and ointments.

Each time they stopped at a stall, Coshelle would spend some time discussing the properties of this or that item for sale with the owner. Findo would crouch by the bags, scan the crowd and listen.

Most conversation revolved around the sale and the purchase of goods, no surprise there. A lot of the chatter was about the fights. He even heard the Untouchables mentioned a few times as people to watch. It seemed their reputation was spreading.

Findo was surprised at how little conversation passed between those wearing white. They very rarely spoke to each other. It was as though it was not allowed. They nodded acknowledgements, said sorry if they bumped into each other and such like but they rarely spoke. With the merchants it was different, they spoke at length, discussing the health of their masters, changes in the households, sizes and weights of new-born children, who their favourite fighters were.

Whilst Coshelle was discussing the viscous properties of certain oils at one stall, and Findo was relaxing taking it all in, he noticed one of the freemen drinking at a table nearby, grab the arm of a man in white walking past.

"Fetch me an orange." the man ordered, and the slave hurried away to the nearest fruit stall and returned shortly afterwards to hand the freeman the required orange. The slave waited for a few moments until the freeman waved his hand and then he continued on his way.

Shortly afterwards, the same freeman, now with orange juice staining his chin, reached out and stopped a young woman in white who was passing. The others in his group all laughed as he ran his hand up inside her tunic. He made her turn around in a circle then ordered her to kneel in front of him. Then he rested his legs on her back.

"Thank you darling. After I have relaxed nicely then you can come with me, and we can relax together a bit more. I'm afraid you might be a bit late returning to your chores today." the freeman said loudly for all to hear as the woman bowed her head so that her hair brushed in the dirt, hiding her shame.

Findo was repulsed at the acquiescence of those in white but also at the presumption of the freemen that it was their right to treat them this way. No one batted an eye lid at this behaviour. It was normalised.

As Findo began to pick up their bags, Coshelle placed a hand on his arm and whispered. "It is not right but you can do nothing. You wear the white now. Do nothing to draw attention to us."

He nodded that he understood, and they moved on.

"You just stole a grape! Guards! This boy just stole from me." Findo and Coshelle moved quickly aside as a skinny boy in white was grabbed by several soldiers.

"What happened here Merchant Jessiah?" One of the tall soldiers asked.

"That filth took a grape from the bunch there and ate it. Just there, you can see the stalk where the grape should be." The merchant Jessiah whined.

"That true boy? Did you steal it?" The guard demanded of the dirty youth.

"I haven't eaten in days boss. I can make up for the loss with work. I'm good with numbers boss." The boy pleaded, his eyes darting everywhere, desperately looking for a way out.

"Merchant. Do you want the boy to work off his debt or should he pay the price for his crime at the pleasure of the Princes?" The soldier asked holding firmly onto the boy's upper arm.

"I have no need for thieves. He should pay for the pleasure of the Princes." The merchant replied gleefully.

The boy seemed to sag in the arms of the soldier at these

words. Another of the guards tried to grasp the boy's hands and the lad suddenly started kicking and bucking, trying to thrash his way free, but the men were much larger than him. They cleared a space on the stall holders table and pulled the lads arms over it.

The boy clenched his fists tight, and the soldiers slowly prised his fingers open. The little finger on his left hand was missing.

"So, lad. This is not your first time. First offence for theft is a finger, to remind you of your crime. Second offence is a hand!"

The boy began to weep. A large crowd had gathered by this time, all watching as the punishment was dealt out.

The merchant waved his new possession in the air as the crowd cheered, a grisly, blood speckled, four fingered hand. The boy slumped to the floor.

"Is there a healer?" the soldier called out sheathing his bloody blade.

Findo reached out a hand to hold Coshelle back. "Don't draw attention you said."

"I'm sorry but I have to." She pulled her arm free and hurried over to crouch over the boy. "I'm a healer. I will see that he survives your butchery to serve another day at the Princes' pleasure."

The soldier back handed her across the face. "Fix him. If I see your insolent face on my watch again you will serve me all night woman. If I hear report that he dies, then you will spend that night with all my men as well! Who is your master?"

"Malthrain." She whispered her reply.

The man's face visibly paled. "Fix him up and be on your way." The soldiers turned and left, hurriedly marching down the street.

Coshelle quickly bound the stump tightly with a bandage and waved for Findo to come over. The crowd were dispersing though trade at the merchant's stall was now brisk. Together they carried the boy and the bags through the bustle to a quiet alleyway. The Stone Druid stripped off the bandage and threw it aside as she inspected the wound.

"Good, his vessels are closing up." She pulled a needle and thread from a hidden pocket in her tunic and sewed a couple of the larger arteries closed. Then she dressed the wound again. "We need to take him back to his master's house."

"How are we supposed to do that? He is out cold. It could be hours until he comes round. We should just leave him here." Findo stood and looked around them, checking to see if they were being watched.

"I can't just leave him to die. I am a healer. In the bag from the first stall we visited, you should find a small brown bottle, pass it to me." Coshelle demanded.

Findo searched the bags and handed her the bottle. Coshelle unstopped it and held it under the boy's nose. He coughed and opened his eyes. Then he struggled to stand up before he paled and sat still.

"Who are you?" he asked, eyeing his stump and wincing in pain.

"I am Coshelle, and this is my friend Findo. I have tried my best to stop you from bleeding out, but you need rest. Where is your master's house? We can carry you there."

"Ain't got no master." The boy shrugged his pained eyes glancing nervously around.

"Then who do you belong to?" Findo felt uneasy sitting in the alley where anyone could see them.

"Don't belong to no one." The boy struggled to sit up, holding his arm just above the stump and staring at it.

"Everyone belongs to someone." Coshelle said softly.

"Not me. I'm a freeman."

"Then where is your home?" Findo asked.

"You're looking at it. I live on the streets."

Coshelle and Findo shared a look of pity for the boy.

"Come on Coshelle, leave him. We still need to finish our mission." Findo began to pick up their bags.

"No. We need to get the boy somewhere safe."

"Lady, thank you and all for the help but I'll be alright. I just need to get back to the others."

Findo stopped in his tracks and turned to face the boy. "Others?"

The boy backed away, realising what he had said was a mistake. "I'm not sayin' nothing mister. You be going on your way now. You don't want to be late getting back to your masters. Thank you very much and all but see you."

He struggled to stand up and leant against the wall with his good hand.

"Let me put that in a sling, you need to keep it raised so the blood will crust over." said Coshelle and she began to put a bandage around him to hold his arm up against his chest. He didn't struggle.

"Do you have someone who can change the bandages for you?"

"No."

"Will you meet us here tomorrow morning? I can check on your wound and see that you're alright." Coshelle asked sincerely.

"You can come if you want. I'll either be here or I won't."

"Can you stay here with my friend for a minute before we go, I would like to give you something."

The lad nodded and Coshelle waved for Findo to stay as she walked off into the market.

"Not like I could get away from you anyway is it." the boy pointed out.

"In your state. Probably not. You know we mentioned a mission. I'm looking for free people like you. I want to stop people being slaves. I have immensely powerful friends, who fight for the King to ensure all men are free. Do you know anyone who could help?" Findo couldn't believe he was asking this of the boy, but he needed to take a chance. If this boy talked to the wrong people, both he and Coshelle would be as good as dead.

"I told you. I got no one." the boy's eyes betrayed the lie.

Coshelle came back and handed the lad a small sack. "Rest and build your strength up. It's the best chance you have to stay healthy. My name is Coshelle. I'll come back and meet you tomorrow."

The boy looked in the bag and snatched out an apple, quickly biting into it as though it might escape him. "Thank you." he mumbled around a mouthful as he turned and began to shuffle away into the dimness of the alley.

"See you tomorrow." Coshelle called as she and Findo made their way back into the busy marketplace.

PART 62

The fighting was brutal.

Findo stood with a small team of healers to the side of the fighters' waiting area. Around them rose the wooden stands set up around the lowest fighting pit located in a cavern carved from the black basalt of the hill. The voices of the cheering crowd rose and fell with the fortunes of the fighters on the sand. When the crowd roared, the sound reverberated around the chamber resonating deep within his bones. It was primal.

He glanced nervously along the faces of the fighters. They all stood stoic and calm on the sand, Serena amongst them. Tall for a girl, but short compared to most of these heavily muscled men. Her armour, as always, made her stand out. She wore her bone knives at her waist, a slim short sword across her back. The hilts of various small throwing knives protruded from their scabbards placed along straps which crisscrossed her chest. Her long hair was tied back in a heavy braid which fell down her back, decorated with black and red ribbons running through it. She seemed calm. He knew she had not fully recovered from the exertions of the previous night, her face still looked drawn, emphasising her high cheek bones.

The team consisted of Serena, Brokenose, Tracks, Woodsy, Den, Girau and Gaz from the Untouchables with Stone, Hammer, Warquan, Tarquin and Desh making up the rest – all experienced fighters who had come from Malthrain's training camps and had joined them at Heartsnest, like Girau. Sir and a group of twelve guards watched over them.

So far, five of the twelve men wearing black and red had fought and won.

Around the pit, the fighters from the other camps stood or sat in their teams wearing their own colours. Behind them rose the stands of freemen, come to watch this first night of the Princes' Festival.

To one side of the arena, on a raised dais, sat the pit boss. It was his job to draw the teams' colours from a chest next to him. He then allowed the chosen teams to select their fighters.

He started each fight and declared the winner if there was any doubt or if someone yielded.

Each team had a small number of slaves who helped the injured or removed the dead from the pit. They then raked the sand ready for the next bout as well as assisting with equipment and seeing to the needs of their team.

The pit boss opened the chest and pulled out two ribbons, one was white and blue, the other red with yellow circles. The two teams whose colours these were quickly selected their fighters and chaos began again as the audience screamed their delight and the fighters pitted their lives against each other.

Findo felt sick. How was such brutality a way of life for these people?

During the fight, the man from the white and blue team had his fingers severed from one hand and yielded. The men in white were quick to gather his fallen digits from the sand and hand them to their team captain who turned to the audience and began haggling with members of the crowd who were desperate for trophies of the night to show to their friends and families.

Findo could not believe it. He shook his head in disgust.

"What's the matter little man? Fights not to your liking?"

One of the guards leant down from the stand above and grabbed Findo's tunic. "Perhaps you need to show more respect for those who honour the Princes."

The guard shoved Findo back, hard. "Fetch me some wine so I can drink to the pleasure of the Princes."

Findo ducked his head and reminded himself to show less reaction in future as he hurried to a wine merchant set up behind the stands.

When he returned, he saw that the pit boss was holding up a black and red ribbon. The fighters did not react. Sir whispered in Serena's ear. The other team drawn selected their fighter, who was a huge man equipped with a big mace and carrying a shield. Serena waited until he stood on the sand of the pit before calmly saying, "Stone."

Malthrain's fighters stood still, unmoving, as Stone stepped from their ranks and jumped onto the sand. He turned and casually faced his opponent who made a great show of roaring at the crowd, swinging his weapon and generally trying to be threatening. Stone acted as if he were his namesake. He was stone. Unshaken, unmoved.

When the pit boss dropped his hand to signal the start of the fight that all changed. Stone ran forward, ducking a high swing from the mace and grabbed his opponent's shield. Surprised the man fell backwards to be pinned to the ground.

Ineffectually, he tried to swing his mace to make contact with Stone, but his own shield hampered his movement as he struggled beneath it. Gradually Stone pushed the shield upwards until the rim pressed against the man's throat.

The audience quieted. This was not the exciting combat they expected. Slowly, the man's eyes began to bulge, and his skin turned red as the life was choked out of him. He had no chance to yield he could not breath to say the word. Time seemed to grind by as everyone waited for him to die. Eventually, Stone stood up. He turned to the pit boss and gave a short bow before walking back to his place in the team line.

As the evening progressed, each of their fights was the same; calm, calculated and ruthless. The team in red and black stood solidly at attention the whole time. Unmoving, unflinching. On the sand they were swift, efficient and bloody. They did not put on a show. They killed without mercy, without a care for the audience's reaction. They were not here to impress the people. They were here to win, and by so doing to get the attention of the Princes.

Serena waited until last to go. She was taking a chance, by going last, she would not be able to size up the opponent and select the right person for the job. She had to face whoever she was given.

Hers was not the last fight of the evening, but it would be remembered that way by all who watched.

When the twelfth black and red ribbon was drawn, she stepped out of line and walked slowly around the pit to stand before the boss. He drew forth a pale green ribbon fringed in orange. A cheer went up from the group of fighters wearing those colours as a mountain of a man stood up from amongst them. He wore shoulder guards studded with small spikes. Over his chest and upper back, articulated plates of steel glimmered. His stomach was bare above a thick boiled leather belt, from which hung a heavy skirt of mail. Upon his head he placed a simple steel helm which covered his ears and the back of his neck and had a wide nose guard. He carried a pair of short swords in his gauntleted hands.

As this goliath made his way into the pit, Serena knelt on one knee before the boss and waited.

The boss raised his hands for silence. "What is this girl. Do you wish to yield now, having seen your opponent?" he drawled for the crowd.

Serena stayed where she was and slowly raised her head to speak.

"No sir. I wanted to show you respect as I will show respect to the Princes in six days' time. I also wanted to ask you a question." She remained on her knee as the audience began to laugh and chatter.

Once more the boss raised his hands. "You are here to fight girl, not to ask favours. If it's my cock you seek, then come to me after the fight, if you survive."

At this the crowd cheered and applauded.

The big man in the pit seemed nervous. Waiting for a fight is no easy thing.

The boss took his time enjoying the applause before quieting the crowd once more. "For the pleasure of the Princes, what is it you ask girl?"

"Where would you like me to strike this man first?"

A whisper passed through the crowd at this, and the boss seemed taken aback. Then he looked around the room and made a great show of considering the question before he replied, "You have more than most of the men here to even be asking the question. I should like you to take his balls!"

At this the audience was in uproar.

The man on the sand seemed unsure what to do as he paced

back and forth.

The pit boss raised his hands again and the audience took a long time to calm and quiet.

"Rise fair maiden of the pits. Fight well this day." The boss feigned a small bow to Serena, and she stood up, waved to the crowd and vaulted the rails into the pit.

The boss raised up the ribbons to signal the fighters to get ready, looked around at the waiting crowd and dropped his hand.

The big fighter warily circled Serena.

She drew her bone daggers testing their weight in her hands.

Findo glanced at the men in black and red. They had not moved and showed no emotion. Behind them, Sir was red faced with anger as the guards all leant forward in anticipation of the first blow.

Her opponent fainted left and then came straight at her. He was fast, blurring as he came. He swung both swords one high and the other low. When he came to a stop, he turned to find Serena standing casually at the opposite end of the pit. No-one had seen her move.

The big man eyed her up.

This time he came slowly. He moved left and right holding his swords wide, trying to shepherd her into a corner. Serena crouched low, dancing lightly on the balls of her feet. Her opponent paused, waiting to see what she would do. Edging backwards slightly until the corner post was at her back, she bided her time.

The big man jabbed his swords in, and she ducked and weaved to avoid the blows, forcing him to come at her. However, he was an experienced fighter, he held his ground just out of her reach. Each time she moved left or right, he sent out a quick jab towards her, hemming her into the corner.

The crowed jeered her. The atmosphere was beginning to turn against her. They shouted for blood.

Serena put her knives away and drew the sword from her back holding it one handed in front of her.

The man slapped at the weapon with his own, looking for an opening in her defences. She raised her arm, so the tip of the blade pointed at his face. He continued to bat at it, each time he swung she was a little faster until he began to miss. He stepped back a pace, she did not follow but kept her blade tip high, aimed at his eyes.

Serena waited. Findo watched breathlessly. He saw the man begin to shift his weight to step forward. She turned her blade so that the light from the braziers flames lighting the room glimmered along its length, then she dropped and twisted, launching herself off the post behind her with unnatural speed. The crowd saw her fly between the man's legs and roll to a stop on one knee in the centre of the pit, her head bowed towards the pit boss. Her opponent seemed frozen in place weight shifted slightly to one side. Then he screamed and toppled to the sand crumpling up to lie like a baby.

Serena looked up at the boss and raised her free hand, palm up. Blood dripped between her fingers and trickled down her arm. Two fleshy masses rested in her hand for all to see.

The crowd went wild.

PART 63

The rough wall rasped against his back as Findo casually leant up against it, watching the people in the market flow by. At his feet sat various bags and sacks full of goods which Coshelle had deemed worth buying. She was talking with an herbalist nearby, looking for ointments and unguents to help heal the wounds of the fighters.

This was the second morning that they had returned to the alleyway where they had last seen the young thief. The previous day they had seen no sign of him. Findo hoped that would change as, although they had tried, so far, he had not managed to make links to any slaves interested in joining a revolt. He had heard no whispers of discontent.

Coshelle returned carrying a few small jars which she placed carefully in one of the sacks. "Any luck?" she asked glancing around.

"No sign yet. It's probably a fool's errand. Perhaps we should try our luck around the cattle markets or even try the slave masters' area. Somewhere, in a city this size with this many people in servitude, there must be some who want freedom and are not afraid to seize it." Findo reached down with a sigh to pick up the bags.

"Perhaps you are right." grated a voice from above them.

Findo looked up and just caught a glimpse of a dark-haired head pulling back behind the roof line. Then a stone bounced along the floor, coming from the shadows in the alleyway, to rest at their feet. Feigning looking in the bags, Coshelle picked it up and unwrapped a piece of parchment tied to it. She handed it to Findo who was nervously glancing all around them.

"What does it say?" she asked.

Findo turned so that the sun was over his shoulder and examined the note. It was written in a rough print and contained only three words. 'Tanner street now.'

From their wanderings in the city, Findo knew where to go.

"Coshelle, I think I'll do this alone. You head back to camp and let the others know that we've made contact. If I don't return, look after Serena. She may have become hardened, but her heart is still good."

"Yes lad. This is your task now. Mine was just to show you the way. Don't you worry. I'll look after that girl. She might put on a good show, but she is still young and inexperienced. In the fights to come, she will need good people, like you and me. Make sure you come back to us." The Stone Druid picked up the sacks and turned to make her way back to the camp.

Findo took a deep breath and wandered off through the market heading for Tanner Street.

It took a while to get there. He had to avoid a couple of patrols and retrace his steps. Tanner street was one of the longest thoroughfares in the city. Towards the palace, it was wide, neatly cobbled, with individual homes set in gardens. Further down the hill, the buildings drew in close, leaning over broken flagstones. Rats scurried along the gutters and filth collected in low spaces. The air was thick and humid. Deeper in, lines were hung between the buildings to dry the clothing and leather was being dyed and treated in the yards behind them. The whole place smelled of urine, and worse, the acidity of it stung the eyes.

Findo made no attempt to conceal himself as he ducked and wove his way further down the street. People in white moved all around him, most with coloured splotches on their tunics and badly stained hands.

He spotted the lad they had helped in a doorway and hurried over. He had to move out of the way as a couple of women stepped in front of him unfolding a freshly dyed sheet and began to hang it up. Once he was clear, he saw that the boy was gone. Findo headed over to the door where he had been.

He hesitated for a moment and then raised his hand to knock.

"I don't know you, so I don't care if you die." A grating

voice spoke from behind him. "Don't bother knocking. We've been expecting you. Make your way in slowly but keep your hands where I can see them."

It was the voice from the roof in the alleyway.

Carefully, Findo reached out and opened the door. Inside was darkness. He stepped forward and let it surround him.

The door behind closed. "Keep walking." the voice like gravel ordered.

After a few paces, the darkness was shattered as a door further down the corridor opened. Light and steam, heavily scented with herbs, spilled out,

"Go on now." the voice behind him encouraged. "You came all this way. Let's find out why."

Findo walked on into the room beyond.

Two men and a woman sat on a long wooden bench. In front of them was a fireplace, above which was suspended a cauldron full of rocks. The woman leaned forward and fished a ladle out of a bucket next to the fire. She poured water over the heated rocks sending a plume of heavily scented steam into the air. The whole place was hot and Findo began to sweat.

All three of them were plain and non-descript, of average height, weight and looks. In a crowd, you would not see them.

One of the men spoke.

"Welcome, King's Messenger. My boy was very excited when he returned, he could speak of little else, my thanks for healing his wounds. Take a seat and we will talk."

The man had the accent of the twin cities, but his skin was paler, more like those Findo had met in Portreath.

Findo moved to sit alongside the man on the bench. When he turned to sit, he saw that the door he had entered through was now closed and that the four of them were alone in the room.

"My name is Wellyn, my companion is Gamon. Our wife is Lydidd." Findo frowned at this.

Gamon spoke, "Don't look like that, we have a rather special relationship. For years we worked the black-markets of the South. When the Princes' men took the cities, we were separated. It took us some time to find our way back together. We chose to never be apart again, the three of us against the world. Time has cost us much. We intend to waste no more, so we are husband, husband and wife."

He spoke like a true southerner, his accent chewed through the consonants allowing the vowels to roll on.

"Everyone should be allowed the freedom to live their lives as they see fit, as long as it brings no harm to others." Findo said.

"Yet you wish to cause harm." Wellyn pointed out.

"Only to those who enslave others. You yourselves wear the white. Who is your master?"

"We bought our lives in blood and tears. No man will ever tell us how to live again." Gamon sounded bitter. Lydidd reached over and held his hand tenderly.

"Is the boy yours?" Findo asked her.

She shook her head and looked away.

"Her last master cut out her tongue when she stayed silent as he raped her. He said that if she refused to cry out in pleasure, she would never cry out again." Wellyn sighed heavily. "He has since paid his debt to us and will never seek to harm another, that is hard to do from the grave. The boy has no mother, like many of the children in this stinking city he was left to die on the streets, the masters do not want too many children, it brings the prices down at the slave markets. We do a little to help those children, and they in turn, help us with our *enterprises*. It is not an easy place to live a life of crime, but we have found a way. What brings a King's Messenger to this filthy corner of the world?"

"I came because I owed a debt to a friend. She seeks to free the people of Havii. People like you. As well as that, I serve the Kingdom. There is trouble brewing. Havii seeks to send an army to Westomere. I hope to slow it down or stop it if I can. My friend seeks to kill the Princes and put an end to Havii." He looked along the line of their faces. "That is all. That is everything I know."

"You risk a lot, telling us this. Your words mean death in this place. We should kill you where you sit and then sell your corpse to the guards." Wellyn signalled for Lydidd to pour more water on the stones. "But we will not. You have powerful friends with ambitions which align with our own. A King, a Stone Druid and a fighter who seems so much more than she is. We have been watching you. At the fights last night, you stood pit-side as Malthrain himself came to watch a girl fighting. A girl who talks to a lowly slave in white who claims he is a Messenger to the King. A girl who kills without mercy, the talk of the town."

"You do your research well. That girl is the one I speak of. She will fight before the Princes soon and when she does this city will go up in flames. With your help we could bring it all down."

"But we will risk our lives."

Findo looked at the door. He needed this to work. The only way he would walk out of here was with them on his side.

"You risk your lives every day. You think you are free, but you are not. One word of you, slipping from the wrong lips, and the guards would be brought here, and your happy life would end. You would each be sold to new masters never to see each other again."

"We know this. It is why we have so many friends. Friends we pay well to keep us informed." Gamon looked like he wanted to say more but hesitated.

"You have been candid with us. We shall be honest with you." Wellyn leaned forward. "We do a little work for the Princes now and again. For this they turn the other way and do not seek us out. But we live under the constant threat that this could change. We try to help where we can. The boy is an example, we have many boys. Yori who brought you to us today - we were lucky to find him, he was our best man back in the old days. When we found him in the pits, we worked to steal him back, we have many Yoris. But it does not matter how many boys or Yoris we have, we are not free.

We cannot leave. We are trapped with no way out."

Lydidd still held Gamon's hand, she reached out and took one of Wellyn's as well, she held their hands firmly and nodded to them.

"We will help you. If your friend kills the Princes, many boys and Yoris will set fire to the city. In the chaos we will leave." Gamon looked hard into Findo's eyes. "You will say thank you and you will never see us again."

Findo sat back for a moment, the warmth of the room had seeped into his bones and relieved the tension in his muscles. He felt better for it. He stood up and stepped towards the door.

"Thank you." he said as he reached for the handle.

INTERLUDE 4: NEW BEGINNINGS

"You have served me well Cxithh and been rewarded amply for your work. Your rooms are large and lavish, close to your offices. You have a healthy salary. Why do you ask for more?" Lord Willhelm sat back in his big oak chair. Upon the beautifully carved desk before him sat a decanter and two cut crystal cups, each held a couple of fingers of deep brown liquor. He reached out and lifted his to his nose and, after inhaling deeply he sighed with delight before taking a small sip of the strong spirit. He hummed his enjoyment softly before swirling the liquid around the glass, watching the way it clung to the sides as the light refracted across his face.

"It is time for our army to make its move. You should be concentrating your energies upon victory. We can talk again of this parcel of land you wish to build an estate upon once our borders are secured." Lord Willhelm dismissed Cxithh's request with finality. "Now tell me, how go the preparations?"

Cxithh looked down at his note pad as he began to work. "As you wish sire. All divisions are in place. The siege is now into its final phase. The people of Holdon weaken. No supplies have gone in since The Cull arrived and the army began to amass."

The advisor paused, put his charcoal down on the table and took a small sip of his drink. It was very good, if a little too oaked, the dry tannin feel of the liquor left him just as thirsty as he had been before it wet his mouth. He placed his cup back on the table precisely, covering the small damp ring it had made upon the wood, and picked up his drawing instrument again. His hand moved deftly over the page as he resumed.

"Scouts have reported that the King's main army still cross the barren lands of the interior. An expeditionary force of cavalry has made it into the high passes and will be engaging our troops in the mountains soon, if they have not already met. The intention is to slow the King's forces allowing the main army to remove the Northerners from their city."

"And my orders to leave the lands undamaged?" Lord Willhelm enquired.

"Still stand. We have only ever wished to expand our borders so that we can bring the light of your rule to more lands. You have already extracted revenge for the Northerners' insults in taking your mines. Now we must make the North see the shining light of your magnificence by showing the common people the splendour that Splitt has to offer. Once the Guilds are removed, the people will see the benefits of your rule." Cxithh spoke smoothly as his hand moved fluidly over the page.

"What of your powers?" the Lord asked, "Will they be needed? Will you be heading north soon?"

Cxithh looked up as Lord Willhelm coughed and reached for his drink. "Are you alright sire?"

"I'm fine. Answer my questions." The Lord of Splitt leant his elbows on the table, resting his head in his hands.

"My powers will be needed soon; have no fear that I will use them wisely." Cxithh sat back and watched as Lord Willhelm tried to loosen his collar, gasping for breath. "They are always needed."

Cxithh began to slowly lean forward, eyes drinking in every fabulous moment as his long-time employer slumped back in his chair, knocking over his glass as convulsions began to shake his body. "As you can see, my powers are now unrivalled in these lands. I can take what I want. Don't worry, I shall leave some small part of you to remain and serve me as I have had to serve you."

Cxithh trickled a little more of the Rush into his work. It flowed through the room. The sketch on the notepad clarifying becoming crisper, the rough sketch transforming to a masterpiece of artistic merit as Lord Willhelm's life force infused the paper. Cxithh allowed a small portion of himself to flow outwards and into the nearly lifeless husk before him. With his mind he tore at the flesh cutting and shaping, sculpting something new. Then he withdrew and allowed the flood of power to slowly drain away.

He ran a thumb lovingly over the page before closing the pad and placing it in a pocket sewn in his coat. He marvelled at what he had accomplished without bloodshed, but at the same time he missed the feel of the slick substance between his fingers, slowly drying and becoming sticky. Still, it would save him having to buy so many new clothes.

He watched and waited.

The cadaver slumped back in its chair. Flesh tight on the bone, shrivelled and dried. Where in life he had been tall and imposing, now he resembled an old man, wrinkled from spending too much time outdoors. Arms drooped to either side with head thrown back as if to ask for help from the skies. Lips peeled away, exposing large yellowing teeth and shrivelled gums.

A small snapping sound came from within the chest of the dead man. Then a wheeze from the mouth was followed by a crackling sound, as of dry autumn leaves being crunched in the hand.

Cxithh was fascinated as the throat began to convulse, the adam's apple bobbing as something pushed its way past. Wet sounds came as the weight of the thing inside made the head slump forward as a reddish pink mass dropped from the distended mouth onto the table. Fleshy protrusions flailed in the air for a moment before slapping down onto the highly polished wooden surface. The thing heaved itself forward towards Cxithh, leaving a red stain on the desk.

"Yes, you will serve me well." he said as he scooped the thing into a porcelain vase taken from a nearby table and stuffed the emerald velvet cloth which had been beneath it down into the neck, trapping the mass inside. A scratching noise came from within the temporary prison which he had fashioned.

He stood and rang a small hand bell, signalling the servants waiting outside to enter.

PART 64

"Perhaps I'll have more luck with the miners." Findo suggested.

Coshelle looked doubtful, "Why would they be any different to the others?"

"I don't know... Harder work, harder men. Greater desperation?" he shook his head. "Where else is there to try?"

In the last few days, Findo had walked the streets of the city, he had talked quietly to labourers laying cobbles in the streets and to hauliers pulling street carts. None were interested in rebellion.

He had received a lead that there were many slaves who were sent out to the fertile fields to the east to plant and gather the crops which fed the city. He had hidden amongst them travelling out to the vast fields where men and women toiled under the sun all day for no reward, watched over by guards who were only too happy to whip a slave if they were deemed too slow in their work. At the end of that day, he had borne fresh welts upon his own back and his palms bled from pulling up crops, removing weeds and turning soil.

The problem was that the slaves he had joined enjoyed their work, they saw it as a release from the grimness of the city. Findo could see that the fire of freedom had gone out of their eyes. They were sheep. He needed to find more wolves.

So, he looked for the place where the workers had the worst deal, where they risked their lives. He had seen chains of men walking through the fields of crops or crowded into carts, all heading further east. In the distance, as he rooted in the soil for beets to fill his basket, he had seen dust and smoke rising. Occasionally, carried upon the wind, he heard the sound of metal striking stone.

"You don't want to pause and gawk for too long lad," one of the other men in the field had pointed out, "They'll whip you and put you in the mine detail. Poor souls. Once you're in the mines you never come out. Not till you're just skin and bone. Best work hard in the fields and enjoy the fresh air."

After his conversation with Coshelle, they had both gone to the fights. The excitement of the event had faded for him. Night after night of violence and bloodshed. All in the name of the Princes.

The beautiful girl he had met in the woods was no more. She was nothing now but a ruthless killer. Cold, emotionless, and deadly. She fought for good reasons and with a noble goal, but it was changing her into a monster. He dreaded the meetings they had in camp at dinner each night. She collected everyone's reports and gave orders, all in her cold calculated voice. It was as though she had taken her soul and locked it away. To look in her eyes was to look into an immense emptiness, which he did not know how to fill.

After the fighting, he slipped away. It was incredible how easy it was to move through the city. No one paid any mind to those in white. Yes, freemen could stop you and give you orders but most were busy with their own business. Guards would do head counts but they were lax. What did it matter if they were short one slave, or if they had one too many, as long as the work got done?

He easily joined a group from the healers' quarters sent to tend to the sick and injured in the miners' encampment. He was glad he had spent some time watching Coshelle and assisting her in her work at the pits. Earlier in the week, he had heard talk of the conditions at the miners' camp and knew that each night healers were sent to aid the sick and to remove those who could no longer work.

Guards led the way through cages full of sleeping slaves to a large tent. Inside, hundreds of men lay on the floor on rough blankets. The healers moved systematically through the area under the watching eyes of the guards. Some of the men slept, others moaned in pain or shook uncontrollably. The healers assessed each quickly and efficiently. Wounds were dressed, salves applied to sores, soft words spoken. Most were given a small portion of bread and a cup of water.

The men were weak, their faces gaunt and haggard. They were literally being worked to the bone.

Occasionally, a healer would raise an arm. Guards would immediately swoop over; the healer would then move on as the guards sank a sword into the chest of the slave. They would then roll the corpse in the blanket it had lain upon and carry it outside. The mines had no place for the weak, if you could not work then you would not live.

Findo did his job well. None doubted he belonged there. His whispered words of encouragement as he dressed wounds were laced with subtle questions, but he doubted he would find support here. He needed to speak with those who were still strong, with those who had not yet had their spirit drained from them by their labours.

When they were done in the tent, the healers were told to check on the cages.

Those around him began to move off and wander through the camp whispering quietly at each cage, "Healing, any with wounds for healing?"

Findo followed. The guards watched from a distance as one of them began to hand out cups and poured wine for them from a bottle he had stashed in his bag soon they were engrossed in a game of dice.

It was hard to make out faces in the darkness. Only dim light from occasional braziers flickered on the dark forms huddled behind the bars.

As the woman in front of Findo rounded the corner of a cage, an arm casually dropped out to bar her way. She reached for her bag of bandages and stepped closer, "Healing?" she whispered. The arm wrapped around her throat cutting off her words.

Findo stepped up quickly. "Let her go friend. She is just doing her job. It was not her who imprisoned you or who makes you work in these terrible conditions."

The man in the cage was all darkness. The arm around the healer's throat was large and muscular. Dust and dirt crusted his skin, the only clean patches were the whites of his eyes. Desperate eyes.

"I'll take what I want, and you will walk away healer.

You're no better than the men you serve. We all know that it is you who choose who lives and who dies in that tent."

"We do not choose friend. We come to help. Most in the tent are too weak and sick to work. We try to get them back on their feet so that they can face death standing up. It is the Princes who choose who will die. In this land everything is done for the pleasure of the Princes is it not?"

Findo paused to let his words sink in. "They are the ones who choose who is a slave and who is free. We all know that to live as a slave is to live as one who is already dead."

"You speak some truth, but it doesn't matter. Before I die, I will take what I want. Tonight, I want her." The bright eyes blinked in the darkness.

"If you take her now then who will heal you when it is you who lies in the tent? Who will keep you alive for another day?" Findo asked.

"I do not want another day. I just want one night with her. One night to forget where I am."

Findo thought fast. "What if I told you that soon you would be free?"

"Do not toy with me, we will never be free." The arm around the terrified woman's throat tightened.

The Messenger took a gamble, "I am a King's Messenger, sent by the King on the orders of The Degan to start a revolution in this land."

Findo reached under his tunic and withdrew a small blade he had sewn to the inside. "Serena, the Untouchable, works alongside me to kill the Princes and free all the slaves of Havii."

He drew the blade along his forearm and covered his palm in red. "I swear this to you in my own blood. May these words be true until my duty is complete."

He reached his arm out towards the man.

A voice from further back in the cage whispered. "Let her go Dea, take his arm. If he lies, then you can have another go at a girl tomorrow. If he speaks the truth and I think he might, then soon you can bed any woman you please. You will be free."

The healer fell to the floor and scrambled away as the arm reached out and grasped Findo's.

PART 65

"Well, my dear, isn't this nice?" Malthrain looked around the mess tent. Guards stood at the doorway, having escorted the rest of the Untouchables outside.

"You and yours have done well by me. You have delivered on your promises." He sat down heavily on the bench opposite hers and rested his hands on the table between them.

He stroked a finger along one of his horns whilst watching her. Then he placed a leather-bound journal between them.

"I was the Princes' champion once. I fought in their grand pit." He almost spat out the words. "It takes more than skill to win them over. So far you have done well. You can do better."

Serena sat still showing no emotion. "I have won every fight. I have put on a show. What more do you ask?"

Malthrain shook his head. "You have put on a show. You are the talk of the town, but I have seen better. You will face better. What you need now is a performance. You need to dazzle the audience and win the hearts of the people."

"Why?"

"Do you think me stupid Serena?" Malthrain's expression darkened.

"Anything but."

"Then don't act as if I do not know what it is you do. You have been spying throughout every camp, you send slaves into the city who meet with an interesting array of low life workers. You plot with your fellows to fight like demons in the pits." Malthrain stood and walked around to stand behind her. "You must know that I now hold no loyalty to the Princes. I despise them. I wish to be free of their shackles."

He stepped over the bench to sit beside her.

"When your moment comes, I will be there. I will stop you for it is I who will kill them." He spoke quietly, with barely contained fury.

Serena placed a hand on his thigh. "That moment will never come for I will not be stopped." Her voice sounded hollow even to her.

He moved to put the journal in front of her. "To even stand a chance, as I said, you need to put on more of a performance. You look like a scruffy soldier in rustic armour. Look at these." Malthrain opened the cover and began to show her images of a woman who it took Serena a moment to realise was her.

Spiked armour, jagged swords, hobnailed leather. Image after image of an athletic woman in a variety of fighting stances dressed in more and more outrageous armour and weaponry.

"Is this how you like to imagine me? When you're alone and the lights are low?" She turned to face him. "You have seen the reality. Why do you need these fantasies?"

"They are not for me. They are for the people. You are too polite in the ring. Bowing to the pit bosses and making polite speeches. You need to be hard and fearsome. The best fighters have seen your stoic act before. They have seen your disciplined men and they have faced worse. No, you need to be someone new. For your last night of fights, you need to be the girl I saw out in the training area covered in mud and blood. You need to be wild and threatening. Men should stand in puddles of their own piss when they see you."

Serena leafed through the pictures. Then she closed the book and handed it back to Malthrain.

"Message understood. I will not disappoint you."

"You say you understand, but you do you really? Look at me. What do you think people see when I walk into a room? Do they see a man who wants only the right to live a free life, or do they see a monster? I have seen plenty of puddles of piss in my life."

Malthrain stood and held his arms wide, accentuating his muscled but deformed frame. "Since the Wizards shaped me and the Princes trained me, I have known no fear. Yet I have also known no love. I have had to be hard."

He lowered his arms and seemed to shrink in upon himself. "It takes it out of you being a monster. I want to be free of all this, to seek a small life for myself somewhere far away from the troubles of the world. I have read every book I can find, seeking escape. Now I wish to live whatever life I can find for myself."

Serena looked up at him. She felt no sorrow, he truly was a monster. But she understood his desire to live a free life. For now, they could be allies.

"When the time comes will you fight with me?" she asked quietly.

"I cannot promise you that my dear. If the time comes, I will fight, but I am too selfish and vain to fight for someone else. I will fight for me."

"That will be enough."

★★★

They all sat around a table. There was a palpable tension in the air.

Malthrain had left, giving instructions that they were to take the day to rest and prepare for the last evening of the Festival.

"Is everything in place?" Serena asked.

Tracks spoke first, "We all know our jobs. First, we need to survive the night. The fights have been getting harder. Our numbers have been severely reduced. Last night alone, we lost another seven fighters in the pits. Coshelle and her healers have done an amazing job keeping so many of us alive and fit to fight but we are exhausted."

He looked down at his hands for a moment before continuing.

"To think that we started with over a hundred men. Eighty-four fought that first night. Malthrain made sure we kept the numbers up through the first four days by reinforcing us, but some of our teams have fared badly. It has been in the top pits we have suffered the worst. As you and the Untouchables have risen through the pits, others have fallen. Tonight, you fight with a full complement. Twelve men have made it to the Princes' Pit. We only have four or five in each of the others and only one man will fight in the lowest pit."

Brokenose shoved his way through the door and into the

room. "Sorry I'm late, but you're going to want to hear this." He made his way to the table and the others squirmed around to make space for him to sit.

"Rule changes. I was talking to a couple of the guards over a game of cards."

"Glass of wine more like!" interrupted Coshelle, waving a hand in in front of her nose.

"OK, so I had a glass, for medicinal purposes. They were sayin' that the Princes will be watching every fight. The pits are opening at midday with the fighting commencing as soon as the sun begins to start its fall. Fights will go from pit to pit starting in the lowest. Any fighter who wins will also progress upwards being given one final chance to rise to the top. Every fighter has been ranked by the Princes' men and placed into a pit. Roll call will be interesting."

Serena looked at their worried expressions. "Nothing changes. We fight the same as always, we offer a chance to yield then we strike without mercy. It matters only that we strive to survive. Tell the men that they should yield rather than risk dying pointlessly, we will need the numbers in the days to come. Findo, how goes the search for friends?"

"As I have already reported, it will come down to trust. The slaves are too scared to discuss rebellion openly, but we have allies. They need to see us strike first, and we will have to hope that it is enough to give them the courage to join us. I wish that I had better news. It will all come down to whether or not you can deliver Serena. This will all come down to you and you alone."

"And that will all depend on you surviving the night. They will want you to fight, but the Princes will want you to lose. Are you really ready?" Coshelle asked reaching out a hand to take Serena's.

"I hope so."

★★★

The others all filed out to get ready, but Serena asked Coshelle to stay.

"I need your help." Serena said looking tired.

"Of course. What is it?" Coshelle sat by her side.

"As a Stone Druid you learned to craft wood into other shapes?"

"Yes, amongst other things. Most shape wood, some can shape stone and bone. Why do you ask?"

"I have shaped wood and bone. I need your help now. I need to become something else." Serena could not look at the Stone Druid's eyes.

"Be careful, you do not want to become him. He is a twisted, broken thing. It is not too late for you."

"I cannot see any other way. I do not think I can win as I am. I need to become someone else."

"It will be hard for you to return to how you are now if you do this, are you certain?" Coshelle squeezed Serena's hand for reassurance.

"You would help me come back, wouldn't you?" Serena looked up and Coshelle saw the tears in her eyes brim over and fall steadily down her cheeks.

"I would do anything for you."

PART 66: MESSAGE FOR A KING

The Degan strode through the camp, his legs aching fiercely, and he knew he would have fresh bruises down his side from his poor landing. The tube strapped to his thigh carried the words which he hoped would convince the King to halt the present war and prepare for the greater threat rising in the South.

He knew now that he should have listened to Findo, whose name had been scratched out of the wall by his own hand, the sign that a Messenger had betrayed his duty. Of the hundreds of names on the wall, most were painted blue to show they had retired. Some were painted red signifying that they had died carrying out their duty. Only a handful were scratched through.

The anger that he had felt when Findo left, disobeying his direct orders, had now died. The Degan felt ashamed that he had not listened to the message that his best man had tried to tell him. He was now consumed by a burning desire to right that wrong.

When Gisselle had returned to the tower without a rider, the novices had not taken long to find the message tube concealed in her saddle. That tube had quickly found its way to The Degan's desk. The report contained within had painted a stark picture of the unseen threat to the Kingdom. With the armies fighting in the west and the north, Westomere and the cities of the east were open to attack. Havii and its slave masters would not miss the opportunity to seize the capital and then the whole of the land.

Only one man had seen it coming, and he was now lost. The Degan had sworn that he would find him again and have his name painted upon the wall once more.

First, the King needed to be warned.

With all the Messengers of the air corps out delivering and given the importance of the message, The Degan had, perhaps rashly, mounted Gisselle himself and flown following the path of the army.

The supply caravans and reserve troops had served as a guide to his hurried flight, spread out in a long line moving along the river and then turning westwards around the peaks of the Scaggs before crossing the barren lands. The main bulk of the army were gathering at the base of The Great Divide, near to Mount Ghastom, preparing to make the march northwards through the northern forests before crossing the high passes to enter Holdon.

The King had led a smaller, fast moving expeditionary force of mounted soldiers and land ships which The Degan had eventually caught up to, camped at the base of one of the passes. With no site for Gisselle to roost, he had had to dismount outside of camp, sending her back to the skies to hunt and await his call.

He brushed the dirt from his heavy coat and winced at the fresh pain in his joints as he approached the ring of men around the command tent.

The King's guides moved constantly. Some jogged, others walked. Some practiced the Movements or jumped and spun athletically through the air. All were watching outwards from the tent they surrounded. As was their way, they wore no clothing, armour or weapons. It struck The Degan as odd that he had never known there were so many of them. At The Gauntlet you only ever saw one or two of the King's elite guards.

He paused for a moment, making way for a huge, armoured ox being led past heading towards the picket lines. From the air, he had counted over two hundred of the animals arrayed around the camp being tended after the long march. Amongst them stood a handful of the King's most prized cavalry, the giant Pangolin. These were large creatures with natural plated armour scales, bred in the deserts of the interior by the nomads who lived there.

The Degan removed his flying cap and goggles and walked quickly through the protective circle of guides. They made no move to stop him, he was not an enemy and his face was well known. Pushing aside the heavy entrance flap, he made his way into the warm interior of the tent where the King and one of his generals were deep in conversation.

"General Veer," said the King as he stood by a large table laid out with a variety of maps and reports, "we cannot afford the delay. We must continue to push on. I cannot allow this siege to continue. We must break through their lines and join the Guild Masters in defence of the city. Our main forces travel slowly but should arrive within a week at which point the enemy will be caught between us and them. If we delay, then Holdon could fall and the forces from Splitt will be able to dig in and it will be us caught between two forces, as their reserve armies move up from the South." said the King as he stood by a large table laid out with a variety of maps and reports.

The General stood opposite him, stern as always, wearing an even deeper frown than usual. "Sir we need to rest the animals and the men, we have not paused for more than a night in the rush to get here. We have no supplies following and the stocks we have are perilously low. The oxen need to graze, and your blasted Pangolin have taken all the feed we brought and broken into one of the waggons with food meant for the soldiers. If we attack in this state, I fear we may not have the energy to see it through!"

The two men turned as The Degan approached, surprise showing in their expressions.

"I hand this to you just as it was given to me. May the words contained within be known to be true and my duty is complete." The Degan gave a small bow of deference to the King and handed him the tube containing the words which weighed so heavily in his heart and mind.

The King placed the tube on the table and reached out an arm which The Degan clasped, "Welcome Degan. You are a long way from where I expect you to be. You should be running the Messenger service, could one of your men not have delivered this?"

"No. You should read that now. Your Kingdom is under threat." As The Degan spoke his tone was all business.

"We have been under threat for a long time. Now we are at war, and in a war-camp is not where you should be, master of words." The General's dislike for The Degan was plain in his tone.

"Sire, the Chancellor agrees. This message changes everything."

The King looked for a moment like he would disagree, "You would not be here if it was not important, tell me."

"I think you should read it for yourself. Make your own judgement without the prejudice of my own ideas." The Degan moved to a side table to pour a glass of water. He had forgotten how hard flying was.

"Sire, can I give the order to put the oxen to pasture?" General Veer stepped forward.

"No. You will wait for my command." The King firmly dismissed his general and unfurled the paper from the message tube.

He moved closer to a lamp hanging from one of the tent's supports. The Degan could see his eyes scanning the page. The silence in the room stretched on as the King read and re-read the message.

"You can confirm that this is his hand?" the King asked.

"Yes, I would know it anywhere."

"You believe what he says to be true?"

"I do."

"Then we are in serious shit."

It was not often that you heard a King swear but somehow, given the problem, it seemed appropriate.

PART 67

Findo waited with a small group of healers. He was beginning to worry. To ease his mind, he checked again through the bag he carried, making sure that there were enough clean bandages and ointments. He flicked open a soft pouch and checked the long-curved needles were prepared and readied with thin, tough twine already threaded. He was sure that they would be needed many times today.

After the morning meeting, Serena had retired to her tent. She had not been seen since. Coshelle had attended her, coming and going, collecting food and drink from the mess and returning empty platters. She assured the rest of them that Serena was alright, that she was just resting and gathering her strength for the fights.

They all knew it was a lie. They had all heard the screams.

Tracks and Brokenose had kept them away from her tent during that miserable hour in the morning. When harsh, ragged screams of pain and torture had wailed forth from behind the heavy canvas.

Coshelle had told them all any number of lies and half-truths in the silence afterwards.

"Serena had an old wound which it pained her to heal."

"She is practicing her roar for the crowds tonight."

"Perhaps if all men quake like you do at the sound, then it will work just as well for her in the pits."

"Hush your fussing boy, it is women's work. Serena will be ready to fight. Will you?"

Now they all waited to see the truth.

Malthrain paced amongst them, offering words of encouragement, checking their armour and inspecting weapons. He was not his usual imperious self. He acted as one of them and they all felt awkward around him.

A distant fanfare sounded from the direction of the Princes' Pit. It was time.

The men all fell in, standing with their designated groups, the slaves at the back. All eyes turned to Serena's tent.

The flaps swept aside as a tall, cloaked figure emerged like a butterfly from its cocoon. Serena strode across the sand of the training camp to take her place in the line with the other eleven Untouchables. The cloak she wore was midnight black with an abstract pattern woven around the edges in bright red. The deep hood was pulled up, covering her head, her face indistinguishable from the shadows within. The cloak covered her body completely, sweeping almost to the floor. Poking out from below it, were her boots. Worn, dark tanned leather, strapped and laced tightly. Her armour appeared bulky beneath the cloak.

So, Findo thought, she has been preparing a surprise. He was fascinated, she did like to surprise. He hoped that whatever she had prepared would prove effective. She was going to need all the help she could get to make this night a success.

Malthrain and the captains led them out of camp and up towards the city. The guards gathered close keeping the cheering throngs of fans and onlookers away from them.

★★★

"Stop staring at her lad, watch your own feet. She is fine. I have never met another woman with as much determination as that one. I fear there is nothing in the world that could stop her." Coshelle jibed at Findo as they followed up the hill. "Do you care for her?"

Findo slapped a grabbing hand away. The guards kept the fighters clear from the crowds lining the streets, but the healers and slaves following them were having to push and fight their way through after the group as the crowd closed in on them in their wake.

"I do." he replied.

"Just make sure you stay around then. She will need good friends after this. I worry that she might be broken. You can help put her pieces back together." Coshelle gave him a stern look. "Keep up lad. We can't afford to get left behind.

They pushed on doing their best to stay with the others and not get caught in the crowd.

***

Malthrain slowed his pace a little so that he walked besides her. "You took my advice?"

"I did." Serena spoke quietly and Malthrain had to lean close to hear her.

"Be the best. Make them bleed for you. Scream at them, taunt them, beat them bloody and crush their bones beneath your boots. Already some will fear you. Ensure that after your first fight, they all do. Fear is a weakness that all can have, all except you. Today you must know only joy. The joy of the kill. Do you understand me, Serena?" He reached to grab her arm.

She turned slightly and moved a pace away. A dry rattling sound came from inside her cloak. "I do not need you to tell me my job Malthrain. Step away from me and leave me to my thoughts. I have no time for your instructions."

Malthrain slowed a step as she swept on. He puzzled at the feeling in his chest. Was that fear? He smiled and strode on. 'She might just be ready.' he thought moving with renewed vigour in his step.

***

Tracks scanned the crowds. They were surrounded by a host of humanity, all flowing in the same direction as them, towards the high hill which housed the Princes' pits. Men were jubilantly calling out to them wishing them luck, calling for the Red and Black, cheering them on. There was a carnival atmosphere. Some were dressed as soldiers. Some in the fine clothes of merchants and freemen. Many more wore the white.

Shockingly, there were also women amongst them. Usually, only seen at the markets and around the homes, today the women of the city were celebrating as well. Most pushed through the crowds quietly, trying to keep close to their men. Others cavorted, brazenly showing their breast or their thighs to the world. Most people held a drink in one hand, frequently toasting 'The Princes.'

Something in the crowd caught Tracks's eye, movement

which did not fit the general pattern.

"Stone, Girau, to the left side. Trouble!" he shouted just as one of the guards suddenly collapsed.

The crowds pushing around them surged in.

The fighting was brief. Two tough looking fellows dressed in rough leather armour had struck at them, but they had been easily dispatched. Malthrain himself had stepped into the fray, throwing men and women aside as though they were rag dolls. The guards had quickly formed up again and the fighters had increased the pace, ploughing through the crowds until they had reached the relative safety of the pit arenas where the Princes' troops had let them through and barred the way behind them.

Malthrain had congratulated them. "You are now truly worthy of being my men. Others fear us so much that they dare try to attack us on the streets, seeking to weaken us before the fights begin. Forget them. You are mine. We are strong. Today you will battle once more on the sand. Will you fight for me, for yourselves, for the Princes? No. Today you fight for your freedom!"

The men in black and red cheered, then lined up. The captains joined their groups and led them on towards the Princes' Pit.

Findo wiped the sweat from his brow and let go of Coshelle's shoulder. He had been hard pressed to keep up, after the assault. Now he needed to stay close to Serena. He had a feeling that she would need him before the day was through.

PART 68

They waited.

The tunnel seemed oppressive and quiet after the colour and rowdiness of the city streets. The fighters fidgeted with their armour and equipment, stretching muscles, trying to keep themselves loose and ready. After what felt like a very long time, they shuffled forward then halted again to wait. A deafening cheer reverberated down the corridor as the crowd celebrated the latest team to enter the sand. The crowds quieted. The sound of a single voice could be heard in the distance, then the cheering rose again, and they shuffled forward once more.

Malthrain stopped them at the tunnel entrance.

"This is it. Be ready!" he called back to them.

The cheering rose and then died. The single voice spoke. Findo caught only a few words.

"....for honour.....freemen......fight........blood........die in vain but be remembered always!"

The crowd cheered. The volume caused Findo to flinch and shy back.

Then they were moving.

Malthrain and the captains led the fighters out into the bright light shining down upon the sand. The guards shepherded the healers to one side, keeping them away from the spotlight. Findo stumbled as he stared wide eyed at the sight surrounding him, a guard grabbed him roughly and shoved him into Coshelle.

The arena was huge. Tier upon tier rose above them, each crowded with the citizens of Havii, come to watch the greatest spectacle the Princes had organised for them.

Malthrain waved to the crowd, he flexed his muscles and walked the sand as if he owned it. The captains paced behind him. Serena and the fighters formed up and stood to attention, eyes on the curtained black tent set on the first tier, the Princes' enclosure.

Four huge men in highly polished, full plate armour stood

either side of the closed front. Further to the sides, surrounding the black tent, armoured soldiers of the Princes' army separated the crowd from their rulers.

The cheering was deafening.

Then the front of the tent began to roll upwards revealing a dark interior. Inside sat three large golden thrones. There were sculpted wings sprouting from the backs of them giving the impression that the three men who sat casually upon them could take flight at any moment.

The man in the central chair waved a hand lazily up and down, signalling the crowd to quiet. It was a wonder he could raise his hand at all, the amount of gold adorning it. Large rings were on every finger, glittering with precious stones and bracelets encircled his arm from wrist to elbow.

The man sitting on the left rose to his feet as the crowd quieted. A jewel encrusted scabbard hung at his hip. He wore a loose-fitting silken shirt and tight leather trousers. While the central Prince was leisurely in his movements, this one moved with purpose. He moved like a true fighter, as though he knew how to use the sword upon whose pommel his hand rested so naturally. He strode forward so that he stood in full view of all the spectators. The Prince on the right seemed to sink further into his chair, relaxing in deep shadows, allowing his brother the limelight. The crowd quieted.

"Malthrain, it is good to see you again. Once you were our greatest champion. You spilled blood and sweat in this very arena. You fought for honour earning the right to be a freeman. You have returned to us as you promised with those who hope to fight and win on this sand. Today they will spill blood, some theirs, with luck and skill, more of their opponents." The Prince turned his attention to the others on the sand before him. "Fighters put on a show for us, do not die in vain but be remembered always!"

The crowd erupted in cheering and applause once more as the Prince waved to them and then turned to return to his seat as the front of the tent lowered once more.

Malthrain did not move off straight away. He stared hard

at the tent for a moment, then turned and waved to the crowd.

The guards began to move and harried Findo and the healers off the sand and into another tunnel. The fighters followed with the captains on their heels. It seemed a long wait until Malthrain finally followed them.

"Remember men. Every voice raised today, every hand that claps, every foot that stamps does so in appreciation of your efforts, live or die, win or lose. To them each of you is a hero, someone to look up to, someone to aspire to be. Show them what you are capable of and milk every moment of praise from the fat cow before you, and she will love you forever more!" Malthrain seemed taller and more powerful than ever. The thrill of the crowd invigorating his every step. "Come men. Let's go prove ourselves for the pleasure of the moment!"

He led them away to the waiting area to prepare for the first round of fights.

Findo glanced nervously at Coshelle. She nodded back to him. There was no going back now.

★★★

The black and red ribbon had been drawn. The men looked down the line to Serena. She did not acknowledge them. Her expression was hidden within her long cloak. Then, slowly, she stepped forward.

Now was not the time for caution.

She walked to the centre of the sand. Her long cloak brushing around her ankles. There she stood, facing the pit boss waiting to see who she would be drawn against.

Just as he was about to dip his hand into the chest of ribbons, a commotion began. People started to point and chatter as a covered palanquin entered the arena.

Sir had led them down to the fourth arena after the display before the Princes. This would be where they would start. The pit boss would announce in which pit each of them would fight next after they had fought.

Findo knew it did not matter. All that mattered was that they won. Only by winning would they rise to the Princes' arena. Only there could Serena meet her destiny.

The four muscular men who carried the palanquin gently lowered it to the ground. Eight more armoured men in the now familiar pointed helms of the Princes' guards formed a defensive shield around the curtained box.

The pit boss hesitated long enough to make sure that nothing else happened and then drew out a ribbon.

It was yellow, a solid bright yellow, the Princes' colour.

The audience gasped. This low down in the pits, they did not often get to see one of the Princes' select fighters. All eyes began to look about. There were no men wearing yellow sitting at the ringside.

Findo looked around. The fighters on the other teams all looked surprised, glancing left and right amongst themselves. There were no fighters wearing yellow.

Everyone's attention turned to the palanquin. There was no sign of movement from the men around it, or from within.

Then sounds of marching came from the same tunnel down which the palanquin had arrived earlier.

Men in scaled mail armour with pointed helmets marched into the arena and formed up to surround the sand of the pit. Behind them followed a strange man.

The first thing that struck Findo was that he was completely bald, no hair on his head or body, no eyebrows and no facial hair. The next was the tone of his skin, he was deathly white. It looked as though he had never seen the sun, his flesh was milky white, his blue veins showing through his skin.

Although muscular, the man was not bulky and he did not strike Findo as being particularly tall, perhaps of a height with himself. He was naked to the waist, around which he wore a broad belt of stiff hide. From his belt hung an array of small, flat daggers. In his hand he carried a simple wooden spear, one end carved and sharpened to a point.

He leaped onto the sand and raised his arms turning before the crowd. It was then that Findo saw the tattoos upon his back, large wings, beautifully and skilfully rendered to appear almost real. They rippled with the movement of the muscles beneath the man's skin.

Serena stood still. She controlled the centre ground as her opponent cavorted around her, forced to the edges of the arena for his display.

The pit boss raised his hands. The crowd stilled.

It was then that Findo saw her move.

She swept the cloak from her in one movement, sending it flying out, fluttering like a bird into the crowd.

No one moved. Findo stared, as did everyone else. There was an audible inhalation of breath from all around.

Serena had changed.

Her boots were the same as was her armour, though it was coloured black and red, each of the individual pieces coloured differently. It should have given the impression of a jester's uniform, but it did not. It looked like the night was bleeding. Her knives were at her sides, her sword strapped to her back and there were various small weapons hanging all about her. Serena had always been broad of shoulder but now she was more so, and her neck was far thicker. Her long hair still flowed but there was more, so much more.

Findo knew the inspiration for the changes immediately.

Flowing from Serena's forehead, through her hair and down to her neck was a thick mane of quills, just like Gisselle's. Her face had also changed, though more subtly. Serena's jaw was now more prominent, her nose appeared more flattened, and her face was slightly extended.

Along each of her forearms, bone protrusions pointed outwards from her flesh in a jagged row, as though the spine of some long dead creature had been fused there.

Serena pushed one leg forward and screamed at the pale man before her, the quills of her mane standing out as she roared her defiance.

The pit boss began to drop his raised hands and she moved.

The man before her was fast. His fist moved fluidly to his belt and flicked a dagger through the air towards her as he began to swing his spear upwards.

Serena was faster.

The blade glanced harmlessly off the quills around her neck as she batted the spearpoint away and swiped her arm across the man's throat. The bone protrusions tore the flesh from his neck in a spray of gore which splattered the side of the palanquin and showered fitfully into the air.

As the pit boss's hands finished their descent, the pale man's body dropped lifelessly to the floor.

Serena stood, fresh blood trickling down her face and roared at the crowd, arms raised in victory.

No one seemed to notice the palanquin leaving as they yelled and applauded their new hero of the arena.

It was Malthrain who started the chant. "Beast! Beast! Beast! Beast!"

It was a long time before the pit boss managed to quieten them.

Findo choked back tears, silently retching as he stared at what Serena had become.

PART 69

"C'mon lovely, dance with me! It is Festival after all." The man spun around her. His many coloured shawl flashed through the air as he twisted and turned.

Serena stood still. Each time the man thrust forward his long thin sword, she batted it away and crouched lower.

"If your wish is to tire me out so we can have a slow dance, then you may find you are disappointed. They don't call me Fast Harndol for no reason!" His spinning ceased and he moved slightly away turning to face the crowd.

"What say you people? Did you come tonight to watch me dance alone?"

A man in the crowd stepped forward and shouted "No!" and his cry was chorused a thousand times.

Serena glanced nervously towards the palanquin and the guards surrounding it.

They were in the second pit. If she won this bout, then she would fight in the finals before the Princes. Her previous fight had lasted slightly longer than the one against the pale man, it had ended with her knife at her opponent's throat with him screaming to yield.

Findo watched Serena. She seemed hesitant for some reason. He glanced around as people began to hiss, a sign of derision and insult. One man near the front, threw something into the pit which rolled to a stop by Serena's feet. She did not spare it a glance, keeping her eyes on her opponent.

"Look my dear at the fine present the crowd has sent for you." The man in the multicoloured shawl began to pace again. "A turd, if I am not mistaken. A gift for 'The Beast' to wallow in. Come now. Let us entertain the crowd together and dance."

He whirled in, sword flashing. Serena stepped back slightly as the blade slid off her quills with a light rasping sound. She turned aside and swept one foot out low. The man spun away.

Crouching close to the ground and using her hands for support, Serena slowly drew her leg back in.

The man laughed at her. "I was right. The Beast loves the turd. Perhaps someone has more for her."

Serena moved her hand out of the warm, moist mess in which it was leaning and stood up, trying her best to look graceful.

The hissing grew louder as more excrement was thrown into the pit. Most landed harmlessly on the sand, but some struck her back and arms.

The man began to spin around the pit, staying clear of Serena. As he spun, his shawl came loose from his neck and danced through the air around his blade. Findo was dazzled by the sight.

The many coloured cloth seemed to fly through the air, controlled by the man. One instant it spun at the end of his arm, then it rolled over his shoulders to twirl about his blade. He threw it up into the air and danced forward, his blade flashing out to leave a small red scar across Serena's upper arm. Then he rolled back and caught the cloth moving out of her reach whilst still juggling the mesmerising movements of the shawl.

Serena moved, lashing out with her own sword but all she found was air as the cloth flew up above her and the man spun away to the side. She reached out to grasp the cloth with her free hand and it twisted around her arm until the tasselled ends wrapped about her shoulder.

Findo saw her wince.

The man spun closer; his blade left a long red line across Serenas thigh as he passed her.

She dropped her sword and began to pull at the cloth entwining her arm. Small hooks concealed within the tassels were sunk in her flesh and the harder she tried to get the cloth off her arm, the deeper she was pulling them into her skin.

The man darted forward and rammed his blade through her calf leaving it buried in her flesh as he danced away drawing a pair of long, curved bladed daggers from his belt.

The crowd were cheering again. They were cheering for him. They were clamouring for her blood.

Serena was losing. She stood in the pit, stinking excrement dribbling down her back, arm trapped in the cloth struggling to get free. The long thin sword jutted out of her calf with the hilt against her skin, blood trickled down both her arm and leg from the long thin slashes.

Findo felt afraid.

He turned to Coshelle. "What can we do?"

She turned sad eyes to him. "If she survives, patch her back together. We cannot help her in this place. You know that."

Looking desperately around the area, Findo's eyes stopped on the palanquin. Perhaps if he could make it over there, he could kill whoever was inside. That might cause a distraction and Serena could get away.

A guard moved across his field of vision. No. Not him. He was only a Messenger. She was the fighter. He needed to trust her.

His eyes ranged across the crowd, and alighted on three familiar faces, two men and a woman. Wellyn nodded. Findo had to do something, everything rested on Serena winning. She had to make it to the Princes' Pit.

He banged his hand down on the bench next to him, "Beast!" He called.

Coshelle stepped closer to his side and the next time his fist fell, hers joined in rhythm as together they shouted, "Beast!"

The fighters in red and black took a small step forward as they stamped in time, "Beast!"

Malthrain stood up, hauling Sir and another captain up with him, "Beast!"

Gradually, the chant was taken up, reverberating around the pit rhythmically. Everyone was on their feet now, stamping and clapping in time, chanting that one word.

Serena breathed it in absorbing the welcome inspiration.

The man came at her fast, his blades glittering and flashing, and together they danced.

It was hard to make out any specific movements. The two fighters became a blur of colour spinning in a kaleidoscope across the sand.

The chanting slowly faded until the crowd was hushed, everyone leaning forward holding their breath trying to see inside the maelstrom of colour in the spectacle before them.

Red and black danced with orange and green, yellow swirled with purple. Silvery flashes of bright light punctuated the storm of action as sand kicked up into the air. A dusty cloud rose and those in the closest seats covered their mouths and noses as they stared on.

The yellowish hue of the dust began to darken slightly, taking on a pink hue. Then those who had leaned too close to the barriers surrounding the sand began to wipe at their faces as trickles of a warm red liquid began to run down their cheeks.

On the sand, the colours changed violently; red now dominated with bursts of black.

Findo wiped at his own face, his palm coming away slick with red blood.

The air of the pit was thick with a fine red mist, and it was beginning to rain down.

The movement in the pit stopped and, as the haze settled, everyone could see Serena standing, head bowed, her bone blades in her hands. Before her were the broken remains of her opponent. Small pieces of bone jutting out of a mess of flesh lying in a pile at her feet.

The palanquin lifted and was carried away surrounded by the guards.

Malthrain himself walked out onto the sand and whispered quietly to Serena before grabbing her wrist and raising her arm in victory.

The pit boss seemed to come out of a trance and raised the hand in which he held the red and black ribbon. "The Beast wins. She will fight next in the big Pit, for the pleasure of the Princes!"

The crowd began to chatter in hushed tones as Malthrain led Serena from the sand and away to one of the waiting rooms. Findo looked back at the faces of the crowd but could see none who were familiar, perhaps he had imagined it. He and Coshelle grabbed their medicine kit and followed in

Malthrain's wake.

PART 70

Coshelle worked swiftly and efficiently. Findo passed her items as she called for them. Wounds were stitched and bandaged. Ointments applied.

First, they had stripped and washed her. Now they had finished piecing her together. Next, they needed to get her to eat and rest.

The problem was that, since the fight, Serena had shut down. She stared straight ahead, moving when told to, but she did not speak or react to anything they did.

Findo was beside himself with worry. They had got this far, but without her they could not execute the plan.

"Is it the Rush? Is she still trapped inside it?" Findo asked.

Coshelle laid a gentle hand on his, "No lad. This is something worse. She is in shock. Her body and mind have closed down for some reason. I think she pushed herself too far. Too much has happened to her in too short a time. She has not had time to adjust to her new life, let alone her new body and the things she has done." The Stone Druid handed him a bowl of sweetened broth. "See if you can get her to drink any of this."

Findo tried his best. He talked to Serena constantly. He told her how amazing she was at fighting, how Giselle would be proud of her. He spooned broth for her, trying to get it into her mouth, but most just dribbled back out, dripping down her chin. He tried giving her orders, nothing. Shouting drew no response. He tried stroking her hand and whispering kindnesses but that just made him feel stupid. In the end he just talked of the things he had seen on his journey to find the King a wife, all the while studying Serena's new and striking appearance.

"Tell me again of the great bear and the land which is always ice."

Her whisper was so faint that at first, he did not notice. Then he told the story again.

She giggled as he blushed telling her about how the Lady

Grey had offered to warm his hands. Then Serena took the bowl from him and drank. She finished off another three bowls before she sat back and looked at him.

"Thank you, Findo. Thank you for being my friend." She rested back on the small camp bed closing her eyes.

"Tell me more of your travels while I try to sleep. I need to recover if I am to fight again."

So, he told her of the lowlands of Singhigh and the people there who made homes deep in the rock, high in the trees and on floating islands in the great lagoon. He spoke of Portreath and the Ry-fell. He described the lands as he had seen them from the air, whispering of the joy and freedom he felt when flying.

Serena slept. He did not mind. He told his stories anyway.

After an hour or so, Malthrain came to check on them. He walked amongst all the wounded, greeting them as victors, wishing those that had further bouts good luck and commiserating with those who would sit them out. Eventually, he thanked the healers and came over to Serena, asking Coshelle to report.

"She seems well. Her wounds will hold for now, she has eaten and sleeps. How long until her last fight?"

"She will be expected to attend the Pit soon. Rouse her and get her ready for combat. She has done well. Make sure she completes this last job." Malthrain stopped as Serena groaned and opened her eyes.

"I'll get it done Malthrain. I just wish I didn't ache as much as I do."

"Have you any Chee bark?" Malthrain asked of Coshelle.

"I would not advise that sir."

"It worked for me when I needed a boost in the pits." he growled.

"It works for most but can leave your mind numb and the Rush flows more slowly. Let the girl stay sharp. A few aches will not stop her now."

"I will be fine, Malthrain. I just need a good meal then I can do some stretches and get ready for what comes next. Are you ready?"

Malthrain leaned in close to Serena and spoke quietly to her for a moment. Findo looked questioningly at Coshelle, but she shook her head to show that she could not hear Malthrain's words.

"If you would just stay out of my way it, it would not be necessary." Serena said hotly as she sat up and swung her legs from the bed.

"I will see you on the sand when you are ready. What comes next is up to you Serena. Be the best fighter they have ever seen, and then be better. I knew you were my girl from the first time I knocked you senseless all those moons ago." Malthrain looked at her for a long moment before turning and lumbering back through the room and out the door.

They helped Serena back into her armour, and Coshelle gave her bowls of spiced and candied nuts and dried fruits laced with her own mix of herbs. When they were finished, the colour had returned to Serena's face, and she looked powerful and self-assured again.

Findo knew that some of it was an act, a face she put on to get through what she must. He held out his arm to her and she clasped it with her own. "Let's go and bring down an empire." he said, and they turned and followed in the direction Malthrain had gone. The fighters and healers all looked up as they passed, offering words of praise and encouragement. Serena waved to each one and called back praise of her own. Then they were out into the tunnels once more, climbing towards the Princes' Pit to face whatever was to come.

When they exited the tunnel into the Pit, there were people crowding in everywhere. Standing in groups talking, sitting on the edges of the flat tiers, moving up and down the ramps and in and out of the tunnels. All the lower pit fights had finished, and the masses had all climbed to get a view in the Princes' Pit. The lowest three tiers, closest to the sand were reserved for the fighters, those who had lived to earn their place there. Findo recognised many of the faces. Most bore injuries of some kind. They sat together in the colours of their masters, strange to see them now without their weapons by their sides. The crowd parted before her as Serena made her way through the throng making her way towards the sands below. Everyone knew her now. Findo could see people whispering and pointing at this exotic and arresting phenomenon before them.

"The first woman in a thousand years…"

"That's The Beast…."

"Killed ten men with her hands before screwing their corpses..."

"I would pay handsomely to screw that..."

Each rumour was more exaggerated, and each fantasy more graphic. Through it all, Serena marched tall and impervious.

They climbed down the nearest ramp and made their way around to where the men in red and black sat. Most were wounded, some more grievously than others.

Stone and Girau were armoured and bearing arms. The others were dressed more casually and sported a host of bandages. Some were still with the healers, more still were not here, having fallen in the pits.

However, Malthrain's men had fared better than most and they made up the largest group. They had all earned the right to be freemen, waiting at the pleasure of the Princes for their official documents. These were to be handed out before the last bouts took place.

Serena took a seat and looked up. The tiers loomed all around her, rising up hundreds of feet to the crater's rim. Behind the fighters were row upon row of colourfully dressed freemen. Higher still, the tiers were lined with men and women wearing the white, above them the sky rose into darkness. Night had fallen and the moon was high.

A hush began to settle over the throng as the Princes' guards filed out to surround the black tent. The men in highly polished armour followed, taking up their positions to either side as the canvas began to roll up.

People rushed to take their seats and settled to look upon the might of the Princes of Havii.

As before, they were seated on their winged thrones, this time they all wore yellow robes as a tribute to their own fighters.

As one, they stood, stepped forward, took a small bow, waved briefly to the crowed and then stepped back to resume their seats.

From the darkness behind their thrones, a familiar figure loomed forth. He paused to turn to the Princes and sweep a low bow before turning once more to face the crowd.

It looked as though someone had taken one of the polished suits of armour from the guards to either side and squeezed Malthrain in, pieces having fallen away from the pressure of trying to contain his muscled bulk. What was left was strapped to him with heavy leather. His chest was bare, but his shoulders and upper back were covered by a pauldron. Over his thighs he wore metal plates or cuisse. In one hand he carried a long-curved axe, in the other was a great war hammer, flat on one end and spiked at the other. Strapped to his left forearm was a small oblong shield like a bracer.

His armour was painted in his colours, red and black, yet his horns were painted yellow and banded with spiked gold hoops, to honour the Princes. He paced for a moment before stopping and looking up at his audience. He raised his weapons above his head and crossed them before he roared at the crowd.

The crowd roared back.

When they quietened, he lowered his weapons.

"Good evening. It has been too long since I faced you all last. I come before you today as the reigning champion of the pits and invite you all to enjoy this evening's spectacle, for the pleasure of the Princes." He spoke loudly in his well cultured accent and, again, the crowd erupted into cheering.

Malthrain made his way down to the sand of the Princes' Pit, once there he spun his weapons briefly before raising them again over his head. He held that position for a time waiting for the crowd to quiet.

"I had my time of victory." He pointed his axe at the

fighters sitting all around. "Most of you have had yours. The reward is to be a freeman. Any who are eligible may now step down and join me to receive your gift, for the pleasure of the Princes."

Around Serena people began to move, only twelve fighters stayed seated, the rest crowded onto the sand surrounding Malthrain.

"Kneel and say the words which will seal your fate!" Malthrain shouted before he himself knelt facing the Princes.

The others followed quickly, looking up towards the black tent and the gilded winged thrones.

It was the Prince on the left who stepped forward, hand resting casually upon the hilt of his sword. "You fought well and have honoured us. I declare you all to be freemen of Havii. These are dangerous times that we live in, and we call upon your service once more. Will you join the army which even now prepares to defend our lands against the evil dictatorship of the King? Will you men fight for the honour of Havii?" he paused to scan the faces on the sand. "Will you crush the city of Westomere beneath your heels and take their folk as your slaves? Will you serve Havii?"

At this Malthrain stood, those around him followed his lead. When all were on their feet, Malthrain shouted and the rest joined him in saying, "I will serve Havii, for the pleasure of the Princes."

"Then take your seats. Your captains have been given your notes of freedom, which you can collect later. Tonight, we will crown a new champion. Who will be first to meet upon the sand?"

A little man wearing white ran down from the Princes' tent and held out a small chest to Malthrain who made a great show of waggling his fingers before dipping them into the chest to pick the ribbons which it contained.

PART 71

Stone and Girau put on a good show against their opponents but eventually, both had yielded to men in yellow. Serena had won her first match against a large man wearing purple. He had obviously suffered in previous fights and had tired quickly, surrendering his weapons and conceding the match.

After the first six fights, there had been only one fatality. Findo began to believe that Serena could really win.

The last matches were to be settled by a system of challenges. The Princes would choose who picked their opponent.

They chose a man who fought only in a loin cloth, armed with a long, hooked dagger and small shield with a spiked boss. Every inch of his exposed skin was heavily tattooed in the style of the spice merchants of Singhigh. He did not hesitate to pick the largest, most heavily armoured man wearing the Princes' colours.

Findo had seen the tattooed man fight before. He had seen how the man had used the Rush and fought tactically, drawing his opponent in close and making precise strikes to weaken them and disable their weapons. This would be an interesting fight.

In the end, the tattooed man won, managing to slide his hooked dagger through a weak spot in his opponent's armour, but it had been a brutal fight and as he made to leave the sand he had stumbled and fallen coughing blood as a seizure wracked his body. Healers quickly carried him from the pit, but he was declared too gravely injured to continue.

That left just four fighters.

Serena – The Beast – armed with sword and knives.

Havan – Warrior of Dawn – specialist in long weapons who fought with a spear and was lightly armoured and fast.

Steppel – Sword of the Princes – armed with longsword and shield who wore armour in the traditional style of Havii.

The Mace – name unknown – strong and muscular yet

exceptionally fast and clever, who wore a leather jerkin reinforced with small circular metal plates and carried a spiked mace in one hand and a studded mace in the other.

These four gathered on the sand for the Princes to choose.

The Prince in the central chair sat caressing the rings on his hands as if in thought. He turned to the Prince with the sword and spoke quietly. They exchanged words for a moment before the third Prince stood. He strode forward as his brothers called to him, but he waved their words away.

He was taller and thinner than the others and he wore a simple black shirt over baggy black trousers, both with a pattern of yellow flowers embroidered upon them. He stopped and looked up at the crowd of people chattering on the many tiers above him.

He raised a hand and the throng quietened.

Although he spoke softly, his words carried to those in the highest and farthest seats. "People of Havii, just three fights remain on this day of Festival, three fights until we crown our new Champion, a Champion for a new age. A Champion who will lead our army to conquer new lands and restore our home city to its rightful place as the centre of the world. Any man who wishes, be they freeman or slave can join that army and fight for Havii. Every man here was once a slave and served their time. These fine fighters," he gestured to the lower tiers, "were all slaves but have now risen to be freemen. Tomorrow they will march forth and free the whole world."

Serena laughed.

The Prince turned to her. "You find that funny?"

He stepped towards her, twisting one of his long, oiled moustaches, as the fighters to either side of her took a step backwards, distancing themselves.

Serena smiled at him, "I only find it funny that the greatest fighter standing on this sand is a woman. Tomorrow your army will be led by a woman. Yet you still do not offer the women here the right to fight."

"Women are weak. They are best left for breeding and looking after the home." The Prince seemed astounded that his word was being challenged.

"Weak. How can you say that to the strongest there is? How can you say that when I have shed so much blood on your sand?" Serena stepped forward as all around people began to glance about nervously.

The dark Prince stood at the edge of the tier, his guards closing in towards his sides.

"You have not proved yourself yet. You do not stand there as the Champion. If you did, then you would have earned the right to question our ways. There are always exceptions. In any beautiful pond, scum sometimes floats to the surface!" The Prince was flustered and angry, his face turning red as he spoke.

In the upper tiers, Findo could hear people shouting and jeering, there were even hisses.

Serena pressed forward, "You deny half the people in your land the right to earn their freedom. I will never fight for your pleasure. I do not wish to be a free man. I fight for the right to be a free person. Free from slavery and oppression!" She shouted the last words, drawing her daggers and holding them high in the air.

A cheer went up from the highest tiers as those in white began to push downwards.

That was when Malthrain attacked. He charged into the guards surrounding the tent, smashing them aside.

Serena turned and darted at the surprised fighters still standing on the sand with her. Her daggers slashed across the throat of the Sword of the Princes, as his knees began to buckle, she whipped around and took the spear from the Warrior of Dawn stabbing the sharp point upwards through the soft flesh behind the chin of The Mace and slamming it on into his brain. She used her momentum to pivot around his collapsing body and swept the legs out from under the Warrior. He rolled in the dirt moving away from her, but she ignored him as she charged for the black tent.

The Warrior was crushed under the boots of the men who ran after Serena. Men who chanted "Beast, Beast, Beast!"

Tracks grabbed Findo by the elbow. "Move!" he shouted.

"Keep close."

Findo grasped hold of Coshelle's arm and together they followed the Untouchables towards the Princes' tent. Above them, the slaves were in full riot, attacking the freemen and pushing them downwards towards the sand of the pit like an unstoppable wave cascading down a waterfall.

Serena slashed lethally at anything in her path. She had set events in motion and now she had one objective. Kill the Princes.

A wall of steel was forming up around the black tent, but it was buckling under the onslaught from Malthrain. He tore into the guards, grabbing and tossing them aside like rag dolls. Other fighters joined him, for a moment Findo thought he saw Sir in the melee, swinging a halberd in mighty arcs.

Serena pulled the Rush to her and then channelled it into her palm, punching forward, sending armoured men flying out of her path as if they were leaves in a gale. She sprinted through the opening and into the darkness of the tent.

The Princes were running towards a low tunnel at its back, led by the one who carried the sword. The four guards in shining plate armour were formed up to protect their retreat. Malthrain crashed into them from the side and Serena vaulted over them catching up to the dark Prince and tackling him to the floor.

He rolled, kicking frantically to get away but she knelt on his arms and sat on his chest, holding her dagger just in front of his eye. "You will die for this, bitch!" he screamed at her as he kicked and struggled ineffectively to get free.

That was when she was knocked aside, a heavy knee slamming into the side of her head. The brunt of the blow was dissipated by her mane of quills, but the force of it threw her a few metres across the room.

Malthrain beat at the Prince with his fists, smashing his ribs and jawbone, turning his flesh to a bloody pulp.

Serena could see that Malthrain was caught in a rage and so she moved on, chasing the Princes down the tunnel.

The Untouchables slowed as they watched Malthrain

screaming his fury at the broken corpse which he still beat at. Then they too were past and charging down the tunnel in pursuit of Serena. She reached a junction and stopped to listen, footsteps could just be heard to the left, so she turned that way, slowing to a jog and using the Rush to help her focus. The tunnel twisted twice and then opened into a chamber carved in the rock.

The two remaining Princes turned to face her. Between them stood the small slave who had held the box of ribbons for Malthrain earlier. They nodded to him and then ran on through a heavy wooden door which they pulled closed behind them.

The small man in white stood before Serena and spoke as he stepped forward to bar her way. His voice was silky smooth, "I regret that you cannot pass this way."

"Who's going to stop me?" Serena pulled her sword from the sheath at her back.

Something about the way the man moved worried her. He stumbled, his skin turning grey. His eyes burned a sickly yellow as they looked straight at her.

"You cannot stop my plan. The Princes will escape to lead their army north. You just delay the inevitable." As he spoke his fingers wove the air before him and a small trickle of inky darkness, like smoke made of blackest night, began to pour towards her.

Then his body seemed to shrivel as though all the moisture had been drawn from it and his eyes went blank. The husk left behind began to topple as the dark cloud billowed towards her.

Serena turned and ran.

PART 72: MESSAGE FROM THE KING

It was a sight to behold.

The Degan stood on a high cliff, watching the King's forces, commanded by General Veer, charge down upon the armies of Splitt.

The oxen led the way, each huge beast in full armour, heads lowered as they stampeded forward. An unstoppable wave of muscle and horns. They formed a tight wedge shape, the largest and strongest animals at the apex.

Inside the wedge, ran a second smaller one, so that, if a hole appeared in their lines, it could be filled immediately. Inside them, ran the Pangolin, three giant armoured animals running on their hind legs. Their awkward gait belied their strength. They carried their forearms close to their chests, each ending in fiercely sharp claws. Their large almost prehensile tails swung pendulously behind them.

Following behind the arrow tip of the wedge was a tight line of unarmoured men surrounding an even tighter group of mounted men on oxen, the King and his guard.

The wedge drove straight for Holdon, aimed at the thinnest part of the enemy's lines. Even so, there were earthworks, defensive structures and thousands of soldiers which the King's forces needed to punch through before they could reach the city.

As the King's Cavalry and Expeditionary Force began to pick up speed, the sound of the drumming of cloven hooves could be heard through the marrow of the earth upon which they charged. Horns began to sound from the enemy lines and The Degan could see men running through the camps, many with long spears and pikes.

The King had hoped that they could cover the distance rapidly enough that the enemy would be unprepared. They were not fast enough. Ranks of soldiers began to fall back to defensive positions revealing a landscape of sharpened poles and deep pits.

Regardless, the King charged on. His troops were

committed now. It was all or nothing. Either they broke through and made it to the safety of Holdon or they would die trying.

The charging oxen lowered their horns, heavy armour on their heads and necks, smashing aside any obstacles in their way. Archers began to fire into their ranks, but they had obviously been ordered to aim at the largest objects, the oxen, and shots glanced off the thick armour. Only a few shots hit the weaker points, the mounted soldiers.

Still, some fell, their bestial screams could be heard over the cries of the men as the forces began to clash.

The wedge smashed into the first line of soldiers throwing them back, the mounted soldiers hacking into enemies with long handled axes. For a while it looked like the enemy would break, but reinforcements were arriving quickly and forming new defensive lines. The charge began to slow and, as it did, the sides of the wedge began to narrow, the outer portion slowing as the centre continued to push forward.

If this continued, then the King would be exposed as the enemy troops pushed around the flanks. Then the front of the wedge opened, and the Pangolin charged into the enemy. Whole swathes of men were swept from their feet by the creatures' claws or were toppled to the ground as their tails swept around. Then the whole wedge began to grind on once again.

The King's guards were a blur of movement around the King. Any who approached them, fallen men trying to stand or the small number of men flanking their formation and running in from behind, were dealt with swiftly and efficiently.

The enemy pulled back.

The King's men charged on across the plain towards the city walls.

The Degan had seen enough. He hummed deeply and then let out a shrill whistle. Then he took a couple of steps back from the drop before him, wishing that he were younger and more foolhardy. He pushed himself forward and leapt off the cliff.

It was not elegant, and he would carry more bruises with him, but Gisselle was there to catch him. As he settled in the saddle and secured his stirrup hooks, he glanced again at the enemy army and the city it still intended to take. The King's Cavalry and Expeditionary Force were approaching the gates, there were less of them now, but they had survived. The Degan wished them good fortune for the coming siege.

Then he turned his attention towards the South and brushed his gloved fingers over Giselle's mane of quills. 'Fly fast.' he thought as he left to carry the King's message to the Pirate Oakhands.

PART 73

Havii was chaos and fire.

Tracks led the Untouchables through the streets, as they cut down anyone who stood in their way. Crowds of people ran down every thoroughfare. Buildings burned. Corpses lay heaped in corners and between buildings.

Men and women wearing white carried makeshift weapons and those they had looted, waving them above their heads and screaming 'Freedom!' They broke into buildings, any they found who did not wear the white, they slaughtered.

Carnage lay all around.

The Untouchables ran on. They ran from what they had seen in the arena.

Serena had found them in the tunnels and warned them to get out before she had left them, saying she would meet them at The Dread. As they had burst from the tunnels and charged down into the city, they had heard the screams from behind. They had all slowed to a stop and stared as that hideous cloud of blackness had flowed upwards through the Princes' Pit rising high into the air before it had collapsed to flow down its sides. They had seen people consumed by that darkness, their flesh shrivelling, coughing up great gouts of blood and collapsing to briefly spasm on the floor before death claimed them.

They had run.

The cloud of death had given chase but had dissipated and dispersed as it had reached the city streets, though Havii now contained enough death of its own.

Here and there they encountered larger complements of well organised fighters and freemen. They did not engage these but instead, back tracked and sought easier streets to pass down. In the end, they found themselves forced out, back towards the training camps. Tracks pushed them faster following the path of least resistance. When those in white saw them, they cheered and followed the friends of The Beast.

★★★

Serena had no time to wonder who the small man had

been, she could feel the destruction and pain that the dark cloud he had summoned brought.

After telling the Untouchables to run, she had made her way back to the black tent. When she arrived, it had been torn to pieces, the mob had not been kind to any they had found inside. She saw no sign of Malthrain but knew he would not have fallen to the mob. She dashed across the sand, dodging through the milling crowd, as the evil black cloud began to seep into the Pit. Serena wasted no time and charged down the tunnels to the lower levels.

She made her way rapidly from pit to pit, sure that somewhere she would find Malthrain. She did not understand why she looked, just that she felt a burning desire to make sure he was free.

As she flew through the seventh and lowest pit, she forced her mind to turn to what came next, she realised that she needed to get out. Others were counting on her. She had made a promise to Bry that she would see him again. The Rush was diminishing in her mind, the torrent had lessened. She knew that she would have to let it go soon before she drained too much. Already she could feel her armour banging loosely against her ribs as her muscle and fat were being burned away. She slowed as she reached the streets.

Did she have to meet the others? It would be far simpler to just sneak away. She could head to the east coast and find passage to Singhigh or Mirror City. Would the world miss her? Would anyone?

No. She owed it to Bry. She needed to know he was safe, make amends for what she had done to him. She thought of Findo. He had saved her twice, she owed him too. He was a King's Messenger, he flew on a beautiful Kystraal, he had travelled the world. Perhaps he would know where she could go now.

At the outskirts of the city, she slowed. So caught up in her thoughts had she been that, only now as she glanced back, did the horror register in her mind. The slavers deserved it all.

But the slaves did not.

From the buildings all around her, she sensed movement as those in white began to step out of doorways and alleys. They whispered amongst themselves cautiously pointing at her. "It's The Beast, she'll save us. She'll know what to do." one man called.

Cautiously the slaves crowded into the street all around her.

"What should we do? Where should we go now?" A woman, with dirt streaking her face and her hair a tangled mess, called to her. A child walked by her side and reached to take the woman's hand.

Others called out.

Serena just stared at them. Why ask her? She didn't know the answers. She was just a tired girl who still wanted to see the world.

"You are free. Stay here and build yourselves a future or leave and make a new home somewhere you feel safe." Serena said, knowing that her words were not the inspiration that they all deserved.

She turned and began to hurry on out of the city and into the camps. She could hear the people following. She dared not look back and see the desperation in their eyes.

As The Dread came into sight, she saw another group coming down the road led by the Untouchables. She ran over and clung tightly to Tracks as he stood there looking awkwardly about. Then she hugged Coshelle and Findo, Girau and even Brokenose. When she broke her grasp and stepped back, she saw that a crowd of slaves in white followed them.

"You saved all these people from the city?" she said to them.

"No, Serena. It is you who saved them, and we have only collected a handful, look how many follow you." Findo gestured behind her.

Serena's knees buckled when she turned and saw the huge crowd gathering all around.

Coshelle was there at her side in an instant with a steadying hand. "It's alright girl. You don't have to do this on your own. You have good friends to help."

"But I..."

Findo stepped in and they began to walk.

"One step at a time. First we follow the plan." he offered her his hand. She looked at it but did not take it and then straightened her back to walk taller. She wasn't ready for that yet.

By the time they stood before The Dread, they had collected over two thousand ragged refugees, fleeing from the city desperate to join 'the cause.' Findo, together with Coshelle, spoke to each group reassuring them that they would be protected and helped with the wounded.

Serena went inside and found Bry and Cobryn on deck giving instructions to the new crew. It took time for them to create some order, but eventually the ship was ready, and they had a plan. Some of the refugees and Untouchables had raided the nearby camps for what food and supplies they could find. It would not last them long, but they could not stay near the city.

The refugees began to walk in a huge column led by some of the Untouchables, as Brokenose and two others unfurled the sails. The big ship shuddered as the wind gusted and hauled at her red and black canvas, the great wheels began to turn. The prow pointed eastwards, sails lit up by the light of the flames rising from the city and the first rays of light coming over the horizon.

Today would be a new day.

ABOUT THE AUTHOR

Steven M Phillips has been many things in his life so far: a student and geologist, owner of a party shop and party organiser, inflator of balloons, bed shop manager, driving instructor, musician and teacher. Throughout everything he has done and all the places he has travelled, he has enjoyed the fantastical tales and magical worlds contained in good books. He plays disc golf when he is not working and finds long walks with Sully the dog to be endless sources of inspiration.

LEVIATHAN

The Beast, The Messenger and The King: Book 2

INTERLUDE 1: BEAUTIFUL PEOPLE

Cxithh waved to the crowds from the comfort of his seat. The magnificent royal carriage, gilded and carved by the finest artisans, was pulled by a team of Eltrath, which also helped to keep the crowds at a distance.

Many in the city had never seen the large insects, common to the deserts of the interior, which he had recently acquired through his contacts with the nomad tribes.

Since he had taken the throne from Lord Wilhelm, the city of Splitt had been in celebration. He was hailed as the greatest ruler the people had ever known. As advisor, he had brought wealth and new ideas to a land which had been stuck in tradition. Then he had stood up to the northern invaders claiming back their ancestral mines in the Great Divide. Now they were at war, their armies fighting for justice against the evil edicts of the King and taking vengeance on the Northern lands.

This was his first outing to see his people. The carriage carried him along the banks of the River Splitt which split the city into two. As he sat back on luxurious pillows and waved lazily at the crowds, he tried not to let his mind dwell on the events in Havii. The death of one of the Princes was only a minor setback. There were two more Princes after all, and he only really needed one to command the army heading to Westomere to dethrone the King.

Ahead of the carriage rode an honour guard of troops mounted on Scalthryn. A poor choice he decided on hindsight, as the Eltrath tended to get a bit skittish if they approached too close, and his carriage driver was struggling to keep control.

It mattered not. He could always trickle a little of the Rush to control them if needed.

The guards threw showers of coins into the crowd, a present from their new ruler, and they in turn cheered for him.

As they approached the shoreline, the soldiers formed up to keep back the joyous people and Cxithh, ruler of Splitt, descended to the sands of the beach. His silken robes fluttered around him as he walked alone to the water's edge. The waves lapped cautiously at his feet.

He turned and motioned the slave forwards. A man wearing a simple white tunic carefully carried a large vase to him and held it out for Cxithh to take, as he did so his eyes kept flicking to the ceramic ware. Small scratching noises came muffled from within it and it moved in his hand as though something inside were struggling to be free. Inside was all that remained of the previous ruler of Splitt, Lord Willhelm.

Cxithh snatched the vase up and the slave all but ran back to the carriage, glad to be rid of his terrible burden.

A green cloth still held the thing trapped within its prison as Cxithh turned to the sea. He held the vase high in front of himself as he reached for his power and began to channel it into the creature. He twisted its simple mind giving it purpose. He gifted flesh to it to help it to thrive. He set it free to achieve his goals.

The cloth came loose, and he took great care as he tipped the mouth towards the water. A pinkish mass of writhing flesh fell from the lip and made a soft 'plop' as it hit the gentle surf. Then it squirmed and a clawed appendage struck out at Cxithh's legs. He channelled more of the Rush and the small horror cowered back into the waves convulsing and thrashing as it began to grow and change.

At his side hung a simple leather satchel, within which he kept his notebook. Cxithh reached out for the power contained within the pages and drew the Rush to him, the stream became a torrent and he shaped it with his mind. A smile cracked his lips as he trembled with the ecstasy of it coursing through him. So much power.

The creature began to move deeper into the water, sending up great clouds of spray as its mass heaved and buckled and Cxithh shaped it to his will.

Stillness came. Their eyes met for a time before the thing he had created thrashed once more as it made its way into the depths of the sea to hunt.

The crowds held back by the soldiers cheered at their ruler's achievement, though it would be some time before they dared to enter the waters again, and Cxithh waved to them as he mounted the carriage once again to continue their grand tour of the city.

The soldiers threw their coins, and the people cheered all the louder for their Lord. Occasionally, Cxithh would lean from the carriage and whisper in his captain's ear, pointing at deserving people in the crowd. Those lucky few were then invited by the captain to a personal meeting with Cxithh, to assist him with his latest artistic project.

The reports confirmed that all was going as planned in the siege of Holdon. The King was trapped inside the northern city and his main army were delayed in the passes of The Great Divide by unseasonably heavy snows. Perhaps it was time to take a more personal approach to the war. Cxithh sank back into the cushions. There was no need to rush things, he could take his time and enjoy every moment.

Printed in Great Britain
by Amazon